FATAL DOSE

By
Russell Atkinson

Chapter 1

The highway patrolman got out of his cruiser and approached the other vehicle, a five-year-old Toyota Corolla with enough patchwork on the body to shame a quilt. As he did so he checked his shoulder radio to be sure it was set to mic on, so that the dashcam in the cruiser could pick up and record the audio.

The officer was a big man – tall, and athletic too. He was in his late thirties but still had the narrow waist and broad shoulders of a college linebacker, which in fact he had once been. His chest was huge, in part from pumping iron, but also due to the thick Kevlar vest he wore under his uniform shirt. He spoke with an air of authority, polite but firm, asking the driver for his license and registration.

The driver of the Toyota was much shorter, but outweighed the officer by fifty pounds. His license identified him as William Houck, male, height 5 ft. 8 in., weight 275. Houck was driving north on I-5 between San Diego and Los Angeles, a known drug transportation route since much of the stuff came from Mexico. This was the real reason the officer had stopped him. He fit the profile of a drug courier – an adult male in his thirties driving alone in midday in the right lane, at exactly 65, the speed limit, in a nondescript car. Everyone else drove 70 or more. He practically screamed that he was trying to avoid drawing attention to himself. The officer had noted that the license plate cover obscured the rear plate a bit, cutting off the bottom of the letters so the E looked like an F. This was the legal reason to stop him in case he needed one.

The officer walked back to his patrol car and ran the driver's license and plate. No wants or warrants on the car. It was registered to someone else, but wasn't reported as stolen. Houck had one DUI stop about five years earlier and a petty theft two years ago, but wasn't on probation or parole. The officer returned to the Toyota and asked the driver to step out of the vehicle. He directed Houck to the rear of the car where he pointed out the plate cover. He did not, however, begin to write up a ticket. Instead he asked the driver what was in the trunk. It appeared to be riding a bit low in back, he commented.

Houck said there was nothing in there. "Then you wouldn't mind me taking a look, now would you?" the patrolman replied. Houck *hesitated and mumbled something unintelligible. The officer demanded the keys, which Houck produced, but continued to state there was nothing in there. "But you don't mind me looking, right?" Houck answered with an animated "Hey no. No…" which legally might have been consent, meaning no, he didn't mind, or might have been refusal to consent, as in "No, don't open it" depending on the lawyer arguing the matter. But it didn't matter here and now. The officer opened the trunk and saw several hundred pounds of cocaine wrapped in plastic bags. He turned to Houck just in time to see the gun, a .32 caliber snub-nosed revolver, a Saturday night special without a lot of stopping power.*

The patrolman batted Houck's gun hand away and shoved him hard as the shot went wide. Houck stumbled backward and fell as the officer, in a smooth, practiced motion, pulled his own gun, a .38 semiautomatic pistol with a four-inch barrel loaded with hollow point rounds, and fired five times into Houck's torso. Houck lay immobile on the ground, blood seeping from his wounds, his gun on the ground a few inches from his hand.

The officer quickly stepped back a few paces onto the shoulder of the road and radioed in for backup, reporting that a man was down from multiple gunshot wounds. He released the mic button so that he could hear the response. As the patrolman turned his head slightly to listen, Houck picked up the gun from the ground and from his supine position fired a single shot in the general direction of the officer. The point of impact was not obvious, but the officer immediately began to stagger and radioed that he had been hit. Desperation could be heard in his voice. Within seconds he crumpled to the ground and died.

The video stopped and the lights came on in the courtroom.

Cliff had watched the video dozens of times by now but it still made him sick to his stomach. A fine young officer, father of three, had his life snuffed out by a single shot from a drug courier, and all caught on dashcam. It was a horrible crime under any circumstances, but this one seemed outrageously, obscenely unfair. The officer's gun had twice the stopping power of the courier's. It had a longer barrel and larger caliber ammunition. His bullets traveled much faster and hit the criminal five times in the body with no ballistic protective vest. Yet Houck had lived and the officer had died; in fact, Houck wasn't even seriously hurt. The hollow point rounds were designed for the safety of the public in mind.

They were supposed to expand in the human body on impact, thus expending all their energy there as the tip flattened, preventing them from penetrating the target's body and hitting innocent persons behind the criminal. That was fine in theory. But Houck's obesity served to stop the bullets in the layers of fat that encased his midsection. Not one of the five shots had penetrated into the vital organs. Houck's single shot, on the other hand, had hit the officer in the left upper arm, ricocheted off the bone through the armhole of his protective vest, and penetrated the aorta, leading to rapid exsanguination. The officer's mistake had been to go for his radio before disarming Houck.

"Officer Knowles," the lawyer began, "from this video it is apparent, is it not, that the officer shot my client three times after he had dropped his gun?"

Technically, this was true. As Houck had fallen, his grip on the gun loosened between the second and third shots and some slight space could be seen between his hand and the butt of the gun as it fell. This could only be seen when the video from the car camera was played in ultra-slow motion. The slow motion, however, was misleading, as the shots were so close together that in real time it was impossible to tell the gun was loose before the fifth shot was fired.

"Counselor, you have my title wrong. I'm not an officer. I was a Special Agent before I retired. An FBI agent. 'Mr. Knowles' will do. Actually, let me correct that. I *am* an officer. An officer of the court, since I'm an active member of the California Bar and I've been appointed as a Judge Pro Tem. If you like we can call each other officer, since as a lawyer you're an officer of the court, too."

The judge, a graying moon-faced woman wearing large hoop earrings, smiled ever so slightly at the answer before resuming her neutral expression.

The defense counsel had been trying to minimize Cliff's expertise by calling him officer, but now he became flustered and sputtered, "Just answer my question. The officer gunned my client down after my client no longer posed a threat, didn't he?"

"Actually, that wasn't your question. You asked if the officer shot the defendant three times after he had dropped his gun. The answer to that is no, for several reasons. First…"

"That's enough," the lawyer barked. "It's a yes-no question. In fact, didn't…"

"Objection. The witness should be allowed to answer the question. Defense counsel is the one who asked for this hearing to provide expert testimony to the court on reasonable force. Now he's trying to prevent the court from hearing that expert testimony." This came from the prosecutor, a sharp-tongued woman with bifocals framed in a severe shade of red. She looked as hard as a cricket bat and could strike with equal force.

"I withdraw the question, your honor." The defense attorney was hoping to change course, but the judge was having none of it.

"I'm going to sustain the objection. You wanted the experts, so now I want to hear what they have to say. I listened to your expert. This is a death penalty case, after all. Let's hear from Mr. Knowles." The judge put a touch of extra emphasis on the word "Mr." to show the prior exchange had not been lost on her. "The witness will complete his answer."

"First," Cliff continued, "the defendant did not drop his weapon. The word drop implies an intentional act. It is obvious from his first shot that he intended to shoot the officer, an intention he quickly carried out, thus showing he never changed that intention. The gun fell from his hand. He didn't drop it. Second, it is only discernible from the slow-motion replay that the gun had begun to separate from his hand between shots two and three. From the officer's angle, that is, above the defendant's hand, he would have been unable to see that separation at that point. He would only have seen that the gun was still pointed in his direction and the defendant, who had shot at him, was moving. It would have been unlikely that he could tell whether the defendant was ducking, dodging, or falling, in the split second between those shots. As to your second question whether the defendant posed a threat when the final shots were fired by the officer, I think that's answered by the fact the defendant shot the officer dead within seconds after that point."

Defense counsel was getting nowhere. This was ground already covered on direct examination and he was just giving the prosecution another chance to put it before the judge. He decided to take another tack.

"Are you familiar with Professor Bernstein's article on reasonable force during police shootings in the Yale Law Review, the one co-authored by Professor Rachel Margolin?" The defense was just name-dropping now, hoping to belittle Knowles by comparing his academic credentials to his own paid expert, Bernstein, a professor at Yale Law School who co-wrote a paper with Margolin, now a judge in the U.S. Court of Appeals who was being touted as a likely Supreme Court nominee.

"I've read it."

"Then you know that Professor Bernstein cited over forty published cases where officers had shot defendants who then fell down and that in the majority of those cases where the victim is brought to the ground with only one or two shots, the court held that police continuing to shoot the victim was unreasonable force."

"I didn't count the cases or the number of gunshots involved when I read that article," Cliff answered calmly.

"And you also know that in Professors Bernstein's and Margolin's opinion, based on this overwhelming body of case law, the victim would be justified in treating the officer who continues to shoot after the second shot as an aggressor and would be legally justified in using deadly force in self-defense." The defense lawyer put on his best smug look, as though he had brushed away a lightweight opponent.

"Actually, that's not a fair characterization of that article, since the good professors said that under some circumstances, a self-defense claim *might* be justified if the shooting victim clearly posed no threat to the officer and the officer knew that but kept shooting. However, I also know that not one of the cases in that article involved an officer who was shot to death while his own gun had been holstered, like this one."

"Move to strike as unresponsive," the defense counsel said desperately.

"Denied."

The prosecutor was smiling broadly now, confident her expert didn't need her help.

The defense counsel paced around for several seconds until the judge prompted him to ask a question or sit down.

"You claim to be an expert on use of reasonable force, yet you've never published a single article on that subject. Isn't that true?"

"That is true." Cliff remained nonchalant.

"How many cases on reasonable force in criminal prosecutions have you read?" This was a mistake, the oldest one known to trial lawyers. He didn't know the answer to the question.

"Scores, maybe hundreds. I instructed FBI agents for almost 25 years on the subject. I never counted them as I read them."

The judge made a note on her pad.

"But you know that Professor Bernstein has read over a thousand such cases."

"I have no idea how many he's read, but I know of one he didn't read."

The defense counsel knew, absolutely knew without one iota of doubt, that he shouldn't ask the next question, but he couldn't help himself.

"What case is that?"

"My case. When I was attacked with lethal force I emptied my gun into my attacker. To me, it all happened in an instant. I didn't even realize I was still shooting until the gun clicked on empty at least three times. There was no way I could judge between shots whether I was still in danger, the shots were coming so fast and I was so pumped full of adrenaline. The forensic team later told me several of my shots missed, too, which meant that I wasn't able to know whether I had hit the target two or three or ten times, or not at all. In law enforcement, your training is to keep shooting until the threat is gone, and the training and adrenaline just take over."

The judge was leaning over the witness stand now, thoroughly engrossed, looking down to jot notes furiously from time to time.

Panicked, the defense counsel had not known a thing about Cliff's background other than his lack of experience as an expert witness or publishing legal articles. Of course he knew he was a retired FBI agent, but he had expected some desk jockey from some ultra-conservative backwater law school with low credibility among left-leaning California judges. He had only found out on direct examination that Cliff had gone to Boalt Hall, the law school at the University of California Berkeley, as liberal as they come and with an academic standing to rival the Ivy League. "That's not a case, that's just an unverified anecdote. What's the citation?" he sputtered.

"No citation. That was never part of a published case. That's how I know Professor Bernstein never read it. That was just me saving my own life by shooting until the threat lay lifeless on the ground. He reads case law in his Ivy League office. I lived life and death on the street."

The defense counsel gave up. "No further questions."

"Any redirect?" the judge asked.

"No, your honor." The prosecutor knew this hearing was won, but it was meaningless anyway.

"Any more witnesses on either side?"

Both lawyers answered no.

Houck was charged with capital murder, which meant every legal stone had to be turned. Appeals were certain and the defense lawyer was protecting his own reputation and livelihood as a death case lawyer by throwing everything he had at it, regardless of how small a chance there was it would work. His client, Houck, had shot first and was trying to kill a peace officer while committing a felony. Houck was going to be convicted of murder. The only question was whether it would be the death penalty. His self-defense theory was doomed to failure and he wouldn't use it at trial, but by floating it in this hearing, he protected against any later ploy by the appellate counsel that Houck had been denied competent trial counsel if he didn't raise it. It would hurt him professionally if he was found to have been incompetent. Besides, he got paid by the hour by deep-pocket taxpayers, so the more work he did, the bigger his paycheck. That was enough reason to request the hearing despite having no chance of success. The prosecutor had at least as much motivation to hold the hearing, which is why she didn't oppose it; she needed to make sure the defendant had every possible crumb of due process to make sure the conviction held up on appeal. The hearing was a necessary evil on both sides. Everyone's tax dollars at work.

"Your honor," defense counsel said, "I move that all evidence on the videotape, both audio and visual, that occurs after the second shot by the officer be excluded from evidence along with any other evidence acquired after that point in time, such as the bullet that killed the officer. All that evidence was acquired as the result of a violation of my client's constitutional rights and should be excluded as a matter of law. As a result, the capital murder charge must be dismissed as the only evidence supporting it is inadmissible. The state has not charged him with attempted murder or assault on an officer, the only violent offenses that arguably might have been supported by the first part of the videotape evidence. Further, we move that the drug charges be dismissed too in that the search of the trunk of his car was illegal. It's the fruit of the poisonous tree."

"Your honor," shrieked the prosecutor, jumping to her feet. "This is outrageous. The…"

"Save it, both of you," the judge ordered. "I've read your motion papers and heard the evidence. I've allowed defense wide latitude in making oral argument in the form of questioning throughout this hearing. I'm not going to hear oral argument yet again. Submit briefs to me by noon Friday of next week and I'll schedule oral argument later if any new points are raised."

The prosecutor motioned Cliff over to her table when the defense counsel had moved away. "Great job. I didn't realize you had been in a gunfight yourself. That was a perfect comeback."

"I was never in a gunfight," Cliff replied.

"But you just testified…"

"I testified about being attacked. I never said it was by a gunman. I was attacked by a mountain lion, which was lunging for my throat when I emptied my gun into him."

"Oh, of course, the lion attack. That's how you gained your notoriety. You said 'attacker', not gunman. Very clever. Your testimony was on point whether the attack was human or not. It was still a nice squelch. Thanks again."

"My pleasure. "

Chapter 2

"How did it go in court?" Maeva asked brightly. Her pale skin and frizzy red hair betrayed her Norse heritage by way of Minnesota and a few generations.

"Fine," Cliff replied dully, heading directly to the coffee pot. Maeva knew how to brew it just the way he liked it, not too strong but very hot. And she wasn't one of those "I don't make coffee" assistants. She wouldn't have gotten the job if she were. In a one-man office her job was to do whatever the boss wanted or needed. As a drop-out from Stanford Law School, she had the brains for a professional career, but she had quickly realized after her first year she didn't want to be a lawyer. She may have been descended from Vikings but she didn't have the killer instinct so she got out early. The job market being what it was, she just felt lucky to have employment. "The prosecutor thinks they'll get the death penalty," he continued.

Maeva, opposed to the death penalty, didn't consider this "fine," but held her tongue. When you're the assistant to a consultant who worked mostly for police agencies or crime victims, you couldn't be too picky about that sort of thing.

"Will you have to fly back down to Orange County?"

"No, I was just hired to testify at the one hearing." He sat down heavily at his desk and set the coffee mug on a coaster. The desktop bore only a small pile of mail, all bills or junk mail, it appeared. After he quickly scanned through the envelopes he opened his browser to check his email. Maeva knew he liked to have the computer on before he arrived so he didn't have to wait for the boot up sequence.

"You got a call yesterday afternoon, about the time you were landing at SFO. I think it's a new client." Maeva said, anticipating that he would see her email about the call momentarily. The fact he hadn't replied told her that he hadn't checked his work email from home last night.

Whether the coffee or the news was responsible, his mood brightened. He could use the business. This whole consultant thing hadn't turned out to be quite what he had hoped. He had run at a negative cash flow for his first eight months and most of the time had been spent with set-up hassles. Only recently had he begun to make a small profit.

He'd tried to operate from his home, but when he'd tried to open his business bank account, the bank needed his business license number. When he'd gone to get that license the city said he couldn't operate a business from his home if he would have customers (their word – he'd used "clients") coming to the location. It had to be zoned commercial for that. So he'd tried to find a decent office nearby, but office space was at a premium in Silicon Valley and there was just nothing for a small solo practitioner anywhere near his home, which was more or less halfway between Google and Apple headquarters. The big companies and startups were gobbling up everything decent out there. He didn't want to have to commute to downtown San Jose or be stuck in some remote strip mall and be squeezed between nail salons and produce stands.

He could have slapped himself for taking so long when he finally realized the solution. He was already a landlord. After his wife had been killed by a drunk driver he had received a sizeable settlement from the lawsuit. He retired soon thereafter and with his FBI pension he hadn't needed the income, so he had invested conservatively. Among other investments his advisor had put him in a partnership that owned a professional building in downtown Los Altos – if you could call four blocks of boutiques and restaurants a downtown, that is. The tenants were a boutique, too – Cross and Silver – a boutique law firm specializing in intellectual property litigation. As it turned out Barry Cross was more than happy to reduce their square footage and rent by giving up their law library, since 98% of legal research was now done online. The books had been moved into new bookcases lining the rest of the space and the library had been converted to a small office, with a wall put in to separate it from Cross and Silver. Fortunately, it already had an outside door to the hallway. Cliff and Maeva were a tight fit, but it suited his purposes. The rent seemed outrageous, but at least he could console himself that one-third of it came back to him through the partnership.

"Really? So who was it?" Cliff asked, interested.

"A Mr. Vogel, from a company called Xlectrix. He said Barry next door gave him the referral. It's all in the email."

Cliff scanned the inbox and quickly determined that the other stuff could wait. He opened her email. The message said little more than what Maeva had just told him, with a telephone number and email address for Vogel. Maeva had thoughtfully looked up the Xlectrix website and provided the link. He clicked on it.

Xlectrix made radiation oncology equipment. Those were machines used to treat cancer by beaming radiation at the tumors. That was about all Cliff could glean from the website. The rest was slick graphics and medico-technical jargon he didn't understand: collimators, megavoltage and orthovoltage options, gamma rays.

"And you have three specials tomorrow," Maeva said when she saw him look up from the screen.

"Specials" were special appearances in civil actions. Cliff had developed an arcane legal niche to bring in regular, easy money, something to count on to pay the rent while between the more interesting consulting or investigation cases. After retiring from the FBI Cliff had become bored with the lonely life of a widowed retiree. His FBI friends his age were all still working, since he'd taken the earliest possible retirement. The older ones who had retired had almost all moved away to parts of the country where the FBI pension went twice as far. He had his hobbies – running, geocaching – and volunteer work, but he found he missed being in the battle, the adrenaline rush. He had realized this only when he became a murder suspect himself and started investigating that case to save his own skin. That was over a year ago and he had solved the case and gotten some good press. So he had paid his bar dues up to active status and taken the private investigator exam.

Now he was officially licensed to practice law as well as hold himself out as a private investigator. He didn't want to represent private clients in court, though. Litigation was a major pain and a pressure cooker on a schedule; it just didn't sound like fun. So he had advertised to the local bar his willingness to appear in court for them on routine status conferences and motion hearings when they're tied up in trial elsewhere. In this county those appearances all took place on Tuesday and Thursday mornings on the Law and Motion calendars. When one lawyer appears for another it's called a special appearance. If the attorney fails to announce he is making a special appearance it is deemed a general appearance, which means the attorney theoretically becomes responsible for the entire case and may even be sued for malpractice if the original attorney has screwed something up. Technically the party – the plaintiff or defendant – was his client, but for practical purposes he worked for the lawyer; by announcing himself as specially appearing, all those headaches were gone.

"Did they send the case info?" Cliff asked.

Cliff could not do a respectable job during these appearances unless he knew the basic procedural status of the case, such as whether discovery was complete, whether the parties had discussed settlement, had all parties been served, and so forth. He didn't really need, or want, to know the details of the underlying facts. Status conferences were easy, but too often his clients were so busy they failed to send him the necessary information – at least a summary email. This being Wednesday, he needed to read through these summaries in order to make the three appearances the next morning. Under the terms of his contract he could refuse to appear for them if they failed to send the necessary summary, but he had become fairly adept at faking it in court, especially if he had previously appeared on the case and already had some of the background, so he generally appeared anyway.

"Two of them did. Hammond didn't. He's on vacation in South America and out of reach.

"Great," Cliff replied, disgust in his voice. "Call his office and get an assistant or someone to look up the status if you can. I think they had a motion to compel scheduled for discovery court which means I can just tell the judge the parties are waiting for that hearing before entering mediation. Check the discovery calendar to confirm that."

Maeva nodded and started to dial the lawyer's office.

This sideline was busy work that didn't pay very well and had low status, but it was steady income, only took two days a week, and was low stress. Mostly it involved sitting in court waiting for the case to be called, standing up for five minutes, and getting out by 11:00. He also got to know a lot of litigators who in turn referred him consulting or investigation cases from time to time. But right now he was more interested in this Vogel thing.

Vogel came on the line promptly when Cliff told his secretary he was returning Vogel's call. "Mr. Knowles, thank you so much for getting back to me so quickly. We were given your name as someone who might be able to help us. I'm the general counsel for Xlectrix and we need an investigator. I understand you're an active member of the California bar."

"I am."

"Good. That's good. This investigation has to be confidential. I want to be very clear that attorney-client confidentiality must be maintained."

"Of course. Can you tell me the nature of the investigation?" Cliff kept his tone neutral. He had no idea whether this case was going to be something he wanted to get involved in, and he didn't want to sound too anxious for the business. Clients sometimes tried to get his fee down if they thought he was desperate for the work.

"We make radiation oncology equipment. That's…"

Cliff interrupted, a habit he knew he should break, but he didn't want a lengthy explanation. "I looked at your website Mr. Vogel. I understand what that is. Machines that zap cancer tumors, is that right?"

"Simplified, yes. Of course there's all kinds of software and protective enclosures, training, and other things that go along with that. We're having problems with some of our machines."

"I see. Well, I'm not an engineer, doctor, or physicist. Why do you think you need an investigator instead of a scientist?"

"We have dozens of engineers, scientists and doctors on our payroll. They haven't been able to find the problem. We think it's a human problem."

"A minute ago you said it was a problem with your machines. Now you say it's a human problem. I think you need to be a bit more specific about the nature of the problem."

"We think someone's been tampering with our machines. We just can't figure out how."

"Sabotage, then. So these machines don't work any more?"

"Oh they work all right," Vogel sighed.

"Then what's the problem?"

"They work too well. They've been killing patients. They've been beaming 100 times the radiation they're supposed to."

Chapter 3

Ellen Kennedy sat in a chair pulled close to the bedside of the young girl. The former nun was only thirty-six, but looked older largely because of her prematurely gray hair and an unbecoming stoutness. The gray was a trait that ran in the family. Her sister Theresa went totally white-haired by age thirty-eight but was still shapely and youthful looking. Theresa's previously unsuccessful modeling career had taken off at that point. She was suddenly in great demand for photo shoots for all sorts of products aimed at the senior set where the manufacturer wanted a still-sexy "older" woman – erectile dysfunction pills, cosmetic surgery, weight loss medications and treatments. Today, however, Theresa sat across the bed from Ellen. Between them was Theresa's daughter Ashley.

"I won!" Ashley exclaimed with delight as she moved her last man into the Home circle on the *Sorry!* board that sat perched precariously on the bed next to her.

"You sure did, Ash," Ellen agreed.

"You were lucky, kiddo," Theresa chided. "I should have used my Sorry card on you instead of on your Aunt Ellen."

"I've got to go," Ellen announced, standing.

"No, Aunt Ellen, you and Mom have to finish the game. To see who comes in last."

"I'm sorry, Ash. I have to get back to work. We can't let the bad guys get away with it, can we?"

"Can I hold your gun?" Ashley asked, looking up adoringly.

Theresa mouthed a virulent "no" to Ellen while making excited motions with her hands resembling a miniature Incomplete Pass signal.

"You can see it, that's all," Ellen replied, holding her jacket out momentarily away from her hip, revealing the butt of a Sig Sauer 9 mm in a leather holster on her belt. The girl's eyes went wide and a huge grin split her face. This glimpse seemed to be illicit enough to satisfy her.

"Thanks for coming by, Sis," Theresa said, coming around the bed and giving Ellen a hug. Ellen returned the hug and then bent over to exchange hugs with her niece.

At that point a tall, lean figure in a white lab coat entered the room and pulled the curtain around Ashley's bed. His name tag read "A.

Maloof M.D." Ellen waved goodbye and left, as the doctor cleared his throat to speak. It was too crowded within the curtain for all four of them anyway.

"Hello, Mrs. Bishop. Hello, Ashley," the doctor said perfunctorily, then bent down quickly to the patient. "Let's see how you are today. Ashley, breathe deeply for me." He listened intently through his stethoscope, both front and back. When done, he took a pulse.

"Your vitals are good. Now please roll over on your side."

The girl complied.

"She seems better today, Doctor," Theresa commented. She noticed a pin on his lab coat that she hadn't seen him wear before. It was clearly a flag – black, white, and green stripes with a red triangle on the left. It looked vaguely familiar to her, but she was never very good at geography. Presumably it was some Arabic country, but she hadn't thought of him as a foreigner since he spoke colloquial English with no accent. It occurred to her now that he had always worn a short beard like many Muslim men, but so what? Lots of men wore beards these days and she didn't care what his religion was. She just wanted him to cure her daughter of the cancer that threatened her life.

"The lab tests are all good. There is still no sign of the cancer. I think we got it all. Surgically it was pretty simple. As we discussed, she'll need these radiation treatments we're starting today to make sure there are no malignant cells left, but I'm very hopeful there will be no lingering effects."

"I'm not going to lose my hair, am I?" Ashley asked, a worried expression fouling her usually cherubic face. At nine years old she was fair-skinned and very blonde, with her mother's good looks. The high cheekbones were starting to make themselves known as she lost her baby fat.

"No, no. That only happens if the radiation is on the head, or with chemotherapy. Your tumor was on your leg. That's where we're going to treat you."

"The technician will be here in just a few minutes to take you in. You should be able to go home in a couple of hours." He smiled benignly at mother and daughter and pulled the curtain open.

"Thank you, doctor," Theresa said as he walked away, trying not to let her voice betray her concern to Ashley.

Chapter 4

Xlectrix was located behind fearsome chain link fences in the heart of Palo Alto's high technology hub, among the most expensive real estate in Silicon Valley. It was just a block off Page Mill Road between Hewlett Packard world headquarters and The Veteran's Administration hospital. The VA hospital here worked in concert with nearby Stanford Medical Canter to conduct cutting edge research of all kinds, but especially for treatments that benefit veterans. It also had a full complement of patients with the usual diseases and ailments.

Cliff pulled into the small visitor parking lot that fronted the street and entered the spacious, modernistic lobby. He was greeted with non-representational art in steel and glass that strained for grandeur and settled for grandiosity. He asked the receptionist, a well-dressed black woman, for Mr. Vogel. She asked if he had an appointment and he answered in the affirmative. With a few efficient clicks she checked a calendar and confirmed the appointment, then called Vogel's extension. Within two minutes he was sitting in Vogel's office.

The room was impressive for its large dimensions and expensive furnishings, a clear success story if dollars were the metrics. One wall had a large display cabinet populated with a mix of golf trophies and a series of Lucite crystals mounted on walnut bases, apparently an ongoing award for charitable activities of some kind. Above the cabinet were professionally-framed certificates – his diploma from Harvard Law (Order of the Coif, of course), his certificate of admission to the California Bar, a certificate of admission to the patent law section, one from a professional society open only to general counsel of major corporations, and one of appreciation from a legal aid society. Less conspicuous were a few others Cliff did not recognize.

The man himself was less impressive, at least to look at. He was medium height and nearly totally bald. Dark blotches dotted his hands, neck, scalp, and ears, presumably from all that sun-drenched California golf at which he seemed to excel. His dull brown eyes were close-set, almost beady, and partly obscured by half glasses, over which he peered intensely at Cliff. His tailored suit was conservative and as expensive as the rest of the surroundings, but did little to conceal a small pot belly. It was also inconsistent with Silicon Valley sartorial culture, where business casual was considered *de rigueur* for corporate lawyers. This told Cliff that Xlectrix was a conservative, traditional firm, not like the start-ups he sometimes dealt with.

"Mr. Knowles," he began, "thank you for coming on such short notice." It had been only two hours since they had spoken on the phone.

"Mr. Vogel. I'm happy to have the opportunity," Cliff replied non-committally.

"Please, call me Roger. May I call you Cliff?"

"Certainly."

"As I told you on the phone, someone is tampering with our systems. We need someone to investigate and find out how this is happening. You come highly recommended."

"I'm glad to hear it. But you realize that if I take this job there's no guarantee of success."

"Of course. Every litigator I've ever hired has that in bold print in the contract. I realize you're not a litigator, but we're all in the same boat. I can't promise my bosses I can prevail on every patent case. You can only do your best."

"How many cases of suspected tampering have there been?"

"Two that have resulted in patient deaths, one other that resulted in the need to amputate a limb that was irradiated. All three have resulted in wrongful death or malpractice claims. Fortunately, none of those have gone to court so it hasn't gotten out to the general public. We settled the death cases quickly. It was tricky because we had doctors and hospitals who also had claims against them and were looking to us for indemnity. The plaintiff's lawyers could see that they had a problem proving damages since the patients were suffering from cancer and had short expected life spans, as well as the fact that their medical bills obviously ceased to accumulate once the patients died. One of the claimant's cause of death was actually from the cancer, not the treatment. The radiation overexposure might have contributed. The amputee case is in negotiations now."

Cliff was not surprised at the bloodless calculation that went into these remarks. This is the way lawyers thought, he knew, from dealing with so many in recent years. Vogel was almost saying his company did the patients a favor by killing them and thus eliminating the high medical bills they would have paid if they had survived for a few years more, medical bills that would have been largely due to the obscenely expensive cancer treatments his company's machines provided. Of course, that was only true if the company was negligent. If someone was tampering with the machines, they would likely be no more responsible than a car manufacturer would be for a death that occurred because someone cut the car's brake lines causing a fatal crash. Even then, though, the company might be negligent for failing to make the machines tamper-proof or at least more tamper resistant.

"Did the patients suffer?" Cliff asked.

"No doubt they did, but death was relatively swift. Pain and suffering were within reasonable limits and we compensated the claimants generously. As I said, we're still negotiating with the amputee."

Cliff was more appalled at this response. He had actually wanted to know whether the patients suffer so that he would have an idea whether a successful investigation could prevent more suffering. Instead, Vogel seemed to think he was asking about the size of damages the company had to incur.

"Why don't we do this," Vogel continued. "I'll take you on a tour downstairs." He rose and motioned toward the door. They walked out of the office and down a long hallway to a different set of elevators from the ones in the lobby. When they emerged, they were in a large area that looked very much like a high-tech factory floor, which in fact it was.

Vogel led Cliff to a corner occupied by a windowless room built within the larger space. As they entered Cliff saw that the room had been divided into two sections. One was a small booth not much larger than a closet, with a window onto the larger section. He surmised that was a control booth of some kind. The larger area was occupied by what appeared to be a doctor's examination table attached to a large machine that looked like it belonged on a *Star Trek* set. In physical configuration it was not unlike the X-ray machines dentists use, only larger and more frightening. It was easily twice the size of a refrigerator, with overhead and underneath projections giving the impression of a gigantic animal's maw. There was a cone-like tip pointing down from the upper structure. The patient's table was more imposing than the corner dentist's office chair as well, with rotating gimbals and straps evident.

"The patient is positioned here," Vogel began, motioning unnecessarily to the padded table. "The straps and joints allow the patient to be oriented in an optimum position for directing the radiation beam.

The beam is produced by the linac, that's short for linear accelerator." He patted the adjacent device affectionately. This model is our most recent. It sells under the name Lilac 4 and, as you would expect, replaces the previous machines, Lilac 1 through 3. We refer to it internally as L4."

"I thought linear accelerators were miles long," Cliff commented, noticing for the first time that the device was a light purple color, presumably to be consistent with the name.

"They can be. You're no doubt thinking of the one at Stanford Linear Accelerator Center just a few miles from here. SLAC does high-energy physics research, splitting the atom and all that. That's many times more powerful than what we use for clinical treatment. But these devices we make are still quite powerful and can be dangerous if used improperly or if they malfunction."

Cliff grunted non-committally.

"The L4 produces both electron beams and X-ray beams. Both are used for various treatments. This makes it very versatile. Clinicians need only one system rather than two. It has sold very well with radiologists all over North America. We have a nearly identical model we sell to Europe. Their standards and regulations are different. We've only had incidents with the L4 in the United States."

Vogel stepped into the control booth and motioned for Cliff to join him. The console looked much like a programmer's cubicle in any of the web startups besieging the region. There were two large monitors attached to a single desktop computer. On the desktop was a microphone connected to a control box with two knobs marked Volume and Gain. Also emanating from the control box was a wire leading to a headset.

"The rad tech, or operator as we call them, has two-way communication with the patient at all times. She controls the settings, the dose, and so forth through the keyboard and mouse."

Cliff thought it interesting that Vogel used the feminine pronoun. He wasn't sure if he was being politically correct, or simply knew that most Lilac operators were female. Perhaps this was one more parallel to dentistry, where all the hygienists Cliff had ever had clean his teeth were women. Knowing how marketing drives most products, he wouldn't even be surprised if the device's floral name was designed to appeal to women, although he assumed most purchasing decisions were made by doctors – male doctors.

"What material, … uh, isotopes do you use?" Cliff asked.

"None. L4 uses only electricity to produce the beams. There are other manufacturers who use radioactive isotopes, but we don't. Just a linear accelerator or linac. This is much safer. No hazardous material, and electricity doesn't decay to uselessness."

"So what goes wrong?" Cliff asked, impatient to get to the point. He still had to get back to the office to review the documents for the court appearances tomorrow.

"One moment. I'll get a Rad Tech in here to demonstrate."

Shortly, he returned with a diminutive Asian woman of middle age. She was carrying a cooler. Cliff watched as she positioned strips of bacon on waxed paper on the patient chair, then placed a cantaloupe on the bacon. On top of the melon she placed some more strips of bacon. Then she flipped a switch by the door to the factory floor and verified that a red warning light was flashing. She closed that outer door, flipped a switch on the Lilac, and then squeezed into the control booth, where she closed the inner door and sat at the console.

She booted up the computer on the console. As the system was loading she lifted a small device from the drawer under the desktop. It looked to Cliff like the male end of the printer cable on his old PC, the big one for the parallel port, back before printers all became wireless or ran from USB ports or network cables. She held this up to Vogel expectantly. He shook his head no. When the system was ready she keyed in some commands. When the enter key was hit for the last one a large warning window appeared in the center of the screen.

Error code 41. Max dosage exceeded.

"Override," Vogel instructed.

The woman held the Alt key and pressed O on the keyboard. Another warning came on the screen again warning of the high dose of radiation and asking if the operator wanted to proceed. The options were Y for Yes or C for Cancel.

"Look at the L4," Vogel said to Cliff. "See that green light on the side near the tip of the delivery cone?"

"Yeah," Cliff replied, once he saw where Vogel was pointing, through the window.

"Okay, go ahead," he said to the operator.

She pressed the Y key and the warning window disappeared, revealing a timer window. It counted down from five seconds to zero. Then the screen flashed a "DPP interrupt 0.024s" message. Cliff didn't know if he was supposed to be watching the screen or the L4, but his gaze shifted from one to the other during the five seconds.

Vogel then opened the door of the booth and led Cliff out to the melon/bacon "patient." Cliff could see no difference. The green light Vogel had pointed out was still shining on the L4.

"So, I don't see anything," he said.

"That's because there's nothing to see," Vogel replied. The radiation was cut off after a fraction of a second because of this." He tapped the plastic housing next to the green light. "That light shows that there is power being fed to the DPP. That's a dose-per-pulse monitor. If the DPP detects a beam that is too powerful to be safe, it closes the beam aperture completely and blocks the radiation from reaching the patient. That's what happened here. Now let's go back inside."

They returned to the booth. This time the woman plugged the small device from the drawer onto the back of the computer in the parallel printer port. She then closed the program on the desktop and reopened it. This time a popup window appeared saying *Diagnostic mode enabled.* She clicked that closed and then repeated the sequence of commands and keystrokes as before, until she got to the final screen. Instead of hitting Y, however, at a signal from Vogel she pressed and held the Alt, Shift, and F1 keys with her left hand. Still nothing happened that Cliff could see. Then Vogel tapped Cliff and again nodded toward the L4. The woman pressed the F12 key and Cliff could see the green light near the cone go dark.

"Okay, now," Vogel said quietly.

Still holding all four of the other keys, the woman pressed the Y key with her thumb, barely able to reach it. She released her thumb but kept the other keys down. When the five second countdown ended, she released all the keys. Instead of the DPP message, this time a simple "Complete dosage" message appeared.

"Let's take another look," Vogel said, once again leading Cliff out of the booth. When they got to the "patient" Cliff could easily see a spot the size of a dime on the bacon that was darker than the rest. He bent down to it and caught a strong whiff of cooking bacon. The woman picked up the melon and the bacon on the underside had a similar circle the size of a quarter. The melon had soft spots on either side. She left with her zapped groceries.

"The beam scatters as it passes through the body," Vogel offered. "That's why the exit beam is larger than the entry. If this were a human being, there would be a cylinder of dead or dying tissue where that beam passed through. You could see the damage to the bacon from the heat, but the real harm is inside. The damage in some ways would resemble gunshot damage, in that it could destroy parts of internal organs, joints, blood vessels, muscle and so forth – whatever is in the path. There would be a tube of cooked flesh. A wound would open on the skin at both entrance and exit points. Attempts to graft over the wounds would fail, as the skin would just rot away. That's what happened with our victims. We just don't understand how the overdose happened."

"Any software can have errors in it," Cliff suggested as tactfully as he could manage.

"True, but we have multiple layers of safeguards. Of course the program is written to give multiple warnings if the operator has keyed in wrong values. You saw those windows appear and the operator must override them. But let's assume the software failed somehow. That DPP isn't software controlled. The circuitry is built in; it's a simple analog circuit. As long as it has power it will automatically shut down the beam once it detects a dose being beamed that is too high. There are only three ways to disable it. You can cut the power to the whole L4, in which case it wouldn't work at all and no harm would occur. You can physically open up the cabinet and detach the power wires to the DPP, which is not easy as they are soldered in, and the connection nodes are covered by metal plates. You'd probably have to cut a wire. The green light wouldn't have been on if that had happened. It's wired in serial with the main power to the DPP. Third, you could put the system in diagnostic mode like we did and use the specific key combination you saw, which isn't easy. It was intentionally designed so that it couldn't be done by accident."

"So that gizmo she plugged in the back puts it in diagnostic mode?"

"That's called a dongle. Yes, among other things, it enables diagnostic mode. It contains an NSA-approved algorithm using a 255-bit key that is unique to each program. The dongle must be plugged in at the time the program is launched. The program queries the parallel port and if the dongle is in place, diagnostic mode is enabled; otherwise it is not and can't be later, not until the program is closed and reopened with the dongle in place. The company that makes the dongles is a specialty contractor that has been providing this type to DOD for decades and there has never been a known breach or hack. The only people who have these dongles are our researchers here and our field service reps."

"The clients don't have them?"

"No. Absolutely not. In addition to enabling diagnostic mode, the dongle is used to decrypt certain highly sensitive files that the service reps use. Things the clients should not be fooling with. The dongle, as I said before, is unique to each computer. The field rep's machine has a specific dongle installed on it here when first set up and all the trade secret files are enciphered with that dongle. Another rep's dongle won't decrypt them and won't put the program into diagnostic mode – not unless he had an exact copy of the first guy's main program and files on his machine."

"I'm not sure I follow. Can you explain that again."

Vogel paused, trying to think how to simplify it. "Let's say service rep John Doe covers five oncology centers with L4s. Each of those L4's have a computer attached to it. Those five would all be installed with the codes from John Doe's dongle. Doe could perform service on those systems either by plugging his dongle into the L4 computer, or by plugging the dongle into his own computer and slaving the L4 system to his. Richard Roe, another service rep, couldn't put those machines into diagnostic mode, not unless he had Doe's computer and dongle, or at least Doe's dongle and access to the computer at the L4. Similarly Doe couldn't access the diagnostic mode on systems that Roe covered."

Cliff was momentarily amused at the use of Doe and Roe. Lawyers used those names in hypothetical cases on tests or moot court questions, even on pleadings to represent unknown parties. "You've done an inventory of all the dongles, I take it?"

"Of course. All accounted for. All our engineers and field reps were able to produce them immediately when asked. We tested each one and each matched the computer it was supposed to match."

"Did you check the Lilacs that were used for the treatment? Check the files to be uncorrupted and the power to the DPPs wasn't interrupted?"

"We did. Everything appeared normal. All attempts to reproduce the dangerous behavior met with failure, other than going through the keyboard sequence you saw here, which would have to be intentional malice by someone with a dongle and the knowledge of how to use it. The operators who administered the overdoses in our three cases are three unrelated individuals at three different radiology centers who swear they did everything right."

"Jesus," Cliff said, whistling softly. "I don't see where to start on this one. Is there anything else about these you haven't told me."

"Well, yes," Vogel sighed. "All three of the technicians at the time of administering the dose said they checked the green DPP light visibly through the window and it was on just before giving the treatment, but they then looked down at their screens or keyboards to enter the commands so they didn't watch it while the beam was active. The doses were all supposed to be much less powerful than the one you saw us do today, of course. A normal dose would be 150 to 200 rads. I just showed you 15,000 rads on the bacon, which is about what we think was administered to the three injured patients. The beam was only active for two seconds or less. One of the three operators, however, said she looked up after pressing the Y and she thinks that when she looked at the L4, that light wasn't on. But it came back on almost immediately."

"So the power was cut to the DPP somehow."

"If she's right, yes. But that alone wouldn't have been enough. The dosage would have had to be altered, too, by a factor of 100. If the dosage is correct the DPP wouldn't ever activate anyway. Remember the DPP just cuts off an overdose. Somehow the dose was increased and the DPP disabled at the same time. Both of those actions require the dongle." Vogel paused for several seconds before continuing. "There's one other thing, too."

Cliff's eyebrows raised in an "Okay, let's hear it" expression.

"All three cases have been local. These machines have been installed all over the continent yet all the problems have been confined to a small geographic area. And all of them are in the territory of a single service rep. His name is Frank Crabbe. He goes by Buster. Of course we interviewed him and he swears he didn't have anything to do with it. He says all the systems are normal at those locations. We've had other service reps go out and confirm that. But we still think he must have done something wrong, either intentionally or accidentally."

Cliff was old enough and enough of a sci-fi fan, to remember the original Buster Crabbe, the Olympic swimmer turned actor. He played Tarzan, then Flash Gordon.

"Have you disciplined him or fired him?"

"No, he's still employed, but we put him on paid leave. His accounts are being serviced by someone else for now. We have his computer and dongle. We reinstalled the Lilac software on those three systems using a different dongle. He's been told to stay available if you want to talk to him."

"I do. Then my first recommendation would be to polygraph him. Once I get those results we'll know where to go from there. Now I really have to get going. Here's my fee agreement." Cliff handed him a copy of his standard contract.

Vogel took a quick look at it. Within seconds he could tell it was all boilerplate, standard language suggested by the California Bar. He flipped right to the hourly rate. "That seems high for an investigator," was his only comment.

"I can give you a referral to some reputable detective agencies if you want something cheaper." He knew his rate was higher than other FBI retirees who did private investigations, but he also knew it was half what Vogel was used to paying for legal specialists like Barry Cross. He also knew other investigators weren't lawyers and weren't as good as he was. Investigators fell into that odd category with perfumes and wine where demand went up as the price went up. Buyers figured that the most expensive one must be the best. They usually had no other way to evaluate, at least not at the time of purchase.

"All right. You're hired. Give me weekly reports." Vogel signed the agreement in duplicate and gave one copy back to Cliff. "Here's a check as a retainer." He'd already had a check made out in Cliff's name. So much for negotiation.

Chapter 5

"Here's Gina now." The speaker was Matt Nguyen. Matt, a senior agent in the Palo Alto Resident Agency of the FBI was addressing Ellen Kennedy, the newest addition to the R.A. He was referring to his wife, the supervisor of the violent crime squad in San Jose. They often met for lunch. Today it was at The Jury Room, a pub-like spot near the San Jose Superior Court building that catered to lawyers. It was all wood paneling and leather-upholstered booths.

When Matt stood to greet his wife, Ellen thought they made an odd couple. Matt was thin, almost painfully so, and of only average height. Gina was at least as tall as her husband and built more solidly. Gina wasn't fat, just solid, Kennedy decided, much like herself, but would definitely outweigh her husband by at least fifteen pounds. At the moment Gina was also frazzled, with her full head of lush black hair in disarray.

"Sorry I'm late," Gina began. "Traffic was terrible. And it's been a horrible morning. You can't believe.... Never mind. Don't ask. Sorry. You must be Ellen." She cast a gracious smile at Kennedy.

"I am. It's nice to meet you. Matt said he wasn't sure you'd be coming."

"He's told me a lot about you, Ellen. You O.P.'ed in from Salt Lake? That's a new one." O.P. referred to Office of Preference transfers, where the agent requests to go to a particular division. Usually O.P. transfers are granted near the end of the fiscal year and only to the most senior agents, using whatever is left of the FBI transfer budget. Ellen only had five years in, despite her gray hair. Not only that, but agents usually O.P.'ed when they were nearing retirement age to transfer out of expensive areas, like Palo Alto, to go to a nice sun belt retirement locale where prices are cheaper and taxes are lower, like Utah, so this was a counterintuitive direction.

"Actually, it was on a hardship, not an O.P.," Ellen replied. "My niece is undergoing cancer treatments at Stanford. My sister has to work. I'm here to help out as much as I can. I'm living with her for now, so it's not that expensive, not yet anyway."

"Oh, I'm so sorry to hear that. What kind of cancer? Will she be okay?"

"Soft tissue cancer on her lower leg. They already operated. The doctor thinks he got it all. She's having radiation treatments now. The surgery itself wasn't bad as those things go."

"Hey guys," Matt broke in. "Let's not get too morbid." He turned to Gina. "Is Cliff coming?"

"He said he should be out of court by 11:30. He should have been here by now. He's the one who picked this place. He's probably on the way."

Right on cue Cliff walked in, huffing and puffing, a scowl marring his forehead. He walked directly to their table, since the small restaurant's entire seating area could be seen from the doorway. As he sat next to Gina he cast a wary eye at the woman across from him in the booth. Was this another setup? Gina was always trying to play matchmaker, never successfully.

"Cliff," Gina gushed. "This is Ellen Kennedy. She just transferred in from Salt Lake. She's on Matt's squad."

Cliff exchanged a polite but unenthusiastic "Nice to meet you" and shook Ellen's hand perfunctorily. He immediately judged Ellen as the kind of woman who, when your mother tries to set you up on a blind date and you ask what she looks like, your mother says has a good personality. Her eyes were a very pretty light blue, but too close set and surmounted by a pair of brows in serious need of a good tweezing. She had a nice complexion and wore little makeup; at least she had that going for her. Her gray hair was cut very short, what some men might call mannish, although short hair was common among law enforcement women for valid professional reasons; then again, there were a lot of mannish women in law enforcement. She had the requisite curves, but they were mounted on an overlarge frame – more burly than girly. Still, even if she wasn't his type, there was no reason to be rude.

"So, do you know Tim Rothman?" he asked. Tim, a pilot, had been Cliff's closest friend and office mate when they both were agents in the San Jose office years earlier. Tim had transferred to Salt Lake City Division after he married a woman who was as rabid as he for camping, horseback riding, and kayaking. They bought a seven-acre spread complete with horses, barn, and corral near Zion National Park when Tim got transferred to the St. George Resident Agency.

"I do. He said to say hi if I ran into you out here. He's flown air support for some of my squad's surveillances. He flew me to Butte on a case once. We had a nice long talk in the plane. I got to sit up front in the co-pilot's seat. He's really a fascinating guy." The women all liked Tim.

Cliff took the opportunity to look at her finger for the first time. No ring. Uh oh. It was time to nip this in the bud. "Tim's a great guy," Cliff mumbled, looking over the menu, avoiding eye contact, although he already knew he would order the club sandwich.

"You look like hell," Matt broke in. "Something bad happen in court?"

"You could say that. The judge sanctioned my client, the lawyer I was appearing for, $500 for failing to appear personally. She's been trying to schedule a trial but the lawyer has sent others to do special appearances three times in a row. I didn't know about the two previous times. I couldn't agree to a trial date, but she set a date anyway at the convenience of the opposing counsel. I thought it was just a routine status conference. Afterward, when I called the lawyer I was appearing for to tell him what happened, he chewed me out like it was my fault and said I cost him $500. He said I could kiss my fee goodbye. He knew this was a trial setting conference and had to know the sanction was coming if he didn't show. He sent me to take the judge's wrath."

"Sounds like fun," Gina said, bored, and not trying to hide it. "Ellen here's a geocacher," she added with more enthusiasm, trying to change the subject to her real purpose. Gina knew Cliff geocached as a hobby. This was obviously a ploy to get him to offer to take Ellen out geocaching. Both Ellen and Cliff squirmed in their seats. An awkward silence followed.

Finally, Cliff announced dutifully that there was a geocaching event planned for later in the month and maybe he'd see her there. He made a mental note not to go. Gina, clearly dissatisfied with his response, kicked him in the ankle at his obstinacy just as the waitress came to take their orders.

In pain, but unintimidated, Cliff gave the waitress his order then asked Matt how things were going on the squad, hoping to change the subject yet again. Palo Alto was a small enough office that there was only one squad. Each agent on the squad had a specialty of sorts – Matt's was terrorism – but they all worked together on all types of cases. Matt couldn't talk about some of the more sensitive case matters, but he began to fill Cliff in on some office gossip. The conversation devolved into a string of Bureau slang and acronyms and hushed murmurings that other diners wouldn't be able to hear or understand. Gina, still ticked at Cliff, silently nibbled the chips while the men ignored the women.

When that was over, Ellen asked Gina what it was like to supervise a bunch of macho men working bank robberies and other violent crimes. Gina made clear that she had no trouble exerting her authority, something Cliff had no difficulty believing, knowing Gina as he did.

When a lull in the conversation descended upon them, Ellen excused herself to go to the ladies' room. When she returned she was chuckling.

"What's so funny?" Gina asked.

"Now I know why they call it The Jury Room."

"Why?"

"The restrooms are labeled Hung and Split."

Gina rolled her eyes and looked at Cliff accusingly.

"What? I didn't name them. It's a good lunch spot."

Gina looked over at Matt, but it was obvious he enjoyed the joke, too.

At that point their food arrived, just in the nick of time so far as Cliff was concerned, and conversation halted for a few minutes. As the meal progressed Gina resumed questioning Ellen. She learned that Ellen had been a nun, that her sister was a widow, which was why Theresa had to work to support the family, a family that now consisted only of herself and her daughter Ashley. Ellen was living with Theresa in Monte Sereno due to the hardship.

When Cliff heard that he joined in, satisfied that he had shown enough disinterest in any dating situation. Monte Sereno was a tiny and very expensive burg squeezed into the western hills between Los Gatos and Saratoga. "I thought you transferred here on an O.P.," he said, glancing up at her gray hair. He had missed the conversation earlier and, like Gina had, assumed that she was senior enough to qualify for an Office of Preference transfer.

"My eyes are down here," Ellen replied, grinning and pointing with her fork at her face.

Cliff blushed as red as the salsa on his enchilada. It was always embarrassing to be caught looking, even though the direction was the opposite from the usual. He fumbled for something to say.

After a beat she let him off the hook, laughing at his discomfiture. "I get that all the time. The gray hair. People always think I'm older. It's a family trait. Theresa's hair went totally white when she hit thirty-eight. At least I'm only starting to show gray. I'm actually here on a hardship transfer to help Theresa with Ashley. She's so busy with her modeling."

Grateful to be let off easily, Cliff smiled back, chagrined. "What happened to Theresa's husband?"

"He had a heart attack running a marathon. Dropped dead right on the street in the middle of the crowd. He was only fifty-two and trim. No history of heart problems."

Bells suddenly went off in Cliff's brain. This sounded like Mark Bishop, which explained a lot. Bishop was a former FBI agent who left the Bureau after five years to pursue a political career. He worked in the San Francisco U.S. Attorney's office and made it up to the position of head of the Criminal Division, then took the same position at the U.S. Department of Justice in Washington. There he became a close friend and golfing buddy of the current FBI Director who was also a DOJ attorney at the time. Finally, Bishop left the DOJ after two years to run for Congress, won, and served on the House Judiciary Committee, the committee that handled the FBI budget among other things. Unsurprisingly, he had a reputation as a staunch FBI advocate. Six months ago Bishop dropped dead of a heart attack at age fifty-two while running a marathon. As a close friend of the Director and of the Bureau, he, or his widow at least, would get every consideration the FBI could offer. If she wanted her FBI agent sister out here to help with a sick child, that sister would be there. Cliff wondered whether Ellen even really wanted the transfer. Salt Lake Division was considered a pretty plush assignment on the whole. She may even have been transferred against her will "for the good of the Bureau." In the FBI you go where they send you.

"Is your sister Mark Bishop's widow?" Cliff asked tentatively, not sure if that was insensitive.

"Yes," she answered simply. "I guess everyone knows about him. Congressmen get good life and health insurance at least." She resumed eating.

Cliff wasn't sure how much concern to show and mulled over this bit of intelligence a while before speaking. He didn't want to pry but didn't want to seem uncaring either. He remembered seeing the news coverage of Bishop's funeral a few months back. Bishop's wife and young daughter standing there in black, evocative of little John John at JFK's funeral. And the wife – Theresa he now recalled was her name – even in black was stunning despite being fiftyish, or at least he assumed then she was in her fifties from her white hair. Now he realized she was probably only in her early forties. He didn't know she worked as a successful model. That hadn't been on the news – at least not that he remembered. That might help explain why a congressman could afford to live in Monte Sereno, although Bishop was the scion of a wealthy family anyway, he knew.

"I'm very sorry to hear about that," he said eventually. "What's Ashley sick with?"

"Cancer. She's being treated over at Louise Packard at Stanford. Everything looks good for a full recovery. The Bureau is being really good about giving me time off on days when she has her treatments."

This news sent a chill up Cliff's spine. Cancer. Treatments locally. He clearly couldn't say anything about Xlectrix, but if he said nothing was he putting Ashley, this girl he didn't even know, at risk? He just hoped that the treatments were chemo, not radiation. Then he wouldn't feel any guilt for staying silent. As much as he wanted to ask, he decided if he didn't ask he could assume it was chemo, not radiation, even while he realized he was rationalizing.

"Jeez, that's a tough break. I hope she's back to normal quickly. Is there anything I can do… I mean, like, is there a fund started? I'd be happy to…"

"No need. Theresa has good insurance," Ellen said curtly. She didn't want charity, especially from someone who seemed to be trying to avoid her on a personal level.

Matt, sensing another awkward moment, then asked Cliff's opinion about the latest smart phone and other high-tech gadgets, an interest they shared. This was something of little interest to either Gina or Ellen, so they began chatting about where to shop and similar topics of interest to a woman moving into the area. The conversation was difficult since Gina and Ellen were sitting diagonally in the booth, as were Matt and Cliff, but they finished the meal this way, talking between bites.

They settled the bill, splitting it four ways. As they filed out of the restaurant to the parking lot Ellen and Matt climbed into his Bureau car to return to Palo Alto, while Gina headed to hers, which was parked only two spots away. Just before Ellen closed her door Gina called over, "I hope your niece does okay with her radiation treatments."

"Thank you. It was nice to meet you," Ellen called back and closed the door.

Cliff, just emerging from the restaurant a few steps behind, stopped cold when he overheard this exchange. His heart sank. So it was radiation, not chemo.

Chapter 6

Cliff sat across the glistening walnut conference table from
Frank Crabbe, the service rep on suspension. Crabbe looked nothing like
his namesake. Frank was on the short side, with stringy black hair and a
swarthy skin tone, resembling an Italian or even Turk with his jumbo
Mediterranean nose. He drummed his fingers nervously on his knee.

"Frank, I want to thank you for taking the time to do this
interview with me. I'm recording this." He placed his Zoom recorder on
the table, red light glowing. "That's okay with you, isn't it?"

"Sure. Well, they pay me my salary and tell me to show up so I
guess I don't have any choice. Who exactly are you again, anyway?"
Vogel had introduced them with only the most cursory mention of Mr.
Knowles being hired to "look into the L4 problem."

"My name again is Cliff Knowles. I'm an attorney hired to try to
find out what is going wrong with the Lilacs. I appreciate that you've
been put on the hot seat over this and I..."

"An attorney?!" Crabbe interrupted, aghast. "How is an attorney
going to help? You're just here to help spin this to avoid liability, like
Vogel. This is an engineering problem."

"It may be. And yes, avoiding liability is a valid goal for any
company and its lawyers. The best way to do that is to find out what is
causing the problem and correct it before there are any more injuries.
That's all I want, just like you."

"They think I screwed up somehow, but I didn't. I didn't. It's a
design issue, but they're trying to pin it on me." Crabbe was clearly
agitated. An artery pulsed noticeably on one side of his neck.

"Frank, calm down. I'm not trying to pin anything on anyone.
I'm just here to find out what's happening."

Crabbe was unconvinced, but paused before speaking, unsure
whether Cliff posed a threat. "Look, call me Buster. Everyone else does.
It's a design issue, but the design engineers won't admit it. They're
pointing their fingers at me."

"What makes you think it's a design issue?"

"It's obvious isn't it? The DPP was disabled somehow. It's not
supposed to be possible without a dongle, but every time it happened I
had the dongle with me, in my computer bag and I was nowhere near the

L4. I was out on the road between calls or at another installation working. If there was no design flaw, this just couldn't have happened. I was 70 miles away. They know that."

This was news to Cliff, but not unsurprising. Why would they think it's you if you had the dongle 70 miles away?"

"I guess they think I stopped at some wifi hot spot or something and did this remotely. But why would I do that? That's crazy. I'd lose my job. I'd probably go to jail for hurting people. Maybe even murder."

"That's possible to put the L4 in diagnostic mode remotely?" Cliff had assumed the L4 was hard-wired to the computer in the control room and could not be accessed any other way.

"Yes, that's new with the L4. Sometimes we have to diagnose problems on an emergency basis from here. But it can only be done if you have both the dongle and computer that can slave the system at the L4. Basically you'd need my laptop and dongle to do it remotely. To do it from the installation you'd only need the dongle since the program is already on their computer. The clients don't have the dongles."

"Okay, so explain this to me again. I'm still not clear about the dongles and programs. I'm no engineer. Dumb it down for me."

"The service rep – me – installs the program at the treatment site using his dongle. The dongle is the key to everything. It's a security device with strong encryption. Once installed the program can run without it to treat patients, but it can only be put into diagnostic mode using the dongle, either at the site, or remotely with my laptop. The DPP, that's the gizmo that shuts down the radiation beam if it's too high, can only be disabled with the dongle and a difficult keyboard combination. None of the other dongles will work on the systems I've installed with mine."

"That doesn't explain how you could control it remotely."

"Several things would have to happen. Let's say I had to do that. Right now I don't have my laptop. It's assigned to my replacement so he can service my accounts while I'm on suspension. But assuming I had it, first I would have to find some place with Internet connectivity. There's a utility to connect with a VPN – a virtual private network – to the desired computer if you know its IP address. All our L4 installations have Internet connections with fixed IP addresses so we can do this."

"Do you have the IP addresses bookmarked or on a drop-down menu of some kind so that a user can just select which one he wants?"

Cliff was already thinking that someone else with access to Crabbe's computer might be able to pick a site by just clicking.

"No. You have to type it in by hand. That's a tough security measure right there."

"So do you have these memorized or are they recorded somewhere?"

"Well, yeah, of course they're recorded. I have seventeen L4s in my territory. There's no way I could memorize seventeen IP addresses which I seldom use. There's an encrypted file on my laptop listing them all, but you'd need the dongle to decrypt that, too. That's a separate application that uses the same dongle. Of course here at HQ we've got paper records for every install, too, so the IP addresses are there."

"Okay, go on. You type in the IP address and then what?"

"The VPN is established so I would then have a secure, encrypted point-to-point connection with the L4. Once that's done I'd make sure my dongle is plugged in and launch the main control program in diagnostic mode on my computer. It would send a request to the L4 computer to slave it to my laptop. That computer would then send the serial number back to my laptop and check for the dongle. If the hash comes back right, that computer releases control to mine. I could then operate it however I wanted, including disabling the DPP. But it couldn't be done accidentally. You have to press four widely spaced keys simultaneously to do that."

"I saw a demonstration. I assume you would get all the same warning messages."

"Of course. I would have to intentionally override them to put in higher dosages." Exasperation crept into Crabbe's tone, but he was trying to keep it from sounding insulting. He was used to talking to engineers and radiation technicians who knew most of this stuff already.

"So do you have to carry seventeen dongles around with you or do you just pack the one you're going to?"

"No, no, no. I only carry one dongle." Crabbe didn't hide his impatience well this time. "Each dongle is unique, but the same dongle is used to install all systems in a single region. I'm the rep for the Bay Area Region and I have one dongle. It would be totally unworkable to manage so many in the field."

"And you had your computer and dongle in your possession each time this happened?"

"I did. Yes, yes, I did. So they're blaming me. That's their theory because they don't want to admit it's a design flaw."

"So do you have a theory as to what kind of flaw?" Cliff was glad he didn't have to take notes. He would have Maeva transcribe it all later.

"I think there must be some condition that cuts power to part of the system, but not all, maybe just for a few seconds."

"So you're saying maybe the linear accelerator could be working at full strength while the DPP power was cut?"

"Exactly. I think there's a short circuit somewhere that's cutting power to both the DPP and the moderating panels."

"What are moderating panels?"

"They're leaves that move in and out of the beam like the iris constricting the pupil, or the f-stop on a camera. Some move all the way across the beam like filters on a camera lens. That's how the dosage is reduced to a safe amount or the specific frequency or type of X-ray or electron beam is blocked or let through. If the leaves and DPP didn't get power at the same time, the full-strength beam would project to the patient." Crabbe was rolling his eyes and spitting out his answers now with a sarcastic edge like he was talking to an inattentive moron.

Cliff was following this, but barely. It was getting too technical for his taste. He could see that Crabbe was becoming hostile. He decided to cut the interview short. He pulled out Crabbe's resume and background form from his personnel file and went over the data there, to verify it. Crabbe didn't become any warmer in his attitude, but remained minimally cooperative.

Cliff gleaned a few extra tidbits – a personal cell phone number in addition to the company one and the land line listed in the personnel file, some personal history. Crabbe had a B.S. in Mechanical Engineering from Chico State, High Honors. He was married with one child, a daughter age three. His wife was a schoolteacher, but quit working when the girl was born. She planned to go back when the girl entered school. He'd had only one prior full-time employment after college, working in a community hospital in a suburb of Sacramento as a Facilities Engineer, but that job disappeared when a huge hospital operator bought it out and then closed it down to eliminate cheap competition to its nearby large hospital. He'd been with Xlectrix for eight years with an excellent work record, first as a Test Engineer in Palo Alto, then as a Field Service

Engineer. Cliff ran out of background questions to ask, thanked him again, and let him get back to getting paid for sitting around waiting to be cleared of wrongdoing.

"One final question, Buster. Do you like working for Xlectrix?"

"Is that a threat?"

"No, no. I didn't mean it that way. I meant that literally. I just want to know if you consider it a good company to work for."

Crabbe took a long time to answer. Finally he grumbled between his teeth, "It *was* a good company to work for. Now I don't *work* for them. I sit around by the phone, 'staying available', for pay. My life is nothing but watching daytime TV and playing solitaire on my computer. It's the worst job I ever had. I might as well be in prison."

The bitterness in his voice was evident. Cliff knew resentment to an employer could be a motive for sabotage, but did this attitude predate the problems? Or was it the result of his treatment and the cloud under which he remained?

Chapter 7

Maeva was none too happy to have an interview recording dumped on her for transcription. That was probably her least favorite part of the job, but one to which she had become accustomed. She stuck out her tongue when Cliff placed the Zoom on her desk. Cliff just smiled an evil grin and retreated to his office.

Cliff pulled out his directory of retired FBI agents. He knew three retirees who had been qualified FBI polygraph examiners, and felt all were competent. But one was vastly superior to the others in evoking confessions when the polygraph subject was guilty: Sol Bergman. He looked up Bergman's number and called. Bergman answered on the third ring.

"Yeah?" It was a bark.

"Sol, is that any way to greet an old friend?"

"Shit. Who is this?" Cliff paused a few seconds without answering. "I mean it. I'm going to hang up."

"You don't want a nice polygraph job?"

"Goddam it. That's you, Cliff, isn't it?" finally recognizing the voice. "I told you I'm retired. I don't do that any more. I'm seventy-two years old. Let me decay in peace." His New York accent was as strong as ever, despite having lived in California for the last forty years.

"Liar."

"Whaddya mean 'liar'? I told cha the last time I don't do that shit any more."

"And yet you did such a great job for me. Have you sold your polygraph?" There was smugness in Cliff's voice.

"What's that got to do with anything? It has sentimental value."

"So you still have it. You still have it because you know you might still need it. Which means you're not retired."

"Mister psychiatrist now, are you? You think you're a hotshot lawyer now? Juris Doctor..." – he pronounced it 'your ass doctor' – "doesn't mean real doctor, moron. It means 'doctor, my ass'."

"So you'll let them die an excruciating death, then?"

"Die.. what? What the hell are you talking about? Who's dying? Delusions are a sign you're the one who needs a psychiatrist."

"Cancer patients. I have a case where some cancer patients are suffering needless pain, death or disfigurement because of a medical device problem. You can help me stop it."

Bergman remained silent for several long seconds and Cliff knew he was hooked. He explained the situation in detail, how he wanted Crabbe polygraphed and how that might lead to removing a saboteur and saving patients. Bergman continued to spit out invective but eventually agreed. He wanted Cliff to send him the transcript of the interview and a summary of the facts first. When he had studied them and felt ready to do the polygraph he would call Cliff to arrange a time.

"How soon do you think that'll be, Sol?" Cliff asked. "This is pretty urgent."

"Two weeks tops. I have tournament finals this weekend, but I'm free after that."

"What tournament? You jousting now? There's not a horse that could hold you." Bergman, only five-seven, had ballooned to over two hundred fifty pounds after retirement.

"Funny man. Lawn bowling. Monterey Lawn Bowling Club. A man's sport. Pure skill. Not like that geode-spotting shit you do."

"Right. Just don't tear an ACL or do any head-butting until after the polygraph. I need you healthy."

"One more thing." Bergman's tone had shifted. He sounded serious.

"What?"

"Thanks, Cliff. I was bored as hell. And now my wife wants me to sell my polygraph and guns so we can move into a retirement community, you know, one of those big condo things with a central dining hall and doctors on site. You know, a place where geezers go to die."

This remark gave Cliff pause. "How is your wife?"

"Healthy as a horse. An arthritic, braying, biting horse."

"You have a wife. You're a lucky man."

Maeva brought in a stack of mail and dropped it in Cliff's In basket. Cliff knew the In and Out baskets were anachronisms in this day and age but they reminded him of his days as an FBI squad supervisor. He enjoyed the nostalgic feeling they gave him. He even used the same gun-metal gray wire baskets the government used.

The mail was mostly junk. Ads for office equipment, ads from other lawyers with specialized services, ads for providers of Mandatory Continuing Legal Education courses.

Near the bottom of the stack of mail was an envelope from one of his clients, an attorney he had appeared for as a special two months earlier. Inside was a check for $300. Cliff shook his head. Sixty days it took to get paid a paltry $300. And that was his only check this week, other than the $10,000 retainer Vogel had handed him. But that ten grand had to go into his client trust account and couldn't be used for expenses or Maeva's salary, at least not until he billed Xlectrix for his time and the bills were approved. Then he could pay himself from the trust account. Maeva didn't know it but she made more with her secretary's salary than Cliff had for the quarter.

Cliff worked through the rest of the mail. When done, he returned some phone calls then began drafting his first weekly report for Vogel.

Chapter 8

Matt Nguyen and Ellen Kennedy watched the SUV pull out of the parking lot of the Home Depot and head north. Ellen pulled her Chevy Malibu into the stream of traffic four cars behind the blue SUV. She was a little nervous today. She'd done many moving surveillances, but this was her first since she'd been transferred here and she did not know the area well yet. In addition, it was a brand new car which she had been assigned only a week earlier, and the nicest Bureau car she'd ever driven. Like anyone with a new car, she was not yet fully used to its handling and the position of all the buttons. To top that, Matt was in the car with her, and it's always a bit nerve-wracking to have a colleague observe your every move.

Normally a physical surveillance, or fisur in FBI lingo, would involve only one agent per car, but Matt knew Ellen would have a hard time by herself in new territory, and it was handy for him to be able to work the radio while she drove. He was the case agent and would be directing today's fisur. He also wanted to ride in the new car. At first he had resented the fact that this new arrival to the squad got assigned a brand new car. Matt was the second most senior agent on the squad, and last year the most senior agent had a new car assigned. That meant Matt would normally be the next to get one since his was over five years old, a base model Dodge Avenger with reliability problems. Instead Matt had to settle for a promise that he would get the next new car. His supervisor had explained to him off the record that the Director himself had called the Special Agent in Charge of the division, and told him to make sure Ellen "got a decent car." Such is life in the Bureau. Matt knew why Ellen was here and understood she was not pulling strings.

"He made that yellow," Matt announced, radio mike in hand, as the SUV scooted through as the light ahead changed. "We're red balled. Unit 2, can you pick him up?"

"I have the eye," a deep male voice responded through the speaker. "No problem."

"Sorry," Ellen began, "I didn't want to bumper lock. He might make us."

"No sweat, Ellen," Matt assured her calmly. "That's why we have a team. I told you to stay back."

They listened as the radio chatter told them the subject had gotten on I-280 south. When the light changed Ellen took off from the line as quickly as was safe and zipped right, into the next lane, weaving dexterously through traffic. She made the next green light just barely and fishtailed onto the freeway on-ramp. Within minutes she caught up with the subject who was in the second lane from the right. She moved into the right lane, which was moving at about the same pace and positioned her car to the SUV's right rear about fifty feet away.

"Okay Unit 2," Matt announced, "We have the eye. You can drop back."

The SUV continued southeast until it reached the Nimitz Freeway, which led up the east side of the bay to Hayward and Oakland. Today, however, the SUV went only one exit north and exited at Bascom, still in San Jose. Ellen dropped back and another car that had not been up close took over the tail position. The team followed the SUV into the neighborhood and saw it pull up and park on Emory, directly across from the Municipal Rose Garden.

The Rose Garden was both a city park, a beautiful gem well-known among rose lovers, and the name of the district. It was one of the nicest neighborhoods in San Jose and had been used as the turnaround point in every Silicon Valley Marathon in recent years. The local schools held their graduation ceremonies here.

The tail car drove on and parked around the corner to avoid being spotted as surveillance by the SUV driver. That agent radioed, "Matt, I had to go past. He was parking his car mid-block. Can someone get an eye to see where he went?"

"Roger, this is Unit 1. We'll take it," Matt responded. To Ellen he barked, "Hurry up and get onto that block."

She turned left off Bascom onto Emory, making the oncoming car hit its brakes and honk angrily, but she didn't slow. She pulled onto the block next to the Rose Garden, finally slowing to normal traffic speed. As they drove down the block looking at the cars parked on either side, the SUV was easily spotted on the right.

"He's parked near the Rose Garden entrance about halfway down," Matt announced to the crew. "He's not in the car. Did anyone see where he went when he got out."

"Unit 2 negative."

"Unit 3 negative."

"Okay, we're going to park and go into the rose garden to see if he's in there. Unit 2, you stay at that end of the block in case he comes out and goes that way. Unit 3, can you park back about four houses from the subject and watch to see if he comes out of one of those houses?"

"10-4."

The others positioned themselves as instructed. Matt and Ellen drove to the far side of the smallish park where they left the car and entered the Rose Garden. They walked at a leisurely pace across the grass toward the SUV, glancing around as they talked, pretending to be just another couple. There was a cluster of teens in one corner and a man throwing a Frisbee for his dog in the center of the grass. Joggers patrolled the outer perimeter beyond the chain link fence that encircled the block, long ago having worn a path in the narrow strip of grass between the fence and the sidewalk. Matt and Ellen could readily see that the subject of the surveillance, an Arab male in his twenties, was not among the current park users on the grass side.

The park was divided in half by a long mound on which a line of redwoods stood in a neat row. The mound was bordered by a stone retaining wall that served as a dais. During ceremonies, the speakers or dignitaries sat or stood on the top level while the audience sat on the flat grass expanse a few feet below in folding chairs. On the other side of the redwoods were rows and rows of roses of almost every variety encircling a large fountain and lovingly cared for by a local flower club and the city staff. Matt and Ellen walked almost to the far side of the park near the Emory entrance and then turned right, passing the rest rooms and entering the rows of roses. There were people everywhere, mostly couples or moms with children, strolling through the aisles, reading the labels and admiring the blooms.

"This is beautiful, Matt," Ellen exclaimed as they passed between the first two columns of flowers. "I had no idea this was here."

"Yup. It's nice. Do you see him?"

Her head snapped up. She was supposed to be working, not sightseeing. "No, where?"

"No, I don't see him. I'm just asking if you see him anywhere."

She looked around. There were too many people in this half of the park to be certain. "No, not yet. Let's keep walking around."

Matt pulled a small handheld radio from his jacket pocket and turned so that no one but Ellen could see him using it as he transmitted. "Anything?"

"Unit 2 negative."

"Nothing, Matt."

"Okay, keep your positions. We don't see him in the park, but we'll keep looking."

They continued to make their way through the rows, moving faster than the other groups around them. After ten minutes they had satisfied themselves that the subject was not in the park. They moved back to the grassy area where they could see the SUV, still parked on the street just on the other side of the chain link fence. They sat on the grass and tried to look natural while keeping an eye on the houses across the street.

"Have you followed Abboud to this area before?" Kennedy asked. Ghalib Abboud was the driver of the SUV, although they refrained from using his true name on the radio for security reasons. He was always just "the package" or "the subject."

"No, I haven't followed him before at all. He was seen back in Alexandria coming out of the national headquarters of the Scimitar Relief Fund. The SRF is a phony charity. On paper it's a Palestinian aid fund but we think it's funneling money to a violent faction of Hamas – a splinter group really. It's probably used to buy weapons or at least that's what we're investigating. They followed him for a couple of days and eventually got a name and address from the hotel where he was staying. He lives out here, in Mountain View. This is just the initial fisur to see if we can figure out where he works and who his contacts are. We're the Office of Origin now."

"How about this area for other subjects? Is this a hot spot for Arabs or anything?"

"No. Maybe some of the San Jose agents have been here on cases, but I haven't had any Peninsula subjects coming down here."

After fifteen minutes Matt's radio crackled. He held it to his ear discreetly, volume low. "Matt. WFJ walking north on Dana approaching Emory. Dark skin, black hair, maybe Arab. With a WMJ. Blond."

"Roger." He turned to Ellen. "White female juvenile, maybe Arab. Watch to see if she turns onto Emory. Blond guy with her."

"Unit 2. Matt, they turned your way."

The girl wore glasses and carried a backpack, obviously a student. The boy with her was skinny, very fair, and on the short side, but taller than the girl, who was petite. They weren't touching, but seemed to be in friendly conversation. They stopped before reaching the park entrance and they appeared to say goodbye. The boy turned around and headed back to Dana. Matt and Ellen watched as the girl walked up Emory on the far side until she was directly across from the SUV. There she turned and walked up the walk of the colonial-style two-story house. She pulled out a key, unlocked the front door, and went in.

"Okay, she went in a house near the subject's vehicle, the white colonial," Matt radioed. He did not give the other units the address since it was theoretically possible the channel could be monitored despite being scrambled. "We don't know if she's connected. We'll keep an eye on this house. You guys watch the rest."

Within minutes, however, they had their answer. Two Arab males walked out onto the front step of that same house. Matt recognized the younger one as Abboud, the driver of the SUV.

"All units. The subject just emerged from the house. There's an older male with him, probably the owner or renter of the house. Wait, they're shaking hands. Our package is returning to his car. We won't be able to get back to our car in time. You guys see if you can follow him out of here."

"10-4."

"Got it, Matt. See you back at the office."

Matt and Ellen headed back to their car, but didn't rush since they knew they had no chance of catching up. Halfway across the park Ellen turned and looked back but the SUV was already gone. Matt turned the radio off.

When they got in the car Ellen asked Matt whether to try to catch up with the surveillance team. He listened to the radio traffic for a few seconds and heard the team say it looked like Abboud was heading home to his house in Mountain View.

"No, we'd have to risk our necks and everyone else's on the road just to prove he drove home. Go back to the R.A. We have the address of a new contact. That should be enough for starters."

Ellen pulled out and headed for the freeway.

Chapter 9

Cliff walked into the bank to deposit his weekly receipts. He also needed to order more business checks. He waited dutifully in line with the other customers until he got to position one. When a young male teller came free Cliff waved the person behind him ahead. He was waiting for Margaret, his favorite teller.

When Cliff had been working on the FBI violent crimes squad fifteen years earlier he had responded to a bank robbery at this same bank when Margaret was a brand new teller. She had been a basket case, since she was the victim teller and that was her first robbery. Cliff had interviewed her. The police had already been there and interviewed her, which was normal since city police patrol cars were always closer than the FBI agents, who cover a much larger area with fewer personnel. What was different about the police and FBI contacts back then, though, was that Cliff had calmed her down patiently, gently joking to make her feel less threatened, emphasizing how she did not have to worry about the robbers coming back to hurt her if she cooperated. He had even called her three days later to find out how she was doing, and when she sounded shaky, drove the fifteen miles from his office to the bank and brought her a small bouquet of flowers. He made her feel safe.

That act of kindness kept her from quitting banking altogether. She was now the assistant manager of the bank, and when Cliff had set up his law office he had made a point to come to her bank. During the busy lunch hour, she filled in as an extra teller. She was a veteran of four bank robberies now, and they had become almost a mundane part of everyday banking life.

Cliff moved to her window, the one farthest from the street, when she came open. He did his transactions, chatting with her about her four kids as she moved with characteristic efficiency. He was just about to leave when all hell broke loose.

Two young punks broke from the line of customers. One, the taller of the two and apparently in charge, wore a hoodie and sunglasses, the other, a do-rag and baggy pants that sagged so low Cliff didn't see how he could walk. Each held a cloth sack in one hand. The taller one announced in a loud voice, almost a scream, that this was a robbery and nobody should move. Immediately a woman customer got faint and sank slowly to the floor.

Cliff whispered to Margaret to hand him a dye pack. Every teller has a bundle of bills, with exploding dye packs embedded between the bills. The packs activate on a time delay when they pass through sensors at the door. Tellers know which bundle that is and they are supposed to give those to any robber, but, of course, not to regular customers. Trusting Cliff implicitly, she quickly handed him a small pack of twenties, which he slipped into his outer suit coat pocket.

"We've got guns," hoodie man shouted, "do as we say and no one gets hurt." He motioned menacingly with his hand under his hoodie. Cliff thought it was a bluff, but couldn't be sure. If there was a gun under there, it had to be a small one. From his experience he knew this was definitely a high-profile robbery. Most were quiet affairs where the robber just passes a note and walks out with maybe two or three thousand dollars. It was obvious here that these guys wanted to clean out all the teller cages of cash. Two-man, multi-teller robberies were rare and usually very dangerous.

The shorter robber was already at the first teller cage demanding all her hundreds and twenties. "No dye packs, bitch, or you're dead," he grunted. The woman complied. He moved to the next. This robber, too, wore sunglasses. His jet black hair was long and on the bushy side. It stuck out of the bottom edge of the do-rag over his ears.

"Everybody back away from the tellers," hoodie commanded. "Put your wallets in the bag. All your cash and credit cards." He walked along the line of customers holding his sack in his left hand while his right hand remained in his hoodie. Customers, numbering around a dozen, stumbled backward until they formed a loose herd in the middle of the lobby around the table that housed all the deposit slips and other forms. They dropped their wallets in the sack.

"You too," hoodie yelled at Cliff, who was slowly walking from the farthest teller window.

Cliff picked up his pace slightly. Do-rag was now at teller number three of the five while hoodie was collecting wallets. Cliff joined the herd and held out his wallet and dropped it in the sack with a show of cooperation along with the pack of twenties. The robber was watching him intently and there was no way to do it discreetly. When he saw the twenties go in the sack, hoodie smelled a rat; he pulled the pack out and threw it on the floor, suspecting it of being a dye pack. He gave Cliff the evil eye, but said nothing. The robber finished with the customers and moved to the desks where the loan officer and manager sat. Cliff picked up the pack and edged his way to the end of the milling herd closest to the door.

Do-rag finished with Margaret and headed back toward the entrance as his partner turned to join him. The two turned their backs on the group and headed to the front door. Cliff, heart racing, sprinted forward and dove onto the back of the shorter robber, taking him to the floor. The other robber turned and pulled a .32-caliber revolver from his hoodie.

Chapter 10

Sol Bergman directed Crabbe to sit in the chair next to the polygraph, but did not attach any of the device's leads or appendages to him.

"I'm recording this conversation," he announced after pushing the *Record* button on his old-fashioned cassette style recorder and watching the reels begin to turn. "You understand that and consent to it. Please confirm that."

"I guess I don't have any choice."

"You do have a choice. I am not operating as a law enforcement officer or with any legal authority. I must have your consent and that consent wouldn't be valid unless it was voluntary."

"My boss said I'd be fired if I didn't cooperate with the investigation this guy Knowles is doing. I wouldn't call that voluntary."

"But that is still your choice. Recording the conversation is part of the polygraph examination so that there will be no question as to what exactly was asked and how you answered at each step in the exam. Do you consent to this process or shall I pack up and go?"

"Yeah, yeah, I consent," Crabbe said resignedly. "Let's get this over with."

Bergman gave him a form to sign, which Crabbe did quickly, without reading it.

Bergman then went on to explain how the polygraph worked. It recorded various body reactions during questioning, such as pulse rate, respiration rate, and skin conductivity. He emphasized how it would detect any lie and that it was important to be truthful. His tone was somber and authoritative, but polite.

Bergman then began a series of questions largely covering the same ground Cliff had, but veering off into some more personal areas unrelated to the investigation. When he was ready, he hooked up the polygraph to Crabbe. One lead went onto the fingers of one hand. A blood pressure cuff was placed on the bicep of the other arm. Bands around his chest measured respiration.

"Beginning the examination. Answer all questions truthfully and promptly yes or no, unless I ask you to explain. Is your name Frank Crabbe?"

"Yes."

"Are you employed as a Field Service Engineer for Xlectrix?"

"Yes."

A series of similar background questions followed, establishing a baseline for the readings. There was a pause after each answer while Bergman examined the readings that followed. It sometimes took several seconds for the nervous reaction to demonstrate itself. The examiner had to determine whether the subject was a quick reactor or slow reactor.

"Do you intend to tell the truth to me during this exam?" The first important question.

"Yes."

"Have you ever taken something from a friend that you shouldn't have?"

"No."

Bergman studied the readings and scowled.

"Frank, it's obvious you lied on that one. I'm going to ask you again, have you ever taken something from a friend you shouldn't have."

Crabbe broke out in a sweat and his body odor filled the small room. "Well, no. I mean he wasn't a friend exactly."

"Explain," commanded Bergman.

"In Little League, I wanted to play catcher, and I was the best catcher on the team, but the coach always played his own son there. So one time I took his catcher's mitt and hid it so that the coach would have to play me. I had the only other catcher's mitt. But he just made me loan Cory, that's his son, my mitt. I hated Cory and gave up baseball after that season. So I was telling the truth. He wasn't a friend so my answer was the truth. But I knew it was wrong. I just felt guilty. That's what you saw." Crabbe's mouth was dry and words were hard to understand.

"And that's the only time?"

"Well, my wife. She used to date a good friend of mine, but she dumped him. And then later I started dating her. I didn't take her from him. She'd already dumped him, but he accused me of stealing his girlfriend." Crabbe was stammering.

"Look me in the eye when you answer," bellowed Bergman. "Yes or no. Other than those two instances you just told me about, have you ever taken anything from a friend that you shouldn't have?"

"No." The voice was barely audible. He managed to make eye contact this time.

Another long pause while Bergman read the output.

"Did you sabotage the Lilac machines that produced the overdoses in this case?"

"No." Crabbe practically shouted this answer.

"Do you know what caused the radiation overdoses?"

A moment's hesitation. "Yes."

"Explain."

"It's a design flaw."

"Yes or no. To the best of your knowledge, do you honestly believe the explanation for the overdoses is a design flaw?"

"Yes."

"Do you know of any other cause?"

"No."

"Do you know of anyone who would intentionally cause those overdoses to happen?"

"No."

"Are these overdoses your fault?"

Another hesitation. "No."

"You reacted to that one. You aren't telling me something. What is it? Explain."

"No, no. Really. I don't know. I think it's a design problem."

"That's not good enough. You're not telling me something. The machine says you're lying."

"I'm not lying. It's just... it's just...they all happened to my clients, no one else's. I keep thinking maybe I somehow did something wrong. But I don't see what. They've sent other engineers, other FSE's, the design team, everyone, to look at those machines and they haven't found anything wrong with them. I'm just afraid that maybe I'm responsible somehow and don't know it."

"Yes or no. That's the only reason you think you might be at fault?"

"Yes." Tears streamed down Crabbe's face.

"Do know of anything else you haven't told Mr. Knowles or me or your own engineers that might help determine the cause of these overdoses?"

"No."

"All right. The test is over." Bergman began to unhook Crabbe.

"Did I pass?" Crabbe was now a nervous wreck. His shirt, a name brand polo shirt, bore dark stains in the armpits. His body odor was even stronger.

"I'll have to study the results before I express any opinion. When I do, I can only tell Mr. Knowles or Mr. Vogel. It's up to them what to tell you and what to use the results for. But if you think of anything that can prevent anyone else from being hurt by these machines, you absolutely must come forward with it. If you conceal anything, it won't go well for you."

Bergman handed Crabbe a tissue, packed up, and left.

Chapter 11

Cliff quickly got the robber's head locked back. He had the robber's neck in a carotid artery hold with his right arm. At the same time, he tried to slip the dye pack into the bag that do-rag carried in his left hand, but in the commotion the bundle fell to the floor. The bag had a drawstring and was closed too tightly for Cliff to manage it.

This frenetic wrestling match lasted no more than three seconds, as the other robber gave Cliff's exposed back a horrendous kick, screaming at him to let go. A shard of pain shot through Cliff's body. He knew instantly his kidney had taken the brunt of the blow; the only thing that saved him from a serious rupture was the fact the robber was wearing Air Jordans instead of boots. Cliff released do-rag and arched his body backward in an involuntary spasmodic response to the blow. He opened his eyes, which he had squeezed shut when the kick landed, and saw a revolver pointed right between his eyes from a distance of no more than a foot. So much for the bluff theory.

"Don't shoot. I'm sorry, I give up," he managed to croak to the taller robber as do-rag got up from the floor.

"I should shoot you just for being a dumb-ass," hoodie declared with a sneer, but turned back to the front and with a jerk of his head signaled the other robber to get out. They both sprinted through the door and then to the right on the sidewalk. Cliff lay writhing in pain. He lay on the floor for another thirty seconds as Margaret and two of the customers rushed to his aid.

They all told him to stay down until help came, but he struggled to his feet anyway, with Margaret helping him as best she could once she realized he wasn't going to listen to reason. When he reached a semi-standing position he noticed for the first time that the dye pack was no longer on the floor. Do-rag must have picked it up, thinking it had fallen from his bag. His back was a wall of flame. He had to brace himself with his elbows on the lobby table until his senses adjusted to this new normal.

"Cliff," Margaret exclaimed, "that was foolish. You could have been killed." She clucked her tongue and scowled like a playground monitor scolding a clutch of rowdy boys.

The first police officer rushed through the front door at that moment, gun drawn, but depressed toward the floor. He was followed immediately by another officer, a fresh-faced rookie type. Both looked around, scanning for signs of danger or medical emergency. Several customers rushed toward them. The woman who had fainted was only now coming to. Like Cliff, she had been surrounded by other good Samaritans as soon as the robbers left.

Cliff made a point to stand up as straight as he could. His back was still afire, but he could tell already that he would be able to tolerate it if he took it easy. He didn't want the police to make him go to the hospital. He wanted no police attention at all. He'd had a lengthy and highly unpleasant hospital stay only a little over a year ago. He didn't want to repeat the experience.

One officer barked some code into his radio, then told everyone to calm down and not to leave until they'd been interviewed. This was as far as he had gotten when a message came over his radio that grabbed his attention. One robber had been apprehended a block away, writhing in pain on the sidewalk, his front pants pocket scorched and bright red.

Cliff couldn't make out the entire transmission, but after the dispatcher stopped talking he heard the younger officer tell the older one, "The little one must have tried to rip off his partner instead of splitting the loot. His partner probably realized it when the pack went off and took off without him. They never learn."

This was exactly the scenario Cliff had hoped the police would adopt. He thought the officer had it slightly wrong; do-rag probably couldn't get the tight drawstring open quickly while running and just stuck the bundle in his front pocket. He wouldn't have been the first bank robber to make that mistake. Cliff wasn't sure whether anyone had seen him try to slip the dye pack in the robber's sack, but he wasn't going to volunteer the information.

A few seconds later two more uniformed officers appeared just outside the front door, visible through the glass, supporting the do-rag robber, who resembled something from a horror movie at this point, charred cloth and red dye completely covering one side of groin. Several customers pointed and most of them yelled "That's him!"

"We have our ID's," the older officer announced to the two standing outside as he opened the bank door. "Take him to the hospital."

The officer turned back and asked who the manager was. A man in the crowd identified himself and the two moved to a desk where the officer was no doubt getting the information on the cameras, security systems, and telling him to prepare a list of serial numbers of the bait money taken and the total dollar loss. Cliff knew the drill. The younger officer began taking down the names of the witnesses, whether they were customers or staff, and so on. Soon he was joined by two more officers and they divided up the people for interview. Several of the witnesses, seeing that this was going to take a long time, declared that they didn't see anything and weren't feeling well so they were going to leave.

Cliff had not yet been interviewed and was looking for a way out. By that time three FBI agents had also shown up. Cliff knew them all. One was from the Palo Alto office and the other two were from Gina's squad in San Jose. Cliff buttonholed the one he knew the best, Woody Braswell, a strapping black fellow Cliff had once supervised, and explained that he really needed to get out of there. Braswell hadn't seen Cliff in several months and wanted to catch up on office news, but Cliff said he's slipped and fallen, hurting his back, and needed to get back to his office and lie down on his couch. Braswell offered to take him to the hospital, but Cliff declined. The agent took pity on him and told the senior police officer that Cliff was ex-FBI and needed medical attention and he, Braswell, was taking him. The officer shook his head and muttered something, pointing to one of the witnesses and then back at Cliff, obviously something about Cliff's tackle of the robber. The agent just shook his head in return and walked back over to Cliff.

"Let's go," he said. "Hang onto my arm. Make it look good."

Cliff didn't need to fake it. He held onto the agent's arm and hobbled out of the bank to the agent's car. When they got there Cliff told him he'd be fine from there, his office being only two blocks away. The agent told him that the second robber had been arrested, too. That message had come over the radio as the agent had driven up. He asked if Cliff could do a line-up later, and Cliff agreed. They shook hands, an act that sent excruciating waves through his torso once more. Braswell again suggested Cliff go to the hospital, but again Cliff begged off and started walking toward his office, thanking the agent once more.

"Say hi to Gina and the gang for me," he called back over his shoulder, not looking.

"I will," he heard Braswell call back.

Chapter 12

Vogel invited Bergman to sit on the plush sofa. Cliff, still in pain from the morning's adventure, stood and sipped at a bottled water, impatient for the results. He'd doped himself with aspirin, which helped a little but the pain was still enough to make him curt and testy.

"So, Sol, let's have it," Cliff blurted out as soon as Bergman was sitting.

"He has very strong responses. He'd make a terrible liar. He should never play poker for money."

"So he's telling the truth?"

"I'll have to study the results and issue a final, written report, which will take another two or three days, but unofficially I don't think he's being deceptive. He really believes it's a design flaw."

"No written report," Vogel declared curtly. "I don't want a paper trail that can be found during litigation."

"It's all privileged," Cliff reminded him.

"Once it's on paper, or worse, a computer, it can show up somewhere – anywhere – and I don't want that."

"That's okay with me," Bergman replied. "But my fee is the same as if I put in the hours writing the report."

"I still want you to put in the hours or whatever it is you do to give me an official final opinion, but make it oral. Can you do it by tomorrow afternoon? If Buster's innocent, I want to put him back to work. He's been through the wringer long enough."

"Well, I'm not sure he's innocent. He reacted to that last question about whether it was his fault. He's afraid he did something wrong, and maybe he did, but he seems honestly not to know what it could be. If he did screw up, he could do it again. I do think he's an honest man, though. I'll get you a final report by tomorrow, three P.M. Will you be here then for my call?"

"I'll make a point of it. Thank you for your help. You may go. Cliff, please stay a minute."

Bergman shook Vogel's hand, picked up his well-worn metal polygraph case, and left.

"Cliff. So what's next?"

"I start interviewing the clients' technicians to see what I can gather there. Maybe it's user error or someone there figured out how to sabotage the L4's."

"Is that absolutely necessary? We've already interviewed them all - repeatedly. If we send in a lawyer to re-interview them, they'll think we're just trying to intimidate them and find a way to shift blame to them. If our clients get a whiff that they're being set up for potential lawsuits, they'll drop us like an Acme anvil. This could literally put us out of business if it becomes known in the industry. Most of them have competitors' devices available. You can read all the notes and talk to our engineers about their interviews."

"Yes, it's absolutely necessary. I've read your engineers' reports. I need to see these things in action myself and judge the attitudes and competence of the users. I don't have to tell them I'm a lawyer. You can get me a name tag like an engineer would wear and I can go in like I'm just one more geek of yours trying to diagnose the problem."

"All right, but under no circumstances are you to let any of the clients know that this has happened anywhere else. So far, each one thinks it's a single incident that's only happened once – to them. You could bankrupt us if you screw this up."

"If we don't get this figured out, you could end up bankrupt anyway. Now I've got to go. My back is killing me."

Cliff spent the next two days at home stretched out in his recliner, recuperating from the kick in the back, self medicating with aspirin and the occasional beer.

He knew he should get checked out by a doctor, but he hadn't detected any blood in his urine or any other symptoms he recognized as serious kidney damage.

He'd had Maeva call off his Thursday special appearances but said he could take business calls at home. One of those was Woody Braswell, the FBI agent who had gotten him out of the bank. Braswell told him he wanted to come by with Cliff's wallet, which the police had released to him since it wasn't needed as evidence. Cliff told him to come on by.

When he got there Braswell said that both robbers were on parole and so were going back to prison without the need for a trial. Each had rolled over on the other one and made quick deals for lighter sentences on the recent robbery, but with their priors they were going to be in for at least ten more years.

"Cliff," the agent finally asked, "what in the world were you doing trying to tackle that guy? It was an armed robbery. You could have taken a bullet. The witnesses identified you as a wacko who tried to take down two guys with guns."

"Okay, it was stupid. I didn't see a weapon and thought they were bluffing with the gun threat. I don't know what got into me. The old FBI instinct, I guess. By the way, I heard one of the robbers got caught because of the dye pack. How did that happen, exactly?" He knew the answer, of course, but he wanted to find out what the police knew.

"We interviewed the tellers, and all of them but one said they didn't give him any dye packs, because he told them not to. They were too afraid. The robber made them point out the dye pack at each window."

"And the one? Let me guess, it was Margaret, the Assistant Manager."

"You know her? Yeah, that's her. She said she put the dye pack bundle in his bag even though he said not to. The unlucky moron must have tried to slip a little extra into his clothing to avoid splitting it with his partner. But he chose the wrong bundle and the wrong place to hide it. That's the current working hypothesis anyway."

"Yeah, what do you know – a stupid bank robber?!" Cliff laughed.

"Those packs get to over 400 degrees when they explode, you know. His pants were set on fire and his love life may be over for good. I have no doubt it's been painful as hell. It sounds like a real civil suit in the making if – and I am saying this purely as a hypothetical – it turned out someone actually put that dye pack there. Say, like someone wrestling around on the floor with him."

"You think I shoved that pack in his clothing? Dream on. He's a bank robber and a lying thief who'll no doubt try to make a buck any way he can. You have the word of a bank teller against that of an armed robber on parole. Who are you going to believe?"

"Margaret. For now anyway."

"There you go then."

The agent eyed Cliff with a sardonic smile. "Oddly, though, the crazy guy who wrestled with the robber left the scene before being interviewed by the police, due to medical necessity. So the police don't have his name in their report. Since the bad guys are back in the slammer for parole violation, and have cut a deal already on the robbery, the cops aren't going to investigate, either." He waited a couple of beats to see if Cliff said any more. When he was met with silence, he handed Cliff his wallet, told him to get well, and said he had to be going.

As soon as Braswell left he picked up the phone and ordered a large bouquet of flowers for Margaret. By the end of the day his back was feeling almost normal.

Chapter 13

Fridays were running days for Cliff and his back was feeling fine. It was expected to hit 90° by mid-afternoon, so Cliff decided to get out for a morning run while it was still cool, but he wasn't a daybreak runner kind of guy. There was nothing pressing at work so he figured he could go in late. He ate a light breakfast and after reading the morning paper, put on his running clothes.

It was 9:30 by the time he reached the parking lot at the county park. He got out and stretched for a few minutes, but it was already warming up so he decided to get going while the shadows were still long and the air cool.

He had a regular route he liked to follow. He was so familiar with this route by now that he tended to run it in a subconscious reverie. He ran on autopilot, vaguely aware of the hikers, the birds, the squirrels and trees, but he relished the zoned out feeling, the vacancy in his mind that running brought. When he got in the zone he achieved a sort of nirvana, a sense of all worries melting away. So it was a bit disturbing when something caught his eye and jerked him back to reality.

He saw a woman and girl twenty feet or so off the trail by a chain link fence that demarcated the edge of the park land. The girl was scowling and talking in an impatient-sounding voice, although he couldn't make out the words. He recognized both the woman and location. It was Ellen Kennedy and the location was that of a notoriously hard geocache in that park, one which he had found a year or two earlier. The girl must be the niece, Ashley. He stopped to watch, amused.

When he had stood there next to the trail for two or three minutes, Ellen noticed him and at first stepped protectively in front of the girl as though to shield her from some pervert's gaze. Almost immediately, though, she recognized Cliff and cocked one of her formidable eyebrows.

"What's so funny?" she called to him as she walked his direction. "Let me guess. You've found this one already."

"I have," he said, laughing, and walked to meet her halfway. "It's pure evil. Not one to break in a newbie. This must be Ashley."

Ashley, hearing her name, looked up and was now watching the two of them.

"Ashley, come on over here," Ellen called to her. "I want you to meet a friend of mine. This is Cliff."

Ashley took the few steps to join them held out her right hand stiffly to shake. "Hello."

"Hello, Ashley. Is this your first time geocaching?"

"No, Aunt Ellen took me once before. It's really fun. Are you a geocacher, too?"

"I sure am. I found this one before. Do you want some help?"

Ashley grinned and looked at Ellen. "Is that okay?"

"Of course. Come on, let's all go back over there." She led them back to the fence and showed Cliff her GPS unit. The distance indicator shrunk to about eight feet as she got to the metal fence post. "This is where it seems to zero out," she said, "I think it's in the fence post, but when I take off the cap there's nothing there. Just a hollow steel pipe." She removed the metal cap from the fence post and held it upside down for Cliff to see. Nothing was glued to the underside of the cap. There was no wire hooked onto the top of the pipe. She peered down the post as though to demonstrate her previous futile attempts.

"You're very, very warm."

At that remark Ashley turned to the post and knocked on it, but she was too short to look into the top.

"The cache page says you don't need any tools, but if it's in there, you'd have to use some sort of tool to get it out." Ellen said this with a stern look of disapproval.

"Does it say you don't need a tool or you don't need to *bring* any tools?" A slight smirk crept over Cliff's visage.

Ellen took a second look at the cache page readout on her smart phone. After a beat she harrumphed. "Oh. You're right. So I guess that means the tool you need is here somewhere."

"Tool or tools, yes."

At this Ashley piped up, "We need tools? What kind of tools?"

Ellen replied, "I've seen caches with metal tops or parts in PVC tubes that you need to retrieve using a magnet, but that's the closest I know of. A magnet wouldn't do any good here. If you tried to dangle a magnet on a string it would just stick right to the steel post."

"Unless the cache had a magnet or piece of metal dead center glued onto a cork or film canister, say, and you had a magnet dead center on a wooden pole that you could stick straight down. The wood would prevent the magnet from sticking to the side and you could make contact with the cache and pull straight up." Cliff grinned as he said this.

Ellen and Ashley immediately started looking around for a wooden pole as described. Cliff let them scour the area for about five minutes before he said, "Of course that would only work if this cache was metal or had a magnet on it. This one's all plastic."

Ellen stood up, shot him the evil eye and punched his shoulder. "You dirty, lowdown ...." She cast an eye at Ashley to signify to Cliff that if her niece weren't present she'd have finished the sentence with stronger language. And maybe a harder punch. "That's for sending us on a wild goose chase."

Cliff laughed gleefully, although his shoulder hurt more than he expected. This gal could throw a punch. Ashley looked on bewildered and maybe just a little shocked that her aunt would hit a friend.

"The tools are right here, just like he said on the cache page." Cliff made an expansive sweeping movement with his arm.

Ellen looked around once more, but quickly looked back up at Cliff. "We've searched all around here. There's nothing but leaf litter, twigs, and these palm fronds."

The California coast may be the only place in the world where conifers, deciduous trees and palms grow side by side. The palms are not native, of course, but the many imported specimens have thrived and even spread in a few places, much as tropical parrots, escapees from birdcages have thrived in San Francisco.

"Bingo!" Cliff replied.

"Bingo? What, the palm fronds?"

Ashley looked on confused.

"Notice anything different about some of them?" Cliff asked.

Ashley and Ellen both bent and picked up a frond base. "I saw these were cut off," Ashley answered brightly. "Is this it? The tool, I mean."

"Oh no. No, no, not that..." Ellen moaned, suddenly realizing the task that lay ahead. Several fronds had been cut so that their broad bases were separated from the leafy part. These particular frond bases were exceptionally curved so as to form natural cups. "How far back was that pond?"

"About a hundred yards," Cliff answered still grinning.

"Carrying water in these fronds is nearly impossible. It'll spill and slosh all over." Ellen was shaking her head in disgust.

"Here, you can borrow my water bottle," Cliff offered. Since the midsummer day was expected to be hot, he had brought a water bottle for the run. He lifted it to his lips and took a big swig then handed it to Ellen, still about half full.

Ellen took it and handed it to Ashley. "Here, Ash, pour this into that pole."

Ashley gushed, "Oh I get it. You pour the water in and it makes the geocache float to the top."

"Smart girl," Cliff replied.

Ashley poured the water into the pole, but almost immediately cried out, "Aunt Ellen, it's leaking out!"

Ellen examined the pole and saw that, indeed, the water poured in was leaking out a neat screw hole near the bottom of the pole. She shot Cliff a look that could have scorched all the ice off Greenland.

Unfazed, he commented, "Now you see why the cache page says to take at least two people for this one."

Ellen handed Cliff a palm frond. "Here. You get the frond. Ashley gets the bottle. I'll stay here and plug the hole." She sat down next to the fence and put her thumb over the screw hole. Some of the water from the bottle was still in the pole.

"Come on Ashley," Cliff said. "It looks like you and I have been elected to go back to that pond and get more water."

Rather than being discouraged, Ashley thought this was a great twist, an adventure of sorts, and immediately took off jogging back toward the pond they had passed. Cliff had to jog to keep up. When they got there, Ashley submerged the bottle in the green algae-filled water and stood up. Cliff dipped the frond in, but his payload was at most a third of hers, and, as Ellen predicted, tended to slosh and spill as he moved. When they made it back to the pole Ashley immediately emptied the bottle into the top. From the increasing pitch it was evident that the pole was filling fairly rapidly. The cache must take up a fairly large part of the volume of the pole. Ellen continued to sit on the ground, thumb over the screw hole, giving Cliff a smug look, like "Who's having fun, now, wise guy?"

Cliff dumped his meager cargo into the pole and then turned back. He had to sprint to catch up with Ashley, who was scampering with a lot more energy than Cliff would have thought a cancer patient would have. By the third round trip he was panting heavily, but the pole was nearly full enough to see the cache. He peeked down inside. Ashley was about to return to the pond, but Cliff stopped her.

"Ashley, hold on," he called. "My fingers are too fat to reach down in there, but maybe yours aren't. Can you try?"

She came back to the fence post. She reached her hand up and slipped three fingers in.

"I can feel something!" she squealed, delighted. With some twisting and considerable effort she finally pulled up a length of PVC pipe obviously chosen to be small enough in diameter to fit loosely in the steel pipe. It had been sealed on both ends with caps, and both caps had projecting loops of nylon cord that had been glued on so that someone could extract the cache. The owner had wisely put loops on both ends so that the cache could be extracted even if put back in either end first, so it couldn't be put in upside down. Ashley began trying to open it, but was unsuccessful.

Ellen stood, letting the water dribble out of the pole through the small screw hole. "Great job, Ash," she said heartily. "Here, let me try."

Ashley handed her the cache. With an effortless twist of her wrists she had unscrewed one cap and handed it back to her niece, who quickly pulled out the log sheet which had been rolled into a cylinder and stuffed in a plastic bag. The log sheet was surprisingly long and had been signed by dozens of geocachers already. Ashley signed her name and handed it to Ellen. Ellen signed and took a moment to read over the names on the sheet.

"What's your geocaching name?" she asked Cliff. "Wait, don't tell me," she added, running her finger down the list until she stopped on one entry. "CliffNotes, I bet."

"You must be a trained detective."

"Har har. Never heard that one."

Ashley took the log sheet back and started rolling it tightly, to fit into the bag and the PVC pipe.

"So how did you get off on a Friday?" he asked Ellen.

"Theresa had to see her agent to sign some papers and then she was going to work out. She spends two hours at that club every day. Models have to do that. She tries to do it mostly in the evening when I'm off work, but I had to watch Ashley while she was at her agent's anyway, so I'm just taking the whole day. Like I said, the Bureau's been very generous with my schedule. I just log this as 199. I don't have to take leave."

Cliff knew that 199 was the FBI classification for terrorism cases. She was logging her time babysitting a deceased congressman's child out of the national counter-terrorism budget. This arrangement bothered him, especially since the widow was living in Monte Sereno, in a home that was probably worth millions. And wasn't Bishop from a wealthy family? His parents must have a trust fund for the granddaughter, mustn't they? At the least, couldn't she sell the house and live modestly on the interest or dividends? He didn't know the answers, but the questions bugged him. Still, he said nothing.

"Well, congratulations on finding the geocache. Like I said, that one is pure evil."

"Seriously, Cliff," she replied *sotto voce*, "thank you for the help. I'm sure this cache is the highlight of her day. Yesterday was rough for her and I'm glad she's feeling so peppy today."

"She's a sweet kid, and smart, too. I'm glad I could help." He turned to Ashley, who was replacing the cache, and called, "Ashley, I have to finish my run. See you around."

She waved at him and called back, "Thanks, Cliff," as he disappeared around a bend in the trail.

Chapter 14

The radiation tech was named Brittany and to Cliff she looked like a teenager. He wondered how a young kid could be given control of a million-dollar machine that had the power to kill someone. He soon learned, however, that she had graduated from San Francisco State in Biology summa cum laude five years earlier and had been a radiation tech for the last three years. Her chubby baby face contributed to the youthful appearance. Strands of mousy brown hair kept struggling to escape from their perch behind her ear and found a natural resting spot in front of her eyes. She continually brushed them back as she spoke, a self-imposed Sisyphean task of which she seemed totally unaware.

"The patient jumped right off the table and yelled at me. She said I burned her skin."

"Where was the radiation being applied, what part of the body?" Cliff had his Zoom recorder going.

"Right there," Brittany replied, touching her chest. "Lung cancer."

"Did you examine her skin?"

"Of course. It was a little bit red and warm to the touch, too. That shouldn't happen with 180 rads."

"What happened next?"

"I got the doctor to come in and he examined her, too. We both agreed something wasn't right. Two months later she was dead. I told all this to the other engineer."

"I know. I read his write-up. I just have some different expertise so they want me to take another look at it. I'd like you to demonstrate exactly what you did."

Brittany led Cliff into the console room and showed him the setup process. It seemed identical to what he had seen at Xlectrix. The tech placed a heavy bowl-like object on the treatment table, then another on top of that, then a small electronic device on top of that.

"These are lead," she explained, "and this is a dosimeter."

Back in the console room she went through the normal process Cliff had witnessed back in Palo Alto, except there was no dongle. The system did not show the diagnostic mode notification and the tech did not get the warning about the dosage being too high. This was as expected since she was showing him how the normal treatment had gone, not how to force an overdose. He watched the DPP light on the Lilac as the beam shot into the lead. It stayed on. When she was done she opened the door to the treatment room and led him back to view the dosimeter.

"One hundred fifty rads," she said triumphantly as she held up the device, "just like it's supposed to be. It's working fine. That's exactly how I did it with the patient. If they told you I messed up that's total BS. I've been…"

"No, Brittany, no one has told me that. I'm sure you're a good tech. Tell me, did the DPP light stay on the whole time?"

"Well, I have to watch my screen, so I wasn't looking through the window at the Lilac. It always came on during all the checklists and has seemed normal."

"Has there been any repeat of this since the incident, any unusual behavior from the system at all?"

"No, everything has seemed normal. The patients have gotten their treatments. We never stopped using the Lilac because the company said it wasn't capable of overdosing like that. They said the woman probably died of cancer, but there was a big exit burn in her back when she came back in a few days later. I saw pictures in a textbook. We're trained in that. That was an exit hole from an X-ray beam. I'll swear to it. She must have had a tube of dead tissue in her body where the beam passed through. The doctor said the dose looked like it was over 10,000 rads. One thousand will kill you if it's spread over the whole body. But ten in a small hole like that? It's like taking an auger and drilling a hole right through the body and filling it with decaying flesh and plugging both ends. Gawd, it was awful."

Cliff tried to shut the image out of his mind. "They reinstalled the software, I understand, is that right?"

"Yes. Since they installed the new release, it's been fine. Better in fact."

"Better? How so?"

"Faster, that's all. It all looks the same on the screen, but it doesn't take quite so long for some of the steps. It's more responsive. Sometimes with the old system there was a hitch, a little delay after you hit a key before the screen refreshed. It could be irritating to wait for it since you want to type the next command. It's immediate now."

"Did the service rep swap in new hardware?" Cliff had not previously heard that the reinstall involved a new release of the software. Vogel had just said they reinstalled the program with a different dongle. If the software and hardware were the same as before, the speed shouldn't change.

"No. He just put that dongle thing in the back and installed on this same system. I was here when he did it. It took half a day. He must have rebooted at least ten times. It was a new guy, Tom somebody. Is Buster in trouble? He's such a nice guy."

The phone on the console rang. Brittany picked it up, listened for a moment and replied with an affirmative grunt, then hung up.

"We've got to get out of here. They have to use it for treatment. These treatment rooms cost thousands of dollars per hour to sit idle. They only gave this to us for fifteen minutes. Patients are waiting. So I've got to get back to work."

They left the treatment area and moved back to an inside office.

Cliff shook her hand and thanked her for her time.

"One last thing," Cliff said. "You mentioned Buster. Did he do anything out of the ordinary around the time this happened?"

"No. Nothing. Just the normal service. I don't think he was even in any time near when the incident occurred, but he could have been here when someone else was on the shift. He's so funny. He has a new joke every time he comes. I really liked him. This new guy Tom is a cold fish. I hope Buster isn't going to lose his job over this. Did he do something wrong?"

"Not that I know of, but I don't have anything to do with personnel decisions. If you think of anything call me at this number." He handed her a business card with the Xlectrix logo on it and a telephone extension there where messages would be recorded. His title was Special Consultant. Vogel had set that up so that the clients would not realize he was working with the legal department.

"OK. Hey, has this happened anywhere else? Is there a problem with the Lilac?"

Damn. The question he was hoping to avoid. He hated lying, but he was bound by attorney-client confidentiality. "God, let's hope not. I'm sure Xlectrix would hear about it if it did." Technically that answer was the truth. Time to get out of there. He was saved by the ringing of his own cell phone. Hurriedly he reached in his pocket and pulled out the phone and held it up in apology. Brittany nodded and Cliff headed for the front lobby. The phone said Unknown Caller. He stopped in the lobby and answered it.

"Hello?"

"Hello, Cliff? This is Ellen Kennedy. Matt gave me your cell number. I hope that's okay."

"Sure," he managed, hoping to mask his insincerity. He hoped she wasn't one of those liberated women who believed in asking the man for a date. He didn't mind liberated women, he just didn't want to have to tell her no. What would be his excuse – he had to wash his hair? For a split second he appreciated how awkward it must be for a woman to reject a man calling to ask her out.

"Sorry to bother you. Ashley forgot to give you back your water bottle. I wanted to know if I should just take it by your house or leave it with Matt or what."

He didn't want to give her his home address, although he realized this was silly since she could get that from FBI or motor vehicle records. At least if he didn't give it to her she couldn't show up there uninvited without looking like a stalker. He didn't really care about the water bottle. He had two others. But he figured that as long as Ellen had it, she would have an excuse to contact him again.

"Where are you now? At the RA?"

"No. I'm at home with Ashley. Monte Sereno."

"Look, I'm near Good Sam," he replied, using the local shorthand for Good Samaritan Hospital. "You're more or less on my way home. I'll just drop by and pick it up. What's the address?"

She gave it to him.

"Okay, I should be there in fifteen minutes or so."

He had nothing further to do at this cancer treatment center so he told the receptionist to thank the office manager for giving him the chance to interview Brittany.

When he pulled up to the residence at the address Ellen had given him, he was awed at the enormity of the estate laid out before his eyes. He had seen some very impressive homes in his day but this one shamed them all. The land alone, several acres at least, must have cost tens of millions by itself. The main house was fashioned after an English manor house, with two looming wings. The faux Jacobethan style reminded him of the castle in Downton Abbey although it wasn't that grand. Despite the expansive front lawn, the house looked totally out of place in the wooded hills, especially since it was accompanied by a smaller "mother-in-law" unit only fifty feet away built in a California ranch house style. That structure alone could have housed a dozen mothers-in-law, and it was unclear to Cliff whether it was intended as servants' quarters or a guest house.

All this he could see through the wrought iron gate as he idled in the driveway, but sturdy brick walls covered in English ivy obscured the manse from the street. After a moment the gate cranked open at some silent command and he drove onto the grounds. As he followed the meandering pavement he reached a point where he could see yet another structure, a Caribbean-style cabana of sorts, in the rear overlooking a massive swimming pool and barbecue complex. If consistency was the hobgoblin of little minds, the Bishop architects were large-minded indeed.

Cliff intended to just knock on the door, grab his bottle and go. He parked his Volvo C-70 convertible next to a Chevy that he immediately recognized as Ellen's Bureau car. A nearby gardener was trimming the immaculate hedges that delineated the pathways through the luxuriant garden. Cliff got out of the car, walked to the front door and knocked. The massive knocker could have doubled as an anchor for the Queen Mary.

The door flew open immediately. Ashley stood there holding the door open, grinning. She wore faded jeans and a Justin Bieber T-shirt. "Cliff! I saw you coming up the driveway."

"Well, hi there, Ashley." He looked to see if she had the water bottle in her hands or within reach. When he didn't see it, he added, "Is Ellen here?"

"She had to pee. She's in the bathroom," she answered without an iota of embarrassment. She grabbed his fingers with both her hands and pulled. "Come in. I got some geocoins. Come see 'em."

Reluctantly, he stepped inside and closed the door behind him. The girl had cancer after all. Disappointing her was out of the question. Ashley ran to a long, low table nearby that looked like it just needed ten pins and a Brunswick ball return to be complete. She scooped up three shiny objects and handed them to Cliff.

Some geocachers have their own personalized coins minted, usually with bright colors and fanciful designs, similar to the coins some military units or motorcycle clubs have minted. These are rarely left in geocaches except occasionally as a first-to-find or FTF prize. More often they are awarded after a geocacher has completed a difficult challenge, or won a contest at a geocaching event. They are not parted with lightly. Cliff was surprised to see she had acquired three so early in her geocaching career. He recognized the patterns on all three and knew the geocachers whose signature items these were.

"Awesome, Ashley," he cooed. "Gimme five." He bent down and held his hand palm out.

She gave him a hearty slap, palm to palm, beaming. At that moment Ellen emerged.

"Oh, hi, Cliff," she said, a bit discomfited, "I didn't hear you arrive. I was in the back of the house." Sorry I wasn't here to answer the door."

"Ashley did fine. She was showing me her geocoins."

"We went to an unevent last night. I met some local geocachers. You have some *really nice* people here in this community. Ashley won three coins playing rock paper scissors."

The significant look she gave Cliff at that moment told him the whole story. An unevent is an informal gathering of geocachers, often for coffee or pizza, with no special purpose other than hanging out, talking, and eating, maybe sharing tips on solving a puzzle cache or finding a particularly hard cache. The name was coined to distinguish it from an event, which is an organized gathering with its own cache page. Geocachers get a "find" for attending an event and logging it online. Unevents may just be arranged by email among friends, but are sometimes announced on the local online geocaching forum. Ellen was a newcomer but was no doubt welcomed. Equally evident was the fact that the geocachers must have discreetly learned of Ashley's interest in geocaching, and, no doubt, her fight with cancer. Cliff was certain those "games" were rigged so Ashley could win. Ellen and Ashley were previously unknown to the group, but that fact would not have been a deterrent to the coin owners parting with their precious prizes. Some things you just do.

Cliff nodded an acknowledgment. "So how does it feel to live in a place like this?" he asked. "I think Barry Bonds would have a hard time knocking a ball out of this living room."

"It's big," Ellen replied evenly, unimpressed with this attempt at humor.

Cliff was waiting for her to produce the water bottle, but it was still nowhere in sight. "Really, I don't get it," he finally said, growing more irritated at the pretentiousness and opulence of his surroundings. "What's with your sister? She could sell this place for eight figures easy. She's got a gardener, an estate from Bishop, a good-paying career. She could hire a nanny or move someplace cheaper and rent this out. I've just never seen a hardship case quite like this."

Ellen's face flushed. She looked as though she was about to tell him off, but bit her tongue since Ashley was still in earshot. "Ashley, honey, why don't you go run and get Cliff's water bottle. It's in the kitchen in the drain rack."

Ashley ran out.

"Just who the hell are you to judge her?" Ellen hissed once Ashley was gone. "Who the hell are you to judge me? Not that it's any of your goddam business, but the house is underwater by at least $3 million. And it's a recourse loan, too. The bank is threatening to foreclose. The bank's paying the gardener to keep it marketable; Theresa doesn't have the money for that. She's trying to negotiate a short sale. Mark's estate is a long way from final distribution. It's tied up in complicated trust arrangements. The money-grubbing lawyers are bleeding her dry and Ashley's cancer treatments are back-breaking financially. There's all kinds of stuff that isn't covered by insurance, like child care. Mark's parents are helping her out and eventually she should come out okay, but she's barely keeping the sheriff from the door right now."

Cliff was completely chagrined. He had made some assumptions he now realized weren't justified. "Okay, I'm sorry, I didn't mean anything. I just…"

His half-hearted apology was interrupted by the sound of tires at the front of the house. He turned to look through the window. A gleaming Mercedes S550 came screeching in much too fast and rolled to a halt right outside the front door. Theresa Bishop stepped out of the Benz and slammed the car door. Even through the ornately leaded and beveled windows Cliff could see she was beautiful. Tall, shapely, with a striking contrast between her deeply tanned skin and white hair. He also recognized her now as one of the inhabitants of those twin bathtubs in those ridiculous Cialis ads.

Bishop shoved the door open roughly and stepped inside. Immediately she lit the cigarette she had fished from her purse as she walked from the car. Then she noticed Cliff.

"Who's this?" she asked Ellen.

"Theresa," she replied stiffly, "this is Cliff Knowles, the geocacher I told you about who helped Ashley the other day."

"Oh, right. The FBI guy," she responded, finally making eye contact with Cliff. "Nice to meet you." She shifted the cigarette to her left hand and extended her right to shake.

He gave her hand a perfunctory shake. Her nails were long and might have had more paint on them than the Mercedes. "Likewise."

Cliff had worn thick glasses throughout his FBI career because he needed them, needed them badly. But after he retired he found a surgeon who could correct his eyesight with laser surgery. He loved the freedom this gave him, since he no longer needed to wear glasses. But his unaided vision now was not quite as good as it had been with glasses before. So sometimes faces were in a slight soft focus, like what cinematographers use to make older actresses look young.

This is why he was shocked when she stepped forward. He was unprepared to discover that the beauty he had seen through the front window was gone. Well, not entirely gone. She still had a breathtaking figure and fine cheekbones. But her face was riddled with the feathery cracks of a middle aged smoker and showed sun damage, too. She looked ten years older close up in person.

"God, the tanning salon was overbooked," she said to Ellen. "Can you believe it? I'm in there three times a week and have a standing reservation and they make we wait fifteen minutes?" Then turning to Ashley, who was just arriving with the water bottle, "Ash, hon, can you get me an ashtray please?"

Ashley seemed just as happy to fetch the ashtray as the water bottle. She took off again.

A $100,000 car, three times a week tanning, and cigarettes. Cliff's desire to apologize for his hasty judgment had entirely evaporated. From his days in New York he knew that virtually all models smoked… when they weren't shooting heroin or puking in the ladies room. Anything to keep the weight off. But smoking in front of her daughter who had cancer? The second-hand smoke couldn't be good for her. He knew if he said anything to Ellen she'd justify the tanning and smoking as necessary for a model. He shot Ellen a scowl which was returned with a small shrug and an expression that told him he wasn't entirely wrong. She handed him the water bottle.

"I'll be going now," he said simply. "Thanks for returning the bottle."

"Thanks for saving me the trip," Ellen replied, her voice equally devoid of warmth. Theresa Bishop ignored the exchange and was already walking back toward the kitchen still muttering about the tanning salon.

Cliff hastened out the door before Ashley could return and beg him to stay. He climbed into his car feeling slightly embarrassed that moments ago he had actually felt relieved he had an upscale car that fit into the milieu. He realized how shallow that was. He turned on the ignition and began driving the circle back around the soccer field of a lawn to the front gate.

As he pulled out onto the street an announcement came over the car radio:

> *We have breaking news. A large explosion occurred in Palo Alto at the Jewish Community Center moments ago. Police and Firefighters are on the scene. Initial reports indicate that it may have been a bomb but that has not been confirmed. There is no official word on casualties yet but witnesses reported seeing a woman running from the building in flames. Another report on Twitter stated that a Palestinian flag was draped over the center's sign. That too is unconfirmed. We have a reporter on the way to the scene now. We'll have more on this as soon as we can.*

He turned up the volume, but the announcer moved on to traffic and weather. He was no more than ten minutes away from the Bishop home when he heard a siren behind him. He pulled over and watched Ellen's Chevy Malibu zoom by him, blue and red lights flashing.

Chapter 15

Matt Nguyen was stopped at the light at Charleston and Fabian, a long block away from the Jewish Community Center when he heard the sound of the explosion. It was surprisingly faint and if he'd had the radio on at the moment he would have missed it. But it was enough to draw his attention to his left. He saw smoke and knew something bad had happened, probably a gas leak exploding. Two seconds later a dark SUV pulled out onto the street in that vicinity and headed north, away from his direction. The way it leaned over as it squealed out of the driveway told him it was going much too fast.

He didn't know for sure that it was coming from the same driveway at that distance, but he decided he'd better take a look. He immediately put on his lights and siren and started to turn left from the through lane, cutting in front of the cars waiting in the left turn lane. When he pulled onto Fabian there was a car between him and the SUV, blocking his view of the lower half and making it hard to identify the make and model, although at this distance he probably could not have anyway.

He floored it, and began to catch up to the car in front, but he had to watch for anyone pulling out of the many driveways since this was a commercial area with parking lots lining both sides. The car driver in front must have heard the siren or seen the lights because it pulled over to let him by. Within seconds he was in front of the Jewish Center, now engulfed in flames, and for an instant he was conflicted whether to stop and render assistance, call 911, or chase the SUV, but it was obvious that there were dozens of people now in the parking lot, some on cell phones, and he doubted he could be of much use there. He was the only one doing this particular task – chasing the SUV – so he kept going.

He got close enough to be confident the car was the same make as Abboud's, but it looked different to him somehow. It looked darker; with the sun reflecting off the back it looked like a shiny black but the lower part was lighter. Maybe it was a different year or different model. Maybe it wasn't Abboud's at all. The SUV wheeled left, out of his sight, clearly fleeing now. Matt continued to accelerate. When he got to that side street the SUV had already turned left again, still out of sight. He came to the cross street and could see it half a block down to his left. He floored it once more, fishtailing and almost hitting a line of parked cars before recovering.

He got close enough to tell the SUV did not have a standard California plate, but it was heavily mud-splattered and impossible to read. There was some color under the mud. It could have been an out-of-state plate or one of the many California specialty plates with artwork on them – the whale tail, the palm trees, Yosemite. Of course, a bomber would not be likely to use his real license plate; it would be a simple matter to steal one off any parked car. The entire lower part of the rear was covered in thick mud, in fact, which Matt assumed was an intentional attempt to hide the license number and any other identifying stickers or marks. Maybe that was why it looked different. He could also tell from the silhouette that the driver was a male.

Finally on a straight stretch, he looked down to grab the microphone off the dash and radio in to the FBI that he was in pursuit. At that moment a bus pulled away from the curb directly in front of him. Passengers on the bus had been making too much noise for the driver to hear the sirens. Matt looked up a split second later, but it was not soon enough. He slammed on his brakes but still hit the rear of the bus at over 30 miles an hour.

The bus driver, a young black woman, stopped the bus immediately, got out and ran back. The front of Matt's car was demolished. She returned to her bus and radioed for help then went back to Matt's car. He still sat, dazed, in the driver's seat. The air bag had deployed and hit him hard in the face, burning his cheeks but saving his life. The white lubricating powder from the airbag covered his head and upper body, bestowing on him a ghostly appearance.

The woman tried to open the door, but it was jammed. She ran around to the passenger side. That door opened, although with difficulty. By this time several passengers had gotten out and gotten close, taking photos or videos with their smart phones. One or two asked if they could help. Matt sat motionless, still stunned. The bus driver touched Matt's right hand and sought a pulse. As soon as he felt her hand he moved his arm. The bus driver helped clear the airbag away and breathed a sigh of relief.

"Are you okay?" She asked the apparition.

Matt took a moment to respond. "I'm not sure," he finally said. He began to move his arms around. His left hand and arm hurt like hell, having been driven by the airbag against the side window. But he could move everything – legs, arms, head. He released his seat belt and tried to open the driver's door, but was just as unsuccessful as the bus driver had been. Slowly, he climbed out the passenger side.

"I'm sorry... I'm sorry... I just didn't hear you," the bus driver stuttered.

"Uh yeah, it's okay," Matt gulped. "I was going too fast. It wasn't your fault."

"I'm sorry," the woman repeated. Several bus passengers videoed the whole exchange. One of them came over to Matt and asked again if he was okay. He assured him he was.

"You'd better call in and get another bus to come out and take your passengers," he told the driver. "The police are going to want to hold this one and you."

She returned to her bus while Matt climbed back in the passenger seat of his Bureau car. He checked the radio and it was still working. He called in that he had been in an accident with a bus and to send another agent. The radio operator asked if he or anyone needed medical attention, and upon being told no, told him that everyone in the area was going to the bombing in Palo Alto and would not be able to respond. So now he knew it was a bombing, not a gas leak.

"My Bureau car is totaled. You'll have to send a tow truck. Tell my supervisor I witnessed a suspect flee the bombing. Male, driving a dark blue or black SUV. He'll send someone here. East Meadow near Louis Drive."

"10-4."

The bus driver pulled her bus over to the side and returned to tell him that they were dispatching an officer. Ten minutes later a Sheriff's Department patrol car rolled up. The officer determined that there was little if any damage to the bus other than some scratches on the rear bumper. Matt and the driver both made statements that the bus driver was not at fault. The deputy chose not to cite anyone and said he would normally do a lot more investigation, talk to the passengers, and so on, but he had to get back over to the Jewish Center to help with crowd control. He laid out two lighted flares behind Matt's car, which was in the lane blocking traffic.

Matt told him about the SUV and the deputy told him he had heard the vehicle description put out by the FBI. When Matt told him the license plate and back of the vehicle was obscured by mud the deputy went back to his patrol car and put that detail out over the air. He made Matt prove to him that he was coherent and physically okay by walking around and answering some questions. Once everyone was satisfied that there was no significant injury they agreed to call it done and go on their way. The bombing had to take priority.

The driver, assured that she was not going to be blamed for the accident, and being told that the deputy could not stay on the scene due to the bombing, obtained permission from her dispatcher to continue on her route. The replacement bus was canceled. The deputy asked the passengers who were still standing around if anyone had a bottle of water they could spare. One young woman did. The deputy took it, handed it to Matt, and told him to wash his face. Then he said he had to go, returned to his patrol car and left.

Matt finally realized what he must look like. He began brushing off the powder from his clothes. He took his sport coat off and shook it violently, sending a plume of cornstarch into the air and revealing his gun to the passengers. This drew a chorus of murmurs and gasps, since apparently all or most of them had not realized Matt was law enforcement. The siren and lights had been totally extinguished by the crash and the car was not a marked car. The airbag and powder coating on the windows had obscured Matt's actions inside the cabin when he radioed in. The bus driver directed the passengers to get back in the bus, which they did.

As the bus pulled away, Ellen drove up and stopped by the curb behind Matt's car, which was still blocking the lane. He was standing on the curb washing the powder off his face. She rushed to his side and assured herself he was okay. Ellen told him that the FBI radio operator had a tow truck on the way. She had a reflective triangle which she put out behind the flares. Traffic was light and had no trouble driving around his car.

"What about the bombing?" Matt asked her.

"Two deaths so far, some major injuries. The fire's been put out. The whole R.A. is there along with the ERT," she replied, referring to the FBI Emergency Response Team. "They're taking statements, doing a neighborhood investigation, looking for any security camera or cell phone videos, the whole nine yards. There was a Palestinian flag found draped on the sign out front. The PD has it in evidence. It looks like a terrorist job. There's Palo Alto PD and Sheriff's and Fire all over the place. I think they have enough manpower. We need to stay here until the tow truck comes anyway. Tell me about this SUV you were chasing."

"It tore out of the scene of the bombing at almost the same time the explosion happened. I was nearby on Charleston, and saw it come out down the block. I started pursuit and almost caught up to it on East Meadow but the bus pulled out in front of me as I was reaching down for the radio."

"Make, model…?

"Same as Abboud's, same color, too, I think, but the back was all splattered with mud. It was definitely dark. It could have been black. I'm sorry. I should have gotten…"

"Whoa. Slow down. It's not a big deal. I'm sure you got what you could. We'll get that out. Did you see for sure it was coming out of the Jewish Center lot?"

Matt had to think about that one for a minute.

"No, I can't really say that. I was a block away and it could have been one of the other nearby driveways. Whoever it was definitely was fleeing, though."

"Fleeing the site of a bombing doesn't mean they were involved in it. Could they have been fleeing you because you chased them?"

"I suppose later, but it took the first turn out of the driveway almost on two wheels while I was still sitting at the light."

"Okay. That's a lead at least."

They sat and speculated for another twenty minutes until the tow truck came. By the time the Bureau car was on its way to the Bureau maintenance facility to be stripped of its radio and anything else that could be salvaged it had been almost two hours since the bombing. Ellen radioed in that they were leaving the scene of the accident and they were directed to return to the Palo Alto Resident Agency.

Chapter 16

The next day Matt, Ellen and the entire surveillance team that had followed Ghalib Abboud to the Rose Garden went to his house, a very small older home near downtown Mountain View that could charitably be described as ramshackle at best. They did not have any sort of warrant, nor any probable cause to get one. The plan was for Matt and one of the other senior agents to interview Abboud. The others were there in case things should go bad. They were to wait outside and to stop Abboud if he tried to flee, since they would then have probable cause, or rush inside as backup if there was any sign of violence.

They wanted to surprise him and to make sure to get there before he left for work, if he had a job, that is. They still didn't know. They formed outside his house at 6:30 A.M. and waited for some sign of life inside. There was none. The SUV that was usually parked in his driveway was still there.

After half an hour the next-door neighbor, an elderly woman originally from El Salvador, came by walking her dog and asked them what they were doing parked in front Abboud's house. Matt showed his FBI credentials and asked her if she knew the man who lived there. The woman told him she did, but not well, and said she was looking after his mail and cat while he was gone. She was surprised he had asked her for the favor since they barely knew each other. He had not left her a key.

"When did he leave?" Matt asked her.

"Last night. He had to go back to Gaza. His father is very ill. He said he was dying. My husband gave him a ride to the airport."

Matt thanked her and relayed the news to the others. He and another agent went to the front door and knocked loudly several times but got no answer. The neighbor stood watching and yelling at them that Gil, as she called him, was not home. After a few minutes they gave up.

Matt asked the neighbor where Abboud worked, but she said she wasn't sure. She thought it was in construction because she had seen lumber and buckets in the back of his SUV once or twice. He followed her back to her house to talk to her husband, who, as it turned out, knew even less. His only contribution was that en route to the airport, the only time he'd ever had much of a conversation with Gil, Abboud talked incessantly about how Israel dropped bombs on Palestinian babies and otherwise oppressed his people.

Abboud was reprioritized to a major case when this investigation was reported back through FBI channels, although he still wasn't directly implicated in the bombing. The explosion had been confirmed as a bombing by the Palo Alto Fire Department Arson Team and the FBI ERT. That case was also assigned to Matt but under a separate title and case number.

There were dozens of people to interview. By the end of the day the first twenty leads had been assigned for these interviews. Ellen had three: one victim who had minor injuries, one employee of the Jewish center, and one of the paramedics. She knew there would be many more to come.

Although Cliff followed the news of the bombing over the next several days, and was as concerned as the next person, it did not involve him directly. He had his own interviews to worry about. The other two Lilac operators who had patients suffer overdoses were located farther east. One was in Milpitas, a bustling city in the northeast corner of the valley where high-tech firms were now overflowing, and the other was in Tracy, over the mountains into the Central Valley.

He had been fortunate. He was able to schedule both interviews on the same day, a Friday. He could do the one in Milpitas early in the morning and then drive on to Tracy for a lunchtime meeting with the other. He should be done by mid-afternoon. This was all arranged on the Wednesday before the interviews.

Once he knew he had the times confirmed he called Bill Porter, a geocacher friend who worked at the Livermore Lab and lived near Tracy. He had only met Bill a few times, all of them at geocaching events, but they had hit it off and stayed in contact through facebook and email. They had talked about kayaking together in some of the lakes in that area, but it had never seemed like a convenient time to get together for it. He got a hold of Porter on the first try and they arranged to go for some caches when Cliff was done with his interviews. Porter could get a day off work and had two kayaks. Cliff would gladly forgo his Friday run for a kayaking trip.

Thursday was another day of special appearances. He spent the morning in court. Back at the office after lunch he reviewed his email and snail mail then watched a training video, taking one small step toward satisfying his continuing legal education requirement. When done, he decided to call it a day. He logged onto the geocaching site to figure out which caches he and Bill would do the next day.

Chapter 17

Friday morning Cliff arrived at the oncology center in Milpitas right on time. He had listened to the radio news en route. There were several minutes of coverage of the bombing, although it was now a week old and not much had been going on; at least the reporting hadn't come up with anything new lately. A man named Ghalid Abboud was declared a "person of interest" and his SUV had been impounded.

The doors to the treatment area opened and Cliff went in for the interview. This technician was the woman who had thought she saw the DPP light go out then on briefly. He questioned her thoroughly about that and went over her entire account once more. It differed little from Brittany's, and was consistent with what this woman had told the Xlectrix engineers who had first talked to her.

Like Brittany, this Lilac operator had to cut the interview short. The machines were so expensive that down time just could not be allowed. Another employee had done the setup and gotten the patient prepped, but this woman was needed to actually operate the device.

"Before you go," Cliff asked, "have you noticed any difference since the new software was installed?"

"Hmm, not really. Well, I guess it's smoother."

"Can you explain that?"

"Well sometimes there was… I don't know how to describe it. It seemed like it wasn't going smoothly."

"Kind of a hitch? A slight delay while you had to wait for it to accept the input?"

"Yes, I guess you could call it that. Why?"

"Just asking. Thank you for your time."

She went inside and Cliff headed on to Tracy for the next interview.

The drive went faster than he had expected, since he was going in the counter-commute direction. That resulted in a long wait at the hospital for the Lilac operator to reach his break. Cliff sat in the Oncology Department waiting room for over an hour, watching the patients get called in and eventually emerge. A malaise engulfed him as he slowly internalized the misery of the worst cases. They were mostly old people, who tended to depress him even when healthy, especially now that he had entered his fifties and saw his own inevitable future in the shuffling gait and stooped posture. But the hairless women with their wan, drawn visages, the sallow sadness painted on their faces, made it all the worse. Then appeared a small blonde girl near the age of Ashley Bishop. She was crying and pleading with her mother that she didn't want to go in. It was when she said it was okay if she died, she didn't mind, that he lost it. The girl was already dry heaving into an emesis basin between her pleas. Her Pavlovian response to the previous treatments had already kicked in.

Cliff told the nurse at the check-in window that he was going to the men's room and would be back precisely at 11:00 for the interview. This was an excuse; he simply could not stay there.

When he returned he learned no more from the radiation tech than he had from the previous interview. This operator was a young male already going bald, sporting numerous tattoos on his biceps and neck. His patient had been the woman who had lost her lower leg to amputation. The patient, it seemed, was doing well, the operator said. A thirtyish marathoner, she had been fitted with a Cheetah leg prosthetic and was quite pleased with the result.

Cliff questioned him thoroughly about any change in the software performance, but the operator said he had noticed no difference. He had never experienced any delays before and none now since the reinstall. The screens and commands were all unchanged. He hadn't been looking at the DPP light when the dose was administered, so he couldn't say whether it went out on that one overdose occasion. He had never noticed it going out during treatment. He had become aware of the overdose only when the patient yelled at him through the intercom that he'd burned her. That had made him look up from the console, but everything had looked normal.

Cliff was getting ready to go when the operator asked, "So is it true that there's a problem with the Lilac 4's?"

Cliff was about to give his evasive denial as before, but then hesitated. He didn't like the way the question was worded. If the man was concerned, why didn't he ask "Is there a problem?" The "Is it true that…" suggested that there was some word out about that already.

"Why do you ask? Have you heard something?" Cliff tried to act shocked as though the very notion was unthinkable.

"Yeah, one of my patients this morning said he had read on an online forum for cancer patients that someone posted that their cousin had suffered burns from an overdose from a Lilac 4. The poster had said those machines were defective."

"Can you give me the patient's name? I'd like to talk to him."

"No, sorry. Patient information is strictly private. Our legal department said I could talk to you about the woman who lost her leg, since we have her waiver on file, but you'd have to go through them for anyone else."

"Did he tell you the name of the website where the post appeared?"

"Yeah, it's one of the more popular forums. I'm a registered user. I was curious so I looked it up myself." He pulled out his smart phone and pushed on the touch screen a few times to bring up the site. He handed the phone to Cliff. Cliff read the post. It was from username ConcernedRelative and time stamped just after midnight earlier that day.

Cliff took his own smart phone and navigated the browser to the site. He couldn't get to the post because he wasn't a registered member, but he bookmarked the home page.

"I don't know what to tell you," he finally answered the operator. This is the first I've heard of this. I'll definitely look into it."

After a hasty goodbye he rushed outside, relieved to be free of the oppressive environment. He got into his car and immediately pulled up the website again and registered. As with most forum sites, it required him to provide a valid email address, username and password, and enter the Captcha text. It took him two tries on the Captcha, he was so anxious. When he succeeded, the screen then told him an email had been sent to the address he had provided and he would have to verify the registration by following the directions in that email. He switched to his email app. Although it was only two minutes, it seemed like an hour before the email came in. He clicked on the link and was taken to a page that said his registration had been verified and asked him to log in. When he finally got to the post he bookmarked it and scrolled across it to copy the text. He went back to his email and sent the text and the link to Vogel. Then he called Vogel's number.

When Cliff got through, Vogel was impatient. "How did the interviews go?" he asked without preliminaries.

"Good, I guess. At least I think I got something, but you're not going to like it."

Silence.

"I just sent you an email," Cliff continued. "A so-called concerned relative says that someone got burned from an overdose from a Lilac 4. It said the machine was defective."

"Hold on. Let me check." There was more silence while Vogel opened his email and read it. "This is not good. How soon can you get back? We have work to do."

"I'm all the way out in Tracy. At least two hours." Cliff cursed inwardly. He was going to have to cancel his kayaking trip. "There's one more thing."

"I'm afraid to ask."

"You need to reinstall the software on all the Lilac 4's in Crabbe's territory. Use a different dongle."

"We're already doing that as part of the annual scheduled service. The clients aren't even aware of the change. The clients would scream bloody murder if we required them to give up an extra half day of billing time, but the annual services are already expected and scheduled in. Most of these places run seven days a week, some of them 24 hours a day."

"Then do it at night or something. Figure it out. There's a problem with the software. I don't know what it is but it goes away when the reinstall is made."

"How do you know this?"

Cliff told him about the delay in the response time, the "hitch" Brittany and the other operator had mentioned.

"I'm not so sure. Was this reported by all three operators?"

"No, just two. But both of them said it disappeared after the reinstall. One of them said the new software was a new release. Was it?"

"No. The program was identical. Maybe some new hardware was installed in those two. It might have been as simple as a faulty keyboard. I'll have to check. The only difference should have been that a different dongle was used."

"I think you have to do all of them. Maybe something about Crabbe's computer, or just the way he installed the software originally, corrupted the file but you shouldn't wait. If you wait for the annual maintenance some systems could be at risk for a full year."

"Cliff, if we did all these at once the clients would find out there's a problem. A lot of these doctors and operators practice at more than one location and would notice since it interrupts their income stream. The word would get out. We can't afford that. We don't even have enough service reps to do that. We'd have to bring someone in from elsewhere."

"You read the post from ConcernedRelative. The word is already out. That ship has sailed. You gotta move. If there are any more cases, you're going to have a much bigger problem."

"I'll have to check with the engineers about the hardware change, if any, and my bosses. Get back here as soon as you can."

"I'll see you later this afternoon."

After they hung up Cliff called Bill Porter, his geocaching buddy, and told him he had to cancel. As he drove back to the Bay Area, he resented this intrusion into his plans. He considered how much geocaching had come to mean to him.

Only four years earlier, when he was still an FBI agent, he could never have imagined he would be kayaking in the Sierra foothills. He had never been much of an outdoorsman. As a high school wrestler, and later an FBI agent, he had been more of a gym rat, concerned with building muscle and stamina in the weight room. In recent years he had mostly enjoyed running in the local parks, but too often he had slacked off and let himself get out of shape. Fitness had been more of a job requirement than a passion. Camping and outdoor sports, however, had never held much appeal for him notwithstanding his submersion in a work culture filled with hunters and fishermen.

Since his retirement, though, he had taken up this strange hobby of geocaching. He had gone kayaking and rock-climbing, made fifteen-mile "death marches," scaled a utility pole without safety gear and crawled through dark, slimy, bug-filled tunnels on several occasions all in pursuit of one more "find." He had become addicted to the constant challenge without fully understanding why. He had also grown to appreciate how fortunate he was to live in California where the outdoors beckoned almost every day of the year. He vowed to himself that he would make it a point to reschedule the kayak trip with Porter.

Chapter 18

Video cameras had not captured anything useful around the scene of the Jewish Community Center bombing. Abboud was still considered a prime suspect, at least by Matt Nguyen, but there was nothing more tying him to the crime after a week.   From his visa papers they had identified his ostensible reason for coming to the United States. He was a student at a local culinary academy, or so the student visa said. An interview with the instructor had confirmed that Abboud showed up sometimes but was a less-than-assiduous student. He would go through the exercises in a haphazard and perfunctory way and obviously had little real interest in becoming a chef.

"He wouldn't even eat the dishes he prepared," the instructor had said. "He'd complain the main dish wasn't halal so he couldn't eat it. How can you learn to be a chef if you don't taste your own cooking? He just said he'd become a pastry chef."

The school had nothing more than Abboud's address, phone number and similar identifying information already in the FBI's possession.

Interviews had determined that a package had been left or dropped right in the lobby of the building by someone unknown. The center had a protocol to deal with suspicious visitors or situations like that, which required the office personnel to call 911 and evacuate but the woman manning the front desk had been on the phone engaged in a heated conversation and not paying attention when he had walked in. If she'd noticed him at all, she hadn't complied with the procedures. She was one of those killed and could not be interviewed. The other office worker there thought she remembered a man coming in and then leaving, but she had only a vague recollection of it being a man with dark hair. They had a security camera but by bad luck it was not working.

Forensics had determined the bomb was relatively simple. It had used a firecracker as a fuse. That sat on a large bed of gunpowder that had been collected from shotgun shells, surrounded by metal scraps that served as shrapnel. That whole arrangement, in a cereal box, had been placed on top of a large can of gasoline. The bomber must have lit the firecracker and immediately left, probably jumping into an idling vehicle. That vehicle, if there was one, must have been very close. There could have been no more than five seconds after the fuse was lit before the bomb went off. Experts determined the bomber was lucky to have escaped without being consumed in flames.

The Palestinian flag could be traced to a Chinese manufacturer who marketed throughout the Middle East and the United States, among other places, but there was no way to trace the specific point of sale for this one. No threats or police warnings had been received by the center. With nothing more to go on, Matt decided to begin interviewing Abboud's contacts. Leads were sent back east to have the Scimitar Relief Fund personnel interviewed and monitoring increased, but out here the only known contact was the man who lived by the Rose Garden: Dr. Akil Maloof.

Friday afternoon was the earliest Maloof could see him, but Matt felt lucky Maloof was willing to see him at all. He brought along squadmate Dave Warner, an ex-Army officer who had served in Iraq and traveled throughout the Middle East. Warner wasn't fluent in Arabic, but he knew a bit and was relatively familiar with the Arab culture. The interview took place at Maloof's office not far from the Stanford Medical Center.

Maloof came to the front and showed them into his office himself.

"Please have a seat, gentlemen. Are you here about the bombing?"

Matt was surprised at his directness and decided to proceed cautiously. "Why do you think that's why we're here?"

"I'm Palestinian. A Jewish target with a Palestinian flag. What else could it be? We're all terrorists to the FBI, aren't we?"

"Of course not. We've made no judgments as to who's responsible, and even if it turns out to be someone affiliated with the Palestinian cause, we don't attribute that to other law-abiding citizens."

This sounded like a lame platitude to Matt even as the words escaped his lips, and he didn't like starting out on the defensive.

"But, OK, you're right," he went on, trying to recover the initiative, "it is about that bombing. Not because you're Palestinian, but because we want to ask you about a specific individual."

"Who might that be?"

"Ghalib Abboud."

"You think he's involved in the bombing?"

"Do you?"

Maloof sighed heavily. "Ghalib is zealous in the Palestinian cause, but I have no reason to think he would resort to violence."

"Do you know where he is?"

"Is he missing?"

"Doctor Maloof," Warner broke in, putting his hand on Matt's knee momentarily, as though in apology for interrupting. His real purpose was to remind Matt to uncross his legs, which Matt quickly did. Matt had inadvertently insulted Maloof by crossing his legs, allowing the sole of one shoe to face Maloof. "Your curiosity is understandable, but we have to ask you to please answer our questions rather than asking us about others. We keep our investigation private, and I'm sure you wouldn't like any information about you that might come into our possession to be revealed to others."

"No, I do not know where he is. I hardly know him. He just called me up one day and said he was a fundraiser for the Scimitar Relief Fund. How do you even know that I know him? Oh, never mind, you won't answer. I'm sure you have all our phones tapped."

Matt, feet planted firmly on the floor, replied, "Doctor, we haven't accused you or anyone else of being involved with the bombing. We do have a vehicle description. Do you know what kind of vehicle Mr. Abboud drives?"

"I do not. He came to my house only once. He said my name was on a list of donors to the fund and he was seeking another, larger donation. I didn't pay any attention to what car he may have driven."

"Do you know any other Palestinians who own or drive a dark SUV?"

"I own a green Ford Explorer. I suppose that makes me a bomber."

Nguyen felt a twinge of guilt at this response. He had forgotten about the Explorer. He had run all registered vehicles to Maloof back when he was first identified, but wasn't thinking about it when he asked the question. "No, I mean dark, like black or dark blue or gray."

"I was in the hospital seeing patients when the bombing occurred. I learned about it for the first time only at the end of my rounds. There's probably a security video of me there if you want proof. But then you probably already know that."

They didn't know that, but his providing them the answer obviated the need to ask. "Dr. Maloof, please don't take that attitude. We never asked you your whereabouts. You're not a suspect and we do not consider you a terrorist. But you are a member of the Palestinian community and we can't ignore the Palestinian flag and the fact that the bombing victim was a Jewish center. Who else should we be asking but Palestinians?"

"The Palestinians are the bombing victims! The Israelis bomb Palestinian homes constantly. If they suspect some Palestinian fighter, a terrorist is what they would call him, of being in a house they will drop a bomb on it even if it is filled with innocent Palestinian babies, even when they don't even know whether he is there. They don't care who they kill. They treat Palestinians like rabid animals. They are the terrorists."

Warner spoke up. "Dr. Maloof, I have seen what suffering the Palestinians have endured. I have seen the Israelis come into the West Bank and demolish your homes and replace them with their own settlements. Even the Israeli government admits Jews are driving your people from their rightful lands there, taking their homes even. They promise to stop the violators, but some Israelis think God has given them the entire Middle East. We are not here to justify the Israelis' actions. We are here only to investigate a terrorist act, the bombing of innocent American civilians. Are you willing to help us or not?"

"The West Bank! That is a paradise compared to Gaza. The Egyptians don't want us and the Israelis starve us. They don't even let us harvest our own crops. Our farmlands are next to the border so the Israelis come in and mine our fields or shoot the farmers who try to reap the crops they have worked on for an entire season. Palestinians starve while their own crops wither on the vine and die under the noses of the Israeli snipers."

It was obvious Warner had a better rapport with Maloof, so Matt stayed silent. Warner continued, "Doctor, as true as that may be, we cannot ignore the bombing. Do you know anything about it? Anything at all?"

"No. I deplore violence. I do not condone what happened. I work side by side with many fine Jewish doctors, some who even use that center. It's terrible what happened, but I know nothing about it."

"Do you know anyone who might have done such a thing, or who might have threatened to do something like that?"

"No. Nothing. I cannot help you at all. I would if I knew anything. This bombing can only bring more discrimination, more prejudice against us."

Warner continued, "Do you know anyone else who might have known Abboud? Any way to help us find him?"

"No, I don't. I've already told you that. Now I will ask you to leave."

They left.

Chapter 19

Cliff stood behind Vogel's desk as they both reread the post from ConcernedRelative.

ConcernedRelative: My cousin was severely burned by a Lilac 4 recently. Those machines are defective. The company needs to recall them but they wont. Their reprehensible. If you need radiation make sure your doctor uses a different system.

"This doesn't smell right," Vogel declared. "I've checked and we haven't had any reports of patients being burned. At least I don't think that's how it would be described. If he was referring to either of the deceased patients why wouldn't he say the cousin was killed? Surely he would know of the death by now. That only leaves the woman whose leg was amputated."

"That was the same one – the one in Tracy. She was a marathoner. The Lilac operator there is the one who told me about the post. He said she was happy with the Cheetah leg prosthesis she got."

"Really? I can use that. I called her lawyer earlier and he was out but I left a message that I would be calling at 5:00. He should be there now. I know they're anxious for a settlement. He's a small-time general practice lawyer with no experience in a medical malpractice case. There's no way he wants to take this to trial."

Cliff stayed silent but formed a doubtful expression. From his experience conducting settlement conferences he knew it was never a good idea to encourage a party as to the strength of his case at trial if you wanted a settlement. Settlements came when you could instill doubt in each party as to a favorable outcome at trial.

Vogel picked up the phone and dialed, then put it on speaker. He was put right through to the attorney in Tracy, a Gerald Farquhar.

"Gerald, Roger Vogel here. How are you today?"

"As well as can be expected. Have you finally decided to take responsibility for causing my client to lose her leg?"

"Well, there have been some disturbing developments with that."

"Like what?" Farquhar's voice cracked ever so slightly. Cliff decided Vogel had correctly assessed the other lawyer as full of bluff.

"Have you seen the forum post about someone's cousin being burned from a Lilac 4? Did you or your client put that up?"

"What? No. I don't know anything about it. Where is this?"

"I'll send you the link." Vogel had already composed the email and now clicked the send button. Within thirty seconds Farquhar had received it and read it.

"This wasn't us," he stated vigorously.

"Gerald, as I made very clear in my last offer, any settlement from us is only going to happen if there is no public claim that our system caused the injury. As you know, her leg was amputated because of the cancer, not the burn she received. An unwarranted accusation against our company's product could have grave financial consequences for us. And a defamation action against you."

"I'll have no problem proving that your machine caused the need for amputation. But look, I understand you want to sweep this under the rug. I've told her to keep quiet and she promised not to say anything about the overdose. So far as her friends and family know, she lost her leg to cancer. Maybe this is another patient who was burned they're talking about in the post. Have there been any others?"

"This could only be your client. There's not a person alive on this planet who was burned by one of our machines, other than your client."

Cliff noticed how Vogel had skirted the question with a misleading truth. The other two victims were dead so they weren't 'persons alive on this planet'."

"I swear, it's not us. Look, I'm reading this posting. The guy says it was a Lilac 4. I didn't even know that. I'm sure she doesn't either. The hospital just told her it's a Lilac. That's all we've ever talked about. How many models are there?"

This caused Vogel to pause. Farquhar was right. All discussions had only been over the hospital's "Lilac" so far as he could remember. The patient had probably not returned for treatment after the burn because her leg had been amputated very quickly after the incident, so she wouldn't have spoken to the staff at the oncology unit or looked at the device. Farquhar was unlikely to have the financial resources to research the models and hire an expert yet. This meant the post had to be from someone else. Someone at the hospital, perhaps, or even inside Xlectrix, who knew the models. It was time to shift tactics.

"How is she doing, Gerald? I hope she's adjusting well."

"What do you think? She lost her leg. She's a runner, for God's sake. Her pain and suffering is indescribable. How would you feel if you lost a limb?"

"I understand her running has been going great with her Cheetah leg. That's good to hear. I'm a golfer, not a runner, but I'd give my right arm for a prosthesis that gave me an extra 20 yards on my drives."

This brought a snort of disgust on the other end followed by a coughing fit. This had obviously shaken the other lawyer who probably was intimidated to discover his client was already being investigated by Xlectrix.

"You'd give an arm? If that's supposed to be a joke, it's a sick one," Farquhar finally said.

"Look, Gerald, for now I'll take your word that the post wasn't from your side. Let's get this whole thing behind us. Three hundred thousand, total confidentiality clause, and you still have your claim against the hospital for the operator's error. That's extremely generous for one week's discomfort in a limb she was going to lose anyway."

"That hardly compensates her for the loss of a limb. She's young. You're talking fifty years or more of dealing with a disability."

"The offer's not going to go up. She'll keep running marathons and look anything but disabled. You know you can't stop her; she's a runner – she's obsessed. And if we find she was behind that libelous post, the deal's off the table."

"I'll talk to her. It's way too low, but she's not the vindictive type. She may want to get it over with too."

They hung up. Vogel beamed at Cliff. "You did it. She'll take it. He's worried we'll find out she spilled the beans and we'll pull the deal. He'll tell her to take the deal now before that can happen. I expect a call back first thing Monday. We were ready to go to five. Our insurance picks up anything over that. Three is a bargain."

"Did she lose the leg due to the cancer or the overdose?" Cliff was curious, and it might be relevant to his investigation, too.

"Hard to say. The doctor told us she had a 60% chance of keeping the leg until the radiation overdose destroyed too much nerve and blood vessel tissue. Necrosis would have set in. Of course he wouldn't have told her that. His malpractice carrier would have told him to attribute it all to the cancer."

The law was a cold, hard business.

"OK, so is that true about the woman not knowing the model number? If so…"

"Yes, I know. It probably is true. I'll have to review our correspondence, but I think they just kept calling it a Lilac, which they spelled L-I-L-L-A-C. He's obviously clueless about the technology. That means the post came from someone else, someone familiar with model numbers at least. I'm adding that to your assignment. Find out who posted that."

Cliff had his doubts about whether he would ever be able to identify ConcernedRelative but he realized Vogel just credited him with saving the company $200,000, so he probably had quite a few billable hours he could rack up before Vogel would protest.

"Fine, I'll work on it. But what about reinstalling the software? There's something funky with the ones Crabbe serviced. You have to fix them. All of them."

"We've been talking it over since you reported the hitch thing. We're going to do that. But we can't do them all overnight. We're going to start with the oldest ones first and work our way forward to the most recently installed systems. We've already reinstalled on the three overdose systems and then two others during the annual service. That's five of seventeen. We're going to have to push at some of these oncology centers. They really hate down time, but we think we can do three a week if we're lucky. In a month we should have all twelve done."

"I'd think two a day would be feasible. A whole month is too long."

"Even if we could get the clients to agree, we don't have the personnel to do that many. We only have one full-time tech dedicated just to doing the reinstalls. The rest are busy with regular installs and service or live out of the area."

"Can't you reactivate Crabbe? With one more tech you could double the rate."

"Too risky. We still don't know if he's the one who screwed up. He could even be ConcernedRelative. We have him working again, rewriting some of the procedures in our Tech Tips file. That's one of the encrypted files the service reps use. He's not to use any service laptop or dongle, though. If you want it sped up, you find out how this happened. If he's in the clear, we can put him back to work."

"You got the final polygraph results. He showed no deception."

"So Sol says, but he also showed inconclusive on that final question. He might be concealing something. I'm afraid I don't put much stock in that stuff anyway."

Cliff shook his head in frustration. "I think he was truthful, but that's your call. If you get another one of these overdoses on a system still waiting for a reinstall, you'll be second-guessing yourself for years."

"Cliff, how about you do your job and I'll do mine. Good work today. Send me your report and your bill."

When he got back to the office Maeva was gone. There was a voice message on his machine. Vogel's voice told him that Farquhar had called back two minutes after Cliff left and they finalized the settlement for $300,000.

Chapter 20

The investigation of the bombing continued for the following week with little to show for it. Abboud's van had been seized and tested for gunpowder or other forensic evidence, but other than traces of gasoline – present in any car – there was nothing.

Victims, witnesses, and Arab sources were all interviewed. The FBI even consulted with the counter-intelligence officer at the Israeli Consulate in San Francisco, but still they had made no significant progress.

They had confirmed that Abboud had traveled to the Middle East, but had not been able to confirm he had arrived in Gaza. His plane reservation had been made only two days before the bombing, which made it very expensive. That might be a sign he knew he was about to bomb the center and wanted a getaway plan, or it might mean he had learned his father was gravely ill, as he had told his neighbor, and had to leave suddenly.

They still didn't have probable cause for a search warrant of his house, but they were able to get a toll records authorization, an order to see the times and numbers of incoming and outgoing calls to Abboud's cell phone. There was no land line to his house. The records showed that he did get a text message from Gaza earlier on the day he had made his airplane reservation, but the text content was not available.

Ellen had conducted several interviews, including Jews who thought the Palestinians should all be exterminated like rats and Arab-Americans who thought Israel should be wiped off the map. One radical Jewish activist supported the Palestinian cause. One of the women who was killed, a staff member there, had a Jewish surname but turned out to be of German Catholic extraction, married to a non-practicing Jew. Both of them were agnostic. Everyone professed personal opposition to violence and no knowledge of anyone who might be the terrorist.

The bomb had been of a style not seen in the Bay Area before. Records of the FBI and the Bureau of Alcohol Tobacco and Firearms (ATF) showed similar bombs being set off in the south in the 1960s by a white hate group against black activists. The manner of construction of those bombs was widely described on the Internet, so anyone could have copied it.

The bottom line for Matt was that they were at a standstill until something broke.

In the week since his last interview with the Lilac operators Cliff had been following the posts on the cancer support forum about the Lilac. ConcernedRelative had not posted any more. There were dozens of replies to his post from others who identified themselves as patients, relatives of patients, doctors, or Lilac operators who countered the original post saying the Lilacs had worked perfectly for them for years and never burned them or anyone they know. Cliff wondered how many of those were real and whether Vogel or some PR flack at Xlectrix was behind the posts.

His job now included trying to find out who had made that post, but he knew the website would never give that information up voluntarily. Vogel could get the information if he really wanted it simply by suing ConcernedRelative and the website owners for defamation and subpoenaing the website operators for the IP address and other registration information of ConcernedRelative. He knew that would probably lead nowhere. The person who posted it had probably used some Internet café or other hot spot and had given a fake email created just for that post.

Vogel was convinced that it was done by a competitor but Cliff wasn't so sure. The language of the post had been inconsistent. The word reprehensible was a ten-dollar word that wasn't likely to be used by someone who misspelled "they're" and "don't". It smelled to him like someone educated trying to appear uneducated. That didn't rule out competitors, though.

Cliff had been studying the histories of the overdose victims for clues during this period. They had all provided various personal information when they filed their claims and waived privacy rights with the treatment centers as to the company so that Xlectrix could get the treatment records there and the doctors and technicians could talk freely to the company. That had been part of the settlement agreements. Cliff had also obtained family history from the attorneys representing them or their families.

One of the victims had no first cousins. Her parents were both only children. Her family didn't even know any more distant cousins and certainly hadn't discussed the case with them. Another victim had two living first cousins, but they were both very old. One had Alzheimer's and the other had been out of touch with the family for decades. Neither knew how to use a computer so far as the families knew. He ruled them out as ConcernedRelative. The third victim, the marathoner, had several young cousins, but her attorney was insistent that she had not discussed the treatment with them or anyone outside her immediate family. He was still adamant that she had not even known the machine was called a Lilac 4. He said he learned the name Lilac through his research and only learned it was a Lilac 4 from Vogel's call. He was now aware of the post in the forum but guaranteed it wasn't from his client.

Assuming all these people were telling the truth, and he tended to think they were, he was beginning to lean toward Vogel's theory of a competitor being behind the post. If true, that meant there was a possible motive for someone to tamper with the machines to cause the malfunctions. Still, it was hard to believe a medical device manufacturer would do such a thing. If it was discovered, that would probably be the end of the company. Why risk that just to get a few more sales?

There were only three other companies that made competing devices used in the United States. He checked stock analyst reports on all of them, but they all appeared to be in financial good health and their devices had their own special advantages and disadvantages, such as technology, price, or size, that made them more suitable for one customer or another. Thus, they weren't competing all that closely. So knocking down a competitor wouldn't help market share much. Of course, even if it was a competitor, that still didn't explain how the sabotage could have been done technically.

Frustrated, he decided to call Vogel and follow up on the reinstallation of the software over the past week. When he got through, Vogel told him they were two-thirds of the way through the process.

"Did any of the clients mention any improvement in the speed, or any elimination of that hitch I reported?" Cliff asked.

"Yes, actually, one did. He said it would 'hiccup' once in a while and that was recent. That stopped after the reinstall."

"Roger, you've got to finish off the rest of those L4's. It's that software from Crabbe's machine. Another one of these incidents could happen any minute. Bring Crabbe back if you need the manpower."

"We still can't risk that, especially now that we know Crabbe's version of the software is probably responsible somehow, but the biggest problem hasn't been manpower. The clients have been reluctant to give us the time. Downtime is very expensive for them; I explained this to you before. They're asking for us to pay them the hourly rate they would charge patients, or, more accurately, knock that off their bills for the regular service contract."

"Pay it. It'll cost you a lot more if another one of these happens."

"I'm well aware of that. We're bringing another tech in from L.A. to help and I think we'll be done in five days or so."

"Are any of the remaining sites here locally?"

"I think so. One in Palo Alto near Lucille Packard Children's Hospital, a pediatric oncology annex, put us off for another three days. I think that's the only one within ten miles or more. We just did one reinstall in Morgan Hill. Why?"

"No reason."

"No reason? Not good enough. Why are you asking?"

"I know someone undergoing radiation treatment, that's all. It would set my mind at ease if I knew they were not at risk."

"A juvenile?"

Cliff hesitated. "Yes."

"Is that where the child is being treated?"

"I don't know. And I don't know specifically what kind of device or treatment, either."

Vogel took on a stern schoolmaster's voice. "You know you can't tell them the Lilacs have had problems, don't you? That's attorney-client privileged."

"I realize that."

"Well, if you have any ability to persuade the people over there to give us our half day any sooner – without telling them why it's urgent – be my guest."

"Have you examined the files on the systems where you reinstalled to see if there are any differences?"

"Yes. The engineers did a file compare on the program files taken from the three overdose machines, from the machines where we've reinstalled, from Crabbe's laptop, and from the laptop we used to reinstall with the different dongle. All the program files from all the systems were identical bit for bit. The new laptop files were all identical except for the single data file that has the unique program key for the new dongle. That would be expected."

"So the new program itself is identical to the old one?"

"Right. There doesn't appear to be any file corruption."

"Maybe Crabbe's right. It could be a design flaw."

Vogel did not like this suggestion and the irritation showed in his voice. "Then why are only his clients being affected?"

"Or maybe Crabbe's dongle is the key to this."

"NSA uses these dongles. I don't think anyone could break them, not any run-of-the-mill hacker. Maybe the Chinese NSA or somebody like that. But that's an idea worth looking into." Vogel obviously liked that idea better since liability would naturally flow to the vendor who sold them the dongles.

"Can you give me the contact information for the vendor?"

"I'll have to look it up. I'll email it to you."

"Okay. I'll be back in touch if I get anything."

Chapter 21

The next morning Cliff called Matt Nguyen. Their regular monthly lunch with Gina was coming up and he wanted to find out if it was still on and confirm the time and place. Matt was in and was able to confirm all the details.

"One more thing, Matt," Cliff said cautiously, unsure how much he could say. "Do you know where Ellen's niece gets her radiation treatments?"

"Somewhere local. Over by Lucille Packard Children's Hospital, I think she said. I know she can get there in less than 15 minutes. She just left for there in fact. Why?"

"She just left? So Ashley is getting a treatment right now?"

"That's what she said. What's going on, Cliff?"

"I'll explain later."

He hung up and dialed Roger Vogel. Vogel was out, but his assistant took the call and was able to look up the name and address of the cancer treatment center.

He reached the center twelve minutes later. Since the annex was separate from the main buildings, he was spared the usual maze wanderings most hospitals entail. He walked up to the gray-haired receptionist, showed his Xlectrix ID, and said he needed to talk to the Lilac operator right away.

The receptionist called back to a treatment room and, after many rings, finally reached someone.

"Someone will be right out," she said pleasantly. She wrote his name in a log book and handed him a Vendor badge to pin on.

Cliff had scanned the waiting room as he came in, and there was no sign of Ellen, Theresa, or Ashley. He guessed they were inside already. There were several other families sitting stoically, with children ranging in age from toddlers to teens. He tried not to pace or look panicky. He had considered just bursting through the doors to the treatment room area but there was a limit to what he could do without compromising his client's privileged information.

After two or three minutes a dark-complected male in a lab coat came out and asked him to follow him. They went through the main doors to the treatment area and as they did so he saw Ellen and Theresa sitting on a cheap sofa in a small room, apparently the waiting area for adults accompanying a child during treatment, right outside the treatment room. He didn't see Ashley, but from his angle he couldn't see whether she was just out of sight in the waiting area. The man led him back to a small office area.

"What's this about?" The man asked, once there.

"Hugo," Cliff said, reading the name from the man's name tag, "I'm with Xlectrix. Has your Lilac 4 been slow to respond to keyboard commands recently?"

"I don't operate it. I just maintain the systems. I'm an engineer, not a rad tech. None of the techs has said anything to me about it. Is this related to the reinstall? You guys already asked me to schedule that. We're doing it the day after tomorrow."

"You really should do it right away. If that causes any inconvenience to your patients, I can explain it to them as being our responsibility, not yours. I can have someone over here later today. Can I just talk to the rad tech now to see if the problem has shown up here? If not, it can wait until the scheduled time."

"She's giving a treatment right now. As soon as she's done we can ask her. What's so urgent about some response time from the keyboard? Is there something serious I should know about? This is pretty irregular."

Suddenly a door slammed and a shaky female voice called out, "Hugo! Come back here. Something's wrong with the L4."

Cliff bolted toward the direction of the voice, Hugo only a step behind. A young woman with purple hair and black fingernails clad in a lab coat similar to Hugo's was holding open a door. The two men reached the open door and Cliff's heart sank through the floor. Ashley Bishop was sitting on the treatment table crying and holding her left calf. She looked up at Cliff with a puzzled expression.

"The patient said I burned her," purple hair said, eyeing Cliff suspiciously.

Seconds later Ellen and Theresa rushed through the open door, too, increasing the crowd to six.

"What's the matter?!" Theresa bellowed. "I heard my daughter crying." She showed no sign of recognizing Cliff. She rushed to her daughter's side and hugged the sobbing girl asking if she was okay.

Ellen, on the other hand, looked Cliff up and down dumbfounded, like she was seeing the Loch Ness Monster emerge from the floor.

"Cliff, what in the world are you doing here?" She muttered from the side of her mouth.

"Call the doctor!" Hugo yelled at the operator, who disappeared into the control booth and picked up a phone.

"I'll tell you later," Cliff replied to Ellen, avoiding eye contact. "It's complicated."

Everyone gathered around Ashley. The skin of her lower leg bore red circles the diameter of a pencil, one on top and one on the bottom. The bottom one was slightly larger. Cliff noticed for the first time a surgical scar that was bisected by the top mark.

Within thirty seconds two more people appeared in the doorway – a pale, pear-shaped woman in her 40's with a Barbra Streisand nose, and a tall Arab-looking male. Both wore white lab coats and had name tags.

"Out! Everyone out but the patient and the operator!" commanded the woman, obviously the doctor in charge. The group began to filter out.

Ellen blanched when she saw the male doctor's name tag. It was Dr. Maloof. She had been by his house near the Rose Garden and knew that Matt had interviewed him, but until now she had not known he was Ashley's treating physician. In her previous trip here she had left before the doctor showed up.

As they stepped outside the room, Hugo informed Cliff that the woman was the chief radiation oncologist and Maloof was the surgical oncologist.

"You knew this could happen, didn't you? That's why you're here," Hugo said accusingly.

Cliff ignored him, as he was paying attention to Ashley and her mother. Theresa had refused to leave the room and was still hugging her daughter. Maloof was bent low, examining the red burn marks closely. There was heated discussion going on inside, but from Cliff's vantage point he could only catch fragments of the conversation. Then he felt a strong grip on his biceps. It was Ellen.

"Is that true? You knew about this and didn't tell me? And what's this?" She flicked her fingernail hard against the Vendor badge.

Cliff remained silent and looked at her helplessly trying hard not to choke up. His heart was racing and his stomach was a roiling mass. But it was the look of accusation on Ellen's face that drove him to turn and start walking toward the lobby. He had braved many things as an FBI agent but this was beyond him. Coward or no, he just had to get out of there.

"Hey, where are you going?" Hugo called after him. "The doctors are going to want to talk to you."

"Cliff!" Ellen chorused.

He kept walking until he got to the reception desk. He threw the Vendor badge on the receptionist's counter and kept on going until he got to the parking lot.

When he got in his car he sat for several minutes, unsure he was in a safe state to drive. Then he spied Hugo stepping out of the front door of the annex, looking around. He decided Hugo was probably looking for him and he did not want to be answering any questions just then. He put the car in gear and took off.

Back at the office Maeva immediately spotted something off in Cliff's demeanor as he walked in. His body language showed defeat and his eyes were watery.

"What's wrong?" she asked anxiously before he said a word.

He didn't answer her. Instead he went into his office, closed the door, and called Vogel, who was still not in. He had the assistant put him through to voice mail, where he left a curt message telling Vogel there was another incident, this time at the Palo Alto location, and to call him right away.

This turned out to be unnecessary, for no more than three minutes later Vogel called him. He picked the line up before Maeva could.

"Cliff, what the hell did you do?" Vogel hissed before any pleasantries. "The company president just called me out of a meeting. The client is saying there's been another malfunction during treatment and that we knew it would happen. They said one of our service reps – they gave your name – was there asking about a keyboard problem and trying to get them to stop treatment."

"I just did exactly what you authorized me to do – to try to get them to expedite the reinstall. I did *not* say it was urgent or to stop treatment."

"I specifically told you not to let them know there had been any other incidents."

"And I didn't. Listen, if you Scrooges recalled the Lilacs or taken them offline remotely immediately this wouldn't have happened. I told you…"

"There's no call for that. We tried but they refused our request to expedite it."

"Because you didn't tell them their patients were at risk of a fatal dose of radiation."

"Cliff, they have your name. You're going to be named in the lawsuit too if there is one. We have to do damage control now if we can. We need to be on the same team. Recriminations aren't going to help. Do you know how bad it is? I don't have any of the details."

"It was a nine-year-old girl. Mark Bishop's daughter."

This brought Vogel to a temporary halt. "Jesus, the Congressman?" he finally managed.

"The same."

"Where was the treatment – what part of the body?"

"Her leg."

"That's good. She'll probably survive. We're only looking at an amputation. That didn't hit us too hard with the other one."

Cliff could hear the gears of the adding machine going in Vogel's brain, computing the likely damages. He was disgusted with Vogel and even more so with himself. This could have been prevented. He realized suddenly that his fingernails were digging into his palm and drawing blood, he was balling his fist so hard.

"'That's good'? Good that a beautiful nine-year-old girl is going to lose her leg and probably won't die, but just maybe she will? She's a bright, sweet-tempered, friendly kid whose life just changed because you were more concerned with liability than saving the patients from harm."

"Damn it, Cliff, that attitude has to stop. If we had told the world that our machines might cause accidental overdoses – had already caused fatal overdoses – that would be the end of our company. No one would buy them. These machines save thousands of lives a year. Other devices can't do the same thing or can't do it as cheaply or require many more treatments, which means there'll be many people who go without treatment if we go under. Keeping the company solvent is my duty and it serves the best interests of the patients, too. So come off your high horse.

You need to understand where your ethical duty lies. Your financial interests, too, for that matter."

"Don't give me that crap about my ethical duty. I'm the one who identified the problem – and the fix. You'd still be doing the reinstalls only as part of the annual service if I hadn't told you about the hitch in response time. And how much did I save you with the marathoner?"

"True. And I'm grateful, but we were already reinstalling the software. You weren't the first to think of that; you just got it expedited. And you still haven't identified how this is being done and who's responsible."

"That's not going to help Ashley now."

"Who's Ashley? Oh, the victim. How do you know… Christ, she's the juvenile you said you knew, isn't she? The one you were telling me about."

"Yes." Cliff's voice cracked on the single syllable.

"I'm sorry. Okay, I must have sounded pretty insensitive there. I didn't realize you knew her. But look, if this girl is as appealing as you make her out to be, she's a plaintiff lawyer's dream client. If they think we, and I'm including you in that 'we', held back information that would have prevented this, there could be punitives in the tens of millions. Maybe hundreds of millions. Punitives aren't covered by your malpractice insurance, either. If, as you say, you only did as I instructed – and I'm not conceding that yet – then you didn't do anything wrong, Cliff, but this could ruin your life, too. Think rationally here."

Cliff slammed his left fist down so hard on his desk Maeva jumped up, despite the closed door muffling the sound. "Screw that! If that little girl dies because I didn't warn her, my life *is* ruined. I'd never forgive myself."

The door opened and Maeva peeked in to see if he was all right. He waved her away.

"Cliff, there are other people still at risk, at least until we finish the reinstalls, and we still need to find out how this is happening. Have you made any progress on finding out who ConcernedRelative is?"

"No."

"Well, you can help Ashley and all the others still at risk by finding out what happened and how. You still owe me a weekly report. I want the whole story of what happened over there down to the last detail. And be sure to mark it attorney-client confidential. Unfortunately this will have to be on paper since I'm going to have to present it to the Executive Committee. Now I have to go. My phone is ringing off the hook and that Committee is waiting for me to report to them. The shit has hit the fan here. Goodbye."

He hung up before Cliff could respond. Cliff sighed and realized Vogel was right about one thing at least. The best thing he could do is find out what happened. He just didn't know how he was going to do that.

Chapter 22

The following morning Cliff reviewed his notes for the umpteenth time, looking for something he may have missed. As he was going through his emails he saw the one from Vogel with the vendor information for the dongle manufacturer: Secryptic Systems. It was located in Livermore, in the East Bay. Cliff recognized the street name. It was within a mile of the Lawrence Livermore National Laboratory, the most highly classified and best secured place in the Bay Area, the same place Bill Porter worked. That was where some of the most sophisticated research of the military-intelligence community was done, including nuclear weapons. Cliff assumed from the location that the lab was a big customer of Secryptic.

He called them, asking by name for the sales representative that handled the Xlectrix account. When the man came on the line Cliff said he was representing Xlectrix and they were considering discontinuing use of the Xlectrix dongles due to some technical problems they were having. The sales rep was certain that the issues could be resolved and wanted to know what he could do to assure them of that. They agreed to a meeting the next afternoon in their facility when the lead engineer could also be available.

No sooner had Cliff put the phone down than he spotted Barry Cross, the lawyer next door, in the "lobby," which consisted of the three feet between the front door and Maeva's desk. He stood and walked out to greet him.

"Barry, to what do we owe the honor?"

"Cliff, I'm glad I caught you in. You do special appearances, don't you?"

"Sure, sometimes. You know someone who needs one?"

"Yeah, me."

"You? But I thought you just did patent and copyright litigation. I don't know anything about patent law."

"You don't need to. It's just a motion to bifurcate. We already submitted briefs and the judge has already posted his tentative ruling. It's going to go our way. The other side will try to argue but we're just submitting it on the papers. I just need a warm body to be present. My mother had a stroke and isn't expected to survive. I'm getting on a plane in two hours. My partner is back east finding housing for his son. He's going to Brandeis in the fall."

"Geez, I'm sorry, Barry. When is this hearing?"

"Tomorrow morning. District Court. Judge Schuler."

To a lawyer "District Court" meant United States District Court, the federal court, as distinct from Superior Court, the state court system. The differences were more than just jurisdictional. Comparing the two would be like comparing a Tesla showroom to a used car lot. Everything in federal court was elevated – the formality, the professionalism, the precision of the pleadings, usually the intelligence of the judges and staff, although there had been some notable exceptions both ways. Cliff had been in District Court many times as an FBI agent, testifying, getting warrants, and meeting with AUSAs, so he knew enough about the civil procedure rules in federal court to get by, but he knew nothing about patent law.

The good news was that he knew Judge Len Schuler well. Schuler had been an Assistant U.S. Attorney when Cliff had been an agent in the San Jose Office and had handled several of Cliff's biggest cases.

"What time? I have an appointment in the afternoon."

"Nine a.m. You'll be out by 11:30 at the latest, probably a lot sooner."

"Okay, if you want me, but I'll have to charge hourly. I do fixed fee in Superior Court, but that's because I can do multiple appearances."

"No problem. Whatever your standard rate is. The client will probably pay you less than they do me. And don't worry about having to counter some last minute argument or ploy by the other counsel. Schuler has never reversed a tentative ruling yet. My client is Cisco. Here."

He handed Cliff a manila folder with some legal documents in it, thanked him and left.

Chapter 23

The next morning Cliff was sitting in the courtroom of the Honorable Leonard Schuler along with a passel of other lawyers. This morning was calendared for all civil cases, but in federal court the judges did not specialize in a single type of case the way they did in state court – family law, juvenile court, criminal court, small claims, and so forth. At one point Schuler interrupted the civil calendar to handle an immigration matter. On another occasion one of the Assistant U.S. Attorneys entered the courtroom and was motioned to the front for the judge to sign something, possibly an order on a criminal case.

It was already past 10:00 and Cliff's Cisco case had yet to be called. He was beginning to wonder if he was going to get out in time. Then he heard Judge Schuler call "Brian Byrne versus Xlectrix." An attractive middle-aged woman with a full, Oprah Winfrey figure clad in an expensive tailored suit walked to the defendant's table and a wizened, plaintiff's lawyer with a crimson nose shuffled to the other table. Cliff recognized him from Superior Court as a plaintiff's lawyer. Cliff had not known there would be an Xlectrix case. He'd never spoken to Vogel about ongoing litigation. This could get interesting.

Without waiting for the judge to ask the lawyers to state their appearances the male spoke, "David Hannity for the plaintiff who is present in the courtroom, your honor." He waved his hand backward to the right without looking. A tall, balding man that direction wearing half glasses, apparently the plaintiff Byrne, sat up straight and looked intensely at the judge. He had piercing blue eyes fixed in a permanent scowl.

The defense lawyer identified herself as Sharon Perry. Cliff did not recognize her.

"Your honor, the conduct by the defendant in discriminating against my client solely because of his age is the most reprehensible form…" the plaintiff's lawyer blurted out, again without being invited to speak by the judge. His cheeks were so lined with veins it looked like a grandchild had gone wild with a red pencil on his face. His pot belly threatened to fall over his belt onto the floor.

"Stow it, counselor," Schuler interrupted. "We're just here to resolve the discovery dispute. Save your closing argument for the jury."

The female attorney suppressed a small smile.

"Ms. Perry, it's your motion," Schuler continued, turning the floor over to her.

"Your honor, we've been trying to schedule a deposition with Mr. Byrne for three months and he refuses to make himself available. We've gotten excuse after excuse from Mr. Hannity."

Hannity replied, "Defendant has been trying to schedule it for an afternoon in Palo Alto. A deposition would take a full day, plus there's travel time. That means it would take two days. Taking two days off his work would be a financial hardship. We've told them Mr. Byrne is available beginning at 8:00 a.m. in our San Jose office, halfway between Palo Alto and Fremont."

The defense lawyer responded that she'd be willing to limit the deposition to four hours. The argument went back and forth awhile and the judge finally ordered Byrne to appear for deposition at Hannity's office at 1:00 p.m. in three days, with questioning limited to four hours.

Cliff had no interest in the deposition timing, but one thing had caught his attention. The plaintiff's attorney had called Xlectrix's conduct "reprehensible." That's a word you didn't hear very often. Cliff saw it in pleadings from time to time, but never outside the courtroom context. Except once. The only place Cliff could recall hearing or reading it in recent memory was the forum post by ConcernedRelative – also applied to Xlectrix.

The two attorneys in Byrne's case filtered out of the courtroom. Schuler called another case, this one with multiple parties on both sides and lawyers galore, so Cliff decided he had a few minutes before his case could be called. He followed the lawyers out and caught up with the woman before she got to the elevator. They were still out of earshot of Byrne and his lawyer.

"Excuse me, Ms. Perry, I'm Cliff Knowles. I'm doing some work for Xlectrix, too. Can I speak to you for a second?"

The woman stopped and looked him up and down. "Pleased to meet you," she said tentatively. "I thought I knew just about all the litigators who work for Xlectrix. They're mostly in my firm, Herrick Morton & Saldini." She was obviously skeptical.

"I'm here for Barry Cross on a patent matter – for another client. I just happened to be here and overheard your case. I'm curious about it. I have to get back in before my case is called, but I'd like to get a copy of the pleadings. Here's my card. You can check with Roger Vogel." The card was his regular attorney-at-law card, not the Xlectrix one Vogel provided.

"The pleadings are public information," she replied, implying that he could get them from the court clerk and save her the trouble of checking him out with Vogel.

"Well, I'd like to talk to you, too. Please check with Roger then I'll call you later today or tomorrow. Congratulations on getting the 1:00 depo time, by the way. I assume you wanted that start time so you'd get Hannity after a liquid lunch."

"Ah, his reputation precedes him," she replied, a twinkle in her eye, pleased that her tactical victory had been recognized. "I'll check with Roger, then we'll talk."

Cliff headed back to the courtroom. The same case was still being argued. After another fifteen minutes Cliff's Cisco case was finally called. He stepped forward and stated his special appearance.

"Ah, Mr. Knowles. This is a rare pleasure," Judge Schuler intoned. The opposing counsel frowned.

The hearing went exactly as Barry Cross had predicted, with the opposing counsel vainly trying to get Schuler to change his tentative ruling. Cliff did nothing but stand there patiently and emerge victorious.

By the time he made his way out of the courtroom it was almost lunchtime. He grabbed a Quarter Pounder from the nearby McDonald's, scolding himself inwardly for doing so, then returned to the car. He buckled up and headed for Livermore.

To say the Secryptic building was low-key would be an understatement. The front of the gray, flat-topped structure bore not a single logo or sign. The landscaping was tasteful and well-tended but only the street address in a small font on the glass door confirmed he was at the right location. He parked in a visitor parking spot on the side and started walking toward the front of the building, only to spot a sign with an arrow stating Entrance In Rear. He walked around to the back where a single solid door was lettered "Please enter". It was unlocked, so he did.

Inside he found himself in a small lobby with two Danish modern chairs and a Plexiglas window behind which a surprised young woman sat. Clearly this company wasn't going for walk-in customers. He asked for Samuel, the sales representative he had spoken to the previous day. The receptionist, or whatever her title was, telephoned someone, then told Cliff to be seated.

Presently two men emerged, one appearing Chinese and one Indian, though neither had any trace of a foreign accent. They ushered him back to a conference room. Cliff explained that he was from Xlectrix and showed the ID that Vogel had given him. Samuel, the Chinese man, examined it closely and nodded to the other. They introduced themselves, both saddled with lengthy titles ending in "engineer." The Indian was Clement something.

Cliff was not about to reveal to them that the Lilacs were overdosing patients. That was still not public and the dongle people did not have a need to know. Instead he told them that one of the dongles seemed to be interfering with the program, causing delays in the program responding to keyboard commands.

"That's impossible," the Indian engineer said. "The dongle is not accessed by the Lilac control program except at program launch." He began explaining something about a modified Rijndael algorithm which lost Cliff within the first five seconds.

"I don't need to know the cryptographic details," Cliff told him, not wanting to let on that he was in over his head. They would wonder why he was the one assigned to deal with this. "I just want to understand how the program interacts with the dongle during operation. One of our service reps says several of the clients who use the program have complained that there's a delayed response time for their typing sometimes. Time is money with our clients. This has happened with several clients, but only ones serviced by that same guy. When the program was reinstalled with another dongle, the problem went away. We think the dongle is defective."

"Did you bring the dongle? We could inspect it," Samuel offered.

"No. We might have you do that in the future, but for now I just want to get your opinion on how that could happen."

"I don't see how it could happen," the Indian replied. "According to the specs you have given us, the dongle isn't even used except by the service reps. The clients do not have them. They should not have them or the security is useless."

"That's true, the clients do not have them. But the programs *installed* with one dongle are the only ones affected. Maybe that one dongle caused a corrupted file or something."

Clement was still adamant. "Impossible. Even if it were somehow true, that would have happened at the time the program was installed. The dongle is removed after that. The problem would have been noticed right away. Was it?"

"No, it's quite recent."

"There's your answer then. It's not the dongle. If you have had no problem after reinstalling with another dongle why don't you just reinstall all of the ones with the suspect dongle?"

Samuel jumped in at that point. "We would be glad to supply you a replacement dongle for no charge if you ship the problem one back to us. We'd like to examine it ourselves. I can tell you NSA, among other government customers, has used many of these and none has ever failed or reported this problem."

Cliff was at a loss where to go from there. He couldn't return the dongle to this company. His gut told him it might be important to keep and only Vogel could make that call. In fact, it was still needed to provide service on the few remaining Lilac sites that had not yet had a reinstall done. Then something struck him about the conversation.

"Clement, didn't you say earlier that the dongle is only queried at program launch?"

"Yes, that's true. Most of the time the program is used by the clients. They don't need the dongle. The program looks for it, but doesn't find it plugged in and cannot be put in diagnostic mode, so it just operates in standard mode. Only the service reps have the dongles, so if they want to diagnose something, the program is shut down, then the rep launches it again with the dongle plugged in. Once the program verifies the right dongle is there, it indicates the program is in diagnostic mode and the dongle is removed."

"Wait, the dongle is removed? It doesn't stay plugged in while the program is used in diagnostic mode?" Cliff was sure the radiation tech at Xlectrix headquarters had left the dongle plugged in while zapping the bacon.

"No, that would be a security flaw," Clement said with confidence. "If the dongle were left in the service reps would forget to retrieve it at the end of the day. There would be dongles left with the clients who could try to do their own maintenance. That would be dangerous. Your company told us this. They wrote the software so that the dongle is queried at launch and once in diagnostic mode the rep is supposed to remove it immediately."

This was disturbing news to Cliff.

"So if someone got his hands on one of these dongles and launched the program, he could continue to use it in diagnostic mode even after the dongle was gone, even after the service rep was gone?"

The two engineers gave each other quizzical looks and leaned over close to each other whispering. Clement shook his head a couple of times. Finally he spoke again.

"That couldn't happen if the service rep restarts the program without the dongle after finishing the service like he is supposed to. If you're talking about someone other than the client, that's only true if the someone you speak of has the program installed for that dongle. Each dongle is unique and is only used on ten or twenty systems – one service rep's territory – I understand. Is that right?"

"Yes," Cliff agreed hesitantly.

"So how many systems are we talking about with this problem of yours?"

"Several." Cliff was intentionally vague.

"Do you think your service rep left his dongle behind at each of those locations? Even if he did, the dongle is still only active at program launch and wouldn't affect the keyboard during clinical operation."

"That seems unlikely," Cliff conceded.

Samuel had mostly been following the conversation silently, but an idea struck him. "Are you sure the service rep isn't doing something wrong, either intentionally or inadvertently, remotely? With his laptop and dongle he could access several different systems."

"Quite certain," Cliff said with as much confidence as he could muster. Crabbe's laptop and dongle were locked safely in Vogel's office and Crabbe safely exiled at home during at least one incident. Still, in the back of his mind he wondered if it was possible.

"Let me ask you something else," he continued. "Hypothetically, if the rep had made a copy of the program on his own personal computer and launched it with the dongle in, then removed the dongle and put it back with his company laptop, could he control his systems from his home computer?"

The two engineers conferred briefly. Clement answered, "Of course, as long as he never closed the program. Anytime he rebooted, or just shut down the program, he would need the dongle again. He would also need the IP addresses of the remote machines if I understand your software correctly, which are in a file with other restricted information. Our dongle is used to encrypt and decrypt sensitive files like that, too, but those are separate programs. Your own software engineers should have explained this to you. He would have to have copied those files onto his home computer, launched the decryption program while the dongle was in, then kept that program open, too, or repeat it with the dongle every time he shut the computer down."

"Couldn't he just print out the IP addresses when they came up on the screen?"

"No, the clipboard, print, and printscreen functions are disabled by your software to prevent that. For security. But I suppose he could copy them down by hand if there's not too many."

This gave Cliff food for thought. He ended the interview with no resolution, leaving the two engineers as unsatisfied as he was. He headed back to the office.

When he got there Maeva told him a check had come in from Orange County. This was his payment for the expert testimony against Houck, the man who killed the patrolman. He picked up the envelope as he sat down, and opened it. He smiled at the nice sum on the check. There was a note in the envelope from the prosecutor asking him to call her.

He called the number on the note. He was lucky to catch her just before quitting time. She wanted to thank him again for his help and confided in him that a plea deal had been struck. Houck had agreed to plead guilty to first degree murder in exchange for a life sentence and identifying all the drug gang leaders and the border agents they had corrupted, including testifying against them.

"He deserved death for killing that patrolman, if you ask me," Cliff opined.

"I agree," the prosecutor replied. "And the jury would have given it to him. This is Orange County. You can get a death sentence for having an Obama sticker on your car. But you know how it is. California judges just won't let it happen. There hasn't been an execution in over a decade. He would have just rotted in a cell until some appellate judge declared our latest procedures unconstitutional and all the death cases would get changed to life sentences anyway. Then we'd tweak the method and go through it all again. This way we get the rest of his crew. He'll probably get whacked by them in prison anyway for ratting them out. Hilarious, isn't it? Death is more likely if he doesn't get the death sentence." She cackled at this.

"I suppose," he replied, nonplussed at her coldness.

"I have another call. Anyway, thanks."

"Okay, goodbye."

Next he scanned his email and saw one from Sharon Perry, the lawyer defending the Byrne lawsuit. It said she had checked with Vogel who gave her the okay to talk to him about the case. He called her.

"Hi, Sharon, it's Cliff Knowles."

"Yes, Cliff, I was expecting your call. How can I help you?"

"Tell me about this Byrne guy. What kind of suit is it?"

"He was laid off by Xlectrix. He's claiming age discrimination."

"How old is he? He didn't look very old to me."

"Forty-two. The minimum age to sue is forty. It's a ridiculous suit. There are a half a dozen field engineers older than he is. There's absolutely no evidence of discrimination against people his age. He has no chance at trial if it ever gets that far."

"He was a field engineer? He installed Lilacs?"

"Lilacs?"

"The cancer treatment machines Xlectrix makes; they're called Lilacs."

"I think so. We haven't taken his depo yet but I believe that's in his job description."

"Where does he work now? His lawyer said somewhere in Fremont."

"Right, at a radiology group there. The doctors lease some Xlectrix equipment, maybe those Lilacs you mentioned. He's the head of their engineering unit I believe."

"When did he get laid off?"

"Three and a half years ago. That's a long time to still be litigating, I know. He filed a discrimination claim right away with the EEOC. He claimed discrimination on every ground he could think of: race, age, religion, disability. But it took him a while to get a right to sue letter from the EEOC for some reason. His claims were so outlandish that I guess they felt they had to look into it. He's very intelligent and can sound credible. Anyway, they finally lost interest and gave him the right to file suit himself. Hannity has been stalling, hoping for a settlement."

"Why was he laid off? Was it a company-wide reduction?" Cliff was getting very interested. If this guy had been a field engineer he would know how to use Xlectrix hardware and software.

"Sort of. Really he was being fired because he was a drunkard. He was showing up at clients' sites with liquor on his breath, and complaints came in he was being rude. The company lumped him in with a couple of other problem employees and some temps and laid them all off, claiming it was a cost savings measure. He wasn't fired for cause. He got his unemployment insurance. They even held their nose and gave him a good reference. He got hired by this doctor's group right away, although at a lower salary. His skills are in demand."

What did he claim his race, religion, and disability were?"

"White, Positive Christianity, and alcoholism."

"Positive Christianity? What's that?"

"A Nazi religious doctrine. Racial purity and all that. I don't know. You can look it up in Wikipedia or wherever. He dropped the claims of race, religion, and alcoholism in the lawsuit. All he has left is age discrimination. I guess he realized no Santa Clara County jury would be sympathetic to a claim the company discriminated against white guys, since 80% of the other field engineers are white and half of the jurors would be minorities. And I suppose he didn't want to publicly declare himself to be a Nazi type or an alcoholic in a court proceeding. I wouldn't advise it if I'd been representing him. It wouldn't have helped his job prospects. Actually, he might have been able to make a case on the disability claim. The courts are pretty sympathetic to treating alcoholism as a disability."

"Did Vogel tell you what I'm doing for him?"

"No. He just said you were investigating another matter. Can you tell me?"

"Probably not. At least not until Vogel says okay. It would help me to know if he's made any threats, been on company grounds recently, or anything like that, though."

"Not that I'm aware of. He has a real temper problem, though, I hear."

"Okay. I'll ask Vogel to keep me informed of any developments in your case. I may be back in touch. Thanks for your help."

"Sure."

Cliff could hear the skritch of her pencil as she marked the end time of the call on her billing sheet.

Chapter 24

"The real problem is the blood supply," Dr. Maloof explained. "Fortunately her tumor was subcutaneous, just under the skin, not on the bone. The radiation beam destroyed some muscle tissue and some nerves, but those should grow back fairly well if we can keep the lower leg blood supply going. The vessels there were badly damaged by the radiation. If we can't restore better circulation, sepsis will set in and the lower leg would have to be amputated. It looks like the first vascular transplant is failing. We used a vein from her other leg and we're going to use another one today, but we can't keep transplanting her own vessels indefinitely. Artificial veins – Gortex – work well above the knee but not below, and the transplant surgeon tells me a cadaver vein is not likely to work in this case because the radiation damage combined with the immunosuppressants would prevent the tissue from healing well. It's highly unusual but we'd like to use a healthy live donor with a good tissue match if we need a third surgery. I'd like you both to be tested in case we need to use your vessels. You're her closest relatives."

"Of course," Ellen immediately replied.

"You want to take our veins?" Theresa asked tentatively. "Of course I'll do whatever it takes to save her leg, but does that leave a scar?"

Maloof gave her an odd look. "Let's not worry about that yet. We can hope that her second vein will do better than the first one. In the meantime let's see if you're a tissue match. Just because you're her mother doesn't guarantee that. All we need is to take a blood sample."

"Can we do that blood test right now? You can take any of my veins you want," Ellen declared stoutly, nudging her sister hard.

Theresa nodded agreement.

It took Roger Vogel three days to return Cliff's call.

"I've been out of town, Cliff. You'll be happy to know we've completed the reinstalls. Every system has been changed over. We've permanently assigned a new service rep to handle all of Crabbe's old clients. He has a new dongle and there have been no further incidents and no more reports of that hitch in response time."

"Did you find out if the latest overdose, with Ashley Bishop, had that delay problem?"

"They aren't sharing a lot of details. Their lawyer has gotten involved. Our field engineer who did the reinstall said the rad tech told him it was behaving a little funny that day but that's all we know. It seems fine now. What have you learned?"

Cliff told him about the interview at Secryptic and how it might have been possible for Crabbe to have copied the program onto his home system, plugged in the dongle, and as long as he kept the program running he theoretically could have controlled the affected machines remotely. Vogel chewed that over but said nothing.

Cliff then asked about Byrne and his lawsuit.

"You think he could be involved? I don't see how." Vogel replied dismissively. "Sure, he's angry about being laid off, and had some technical knowledge, but he left over three years ago. The L4 didn't come out until after he left. He's never been trained how to service one. We got his old laptop when he left and it didn't have the necessary instructions and specifications anyway. He never even had a dongle issued to him. I doubt he even knows what a dongle is. They weren't used on the L3's or earlier models. I'm pretty sure the doctor group he works for now doesn't even have one of our L4's, just the L3."

"Why did you fire him?" Cliff had already heard from Sharon Perry but he wanted to see if Vogel gave the same story.

"Bizarre behavior. He has an alcohol problem. When he gets drunk he gets belligerent. He was okay during regular work hours, but he'd get called out to service machines after hours sometimes. Back then, with the L3's or earlier, there was no remote access. The rep couldn't fix anything from the office or home with his laptop. He'd have to jump in the car and go. These cancer centers or hospitals sometimes work twenty-four hours a day. If he got a call in the evening, he'd be out on the road driving drunk, and he'd for sure do something to alienate one of our clients. He had to go."

"Give me an example."

"Well, he was working up in Idaho at the time and serviced Montana, too. One time he got called to a site in Bozeman in the evening and was drunk as usual. When he got there he found out someone there had accidentally disconnected a cable. He blew up for having been called out that late over something that simple. The rad tech was from one of those Indian tribes up there, I guess, and he began chewing her out, saying things like he should have expected as much from an inferior breed like her. Of course the client complained. We yanked him back here and had him work with our software design team for a few months.

"He's a good software engineer. He seemed okay at first, but was angry about being transferred. He had come to like that mountain environment. I think he'd gotten into one of those white hate groups. The cost of housing here was killing him, even with us paying the transfer costs and giving him a cost of living adjustment. Housing here is at least three times the cost of Boise. He had to rent some shack way up in the hills above Morgan Hill, a two-hour commute. He'd come in late and angry, leave early. He was pretty good with coding they said, but was real disruptive to the group, especially the minorities. It wasn't working so his boss let him go."

"I want to be kept informed of all developments in that case. Can you send me all the pleadings and discovery, his current work details and so on."

"Okay, I'll have my assistant send that to you, but really I think that's a waste. He's an L3 guy, not an L4 guy."

"That reminds me. Who services the L3's? Would that have been Crabbe?"

This made Vogel think for a moment. "Yes, I think it would. It's geographical, not by product line. Crabbe serviced all our clients in the Bay Area. There are even a couple of L2's still around somewhere."

Chapter 25

Cliff spent the next morning researching Brian Byrne online. There were too many Brian Byrnes on facebook and Google+ to identify him, assuming he was even there, but Cliff found his profile on LinkedIn. Byrne apparently considered that site useful for his job search. Cliff also had a credit agency account and found a report there.

Byrne was 45 and unmarried, mediocre credit. Sharon Perry had told him 42, but that was the age he was when laid off, close to the minimum of 40 to claim age discrimination. He lived on Finley Ridge Road in Morgan Hill. Cliff looked that up and found it was a short, sparsely built two-lane road in the eastern hills just before the entrance to Henry Coe State Park.

He knew the area only vaguely. Henry Coe was the largest state park in northern California, but not so well known or frequented as the more scenic and accessible parks in the western hills, ones with redwoods, or the ones at the shore. Coe was dry and very hot during the summer and had very little development. It was thirty minutes of winding mountain driving from the nearest freeway entrance and then once at the park, it was two days' hike to some of the more interesting spots. Byrne's house wasn't as far as the park, but it was still a good distance from the beaten path.

Byrne's LinkedIn profile claimed he graduated from Rensselaer Polytechnic Institute with a degree in Electrical Engineering and a minor in Physics. His prior employments looked impressive until one considered that most of them did not last long. His listed current employment, as Cliff expected, was at Fremont Radiology Group as Director of Engineering. Cliff printed out the page and added it to the growing file he had on the case. Cliff then looked up the website of that group and saw that it consisted of five doctors who did both diagnostic radiology and radiation oncology. Another page added to the file.

Vogel had emailed over some of the basic data on the radiology group's contract with Xlectrix. As Vogel had told him, the group had a Lilac 3, but no Lilac 4. The technical contact was shown as Byrne. No surprise there. The billing contact was shown as a Lynda Satterlee. Cliff noticed something else: the service contract was due to expire in six weeks. He called Vogel, but only got voicemail, so he decided to call Buster Crabbe. He got through.

"Hi, Buster, this is Cliff Knowles. I'm the ..."

"I remember who you are," Crabbe interrupted. "I suppose you expect me to be grateful that your investigation got me back to work. Don't hold your breath. I'm in a lower paid job and everyone still treats me like a pariah. They still don't trust me."

"They cut your pay? I didn't know. I told Vogel to put you back to work. You passed the polygraph."

"They're still paying me the field engineer rate, but that can't last. This is a make-work position that could be done by someone right out of college. It's gotta be temporary."

"I'm sorry. At least you're actually working and not fired. If you want to get this all back to normal you can still help yourself by helping me solve it."

"How?"

"Do you remember a guy named Brian Byrne?"

"Of course. He was a field service engineer like me. Got laid off three or four years ago. He was up north somewhere, so I didn't really get to know him until they transferred him back here to headquarters. He only lasted here for a year. Maybe less."

"What do you think of him?"

The long pause on the other end told Cliff that Crabbe was weighing what to say. Finally came a tentative, "Why?"

"The why isn't important. Just tell me your impression."

"He was kinda weird. A jerk, if you must know, but don't quote me on that. But he did his job."

"Weird in what way?"

"He was into those online role-playing games, the violent ones. He talked about those a lot, bragged about what a good shot he was. He was into guns and always going on about the Second Amendment. He told me once he shot a red-tailed hawk from his porch with a rifle. Not a shotgun, a rifle. I guess that's hard; at least he seemed to think it was something to brag about. I'm not a hunter."

This gave Cliff pause. He hadn't heard of this aspect of Byrne. It's something he would have to take into account if he decided to investigate the man.

"You say he did his job. I heard there were some complaints."

"He did his job. Well, he pissed off whoever he was with so I'm sure there were complaints. He was very sarcastic and bitter about being transferred here. He was always running down management and almost everyone else."

"How do you know this? Did he talk to you at work or did you go drinking after work or what?"

"Mostly other employees would tell me about the latest episode. In emails they'd say things like who's the latest to get 'Byrned' – stuff like that."

"So you never socialized – went to lunch with him, or out for a beer?"

"Lunch a couple of times with a few other employees – you know, for someone's birthday or like that. Once when he was new he got invited to go with a couple of other guys and me over to the local sports bar on El Camino. The Giants were playing a night game and in a tight race for the playoffs. He got drunk and got nasty. That was the last time I ever went after work if he was going to be there, but I don't think anyone else ever invited him after that."

"How nasty?"

"He was making fun of the Giants' players when they screwed up, calling them faggots and like that, the usual racial names. And loud. Geez, this is a sports bar. Everyone there was probably a big Giants fan. People were giving us the evil eye."

"So would you say he had a drinking problem?"

"That night he did. I didn't see it at work, though."

"You know he still works locally – over at one of your clients."

"One of my former clients, you mean. I've been handcuffed to a desk."

"Have you seen him over there at the Fremont Radiology Group?"

"When I have to. There's a lower-level guy I try to deal with when I'm there. His name's Mel. The Lilac is actually at the local hospital, not at their own facility. They own it but it's used by the hospital staff. They have some X-ray machines and other hardware at their offices, but I go to the hospital to do the service, so I usually just see the radiation tech or one of the engineering guys comes over. Byrne doesn't usually hang out at the hospital."

"When's the last time you were there?"

"Six months or so."

Cliff checked the file that Vogel had sent. It was slightly over six months. He did the mental math. That was about three weeks before the first overdose.

"Did you see him then?"

"Yeah, actually I did. Not the first time, but he was there the second time."

"Second time?"

"I serviced the L3 on the first day, but couldn't fix it without a part I needed, so I came back the next day. He was there the second day for a little bit. We talked about the problem. He's a former service rep so he was interested in how I fixed it, what the failure rate was. That kind of thing. We only talked maybe five minutes."

"Did you ever discuss the Lilac 4 with him?"

"I didn't. Maybe our sales people did. They only have an L3 so I didn't have any reason to."

"Did he ever ask you about it, or about the dongle?"

"The dongle?" Crabbe asked, his tone making clear he thought Cliff must be insane. "No, of course not. The L3 doesn't even use a dongle. You can't remotely access the L3's. Why would he have any interest in my dongle?"

"So you kept your laptop and dongle with you the whole time?"

"Yes, of course... well, essentially yes."

"Essentially yes? Meaning?" This time it was Cliff whose tone betrayed skepticism.

"Look, it was late when I finished up the first day and I was going to drive directly to a restaurant to meet my wife. I don't like to leave my laptop in the car, especially if I have to leave it with a valet to park. Laptops get stolen all the time and this had all kinds of sensitive company information on it, although that was all encrypted. So I asked the other engineer there, Mel, if he had a secure place to keep it overnight. I knew I was coming back first thing the next day. I couldn't leave it in the hospital treatment room. He said he did. He kept it locked up over at the engineering room at the radiology group. But I pulled the dongle out before I gave it to him. Without the dongle there's nothing. I'm positive I kept it with me. The next day I came back and put the dongle in the bag. I double-checked it when I left, too. It was there with me the whole time."

This explanation came rushing out and acquired a more defensive tone to it as he got to the end. Cliff smelled a vole at least, if not quite a rat.

"Buster, is that the normal protocol? Leaving a company laptop at a client's, I mean?"

"We do it sometimes. I'm not the only one."

"Which means no, doesn't it," Cliff said, sounding like a school principal confronting a spitball thrower.

"Technically, I'm supposed to return to my office and lock the computer there overnight or take it directly home. But without the dongle, there's nothing useful on it. Even most of the stuff on it that is encrypted is stuff Byrne already knows from being a field engineer himself. Other than the L4 stuff and the updated Tech Tips and client information, he probably knows all of it."

"Is that what you were nervous about during the polygraph? What you meant when you said you were afraid you might be responsible somehow?"

"No," Crabbe almost spit out. "No. I never even thought about Byrne. What does he have to do with it anyway? You think he's involved? He'd need my laptop and the dongle to remotely access those other machines, and the IP addresses of the other clients' machines. He didn't have any of those. I... I was just worried that somehow if I skirted their rules a little bit, like that time, somehow I might have caused a problem. But I kept the dongle that time; I know I did. And I had the laptop with me every time the overdoses happened, except this last time and then it was at the office in Vogel's safe or with my replacement. Are you going to report this?"

"I have to. But if you're telling the truth, then I don't see how that incident could have led to the overdoses."

"Jesus, just when I thought I was in the clear."

"Take it easy. You should come out of it fine. It doesn't seem like a big deal to me, especially if other field service reps do it, too."

"They do, I swear."

"Okay, you go back to work. I may be back in touch if I need more."

They hung up.

Chapter 26

Ellen took the news stoically, but Theresa was on the brink of a nervous breakdown. Ashley had already had two vascular transplants in the last month to try to save the leg. Both had worked for a time, but then the grafts began to fail because the tissue around them was so damaged from the radiation overdose. Theresa wasn't a tissue match; Ellen was a fair match, and might be possible. It was all but certain that Ashley would lose her lower leg if a matching donor could not be found. For the time being Ashley was not told of this.

When they came from the doctor's office, Ellen headed directly to the FBI's Palo Alto Resident Agency. Although she was a relative newcomer she knew her fellow agents would come through. Time was of the essence. She marched right into the squad supervisor's office even though he was on the phone. He was surprised but put the caller on hold to ask what was the matter. He trusted his agents to know when a matter was important or urgent enough to interrupt him. She explained the situation and asked him to call a squad conference as soon as possible. She wanted to ask for her co-workers to get tested for a tissue match. The supervisor agreed, and put a message out over the radio for all the Palo Alto R.A. agents to be present for a squad conference at 4:00. Many agents were out covering leads and that was the earliest possible time.

When Ellen presented the doctor's findings to the squad there was a nearly universal response by the agents. Every agent but one volunteered to get tested. The one who didn't was pregnant and knew she could not be a suitable donor at this time.

The next day Cliff, Gina, and Matt sat at The Red Pepper, one of their regular lunch spots. Cliff ordered his usual two enchilada lunch. His morning had consisted of more special appearances in Superior Court, none of the details worth sharing with Matt and Gina.

The initial conversation was awkward. By now both Gina and Matt were aware in general terms of the incident at the hospital involving Cliff, Ashley, and Ellen, but no one wanted to be the first one to broach the subject.

Cliff broke the ice, directing the question at Matt. "Have you heard how Ashley Bishop is doing?"

"Not so good. Ellen said the vein graft is failing and they'll have to find a blood vessel donor who's a good tissue match or she'll lose the lower part of her leg."

"Oh, Christ, no," Cliff muttered, shaking his head. He looked away.

Gina had already heard this news. In fact it had begun to spread throughout the whole division and FBI volunteers were signing up from all over the Bay Area. Ashley Bishop was not only the niece of an agent and the daughter of a former agent, but also the goddaughter of the Director. Gina felt a pang of sympathy for Cliff, but her curiosity was even stronger.

"Cliff," she said. "What happened over there? Ellen thinks you knew about the problem with the radiation machine and didn't say anything. She blames you for this."

"That's not true, Gina," Cliff replied, shaking his head vigorously. "I did everything I could to prevent it. That's… it's… that's all I can say. Everything else I know about this is attorney-client privileged. You'll just have to take my word for it."

Gina and Matt exchanged uneasy glances. Cliff had mentored them both when he was a senior agent in San Jose and they were new agents on his squad. They trusted him implicitly, but he had not given them a satisfactory explanation, not one they could take to Ellen anyway.

"Sure, Cliff," Matt finally said. "I'm sure you did what you could." He didn't sound all that sincere.

"How are you doing on Palobom?" Cliff had heard from them the code name of the bombing case.

"Stymied," Matt replied. "It's really frustrating. Our only real suspect has been out of the country since right after the bombing."

"That sounds like you have the right guy."

"Not necessarily. We seized his car and tested it every which way from Sunday. We couldn't match up any residue or forensic evidence with the bombing."

Cliff asked what kind of bomb it was. Matt told him the forensic details. Even though that was not public knowledge, he knew Cliff would not reveal the information. More importantly, Cliff was a smart guy who knew more about solving crimes than anyone else Matt had ever met.

"That sounds like some of those bombs the KKK used in the south," Cliff opined. "I don't remember hearing of Middle Eastern terrorists using that kind. That's sort of old school. Good for setting fire, but not much of a bang. I'd expect a pressure cooker or something like that from Palestinians."

"You have a good memory. But the recipe is all over the Internet. Anyone could copy it. We think this is a loner – someone operating by himself without guidance from any group. It is unusual for a Palestinian group, though. They've never targeted anyone in the U.S. Their U.N. status and financial support is too important. It's typically Al Qaeda that does this kind of stuff, or individuals inspired by Al Qaeda – the wannabes – who do it. There's a first time for everything, though. The underwear bomber, the shoe bomber, the toner cartridge bomb, they were all things we hadn't seen before."

"True. Have any groups claimed credit?"

"No. To the contrary. They've all denied being involved."

"Have you considered the possibility that someone else did it and is trying to shift blame with that flag? Maybe someone with a personal grudge against the center or someone who works there. Someone who got fired, for example."

"We can't rule it out, but we haven't been able to identify anyone else who would have a motive. There haven't been any threats or prior incidents. No paid staff firings ever. It's mostly volunteers over there."

"How do I volunteer?" Cliff asked.

Nonplussed, Matt replied, "Volunteer for what? You want to become Jewish?"

"To get tested, for a tissue match."

"For Ellen's niece? Are you sure that's a good idea. Like I said, Ellen blames you."

"All the more reason. I'm not doing this out of guilt, because I didn't do anything wrong, but I want to help. I'm still part of the Bureau family."

Gina and Matt exchanged uneasy glances again. Finally Gina replied, "Okay, I suppose if you're a match they'd be happy enough to have your veins. Here's the contact information for the hospital official coordinating this." She pulled it up on her phone from her email and forwarded it to Cliff.

As Gina did that Matt looked across the room and emitted a soft "Uh oh." He spotted someone getting up from his table after paying his bill and recognized him.

"What is it?" Gina asked.

But she didn't require a response. As she turned to see where he was looking she saw Dr. Akil Maloof walking to their table. He had spotted Matt and was approaching with anger painted all over his face.

Even before he got to their table he pointed accusingly at Matt and called out in a loud voice, "This is harassment. It is bad enough you come to my house and accuse me of being a terrorist, but you follow me around when I go to lunch. Do you have a GPS on my car? Are you following my kids?"

"I didn't follow you. We…" but that was all Matt got out.

"You!" bellowed Maloof, now pointing at Cliff, whom he only now recognized since Cliff's back had been toward him before. "So you're with the FBI, too. You rigged that Lilac to injure the patient so you could accuse me of being a terrorist, is that it?"

"No, I didn't, I…" Cliff started, but he had no better luck than Matt.

"You're going to tell me it's all coincidence? You just happen to show up where I work and where I eat!? How stupid do you think I am? Here I am trying to save children's lives and you're using them as sacrificial lambs just so you can make a trumped up terrorism case against me because I'm an Arab American! How do you even look at yourself in the mirror at night. You're despicable."

By this point everyone in the restaurant was looking at them. The waiter stood there nervously wondering what he should do. Murmurs buzzed everywhere.

"No, it's not like that at all," Matt said, pleading. "We just came here for lunch. We're regulars here. You can check with the waiter."

"He's not with us," Gina added, indicating Cliff with her thumb. Even as she said it, she realized how ridiculous it sounded, since Cliff was sitting right next to her. "I mean, he's retired. He's just a friend."

"Retired? From the FBI. Hugo said you told him you were an engineer for Xlectrix. You had a vendor badge. Since when does the FBI hire radiological engineers? You were sent to spy on me." The scorn in Maloof's voice was palpable.

"No, I wasn't," Cliff replied weakly, but realized he couldn't say more. Without any further explanation the denial rang hollow.

Maloof turned and stormed out. The entire restaurant stared at the trio still seated in their booth. The three of them silently watched Maloof through the window for a moment.

"Well, that was awkward," Gina said, breaking the silence. She looked around and saw the other diners watching them. "Nothing to see here folks. Eat your meals and mind your own business," she bellowed in her command voice. Everybody stopped staring.

Cliff leaned in and whispered to Matt, "That was Ashley's doctor. Is he one of your subjects?"

"No, just someone I interviewed." Matt had only recently become aware, from Ellen, that Maloof was Ashley's doctor. This was information he hadn't even shared with Gina.

"Great," Gina said disgustedly, "so this Arab doctor you interviewed thinks the FBI is spying on him and now we find out he's the guy treating Ellen's niece. I wonder how many tweets have already gone out from this restaurant. Let's hope no one got video or it'll be on YouTube in minutes."

"Worse," Matt replied, "he thinks the FBI sabotaged the machine that burned Ashley as part of our arsenal of dirty tricks. Sure, we sacrifice children all the time just to make cases against innocent citizens. For Christ sakes, Cliff, what were you doing there?"

Cliff knew he would be violating attorney-client privilege, but he also knew Matt had already shared FBI information with him on the bombing that shouldn't have been revealed outside the Bureau. His status as ex-FBI wasn't really so "ex" in any of their minds.

"Okay, look, you can't tell anyone. It's attorney-client privileged. I'd be disbarred. I was there to try to prevent that very thing. I'm on a consulting job for the company that makes the cancer radiation machine. They thought someone was sabotaging the machines and causing patients harm. I found that the problem could be solved with a software update, but Ashley's treatment facility was delaying the update. I was there trying to get them to do it before any further treatment took place. I was minutes too late. It was a horrible coincidence that the patient there was Ashley Bishop. Until I showed up there I didn't know she was even being treated by that machine."

"Ellen should know this," Gina replied.

"You can't tell her," Cliff retorted. "Don't even think it."

"Okay, okay, we won't," Matt assured him, starting to pick at his food again.

None of them had much appetite after this but they finished their meal, paid, and went on their separate ways.

Chapter 27

Right after lunch Cliff called the hospital and arranged to be tested for tissue matching to Ashley Bishop. The woman in charge of that program told him to come in right away, which he did. They took blood samples, and it was over in a few minutes.

When he got back to the office he called Vogel to let him know about the scene in the restaurant. He told him that Maloof was there and recognized him sitting with an FBI agent who had interviewed him and somehow reached the conclusion that he was spying for the FBI and that the FBI had sabotaged the Lilac. Vogel's main concern was whether the company name was mentioned. When Cliff assured him it wasn't, Vogel seemed less concerned. Still, he was worried that the doctor, and anyone he confided in, would think the company would cooperate with the FBI in any such thing.

The conversation shifted to Cliff's contract. Vogel said now that the problem seems to have been resolved, it may be time to call off the investigation. After all, it was costing money and there was little to show for it.

"First of all," Cliff countered, "this is resolved because I'm the one who found out about the delay in keyboard response and that reinstalling the software solved. And second, we still don't know how it happened or who ConcernedRelative is."

"Cliff, we've been over this. You earned your pay. I'm not arguing. But we were already in the process of reinstalling; you just sped it up. And I asked you to find out who ConcernedRelative is and you haven't been able to. So can you or can't you?"

"I told you about my interview out at Secryptic. I think I know how this has been done... sort of. I just need a little more time."

"I'm listening."

"I think when Crabbe went to the Fremont Clinic where Byrne works, his computer was compromised in some way that allowed Byrne or someone else there to gain access to the other computers, the ones that control all his clients' L4's."

"That seems awfully far-fetched to me. You told me Crabbe says he took the dongle with him when he left."

"I'd like to re-polygraph him on that specific point."

"That still means that you think Byrne would remotely kill patients in other clinics just to get revenge on us for laying him off? I just don't see it. We gave him a good recommendation when he left and he got rehired quickly."

"He's suing you. He can't be all that satisfied. And maybe he's trying to drive patients to his clinic. If he's ConcernedRelative, that would explain why he had to say it was a Lilac 4, not just a Lilac. His clinic has an L3 and several other machines from different manufacturers."

"Oh come on. Patients don't even know the model numbers of the machines that treat them. Even if people knew of the post and believed it, they still wouldn't know where to go."

"But the doctors do. Most oncologists have admitting privileges in more than one hospital, and may have offices in two or more cities. They can send their patients to the places they feel are safest. And look at where the incidents have happened. Palo Alto, Milpitas, Tracy, San Jose. Fremont is almost dead center. Fremont is just about the closest unaffected clinic to each of those."

"I don't buy it. Vengeance is a better motive, although not a good one. I'm sure he's salaried and wouldn't even benefit financially from driving traffic to his site. Besides, how could he do it? Assuming Crabbe kept the dongle, I mean. I've got the dongle right here in my safe."

"Maybe Crabbe didn't keep the dongle. We'll find that out with the polygraph. Or maybe he really thought he had, but actually left it with the laptop that evening. We already know that if you can copy all the files and get the dongle you can boot up the copied file with the dongle in and remove the dongle later but the program works until closed. If Byrne copied his laptop and had the dongle for even a short time he could have launched the program, removed the dongle and put it back in the bag and returned it to Crabbe. As long as he kept the program running, he wouldn't need the dongle."

"You think he's kept the program running for months? Look, you just came up with Byrne out of nowhere based on that one word, 'reprehensible.' I just think that's too tenuous."

"Is there anyone else you think hates Xlectrix enough to kill your patients? Your competitors even?"

"No."

"Give me a few more days to work on this."

"How would you do it?"

"Go out to Fremont, for starters."

"That didn't work out so well over at Lucille Packard. They're a customer, too, you know."

"Trust me."

"You have two days."

After they hung up, Cliff looked at his watch. It was late in the afternoon, but he could make it to Fremont before normal office closing time. He grabbed his Xlectrix ID, told Maeva he'd be gone for two or three hours, and headed out the door.

The weather was still spectacular, so he left the top down on his C-70 as he drove east on Highway 237. Traffic was heavy, but he made it in less than an hour. He saw the main entrance, marked "Patient Entrance" but remembered from the notes in Crabbe's file on this facility that there was a separate business office entrance on the north side of the building, where Xlectrix employees should go. He parked near there and went in.

The small lobby held two chairs, one of which was occupied by a voluptuous young woman, heavily made up, wearing spike heels and carrying a valise or sample case of some kind. She had a name tag on her blouse with the name of one of the major drug companies. Subtlety wasn't her middle name. Cliff had heard that drug companies used attractive female sales reps to push their wares on male doctors but he hadn't realized it was quite that blatant.

A thirtyish Asian woman sat at the reception desk with scissors in one hand and a sheet of paper in the other. Her hair was cut in a Buster Brown, and she wore thick glasses with round lenses and heavy black frames. Cliff thought that if she were wearing a Mao suit she would look exactly like Duke's girlfriend Honey in the Doonesbury comic strip. The woman looked up expectantly, but said nothing.

"Hi, I'm from Xlectrix. I'd like to see Brian Byrne," Cliff said cheerfully. He showed her his ID.

"Is he expecting you?" the woman replied.

"I didn't have an appointment, but I was nearby and I realized there's an important technical issue I need to discuss with your engineering department."

"He went out. He should be back in fifteen minutes or so. Do you want to talk to Mel?"

Cliff remembered Mel as the second engineer Crabbe had mentioned. "Sure."

"Have a seat. I'll see if he's available."

Cliff sat and pulled out his cell phone. He pretended to make a call, but in fact was snapping pictures. The drug rep caught on fairly quickly and began smiling. Cliff noticed and pointed the camera her way. She shot him a grin and, after looking back at Honey or whatever her name was, who was paying no attention, struck a sexy pose, her impressive chest thrust forward. Cliff snapped several quick shots. The rep immediately wagged her finger at him like he'd been a naughty boy, although her smile said she'd enjoyed every second of the attention.

Still talking on the phone to no one, he stood up and walked around the lobby. When he got over the reception desk he snapped several shots of Honey's activity. She was trimming the edges off some computer printouts, then stacking those to one side. She paid him no attention.

Within a few minutes a short thin man with an equally thin mustache came up to the reception desk. He didn't enter the lobby. Standing over Honey, he asked Cliff, "Who are you?"

"Cliff Knowles, Xlectrix. You must be Mel. I need to talk to you." Cliff held out his ID as he spoke and handed him his Xlectrix business card.

"Why did you come here? The Lilac's over at the hospital."

"Can I come inside, Mel? I need to explain some technical issues that have come up."

Mel was obviously nervous. He made no move to open the door to the lobby. "What issues? I haven't heard anything about this."

"I e-mailed Brian, " Cliff lied. "I told him I'd be coming by. Maybe he didn't read the email or forgot to tell you."

Mel was still hesitant.

"Mel," Cliff said more forcefully, stretching up to his full six-foot-plus height and leaning over the desk into Mel's face. "This is important or I wouldn't be here. Now let me in."

Intimidated, or perhaps swayed by the use of Brian Byrne's name, Mel complied. They walked back to an office that resembled an electronics lab, with workbenches covered with various gizmos and a lot of computer parts. As they walked, Cliff continued to snap pictures with his phone, being sure to hold it on the opposite side of his body from Mel so as to be out of sight. Mel had a small desk against one wall. There was only one chair in that part of the workspace, and Mel sat in it. Cliff remained standing.

"Mel, have you had any reports of problems with the Lilac?" Cliff asked.

"Like what?"

"Like anything," Cliff responded in an exasperated tone.

"Well, I'm not sure what you mean," Mel mumbled.

"For Pete's sake, Mel, you know what I'm asking. Anything. Anything at all. We've had some complaints about some of our other Lilacs and want to know if you've experienced the same thing."

"What happened with the others?"

"Mel, cut it out. I need to know what you've experienced. Patient safety could be at stake. Have you had reports of problems or not?"

"You mean like the overdoses on the L4's? No, we only have the L3. They're immune. Just the usual calibration problems, but those are easy enough to deal with."

Eureka! Now he was getting somewhere. "Overdoses? I never said anything about overdoses. Where'd you hear about overdoses?"

"Brian said one of the rad techs at the hospital told him the L4's had burned some people. It was going around the community. He said we didn't have to worry since ours was an L3."

"I thought the local hospital didn't have an L4."

"They don't. They must have heard it from someone at another facility. Or maybe they work at another site."

"I don't know about any overdoses," Cliff continued. "I was investigating a delayed response from the keyboard, a reported pause when the screen doesn't seem to refresh normally when the operator enters a command. I think Brian must have gotten some bogus information there."

"He even knew the locations—one in Tracy, one in San Jose. I forget where the other one was."

"When did he tell you this?"

"Maybe a month ago. What's so important about keyboard delay? That sounds like an IT problem. How is patient safety involved?"

A month ago. If accurate, that was after the first two overdoses, but before the post by ConcernedRelative. Neither Byrne nor any radiation technician could have heard about it from the forum post. Byrne had to have personal knowledge.

"Where's Byrne's desk?" Cliff suddenly demanded.

"You can't…" Mel protested, but Cliff was already storming around the workspace.

It took him only seconds to spy the largest, nicest desk which also had a cubicle arrangement around it, something Mel's did not. Since there were only two, he assumed it was Byrne's. Cliff strode to it, Mel straggling behind. There were two computer systems there with giant monitors. Above it was a bookshelf mounted on the wall, filled with technical manuals and engineering books. One of them was clearly labeled "Xlectrix L3 Service Manual. Proprietary." Cliff spotted yet another, shorter, book, really a ring binder, that also bore the Xlectrix logo. On the desk was a paperweight made of solid metal ornamented on top with a tiny model of an AK-47 style assault weapon. He snapped photos of the whole bookshelf and desk.

Mel put his hand on Cliff's shoulder and squeaked, "You can't do that. This is private property. You need Brian's permission. You'd better leave now."

Cliff whirled, throwing off Mel's hand with an effortless swipe of his arm. He bellied up to Mel and stared down at him.

"Where'd you get the dongle? Did Crabbe give it to you?"

At the mention of the word dongle Mel cowered and shrank visibly. His lip quivered momentarily and he backpedaled to the doorway. Then he flung open the door and called out to the receptionist to get Mrs. Satterlee.

Cliff recognized the name as the billing contact. He walked to the doorway and was surprised to see Brian Byrne walk in the front door of the lobby. The receptionist pushed an intercom button and told the female voice that answered that she was needed in Engineering right away. Byrne walked up to the desk and asked what was going on. The sales rep was still sitting in the waiting room watching the drama.

Cliff walked back out to the reception desk and arrived just as a trim, gray-haired, no-nonsense woman in a black skirt and tasteful mauve blouse reached the area. Byrne, Cliff, Mel and the woman all hovered over the receptionist's desk.

The woman, recognizing Cliff as the only non-employee, announced, "I'm Lynda Satterlee, the manager. What seems to be the problem?"

"Hello," Cliff said politely, "I'm Cliff Knowles, from Xlectrix. There seems to be an issue here. I was just discussing an engineering issue here with Mel and noticed that there are a number of our proprietary manuals here. I'm afraid I must ask for an explanation."

Byrne snapped, "What the hell were you doing back in Engineering?"

"Brian, let me handle this," Satterlee said calmly. "Why don't we go back to my office."

Cliff followed her down the hallway. Mel immediately retreated to Engineering, but Byrne started to follow Cliff. When they got to her office Satterlee motioned for Cliff to have a seat and whispered something to Byrne. He shook his head vigorously but it was clear to Cliff that she was the boss and was directing him to butt out. He headed back to Engineering. She closed the door.

"Mr. Knowles, this is an unexpected visit. So what is this about proprietary manuals?"

Cliff pulled out his phone and brought up one of the shots of the bookshelf. He displayed it to her without a word.

She seemed unimpressed. "As you know, we have a license for those manuals," she replied evenly and smiled.

Oh shit. A license. He hadn't thought of that. The clients might be permitted to have the manuals if they paid an annual fee or as part of the purchase of the Lilac. Maybe she was bluffing. He had to hope he hadn't ruined yet another client relation for Xlectrix.

"A current license?" he said incredulously. He could bluff, too.

"Well, of course we didn't renew the license after last June. That's separate from the service contract. You know we hired Brian and he knows your system inside and out. I know the contract calls for us to return the manuals, but you aren't really here for that are you? Brian offered to return them last fall but he said you told him to keep them. Your service rep, Mr. Crabbe is it, said it was better to have Brian having a reliable reference source than trying to do maintenance from memory. He said something about it being easier for him than trying to fix Brian's mistakes. At least that's what Brian told me. Are you saying that's not true?"

"I see. Buster didn't mention that to me. If he said that, he really didn't have the authority." Cliff felt relieved. Technically they didn't have a valid license. At least he was on solid legal footing.

"Is this really about trying to get us to re-up the maintenance contract? That's a rather aggressive sales tactic – not like your company. I know you're losing a lot of revenue just providing repairs on an as needed basis rather than the annual warranty service, but business is business after all. It's cheaper for us to have Brian and Mel do it in house."

"Mr. Crabbe has been reassigned. I'm new on this contract and just wasn't aware. I'm sorry to have caused a stir. I'm really not here to generate sales. Perhaps you could enlighten me as to everyone's role here. You're in charge, I take it?"

"The business is owned by the doctors. They're in charge, but they spend their time doing doctor stuff – you know, saving lives and so on." Her tone dripped with sarcasm. "I'm the office manager. I run the business end. I work for the doctors and everyone else works for me. Brian is the head of Engineering and Mel reports to him. The Lilac is over at the hospital, though, not here. Why did you even come here?"

"It was a technical issue. A problem with keyboard response time on some Lilacs. I'm trying to troubleshoot it. Mel told me it hasn't been a problem with your system. It sounds like this trip was wasted. I'll check with our legal people to make sure it's okay for you to have those manuals and we can just consider this a meet and greet." Cliff handed her his Xlectrix business card.

"If you want the manuals back, we'll be glad to return them," Satterlee said pleasantly. She stood, signaling that the conversation was over. Cliff had what he needed and was just as anxious to get out of there as she was to get rid of him. He stood, too, and turned to the door.

Satterlee walked him to the reception area. Cliff noticed on his way out that Honey was no longer clipping paper and the stacks of finished pages was gone. The sales rep was no longer in the waiting room. Apparently some doctor was in the process of getting a close personal demonstration of the therapeutic benefits of some pharmaceutical. He exited to the parking lot.

Just outside the door stood Brian Byrne. This was the first close look Cliff had gotten of Byrne. He'd been largely obscured in the courtroom by all the others in the room. The man was even taller than

Cliff, and heavier, too, by at least fifty pounds. Still, he didn't look so formidable; his weight was mostly in his gut and his butt. He had narrow shoulders and an ugly dewlap of fat hanging from his neck. The redness of his facial veins wasn't as bad as his lawyer's, but would be in a few more years. His drinking habit was obvious anyway from his breath. He was clearly a whiskey man.

"I'm Brian Byrne," he announced, thick tongued but somehow more menacing that comical. "Don't ever come here again."

Cliff put his face into Byrne's. "Well, Brian, you seem concerned – *relatively* concerned. Or should I say ConcernedRelative...ly?"

"You'd better watch your step, Knowles. You've been warned." Byrne pulled from his pocket a box cutter, blade retracted, and flipped it in the air once before returning it to his pocket. He then brushed hard against Cliff as he went back inside the lobby.

Cliff stepped back to let him by and stood watching Byrne disappear into the building. He then walked back to his car. When he got there, his heart sank. The driver's seat, expensive leather, of course, had been slit in a big X across the entire seating surface. He cursed himself for driving his own car out here. He should have rented something and taken out the insurance. There was nothing to be done about it now, so he climbed in and drove back to the office.

He parked in his usual spot in his lot and got out. He had noticed an uncomfortable lump in his rear on the drive back and had assumed he was being poked by a spring that had been exposed by the sliced X. He bent over to look more closely and was surprised to see there was something wedged in the stuffing at the crossing point of the X. He fished it out. It was a small metallic cylinder, like a miniature barrel. He had not seen anything like it that he could remember. It was about the size of a ring box. The top had been removed. Inside was a small pebble about the size of a peppercorn. He picked it out and examined it, but had no idea what it was. He turned the box over in his other hand to see if there any markings on the bottom.

Indeed there were – markings that gave him the shock of his life. Unmistakable on the bottom of the cylinder was the black and yellow radiation warning symbol. Instinctively, he dropped it. Then came the sickening realization that he had driven for an hour with that pebble directly underneath his thighs and private parts, unshielded by the top that had been removed. The only thing between him and the rock had been the seat stuffing that had been pulled up around the cylinder to hide it. Then he cursed himself for dropping the pebble. He looked down at the ground but there was loose gravel all over the parking lot. The cylinder was easily retrieved, but he had no chance of identifying the pebble.

He whipped out his phone to call Vogel and saw that there was one text message. He retrieved it. The hospital was notifying him that he was a perfect tissue match for Ashley Bishop. They wanted to do the transplant surgery on Saturday, the day after tomorrow and to call immediately on getting the text.

He wasn't ready to deal with that, especially not now. He might not even be an eligible donor if he had been irradiated. He called Vogel's office but only got voice mail. This couldn't wait. He considered calling Crabbe, the only other person at Xlectrix he knew, but he still didn't know if Crabbe was in on the scheme with Byrne. He decided to call Matt Nguyen.

"Call 911, Cliff," Matt said after Cliff explained the situation. "They have hazmat teams in every county. I know they have Geiger counters and ways to search for radioactive materials. Don't let anyone drive or walk over that area. Can you get someone there right away to watch it? You need to get to the hospital to be tested. And don't drive your own car. Take an ambulance."

"Matt, I feel fine. I can get Maeva to drive me in her car."

"That's not the point. It's important to get treatment right away if you've been exposed, I'm pretty sure. If you drive or walk in to the emergency room you may sit for hours, especially if you look fine. They may even send you to another hospital if they're busy. By law they have to see you if you come in by ambulance. Take the container with you."

This was all good advice that Cliff hadn't considered. He knew he wasn't thinking clearly. Byrne had gotten to him. He was off his game.

He called 911. The conversation was awkward since the operator had never handled an accidental radiation exposure case before, but she rolled police, fire, and ambulance to the scene. The operator wanted him to stay on the line until help arrived, so he did.

Los Altos police were on the scene within two minutes, sirens wailing. Cliff explained the situation and pointed out the small cylinder, still on the ground. One officer started to pick it up, but the other one stopped him, saying it could be dangerous.

At this point Maeva came down the stairs out to the lot to see what the commotion was, only to find her boss standing there talking with officers. Within another minute two fire engines rolled up, also with sirens blaring. Soon the parking lot was milling with all the tenants of the building and various passersby. The police were struggling to keep people away from the possibly contaminated scene. The fire crew wanted to know the situation and Cliff was trying to explain to them, the police, and Maeva all at the same time. Maeva, upset, kept asking why he didn't call her immediately.

The fire crew had to send for their hazardous materials team. The ambulance crew arrived last, sirens and lights once more calling attention to the scene. When they were informed of the nature of the call they agreed Cliff should get to the hospital immediately. Then debate broke out about the cylinder. The police wanted it left there as crime scene evidence. The ambulance crew said it would be important for the doctors to have it to be able to determine the best treatment, but they didn't want it in their ambulance. Finally it was agreed that the medical need outweighed everything else. It was decided to have the container placed in the very back of the longest fire truck, farthest from where anyone might sit or stand, and have that truck follow the ambulance to the hospital. An intrepid female firefighter, fed up with all the talk, walked over, picked it up and placed it inside the back of the truck and yelled at everyone to get the hell moving.

At this the ambulance crew led Cliff into the ambulance, making him lie down, and they took off for the Stanford Hospital Emergency Room, fire truck right behind. The officers and one fire truck stayed behind guarding the scene. Maeva stood there dumbfounded. Matt Nguyen showed up and began talking to the first responders.

The other tenants of the building were now giving the officers a hard time, wanting to get their cars out of the lot so they could go home. The small lot had only one entrance/exit.

Finally the fire department's hazmat team showed up and took charge of the scene. When the first member of the team emerged in what looked like a space suit, the crowd drew back. Self-preservation finally took sway over getting home.

It didn't take long for the hazmat team to confirm that there was an elevated level of radiation in the vandalized car seat, but it was very slight and not at hazardous levels. They determined that it was almost certainly from the cylinder which at some point in the past had held a radioactive substance, but probably not from the pebble. They scanned the gravel area around the car and eventually found one tiny piece of rock that registered on the Geiger counter slightly higher than anything else. They decided this was probably what had been in the box. The most likely explanation, they explained to Matt and the officers, was that someone had placed an ordinary piece of gravel in an old container that had once held a radioactive isotope. The gravel had picked up just enough radioactivity to register at a slightly elevated level, but neither the seat nor the gravel were considered dangerous. Without the cylinder they could not be sure, but they believed it, too, was probably not dangerous. The bottom line: this was a cruel joke meant to throw a scare into the victim. The police called this information over to the hospital.

Meanwhile, in the emergency room, Cliff had been subjected to the indignity of having to strip and have his genitals and thigh area scanned with a radiation detector. The box was identified by a radiation tech as a common type, known as a pig, used to store and transport certain isotopes used in X-ray machines, but the top was missing. The labeling that would tell exactly what had been inside would have been there. There were a number of different elements used for diagnostic or therapeutic purposes. The level of residual radioactivity was so slight that it had probably been one with a short half-life and that had probably been quite a long time ago. The radioactivity was barely higher than that of a granite countertop. The doctors pronounced Cliff healthy and released him.

It was 8:30 by the time Cliff got home, tired, hungry, and very angry. He wolfed down a peanut butter sandwich and glass of milk and climbed in the shower for a long soak. When he finally got out and dressed he flopped down in his recliner and opened up the bag the hospital had given him containing his wallet and phone. When he turned on the phone there were nine missed calls, seven voice messages, and thirteen texts. He slowly read or listened to all of them, jotting down the names. Nearly all of them were people, like Maeva and Matt, asking him if he was okay and offering to help.

He composed one email to the effect that he was fine and back home and thanked everyone involved. He copied all the well-wishers with bcc's so he wouldn't have to retype it or retell the story over the phone.

That left only three he had to deal with. First was from the Los Altos police asking him to call the detectives. He decided to do that one the next day. Next was the hospital who had called about the vein donation surgery. He called them back and said he was ready, willing, and able. He got the address and time to show up. The hospital coordinator said the vascular surgeon would be calling him tomorrow about prep for the surgery and the risks.

Last was Vogel. His message to Vogel had only said it was important, but had not provided any detail. He wasn't sure Vogel would answer after hours, but he tried Vogel's cell. After six rings Vogel had still not answered, but then suddenly he came on the line. Cliff figured Vogel was looking at his display and debating whether to answer or let it wait until the next day.

"Yes, Cliff, how'd it go today?" Vogel asked casually, a hint of impatience coloring his tone.

"Bull's-eye. We got our man."

Cliff could almost see the enthusiasm flowing from the phone. "Tell me more."

Cliff relayed the whole story all the way down to the chaos in the parking lot and the trip to the hospital. It took twenty minutes of non-stop talking. Vogel didn't interrupt him once.

When Cliff was done Vogel exclaimed, "So Byrne must have copied Crabbe's laptop onto a computer there and had the dongle, too. That must have happened when Buster left it that night. Byrne set up a complete clone of his system, then used that to remotely manipulate the L4's. With the dongle he could have decrypted the IP addresses and read the instructions for the L4's."

Cliff agreed. "Assuming that's all true, I can only see three possibilities. One, Crabbe is not in on it, but is lying to cover up the fact he left the dongle there with the laptop; two, he's not in on it, but mistakenly believes he didn't leave the dongle; or three, he's in on it and helped Byrne do this. We need to do that polygraph again to nail down which it is."

"Fine. I authorize it. Do what you have to do. And send me those pictures you took. I'll have to review our licensing contract with the Fremont group, and talk to Crabbe to see if he really told them they could keep those manuals, but I think we may have a solid case against them. We should have some leverage anyway. Even if Buster told them to keep it, the contract makes clear that it can only be altered in writing and only if it's signed by an authorized sales representative. It's at least a contract violation, maybe a theft of trade secrets."

"Why don't I send them to Sharon Perry, too," Cliff suggested. "Maybe she can file a cross-complaint against Byrne and his employer."

"Good idea. Go ahead. I'll let her know not to do anything with them until I've reviewed them."

"Will do."

As soon as he was off the line Cliff went to his home computer and uploaded the photos from his phone. He'd taken over fifty shots. He was just about to upload them en masse to Xlectrix's internal site when he noticed the ones of the pharmaceutical sales rep. Hmm, she was definitely photogenic, but probably not ideal as evidence. After deleting those he uploaded the rest and sent the link to Vogel and Sharon Perry.

The "message sent" notice flashed on his screen and he sat back, savoring a certain satisfaction that he finally had the case under control. It wasn't fully solved. He still had to find out whether Crabbe was involved, or for that matter, Mel or anyone else at the Fremont facility. Could Byrne have been operating at the direction of the doctors? As Vogel had pointed out, Byrne probably had no financial motive in driving patients to his facility.

An email appeared on his screen. For a moment he thought it was a reply from Vogel acknowledging the link to the photos, since it came from the Xlectrix domain. As soon as he read the subject line, though, he realized it was an automated notification that he had received an email on his Xlectrix account. Vogel had had his IT people create an email address there for him as a consultant, but no one had yet used it. He had set it up to notify him at his personal email account of any incoming mail. He logged onto the Xlectrix site and opened his email Inbox. There was one new message.

To: Cliff Knowles
From: ConcernedPerson
Subject: How is your health?
You must have had quite a scare today. I hope you are fine. You need to take better care. Next time you might not be so lucky.

Cliff immediately checked the header information. It was mailed through an anonymous remailer in Serbia. He knew tracing it back to Byrne would be impossible. It would never qualify as a threat, either, not for purposes of a criminal case. Still, he printed out a copy. He would give it to the police the next day for what it was worth.

So, the fight was on. Whether Vogel authorized payment or not, this wasn't going to be over until Byrne got paid back. How exactly, he didn't know, but it wasn't going to be pretty.

Chapter 28

The next day was hectic. All the signs of yesterday's commotion were gone from the parking lot of his office when Cliff arrived. Maeva gave him a big hug when he walked in the door. He called the Los Altos Police as his first order of business after prying her off. The detective asked if he could come by and take a full report and Cliff agreed.

The detective turned out to be surprisingly young. He was a well-built fellow, blond and fair, with a crooked nose that betrayed some past boxing experience. His erect posture and buzz cut suggested he was ex-military. He identified himself as Sergeant Hanssen.

Cliff went through the previous day's experience, keeping vague about the reason for his visit to the Fremont Radiology Group. He gave him the printout of the email from ConcernedPerson.

When he was done the detective told him the tests of the cylinder showed that it had probably held some radioactive isotopes used by radiologists, but did not qualify as a weapon or even as hazardous material. There was too little residual radioactivity detected. It was just trash. Basically, from a criminal standpoint, he said, it was equivalent to an empty Kleenex box being stuck in Cliff's car seat.

The vandalism of the seat was a crime, of course, but it did not take place in Los Altos, so he had no jurisdiction. He suggested Cliff file a report with the Fremont police, but he also advised that without proof Byrne did it, there was little chance the police or prosecutors would pursue a car vandalism case. The display of the box cutter and the statement to Cliff not to come back did not constitute threats legally, and in any event probably could not be proven. It was just Cliff's word, and the car had been parked in a publicly accessible lot. Anyone could have found the pig in the trash bin of the facility and slashed his car seat.

Cliff thanked him and said he understood. He had already concluded it would be a waste of time to report it to the Fremont police. As the officer was getting ready to leave Maeva appeared at the doorway with a cup of freshly brewed coffee for the officer. He politely accepted it, despite the fact he had just told Cliff he had to get back. He walked over to Maeva's desk and admired the picture of her cat on her desk.

Cliff closed his office door and called his insurance agent and filed a claim for the car seat vandalism. The agent assured him the comprehensive would cover it and gave him the name of the repair facility to take it to. When he got off the phone, Sgt. Hanssen was still there, laughing at something Maeva's had said. Cliff told her he had to take the car to be repaired and left.

When he returned an hour later driving a loaner, the officer was gone and he had a message from Sharon Perry, the lawyer handling the defense of Byrne's case and one from Roger Vogel. He called Vogel first.

"Cliff," Vogel said enthusiastically. "The pictures you got are a gold mine."

"So those manuals were proprietary?"

"Actually, there were two manuals shown in the photos. The one you thought was the problem turned out to be okay for them to have. It was licensed to them when they bought the Lilac 3. It's the usual manual any user needs – how to calibrate it, all the keyboard instructions, and so forth. I thought that they should have returned it when they terminated our maintenance contract, but I found out from Crabbe that he did tell them to keep it, and it turns out that is the standard practice with all our service reps. The medical safety people determined it was unsafe for them to have the Lilac and not the manual, and to disregard the clause in the contract. So Satterlee was right."

"So it was the second manual that was the problem? What was it?"

"Actually, no. That was the Tech Tips binder for the Lilac 2 and Lilac 3 but, about seven years old. Tech Tips is our term for what you might call a troubleshooting procedure manual. Only the service reps are supposed to have those, but the old ones were not always shredded. Those have been revised many times. Byrne must have kept his when he was laid off. It's all outdated and harmless. We couldn't prove it's a trade secret or caused us any damages."

"Then what's the gold mine?"

"The photos of the receptionist doing the cutting. It turns out she had printouts of the Tech Tips for the L4. She was trimming off the edges with our logo and 'Property of Xlectrix Corp.' statements. Apparently she was in the process of copying the sheets and mounting them in a binder, in effect cleaned of any evidence the pages were stolen property. Unlike the old printed L3 Tech Tips binder, the L4 ones are encrypted and do not exist in paper form. They're only digital and enciphered. They're also up-to-date and valuable. This shot of her with scissors in hand trimming off the markings is a litigator's dream. It proves she was trying to conceal the origin of the document. She'd have been smarter just to scan them as is, use OCR, and then use search and replace to get rid of them. That's so much quicker. You can even see a scanner in one of the shots. The photo might still show that they had the documents, but wouldn't show her trying to conceal the evidence of theft."

Cliff studied the photos for a few seconds. "It wouldn't work. See how the proprietary markings appear sideways on the edge of the screen shots, too? If you run that through an optical character recognition program it would try to interpret those letters at a ninety degree angle and fail. There would be random wrong characters stuck at the ends of most lines. Someone would have to go through and edit every line by hand. It's much easier just to snip off the warnings with scissors before scanning."

"Hmm, I hadn't thought of that. Well, he must have gotten these files from Crabbe's laptop."

"So that means he must have had Crabbe's dongle, too."

"That's what the scientists tell me. So we really need to find out if Crabbe is in on it. How soon can you arrange that polygraph?"

"I'll call today to find out when Sol can be available."

"That also means we have grounds for a theft of trade secrets case against Byrne and the Fremont doctors group. I've authorized Sharon Perry to go ahead and file a cross-complaint. She doesn't know about the overdoses; let's keep it that way. She should be calling you soon."

"She already has."

"Most importantly, this gets us off the hook for the liability on these overdose cases, even if the word spreads about them. An intervening criminal act breaks proximate cause."

Cliff understood that Vogel cared most about whether his employer could be held liable, but he wasn't much interested in that. He was just relieved that they now knew for sure that Byrne, and maybe others in Fremont, had the dongle at some point, but, more importantly, it was now useless since all Crabbe's customers had the software reinstalled with a new dongle. Byrne could no longer remotely access any Lilac systems and couldn't hurt anyone.

"That's great Roger," Cliff replied, mustering some faux sincerity. "Tell me, did you ask Buster flat out about whether he was sure he took the dongle with him when he left the laptop that night?"

"Yes, and he told me the same thing he told you. He is positive he took it with him to the restaurant. He even offered to take a polygraph on it without me asking."

"Okay, I'll call Sol right now and set it up. One more thing, Roger. This now looks like intentional acts of overdosing, either for revenge or for financial gain. We need to bring this to the attention of law enforcement."

"Cliff, once they're involved it's out of our control. It'll hit the press and everyone will be scared to death of using our systems, even if it was just one rogue guy. They'll think it could happen again."

"Maybe it could. We still don't know exactly how this happened."

"I can't authorize bringing in police yet. We'll do that when you find out what happened. No one's at risk now. If we get the police involved in a murder case this will be sensationalized by the press so much patients will be stopping their cancer treatments right and left, afraid of some hacker zapping holes in their bodies. Cliff, we're saving lives by keeping this off the airwaves and Internet."

"Roger, you have a point, but we can't just ignore this. We have a psychopath on the loose."

"Okay I'll authorize this much. You have the photographic evidence of trade secret theft. We're about to go public in our cross complaint on that anyway. That's a federal crime, isn't it?"

"Yes. The FBI investigates that."

"Find a discreet FBI agent and arrange for them to take a complaint for that. We can bring them in to the overdose thing later when we see what you come up with."

"Okay, that's a start."

As soon as he got off the phone he made the call to Sol Bergman, who was as crusty and profane as ever. Cliff brought him up to date on the investigation. When Sol heard that the dongle had been used to remotely overdose an agent's niece, and as a result she may lose her leg, his tone changed completely.

"Set it up for this afternoon," he instructed.

"This afternoon? That's fast. What about your lawn bowling?"

"Screw that! This is Bureau family. Someone hurt one of our own. If this guy had a hand in it, I'll find out. No charge. This one's on me."

"Down, boy. I need you to remain objective. Crabbe may be innocent. Maybe his memory is playing tricks on him and he really thought he took the dongle with him. I don't need a lynch mob mentality."

"I'm insulted you'd say that. You think I don't know that? Like I said, if he had a hand in it, I'll find that out. If he didn't, I'll find that out, too."

"Okay, I'll set it up."

A series of quick calls to Crabbe, Vogel, and Bergman resulted in the second polygraph being arranged for 3:00 that afternoon.

Next Cliff returned Sharon Perry's call.

"Cliff, you're a prince," she gushed. "I'm going to nail these bastards, thanks to you. Roger gave me the go-ahead to file a cross-complaint."

"Are you filing against Byrne and the doctor's group?"

"No, just Byrne for now. Roger doesn't want to antagonize a client if he doesn't have to, and naming new parties now would be a problem in the suit – delays and so forth. A cross-complaint against Byrne is easy. We think the doctors probably didn't know anything about it. It doesn't even make sense financially."

"I tend to agree, but I'm still not sure about Crabbe or Mel. Or Honey, for that matter."

"Who are Mel and Honey?"

"Mel's the second engineer. His eyes went as wide as the proverbial saucers when I mentioned the dongle. He had to know. Honey is my name for the receptionist who was doing the clipping and copying of the pages. She looks like Honey Huan from the Doonesbury strip. I don't know her real name."

"We can worry about them later. We're going to throw the fear of God into them, though. When we file against Byrne we're also going to contact his employer and show them our evidence. They'll have to investigate and everyone there involved is likely to get fired or at least their jobs will be in jeopardy. We have reason to subpoena everyone from the top down now as witnesses to Byrne's case. All their financial records, too."

"That should ruin Byrne's life. How soon will this happen?"

"I'll file on Monday. I may need you as a witness eventually, but we should be able to keep you from any subpoenas for now with attorney-client and attorney work product privilege."

"Okay, that's good news. Let me know."

"I will. If you can find out any more about these Mel or Honey characters, let me know. Roger has authorized unlimited investigation on this."

"All right. I'll get on that."

"Can you tell me why he wanted the Tech Tips on the Lilac 4? Didn't you tell me they only had a model 3?"

"That's a good question. I'm not sure. I've got some work cut out for me, I guess. I'll get back to you when I have more."

"Super." There was a pause and a change of tone. "You should come by our office. Have you been here before?"

"I don't think so."

"If we're going to be working together, we should get better acquainted. I can introduce you to my associates here and they may even have additional work for you. Good investigators are hard to come by. I can take you to lunch. On Roger."

"Uh, sure, that sounds great. I'll have my assistant look at my calendar and find a day next week."

"Great, see you then."

When he finished the call he walked out to Maeva's desk. She was humming.

"You're in a good mood," he said.

"I am in a good mood. It's a nice day. Why not?"

"Any particular reason?"

"What do you mean?" Maeva replied, looking genuinely perplexed.

"Never mind. Do I have any special appearances scheduled for next week?"

"You had two inquiries for Tuesday, but I haven't confirmed them yet."

"Call them back and tell them I can't. I'm going to be busy all week on this Xlectrix thing. Then find a day next week for lunch with Sharon Perry over at Herrick. You'll have to call her assistant and find a time we're both free."

"No problem."

"One more thing. Can you look through the computer files and notes from Vogel and Crabbe for any mention of Mel or Melvin at the Fremont Radiology Group and try to get a last name or other identifying information. If you do, see what you can dig up from the Internet on him. He's a white male engineer, little, with a thin mustache."

"I'm on it," she said beaming. She always enjoyed getting assigned investigation. It was more interesting than the clerical work.

"I'm going out running. It may be my last chance for a while."

"Why?"

He didn't want to tell her about the vein surgery. "I'll be too busy with this case."

"Okay. Have a good run."

He headed out the door to his fitness club and changed clothes there. He decided to run through the neighborhoods of north Los Altos. The pavement was hard on his joints, but he enjoyed looking at the beautifully landscaped yards and tasteful homes and he just didn't have time to drive over to one of the large parks to run trails. The route was hilly, but he felt strong and finished the five miles with no trouble. He'd worked up a good sweat and felt tension-free.

Afterward he showered, changed and walked over to the local pizza joint. He knew he wouldn't be able to eat solid food after 7:00 because of the surgery, so he treated himself to two large slices, loaded with salami and pepperoni.

When he got back to the office he had a message from the vascular surgeon who would be doing the transplant tomorrow. He returned the call.

The doctor told him of the risks of the procedure, which he said were relatively small. He would be taking out a portion of a major leg vein. It was very similar to varicose vein surgery, although they would be taking a smaller piece than was typical for that so recovery should be fast. He said most people are up and walking the same day and he could be back to running in two or three days. Then he launched into the things the lawyers made him say – that sometimes people had bad reactions and he could experience pain for weeks or months, his feet could lose sensation, turn blue, general anesthesia carried its own risks, he could die an agonizing death, yada, yada, yada. Cliff began to wonder whether he was really feeling that noble.

"In transplant cases it's normal to withhold the identity of the donor from the recipient unless both parties agree to share that information. Do you want your name to be shared?"

"No. I already know who the recipient is – Ashley Bishop. I don't want her family to know who I am or think of me as anyone special. I know that hundreds of FBI employees and their families have volunteered to be a donor for her, so she doesn't need to know any more than the vein came from the FBI family."

"As you wish."

By the time this conversation was over Maeva had emailed him some results on her search for Mel. Buried deep in the Xlectrix file was a report from the initial salesman who landed the account, the sale of the Lilac 3. The technical contact at that time was Melvin Wagner. She had found two possible Melvin Wagners, both in the East Bay, but couldn't guarantee it was one of those. She had already used Cliff's commercial requester account with the Department of Motor Vehicles to obtain the vehicles registered to both. The make, model, and license of each was in the email along with the driver's license information.

He pulled up the photos from his visit to the facility and matched one of the cars in the lot with one from the list. Now he knew Mel's full name, address, date of birth, and registered vehicles. He had already pegged Mel as a weak link. Now he was beginning to form a plan of attack.

It was time to get over to Xlectrix for the polygraph. He told Maeva where he was going, and headed over. When he got there, Sol Bergman was in a conference room waiting for him. Crabbe was right outside.

"Bad news, Cliff," Sol said in a matter-of-fact tone and handed him a glossy 8"x10" photo.

Cliff inspected it for a minute. It was a shot of Crabbe in a nice suit with a woman, presumably his wife, who was appropriately gussied up. They were sitting at a restaurant table. Judging from the tablecloth, overabundant tableware, oversized menus with leather covers, and floral centerpiece it appeared to be an expensive place. They were smiling at the camera. It looked like one of those shots done by roving photographers to commemorate special occasions.

"So that's Crabbe. His wife, too, I guess. What's the problem?"

"Flip it over."

On the back was a stamp from the photographer with his name, logo and the date. Cliff recognized the date as the one Crabbe had serviced the Fremont facility, the time he had left his laptop bag behind. Cliff had verified that date with the service records.

"So this proves he went to the restaurant like he said. I don't see the problem. It doesn't prove that he had the dongle with him."

"Take another look. Shirt pocket."

Cliff flipped it over again and examined Crabbe's shirt pocket. The quintessential nerdy engineer had a pocket protector with two pens clipped in it. Barely visible protruding from the protector was the end of a silvery object. It looked like a computer part. He couldn't swear he knew what it was, but from the conversation, it could only be one thing.

"Don't tell me – the dongle."

"The dongle. When he found out what this second polygraph was going to be for, he went back and checked everything he could about that night. It was his tenth wedding anniversary. They went to this fancy place and paid for the photo. By chance, the dongle happened to be caught in this photo. I've already had Vogel verify that's one of their dongles. It has a unique design. If you look with a magnifying glass you can actually see the Xlectrix logo stamped on the metal. I'm still going to polygraph him but it looks like he's telling the truth. He left the laptop but took the dongle, at least on this occasion."

"Jesus, that blows up our entire working theory. Maybe he left the laptop another time, with the dongle."

"I'll find out."

Cliff left the conference room and went to talk to Vogel. He told Crabbe to go on in as he left. When he got to Vogel's office the lawyer confirmed everything Sol had told him.

"He must have left the dongle on another occasion," Cliff said. "Either that or Byrne is a better codebreaker than the NSA."

"Let's hope so, and hope we can prove that. This puts a serious dent in our case. If Crabbe didn't leave the dongle, then that means our trade secrets are not secure. We can prove they had the encrypted Tech Tips file from your photos, but if we left them there accessible on the laptop then it would be impossible to make a case for theft of trade secrets. They have to be protected information or there's no case."

Cliff was getting seriously upset with Vogel's concentration on his litigation strategy. He replied, "More important – if anyone with access to the laptop alone, without the dongle, can remotely control dosages of other systems, that means anyone could cause radiation overdoses in distant locations, anonymously."

"Of course. But I'm sure our system is more secure than that."

Cliff told him about the progress in identifying Mel and about his contact with Sharon Perry. He also pointed out that the clipping of the Xlectrix logos and warnings about it being proprietary information proved knowledge by the Fremont people that it was protected information.

"It has 'Do Not Copy' all over it in the edges of the screen. Let Sharon do her job. Me too. We'll make a case."

"Have you talked to the FBI yet?"

"No," Cliff replied, "I plan to do that first thing Monday."

"Do you want to walk with me to the cafeteria?" Vogel asked. "We can be right next to the conference room when Sol finishes. Plus they have some really good scones in right now."

They walked downstairs to the cafeteria and sampled the scones while they waited. Eventually Sol and Crabbe emerged across the hall. Crabbe had a big smile on his face. Sol told him to go back to his normal work and he would talk with Vogel, whom he spotted waiting with Cliff.

"He's telling the truth. He had the dongle with him the whole time. That night and every other time he was ever there in Fremont, at least to the best of his recollection. He showed no deception. I don't usually do it but I told him he passed 100%."

Vogel and Cliff exchanged glances. That meant there was no explanation for how Byrne accessed the Tech Tips file and how he controlled the remote Lilacs that overdosed – if in fact he did control them remotely.

"Okay, Sol," Vogel said softly. "Thank you. Let's all think about this and we'll regroup on Monday. Sharon is filing her cross-complaint then and is going to hit the doctor's group over there with a big fat subpoena for the records. That should shake things up."

Chapter 29

Cliff woke up early Saturday. He was hungry but he was under orders to ingest nothing for the twelve hours before surgery. Since he was going to be put under general anesthesia he knew he shouldn't be driving back so he called a cab company to get a ride to the hospital. He could have called a friend, but he wanted this vein donation to be anonymous.

He took a quick shower and dressed in jeans and a polo shirt. By the time he was ready the cab was at the door. Fifteen minutes later he was at the hospital.

When he arrived the admitting nurse led him back to a small patient exam room. She assured him that the donation would be anonymous so he was being isolated from the recipient and her family. She left him a hospital gown to put on. He dutifully changed into it.

There he sat for almost half an hour. He was kicking himself for not bringing a book, but there was a selection of old magazines in a rack. He leafed through two-year-old copies of *People*. He didn't even know who two-thirds of the "celebrities" were. He must be getting old.

The vascular surgeon finally made an appearance. He was younger than Cliff had expected, dark-complected with thick hammy fingers and the hairiest arms he'd seen outside a zoo. Cliff wondered how he could do the delicate surgical work with those hands. The doctor told him there could be a delay. There was actually a second donor, a family member present who might be a better match.

"Why didn't you tell me this before?" Cliff asked.

"I'm sorry, but we weren't sure until this morning that we could use... this other person. We still aren't."

Cliff figured this was probably Theresa. "You mean she didn't consent right away?"

This was met with a nervous shuffle of feet. "I can't go into the medical reasons. And I didn't say it was a female."

"Never mind," Cliff said disgustedly. "Can I go now?"

"No, no. We may still need you. We're doing some more tissue matching. Everything has to be just right for this. Since the patient has had two previous transplants this one is..." He started to say "do or die" but thought better of it. "...may be our last chance to get it right. I'm sorry but it means you'll just have to wait a bit longer. Do you want something to read? I can have the nurse bring you something."

Exasperated, Cliff replied, "Yes, okay. Have her bring me something else to read."

The doctor left and shortly thereafter a male nurse, very black and very thin, brought him a pile of magazines, newer than the ones in the room. *Time. The New Yorker. Outdoor Life.*

Two more hours came and went. Cliff had read everything he had any interest in and still there was no word. He snagged the male nurse as he passed by the exam room and asked if he could at least have something to drink, something with a few calories, 7-Up or chicken broth or something. He was famished and getting a headache from low blood sugar. The nurse said he would check. A few minutes later he returned with a small plastic glass of water.

"So what's the deal," Cliff pressed him "How much longer?"

"I'm so sorry," the nurse said in a beautiful lilting African accent. "Nothing by mouth before the surgery. They let me give you this water, but only this much. They had to give up the operating theaters. You can't hold them. Other surgeries are scheduled. But the three o'clock slot is open. If it's needed."

"What do you mean, 'if it's needed'? Is she going to get the transplant or not."

"Really the doctor should tell you, but it's looking like maybe not. The recipient is doing much better. The doctors are trying to decide if the transplant is needed at all now."

"You mean her leg may be saved after all? She's okay?"

"I really cannot say. You will have to talk to the doctor." The nurse scooted out.

Cliff could concentrate on nothing else after that. He stood and began pacing the room. He kept poking his head out, looking for the doctor. After another twenty minutes the surgeon reappeared.

"I guess the nurse told you. The girl's leg is looking very good today. Much pinker. It was blue at the toe just yesterday. It's a remarkable turnaround. We are now doing tests on the circulation. We, the oncologist and I, have to consult with the radiologist before we can cancel the surgery, but it's looking very good. I'm afraid I'm going to have to ask you to wait another couple of hours before we can be sure."

"That's fantastic!" Cliff practically shouted. "That's very good news. Thank you for telling me."

The doctor had expected Cliff to be angry at being made to wait without eating another two hours, since it was after lunchtime now, and was gratified at the good reception to the news. "You must be starving. I can authorize more clear liquids. Can you survive a bit longer?"

"Of course."

Whether from the lack of sustenance or the good news, Cliff began to feel very light-headed. He lay down on the examining table. A heavy weight was slowly lifting from him. It reminded him of his high school wrestling days when he'd been pinned and the victorious opponent finally let him up. The ignominy of defeat still weighed on him, but it felt so good finally to have the real pressure off, the thing over. Or, in this case, almost over.

It was 5:30 by the time the doctor finally came in and told him there would be no transplant. It was remarkable, he said, how well the girl's own vein graft had taken hold in the last 24 hours. All the tests showed excellent blood flow and all the blood gases were good. She said the pain had stopped. He expected a full recovery.

Cliff's stomach growled loudly in response, but the noise did nothing to suppress his delight at the news.

"So can I go now?" he asked.

"You can. Thank you again. You should at least stay and get a decent meal on us. No charge for donors. You haven't had anything since last night."

"Hospital food? No thanks. I'm heading for a restaurant as soon as I get out of here."

"That's funny," the doctor said, chuckling. "That's exactly what the aunt said... I mean the other donor. I don't blame either of you."

So it was Ellen, not Theresa, who was the other donor. Cliff almost made a remark, but felt the doctor might realize he had said too much.

The doctor made him sign some form on his clipboard and wished him well. As soon as the doctor was out of the room Cliff stripped off his hospital gown and grabbed his clothes. He put on his jeans and shoes, and walked out into the waiting room still tucking in his polo shirt. He knew the fashion today was to leave shirts untucked, but he had total disdain for whatever kids today thought was cool or uncool.

When he neared the doorway to the parking lot he stopped for a moment to finish tucking in the shirt and was surprised to feel someone pull on the shirttail. He turned to see Ashley Bishop. She had run ahead of her mother and aunt, who were ten yards or so behind.

"Cliff! My leg's okay," Ashley gushed. It didn't seem odd to her that this friend of her aunt would be in the hospital lobby.

"That's wonderful," he gushed back and lifted her up, shaking her gently until she giggled. He heard her stomach rumble with hunger and his own did the same thing as if in reply. They both laughed as the two women came up to them.

"Oh no, not you," Ellen said scornfully. "Don't tell me you were the other donor."

"I don't know what you're talking about," he replied, but his stomach betrayed the lie with its loudest rumble yet, one so loud that others in the waiting room turned to look at him.

"The FBI guy," Theresa said, finally placing him. "The doctor said it was someone from the FBI family."

"It could have been anybody," Cliff replied non-committally.

"Yeah, right," she said. "Well, I want to thank you personally. I wasn't a match as it turned out and Ellen, the best match, is just getting over an infection. They didn't think she could donate yet. You'll join us for dinner, of course."

"That's not necessary. I – "

"Of course it is. Mark's father just told me to splurge. He's got a regular table at *Hôtel de Montparnasse*. Mark's parents came to the first two surgeries but just couldn't stand to go through that again, so they're at home. When I told them how long this day has been, how it turned out, and how Ashley and Ellen haven't had a bite to eat since last night, he insisted I take them there, his treat. He even said it was a shame I didn't know who the other donor was, so I know he'd want you to be included. You have to come."

Cliff knew *Hôtel de Montparnasse* was a four-star hotel with a five-star restaurant just a mile or so away. He had eaten there only once, years ago on his wife's birthday. The food was fabulous and the prices astronomical. The very thought of it made his mouth water, but then the thought of a Big Mac did too at this point. He looked at Ellen, wondering what her preference was. She was probably still furious at him. If his presence would ruin her experience, he would refuse the invitation.

As if reading his mind Ellen said, "Oh come on. Let's eat."

"I'm not exactly dressed for it…" he protested.

"For Christ sakes," Theresa countered, "Steve Jobs used to eat there regularly in ratty ripped up jeans. This is Silicon Valley. You're fine."

They all piled into the Mercedes, Theresa smoking the whole way, but holding the cigarette out the window, driving with the other hand.

It was early and the restaurant was almost empty. The maître d' greeted them at the entrance.

"Mrs. Bishop, we were expecting you. Mr. Bishop called ahead. Please, this way."

"Thank you, Marcel," Theresa replied. "Get something on the table quick for Ashley. She just came from the hospital and hasn't eaten since last night. None of that fancy French food. Something for a kid."

"Of course. Mr. Bishop told us what to expect."

As they sat down a waiter arrived with a silver tray bearing two plates. One had an assortment of crackers, from Ritz to some European things Cliff didn't recognize, and several small silver dishes of various jams and jellies. He was pleased to see one held peanut butter. The other platter had an assortment of French *hors d'oeuvres*, including shrimp and oyster specialties Cliff couldn't name.

As soon as the first waiter had put down his cargo, a second one arrived with a glass of milk for Ashley, three wine glasses, and a bottle of red wine. Marcel was still standing by, at a discreet distance. The waiter placed the wine glasses down before the adults.

Cliff was already wolfing down some of the offerings. Theresa was spreading peanut butter and jelly on a Ritz cracker for Ashley who had already started on her milk.

When Theresa glanced at the wine bottle she looked up at Marcel, delight suffusing her features.

"Mr. Bishop insisted," Marcel explained, stepping forward.

"Cliff, you have to try this," Theresa said. "Mark's father keeps a full supply from his own collection here in the restaurant wine cellar. The corkage fee alone is $25. The wine collection is somewhere in the thousands. This is the Bordeaux he had imported two years ago. He knows it's my favorite. It is by far the best wine I've ever had." She poured him a glass, then one for Ellen, then her own.

Cliff liked wine well enough, although he rarely drank it. Beer was his libation of choice. He liked beer better than cheap wine, and the really good wine was ridiculously expensive. It also tended to lead him to overindulge. He was a big man who liked to guzzle, not sip. Still, he was certainly curious about this one with such an introduction.

They lifted their glasses and clicked them together. Theresa declared a toast to modern medicine, which Cliff seconded. He noticed Ellen cross herself and silently mouth a "Thank you, Lord." He remembered then that she used to be a nun. They all sipped the wine.

After the first taste, Cliff knew why Theresa had been so excited. This was, bar none, the best wine he'd ever had. He picked up some paper-thin marinated beef thingy from the platter and munched on it, sipping the wine gratefully. Maybe beer was overrated, he began to wonder.

By this time Ashley had wolfed down half of her cracker platter and all of her milk. The first waiter came back with menus and handed them out. Cliff's was the woman's menu, the one without the prices. When he had been here years ago he had gotten the man's version along with considerable sticker shock. He looked over at Theresa and turned his menu so she could see. He pointed to the missing prices. She turned hers to him, too, showing that hers was also missing the prices. Ashley's grandfather must have instructed Marcel not to let them see how much it was costing.

Theresa launched into a long account of what Ashley has been through over the last two weeks with her leg and the two operations. Then she switched to her financial woes, then the things models have to put up with. Cliff tuned her out but nodded politely and kept sipping the wine. It was *really good* wine.

When Theresa stopped her complaining Cliff asked Ellen why she had become a nun, and why she had quit.

"I wanted to help people. It's that simple. I had a degree in health administration and wanted to work in a hospital setting. There was an order of nuns who did nursing work in a poor area near where I lived back in Buffalo. I learned about them and their work and decided to join the order, to help the poor and sick. I wasn't a nurse, but I got hired by the hospital they supported to help on the staff. But after a while I realized it wasn't for me."

"Why's that?" Cliff asked, noticing for the first time how much the sisters looked alike. The coloring, the hair, the striking blue eyes. If only Ellen would grow out her hair the resemblance could be quite strong despite the different body builds.

"I was cooped up in an office pushing paper. I didn't see how I was helping people. I didn't have direct contact with the patients, with the people I wanted to help. And it obviously wasn't good for my social life. I wasn't sure I was ready to commit to... what a nun commits to."

She took another sip of wine, emptying her glass. "Boy, Theresa, this really is nice," she said. She reached for the bottle only to find it empty.

Cliff realized that they had polished off the bottle and hadn't even ordered yet. He looked over at Theresa, whose wine glass was still half full. She was sipping water. Good, he thought, we need a designated driver.

"We really should order," he said to Theresa, who was motioning the waiter over.

"You're right, Cliff," she said, then to the waiter, "Can you bring us another bottle of this? We're ready to order now."

"Of course," he replied. He took their orders. Cliff and Ellen both ordered beef dishes with heavy-sounding sauces. Theresa ordered a small salad, dressing on the side. Ashley ordered a kid's plate hamburger and a milkshake.

Within minutes another bottle of Bordeaux appeared. The waiter filled his glass and Ellen's but Theresa waved him off.

During the ensuing twenty minutes they chatted, nibbled, and laughed. Everyone was in a good mood. It was almost like a family and Cliff had a momentary pang of nostalgia of sorts. His own childhood had not been happy. His mother was an alcoholic and his father a self-absorbed narcissist with no interest in his children. There were some good times at holiday meals, but everyday meals were simply a venue for arguing, scolding, and recriminations. Cliff and his wife had tried to have a family, but his wife could not become pregnant. This was the kind of family meal he had always yearned for, but seldom experienced.

"My egg lakes," Ashley suddenly blurted out.

"Your what?" Theresa asked, confused.

"My leg. It aches."

With that, all the adults at the table broke out in giggles, but Theresa scooted over closer to Ashley and gave her a hug at the same time.

"Honey, the doctor said to expect that. The healing is going so fast now, and the body is getting rid of some of the dead tissue."

"But it hurrrts!"

"How about if I rub it?" Theresa started to massage the leg.

"Oww! That hurts more. I'm full. I want to go home." Even as she spoke the waiter began bringing the first tray of food.

Theresa looked at the others. "I think maybe I should take her home," she said apologetically. "You two should stay and eat. Will you two be okay if I leave you here?"

"We can get a gab... get a cab," Ellen said, laughing even more heavily at her own flub. "I guess none of us can talk. But what about your dinner?"

"The hors d'oeuvres and glass of wine had as many calories as I should take in anyway. You can have the salad. I'll take the burger for Ashley for when she's feeling better. She filled up on peanut butter and jelly."

With that she instructed the waiter to bring a box for the hamburger, which he did without further ado. Theresa and Ashley left as the waiter served Cliff and Ellen.

" 'My egg lakes.' Can you believe that?" Cliff said, chuckling. "That's precious. You'll have to remember that to embarrass her with when she gets older and starts dating."

"Too funny."

They began to dig into their meals. The edge had been taken off their hunger by the hors d'oeuvres and wine, but they were still both hungry and the food was exquisite.

After several minutes of enjoying the food Ellen remarked, "Cliff, I know it wasn't your fault. What happened to Ashley, I mean. Matt told me."

"What did he tell you?" Cliff said, alarmed.

"No details. He just said he knew you did everything you could to prevent Ashley – or anyone – from getting hurt. When I asked how he knew, he said he couldn't tell me. He said to trust him. I do trust him. And then you turned out to volunteer to be a donor for Ashley."

"You weren't supposed to find out. I didn't do it because I felt responsible, I –"

"I know, I know. You did it because you're just a good guy. That was a really unselfish thing to do. Thank you. For all of us."

She raised her glass to him. He clinked her glass as he blushed. His coloration made a good run at matching the Bordeaux. He realized he was enjoying the evening much more than he had expected. He was off the hook with Ellen. Ashley was fine and he didn't even have to undergo the surgery. The food and wine were delicious. He sat back and took another long sip. Even Ellen was surprisingly good company. She was smart and funny and not nearly so unattractive as he had first thought. Sure, she had the shoulders of a boxer, but she had other parts better suited to the cheerleading squad. She and her sister had that in common.

"So are you fully adjusted to Silicon Valley?" Cliff asked.

"It's a great place to live if you can afford it, but I still haven't mastered the geography. And the roads! they're in terrible condition, traffic's horrible. Then the directional signs! You're going south on 280 then suddenly you're going north on 680 without changing direction! How can that be?"

Cliff chuckled, since he knew it was all true. "True, all true. It's the weird shape of the valley, a bulging triangle sort of. It's like a ... I don't know, a big womb or something."

"A womb?" Ellen repeated dubiously. "That's not the first metaphor I would have thought of. Palo Alto doesn't feel so womb-like to me."

"That's the northwest corner, out of the warm enveloping valley center. That's more of a ... the right ovary I guess." Cliff fumbled a bit with the answer, vaguely knowing he was getting into dicey territory but somehow not caring. He took another swig of wine.

"The right side is the west? Just how are you visualizing this female?"

"Uh, well the left, ... the west ovary, then."

She rolled her eyes. "West Ovary, California. Very catchy. Maybe we should start a petition to the city council to change the name. I'm glad I didn't mention Gilroy."

Cliff's wine-addled brain took a moment to process the comment, then he blushed crimson realizing the significance to her comment about Gilroy, the southern outlet to the valley. They both began chuckling.

They continued eating, drinking and talking, sharing geocaching stories, and FBI war stories. The food ran out as they polished off the second bottle of wine. Or was it the third? He couldn't remember for sure. The waiter appeared with a dessert tray.

"I'm stotally tuffed," Cliff declared, waving him off, then cracked up when he realized what he had said.

Ellen began cackling. "I'll bet your egg lakes, too." She gave him a playful nudge on his leg with her foot. His reaction time was dulled by the wine, but he suddenly realized with some chagrin that the touch had given him a small erotic thrill. But it was already gone.

The waiter was quite insistent, though, claiming that Mr. Bishop would never forgive him if they did not try any of the desserts. They were the specialty of the house. Eventually he prevailed and they agreed to share the chocolate mousse. The waiter placed it on the table, producing two elegant tiny dessert spoons, and two glasses of some dessert liqueur Cliff had never heard of.

It all went down with surprising ease.

He woke up with a splitting headache. He hadn't experienced one like it since college, but he instantly knew what it was. As soon as he lifted his head to get out of bed a wave of nausea hit him. The wine was good, but was it really worth this? He had only vague memories of the previous evening after dessert, but he remembered staggering from the taxi to his front door.

He managed to keep down some juice and coffee. He took aspirin but it did little to help. The water he drank with it probably did more good. He wondered how Ellen was feeling. Should he call her? He debated the question, but decided discretion was the better part of valor. He moped around the house until noon, then made his way to the gym for a long workout with heavy weights. Sunday turned into a wasted day.

Chapter 30

By Monday morning Cliff was recovered. He was anxious to see how Byrne and his employer would react when the civil counterclaim got filed, but he had his own business to attend to at first. He called Matt Nguyen to ask who in the Palo Alto office handled trade secret theft matters.

"That would be Ellen. She's been handling all the intellectual property crimes," Matt answered.

"Really! That's a coincidence."

"How so?"

"No particular reason," Cliff answered, not wanting to go into their encounter over the weekend. "It doesn't matter. I have to report something for a client. Can you transfer me?"

"Sure. Hey, before you go, I wanted to let you know that I told her you were trying to save Ashley from harm, and that you weren't to blame for the injury. I think she believed me. I did *not* tell her any more details… nothing that…" He lowered his voice to a whisper so no eavesdropper could hear. "…would get you in trouble with the bar or anyone."

"Okay, Matt, thanks. I've spoken to her. I think we're good."

"That's good to hear. Also, did you hear that her niece is recovering. The doctors think her leg will be fine. They were worried about needing to amputate it there for a while."

"That's super."

"All right. I'll transfer you now."

There was a click, then two seconds later, "Ellen Kennedy."

"Hi, this is Cliff."

"Cliff. Uh, I see." She lowered her voice, too. "Look, that's sweet of you to call and all, but really that's not necessary. Maybe… maybe it seemed like I was flirting, but really you're just not my type. We both had too much to drink. We probably said some things…"

"No, I'm not calling about that," he interrupted. "I have a case to report. On behalf of a client. I was planning to report this today no matter what, but I just found out from Matt that you handle trade secret theft and economic espionage."

"I do," she replied skeptically, not willing to believe this was unrelated to what had happened Saturday.

"Look, it's a good case. We have photographic evidence that a former employee of a high-tech company somehow acquired encrypted trade secrets from his ex-employer, decrypted them, and now is using them for his own ends. A civil claim is going to be filed today by the victim company."

"Really. What's the name of the company?"

"Xlectrix."

The name did not ring a bell with Ellen. She was new to the valley and there were hundreds of high-tech firms, the mix constantly changing. Firms merged, closed down for lack of funding, or changed names every day.

"What do they do?"

"They make medical devices. Radiological devices for treating cancer."

This news sent an electric shock up Ellen's spine. "You mean like what was treating Ashley, the machine that went bad?"

Cliff had to tread carefully here. He was under orders from Vogel to report only the trade secret theft – the clipped Tech Tips – not the possible compromise of the Lilacs and the deaths.

"The machine did not go bad. There was an overdose, but we're still investigating how that happened. It could have been operator error, a lot of things. But yes, that's the company. But what I'm reporting is that the employee possessed documents of ours, ones that were encrypted by NSA-approved hardware and which were clearly marked as proprietary. We have photographs of the documents in the thief's company's possession. He was having an employee trim off the proprietary markings."

Cliff knew that to prove a trade secret theft case you had to prove the thing stolen was really a secret, that is, sufficient protections were afforded it so that it was not accessible to non-authorized personnel or the general public. Defense lawyers almost always defended these cases by saying, in essence, if my client was able to steal it, it must not have been a secret. It was important to emphasize when reporting to the FBI that these protections existed, that it would be possible to prove the defendant knew that what he was taking was someone else's property, not an innocent copying error.

Ellen mulled this over for a few seconds. "Cliff, are you saying this doesn't have anything to do with how Ashley was hurt?"

"The provable cash damages in this case are in the millions."

Cliff's answer was intended to do two things. First, he knew the United States Attorney's Office didn't like to prosecute white collar cases. They were too hard to prove to lay juries and weren't as sexy as violent crimes. But large dollar damages made the case a lot more attractive to the prosecutors, especially if the loss was easily proved as cash losses, like the damages paid in this case to the overdose victims, rather than, say, lost market share. But his real reason for the answer was that by dodging her question, he knew she would read between the lines and conclude that the theft did have something to do with Ashley's injury, while at the same time he could stay within his orders not to reveal privileged information. That would be a motivator for her to open a case if anything was.

"So who's the subject?"

Cliff began laying out the case, how he'd gone to the Fremont Radiology Group as part of an investigation on behalf of his client and saw the receptionist clipping sheets of paper, how he confronted Mel and the office manager. He explained how the photos had revealed that these were the Tech Tips.

"How are those protected?" she asked.

"With a dongle."

"They used protection with their dongle? Is this where I'm supposed to say I love it when you talk dirty?"

Despite himself, Cliff laughed out loud. "You're good at badinage. I guess that's why it was so fun the other night."

"Good badinage? That sounds like an oxymoron."

"QED," he replied, laughing again. "A dongle is a device that plugs into a computer for security. It's like a super password in hardware form."

"I know what a dongle is. I was just badinaging."

"That's not a word."

"It is now."

Cliff laughed again then went on to explain about how the information was encrypted by the dongle, and how Crabbe had admitted leaving his laptop there overnight once – although without the dongle.

He told her about Byrne being laid off by Xlectrix and how he was suing them, obviously bitter about it.

"Civil suits can complicate these things," she told him, although he knew this better than she did from his years as a white collar supervisor. "The defense in the civil case claims that the victim is using the government, the big bad FBI, to intimidate a business rival over what is just a licensing dispute. The criminal defense claims that the FBI is circumventing the constitution by forcing the defendant to testify against himself in civil depositions or doing searches through the private company's subpoenas. Either the company is the pawn of the FBI or vice versa, or both."

"I'm well aware of that."

"Cliff, you know the U.S. Attorney doesn't like to prosecute business cases. The victims have their civil remedies. The case would have a lot better chance of getting prosecuted if there was an element of violence, or harm, especially to some innocent victim."

Cliff knew she was fishing for him to confirm that Byrne caused Ashley's injury, but he still had to follow Vogel's directive. "Ellen, there are some things I can't tell you. Attorney-client privileged things. But I can tell you this. I was the victim of violence in this case."

He launched into the story of the vandalism to his car and the isotope container that was stuffed in his seat, his trip to the emergency room.

"That's terrible, Cliff. I hadn't heard anything about that. I'm sorry you went through that, but it sounds like you don't have any proof Byrne did that, and there was no actual physical harm to you. For that matter, your evidence on the theft right now seems to be limited to the receptionist. She's the one who had the documents in her possession. Did you ever see Byrne with those Tech Tips?"

"No."

"And the dongle. If Crabbe didn't leave the dongle, then how did Byrne decrypt the Tech Tips? The defense is just going to argue that the Tech Tips were left unencrypted on a laptop that was knowingly left behind by an Xlectrix employee. Not a secret. Copying at best. I'm not sure that's even a misdemeanor."

"That, I admit, is a problem. We still don't know how. But Mel's eyes went as wide as pancakes when I said the word dongle. He knows something. I think we need to go after him."

"We? Cliff, we can't work together on this. I just explained about the problem with a civil case going on at the same time. Our priority has to be catching the thief, not your client's damages. Which, by the way, you haven't explained. How did they suffer millions of dollars in damages? Did Byrne set up his own consulting company to provide service contracts on these radiology devices? Did he steal business from them?"

"I'm sorry, that's one thing I can't explain just yet." He wasn't sure he would ever be able to explain, either. Vogel didn't want the world to know that there had been the fatal overdoses. The civil damage claims had all been paid with iron-clad confidentiality clauses. The company would be hurt much more by word of the Lilac's vulnerability that the few million it lost in damage claims.

"That's not going to fly if you want this prosecuted, but we can let that slide for now. Here's what I'll do. I'll write this up and get my supervisor to open it and assign it to me. I'll do an initial interview with your client, get the photos, and then get a preliminary prosecutive opinion from an AUSA. We'll see where we can go from there. When can I do the interview at Xlectrix?"

"I'll have to check. The General Counsel there is Roger Vogel. He'll be the one to interview."

"And this guy Crabbe, too, it sounds like."

"Okay, Crabbe, too. That might be a little harder to arrange. I'll call you back today or tomorrow."

As soon as Cliff was off the phone Ellen typed up an FD-302 of the interview and a cover memo recommending opening the case. Although Cliff wouldn't officially confirm it, she had no doubt that this was going to lead to whoever was responsible for Ashley's overdose. She was going to work this case no matter what.

She took her paperwork into her supervisor's office and stood there with it in her hand. The supervisor was a bespectacled, gray-haired veteran of seven different geographic assignments in the FBI, from Anchorage, Alaska to Valdosta, Georgia, with several stops at FBIHQ. Ellen knew he had put in a request to step down from his supervisory desk and take an Office of Preference transfer back to Tennessee, where he was from originally. He was busy typing something on his computer.

"I've got a new trade secret theft case."

"Okay, you can leave it in my In box," he said without taking his attention from his screen.

"I need it opened and assigned right away."

This caused him to look up, finally making eye contact. One look at Ellen and he knew this was not a routine matter. "Why, what's up?"

"The victim is the company that makes the machine that gave the overdose to my niece Ashley."

"And the theft had something to do with that?"

"Officially, no. But my nose tells me yes. Something smells."

The supervisor took the papers from her hand and quickly skimmed them. Without a further word he marked "O + A 285-new Kennedy" on the cover memo, initialed it, and handed them back. She took them to the file clerk and went through the same exercise, getting her to stop what she was doing and open the case immediately.

It was almost lunch hour by the time Sharon Perry called Cliff.

"Cliff, we've filed our counterclaim. I'll serve it by fax on Byrne's lawyer right before 5:00 when he'll be potted. That will give us an extra day. I've also got several deposition subpoenas to be served on the witnesses at the Fremont Radiology Group. One for Lynda Satterlee and one for Mel for starters. Later I'll get the full name of the receptionist, the one you called Honey, through discovery and we can do one for her, too. Do you want to serve them?"

"It would be my pleasure. Can I come by and pick them up now?"

"They're here. In fact, we can do that lunch I talked about if you're coming over, and you can meet the other lawyers here."

"Okay. I'll be there in fifteen minutes."

He told Maeva he was going out for lunch. He climbed in his rental car and headed over to Herrick in Menlo Park. Herrick was one of the largest and oldest corporate firms in the Bay Area. It started in San Francisco decades earlier and was still headquartered there, but it was one of the success stories of Silicon Valley, getting in on the original semiconductor boom, then the dot com boom, onto the whole Internet craze, and now its Menlo Park office, in the heart of Silicon Valley, generated as much revenue as the larger San Francisco office.

When he got there he was quite impressed. Although the San Francisco office was in a skyscraper, typical of that venue, here the office was an expansive ground floor campus nestled on the edge of a residential area. The décor was corporate modern with artwork rivaling the local art museum. When he told the receptionist, a woman named Keiko, his name she virtually gushed that Sharon was expecting him and to have a seat. She rang some assistant, a handsome young Latino man as it turned out, who came out immediately and walked Cliff back to Sharon's office. As a full partner her digs were in scale with the rest of the place, making Cliff's converted library annex look like a broom closet.

In the room with Sharon were two clean-cut young people dressed in the usual business casual. Asian and Latino out front, now a black and a white female on display for his admiration like it was some sort of diversity contest. This was a little too much political correctness for his taste, but he said nothing.

"Cliff, thanks for coming by," Sharon greeted him, extending her hand. "Please meet Lisa Goodwin and Robert Jackson, two associates here. They're helping me with the case."

Cliff shook their hands and everyone exchanged "pleased to meet you"s.

"It's such an honor," Goodwin cooed. "I read about you back when that mountain lion attacked you. That's so cool how you saved the woman. I don't know how you did it."

"Mostly by imitating a cat toy," Cliff replied, and pulled up his pant leg a few inches to show a few of the nastiest scars from that encounter. "Are you two joining us for lunch?"

They both smiled hesitantly and looked expectantly at Perry, who shook her head. "No, they've got work to do, I'm afraid. We don't want to pad the client's bill, now do we?"

This surprised Cliff a bit, since padding the client's bill was generally considered the primary job of a corporate lawyer, at least for the full partners. Why bill Xlectrix for just her time when they could bill for three lawyers to sit around and trade stories? Maybe she was just more conscientious than most. From the looks on their faces, they were surprised, too.

"Here are the subpoenas," Perry announced, and handed some envelopes to Cliff. "Let's do our talking over lunch. I'm famished." She stood to go.

The associates took their cue and left. So much for the team-building. Perry gestured toward the door as she came around the desk. As they passed through the lobby she commented knowledgeably on some of the artwork. They bumped into two gray-haired men. Perry introduced them as partners in the firm. Cliff shook hands and made a mental note of them; he could always use good sources of business. One of them said something about him being "the FBI agent" which he acknowledged demurely. Apparently his reputation had already preceded him. One partner asked him how he liked the Pinafore.

Confused, Cliff stood mute for several seconds, and looked over to Sharon, but before she could explain the inside joke, it hit him: Herrick Morton & Saldini – HMS – as in HMS Pinafore. He'd been forced to listen to Gilbert and Sullivan in music class in junior high and even sing it.

"It's great!" he replied heartily. "The handle on the big front door was polished so carefully." Somehow he'd managed to remember not only one of its songs, but one pertaining to a law firm and its pretentiousness.

This retort elicited from the partner a hearty chuckle. "Well played! I like your style." As they left Perry gave him a furtive thumbs up.

As he and Perry walked into the parking lot she pushed a button on her car key fob and the door to a BMW 7 series sedan clicked open. He climbed in the passenger side. She drove him to a nearby Thai restaurant where they were quickly seated. Thai wasn't his favorite, but he could eat almost anything with gusto, so it didn't matter to him.

After they ordered and the waitress left them with some privacy Perry said, "I've put a cover letter in with the subpoena for Satterlee. It's not a formal discovery request since they're not a party – not yet anyway – but I requested certain information. If I can get it informally there'll be no need for me to subpoena the doctors who own the business."

"The doctors'll hit the roof when they get word of that."

"I think the proper expression is 'shit bricks'." She cast him a wicked grin.

"Are you planning to file against the radiology group?"

"That'll be up to the client, but I don't think so. Most businesses don't want to sue their customers as long as they're still getting paid and doing business with them."

"Makes sense. So do you want me to try to interview Satterlee or Mel Wagner when I serve them?"

"Anything you get is gravy, so feel free to go for it. Just remember that they'll associate you with Xlectrix and you don't want to get in the way of that business relationship. It's a little easier for me since I'm just the lawyer. Everyone thinks lawyers are nasty jerks. But you went in there with an Xlectrix ID the last time."

"I'll bear that in mind," he replied, not entirely pleased she was telling him how to do his job. Still, he had asked for direction.

The food came and the conversation turned to the personal. They ate and enjoyed their food as they conversed. Perry made no effort to speed things along. She asked about his FBI experience and seemed genuinely interested in some of the cases, especially the white collar ones. Her questions made it obvious that she understood the subtleties of the legal problems and strategies of investigating and prosecuting such cases. She marveled at how he had managed to get the goods on some insider traders. It was the first time in a long time that anyone outside the FBI seemed to really appreciate what he had accomplished and how hard it was sometimes. He asked about her practice, which was centered on labor and employment matters, cases like Byrne's. She regaled him with some tales of the quirks of some of the labor arbitrators she had appeared before and appalled him with stories of how some of the worst union leaders took advantage of their members.

The check came and she grabbed it. Xlectrix was going to end up paying it, as they both knew. When the waitress took her credit card away, she cleared her throat and spoke. "Cliff, I have a personal favor to ask. Do you mind?"

"What is it?"

"My brother's son is getting married next month and I really don't want to go unaccompanied. Since my divorce I just haven't developed a relationship with anyone…. Well, you understand. I can't go with another member of the firm; none of the men my age are single anyway. And especially not a client. That's kind of my world right now. Would you be willing to go with me?"

"When is it?" he answered uneasily.

She gave him the date. "It's a Saturday," she added helpfully.

Cliff had not seen this coming and was unsure what to say. The Saturday that far off made it difficult to demur on the grounds of a previous engagement. The professional relationship could be tricky whether he said yes or no. Then there was the personal. Now he realized why she had shooed away the associates. He did hit it off with her at lunch today, and he was unattached. It was clear she had once been a real beauty – big corporate law firms just didn't hire ugly people, especially not ugly women, he knew – and she had held up better than he had over the years, truth be told.

"Well, that's an attractive offer. I don't have my calendar here right now, but it might work. Where is this going to be held?"

"Santa Barbara."

Whoa. That was over 150 miles away, with no air service from a major carrier. Driving both ways and attending a wedding and reception would be an all-day affair, assuming the wedding was held midday.

As if reading his thoughts, she added, "The wedding's in the evening. Don't worry, my brother has an enormous house and has already offered to let me and my guest stay there."

Now this was getting complicated. She was inviting him for a weekend, he realized. She hadn't said whether the brother had offered her a room or rooms, plural. Was she thinking of a romantic getaway or strictly a family obligation? He squirmed inwardly, but still, it didn't sound entirely bad.

"Sharon, I think I'd like to go, but I'll have to check my calendar. Let's treat it as a tentative yes. Can I get back to you tomorrow on that before we make it definite?"

"Of course," she said beaming, and placed her hand on his arm to give it a little squeeze of thanks.

They left the restaurant chatting and making jokes about some of the local judges. She laughed heartily at Cliff's story about Judge Schuler when he was a new Assistant United States Attorney and first assigned to prosecute Asian gang matters, something with which he'd had no previous experience. When he'd first seen some FBI memo titled "FNU LNU, Racketeering, Unlawful flight – Murder" he had wanted to get an arrest warrant immediately, assuming this was a Cambodian gangster. They all had crazy, short names. Cliff had had to explain that FNU LNU was an FBI acronym for First Name Unknown, Last Name Unknown. Basically, the killer hadn't been identified yet.

When they got back to the office, Cliff took the subpoenas and returned to his office. He threw on a sport coat and grabbed a sporty fedora he kept for such occasions. This changed his look so that he wouldn't be immediately recognized at the Fremont clinic, at least so he hoped. Once again he told Maeva where he was going and headed out.

When he got to the Fremont clinic he checked the cars in the lot. He'd had Maeva run Satterlee's name in addition to Mel's and Byrne's through DMV. All three had vehicles parked in the employee parking area. Good. Everyone was there.

He walked into the reception area and there was Honey, once again clipping the edges off Xlectrix documents. She was also talking to another employee over her shoulder and did not immediately look at him as he entered. Cliff heard the other employee address her as Alice. He snapped another photo with his cell phone. The other employee left.

"Ni hao ma? Nin gui xing?" Cliff almost bellowed in a hearty voice. He'd worked Chinese counterintelligence cases in the FBI enough to know how to say "how are you" and "what's your name."

Alice looked up, amazed. This was apparently the first time a white guy had addressed her in Mandarin.

"Wo hao. Bixing Wang." *I'm fine. My name is Wang.* She showed no sign of recognizing him. "Where'd you learn Chinese?"

"I deal with a lot of doctors," he lied. "Chinese comes in handy." This seemed to satisfy her. "Is Lynda here? I have something for her." He held up a small gift-wrapped box, apparently candy, he used for such purposes.

"I can take it." She held out her hand.

"Sorry, Alice. I have to give it to her personally."

The receptionist picked up the phone and called back to Satterlee. Luckily, Cliff didn't have to wait. Satterlee came right out. When she got to the front desk she recognized Cliff and took on a wary look.

Cliff reached over Alice's desk and handed her the envelope with her subpoena. She took it reluctantly. "What's this?" she asked.

"You've been served. Now I think we should talk."

The cold stare he got in return was worthy of Frozone from *The Incredibles*.

"You can talk to our lawyers."

"So you'd rather we subpoena all the partners in the practice? I'll be sure to tell them it could have been avoided but you refused to talk to me."

Her demeanor became even frostier, but she relented and told him to come in and say what he had to say. They went back to her office.

"Xlectrix is countersuing Byrne for theft of trade secrets. The only question is whether he was doing it on his own or with the approval of you, the doctors, or someone else in this clinic."

"I already told you, the manuals were properly licensed."

"I'm not talking about the manuals. I'm talking about the L4 Tech Tips. At a minimum. There may be more we don't know about. The things Alice out there is clipping the borders off of, the borders that say 'Property of Xlectrix Corporation Do Not Copy'."

"If you think threatening to subpoena the doctors is going to impress anyone, you thought wrong. They get paid $800 an hour for their testimony. I'm sure they'd be happy to appear. I know. I see the revenue figures."

"Maybe they get paid that for expert testimony, but they'd get paid nothing other than travel expenses. If we subpoena them it would be either as defendants or as percipient witnesses."

"Percipient witnesses?"

"You know, people who perceive something. Eyewitnesses. If you witness an auto accident, or see someone steal something, you can be subpoenaed to testify, whether you're a homeless bum or the highest paid doctor in the world. You don't get paid for that."

This brought Satterlee to a grinding halt. She knew the doctors would be outraged at being subpoenaed, and apoplectic if they became defendants. She was also worried about her own liability.

"I don't know what that project is that Alice is doing. It's something Byrne gave her to do."

Bingo. That could be used. Cliff knew Satterlee was ready to throw Byrne overboard without a life raft.

"What do you want?" she went on, resignedly.

"For starters, you aren't to destroy those documents she is working on. I have photos of her clipping them, both the first time I was here and now, so we can prove you're in possession of them. We'd like you to return them to Xlectrix unaltered. If you destroy them, then that's obstruction of justice and is also evidence of guilt. The case has been referred to the FBI for criminal investigation. Second, I'd like you to call Mel Wagner in here so I can serve him. I have a subpoena for him, too. Third, we want to know everything that's on Byrne's computers. We aren't interested in your clinical, patient, or financial information at this point, just whatever he's got in the engineering section. We think he's got Xlectrix information there and we want that preserved. Again, if you destroy it, or allow him to do so, that's obstruction of justice. Last, I'd like you to call our attorney in this case, Sharon Perry, and, if you provide the information in her cover letter, it may be possible to avoid you testifying under oath at a deposition – and the doctors, too. No guarantees. That will be up to Ms. Perry. Don't tell Byrne about that. Of course, as plaintiff he could subpoena you, too, but I doubt he will."

Satterlee kept staring down unblinking at the documents as though in shock. "Is that it?" she finally asked.

"For now."

She picked up her phone, put it on speaker, and pressed a button. After a moment Mel's voice came on. "Mel here."

"Mel, can you come into my office."

"Be right there."

Within a minute there was a knock on the door and then Mel opened it and stepped in. When he saw Cliff, he scowled.

"You've been served," Cliff said, handing him the subpoena.

Mel stood there stunned for a second then looked over at Satterlee.

"Don't say anything, Mel," she ordered. Then, turning back to Cliff, "All right Mr. Knowles, I understand what you're seeking. I'll talk to our lawyers and we'll be in touch. I don't want you talking to any of our employees. They're on duty. You've served us, now please leave."

Cliff stood, tipped his hat, which he had never taken off, and said, "I'll be going then." He gave Wagner a satisfied grin and headed for the door. Satterlee rose and followed him out to the front, apparently wanting to make sure he didn't talk to Alice Wang or anyone else. Wagner came out of her office, trailing like a puppy dog, but she told him to go back in and wait for her.

When they got to the reception desk, Alice was still clipping the Tech Tips. Cliff looked at Satterlee and nodded his head toward Wang. Satterlee sighed and said to Wang, "Alice, I need you to stop what you're doing. Don't work on that project any more. Put it all in boxes and bring it to me in my office. All of it, including the completed work."

At that moment Byrne stepped out of the engineering office and saw Cliff and Satterlee at Alice's desk. Satterlee barked at him to go back to her office and stay there.

Cliff looked at Byrne, tipped his fedora once more, and left. His rental car, which he had carefully parked in the crowded patient lot this time, was untouched. Not a bad day's work.

Satterlee stormed into her office and slammed the door behind her. "Okay, what the hell is this project you two have got Alice doing? This Tech Tips thing." She waved one of the sheets she had taken from Wang's desk.

"It was Brian's idea..." Wagner began.

"We thought it would save the doctors money," Byrne cut in, emphasizing the 'we' as he glared at Wagner. "We briefed you on it, remember?"

"You told me you were organizing some of your institutional knowledge from your employment at Xlectrix and putting it in written form. You didn't tell me you were copying proprietary information."

"You said Dr. Gaur approved it." Dr. Gaur was the managing partner in the firm.

"Dr. Gaur approved of you putting into written form your knowledge for future reference of your department. You were supposed to do that from the time you were hired. That's partly why you got the job. She didn't know anything about copying documents." She again waved the sheet. "How'd you get these anyway?"

For a moment there was silence. Wagner looked like he was about to speak, but Byrne stared him down again. "Oh, that doesn't mean anything. All the ex-service reps keep those when they leave Xlectrix. There are half a dozen third-party service firms that compete with Xlectrix for servicing the Lilacs. You even took bids from a couple of them. Those are not trade secrets. They're common knowledge in the trade."

Satterlee looked at the sheet again, uncertain whether to believe him, and in any event wasn't about to take his word for the legal ramifications, even if what he said was true.

"This chart says 'L4 keyboard shortcuts.' We only have an L3. The L4 is the new model, only two years old, I think. You had the documentation on the L4 when you left Xlectrix?"

"I thought we might want to get an L4 at some point in the future. This gives us the ability to assess the effectiveness of the L4 and if we got one, to curb our service costs if Mel and I could do it in house."

This didn't answer her question. The evasion told her enough. She reached for the phone and dialed an extension. After a moment she asked whoever was on the other end if Dr. Gaur was available. Apparently receiving a negative answer, she replied, "When she gets off the phone, can you buzz me? I need to see her. As soon as possible. Tell her it's important. And send Cezar over here immediately." Cezar was a combination handyman, janitor, and on rare occasions, doubled as security. As a former lineman on his high school football team and tipping the scales at over 250 pounds he was big enough to dissuade Byrne from disregarding her orders, although Byrne was no midget himself.

Turning back to the engineers she told them both they were on administrative leave until further notice, paid for the time being. They were not to go back into the engineering office and not to touch the computers or anything else. She told them not to return to the office until instructed to do so and not to talk to anyone. Byrne protested that his jacket and laptop were in there.

As soon as Cezar arrived she had him go in and get the jackets and personal items of the two engineers, then stand guarding the door to Engineering. She pointed out that the laptop was property of the clinic so that was to stay. Then she walked them out to the employee parking area herself. Returning to reception she told Alice Wang to call their security firm and have them rekey the door locks and recode the security access keypads. Then she returned to her office to wait for the word from her boss, Dr. Gaur.

Chapter 31

The next morning Cliff spent at Xlectrix in a legal training seminar the company was holding to help satisfy the mandatory legal education requirements for its lawyers. The conference room held eight people in addition to the lecturer. The other seven lawyers, Cliff learned, were regulatory, licensing, or contract lawyers except for one who handled the 401k plan, the executive pension system, and other tax or internal employment matters.

The lecturer was some nebbish who had a degree in psychology and was showing a *PowerPoint* presentation full of statistics about how many disbarred lawyers had substance abuse problems, mostly from alcohol. This was hardly news to the assemblage, especially since none of the lawyers heard a word of it anyway. They were all talking among themselves about their legal work, eating, or on their laptops doing email. The buzz in the room from the employees was much louder than the drone from the weak-voiced lecturer, who ignored the fact he was being ignored and plowed on in a monotone. He was an authorized provider of legal education by the state bar and got paid whether anyone listened to him or not.

Cliff stewed at being forced by state bar rules to undergo this mandatory in-person training. What a waste of everyone's time and money. At the far end of the room, he gave up trying to hear, and pulled out his phone to check with Sharon Perry. Still no word from the Fremont clinic's lawyer she said. Cliff told her he'd checked his calendar and would be happy to join her for the trip to Santa Barbara. He also told her the receptionist's name was Alice Wang, so she didn't have to do a formal request for that information.

No sooner had he hung up when he got a call from Ellen Kennedy.

"Cliff, I thought you'd want to know that the case is opened and assigned."

"To you?"

"To me."

"That's great. I was out at the clinic yesterday. I told them we had referred the case to the FBI."

"Who'd you talk to?"

"Satterlee, the office manager. I also served her with a civil subpoena and told her not to destroy any documents and to preserve whatever is on the engineering computers."

"Well, that kills our element of surprise if we want to do a search warrant." Ellen did not sound happy. "I'm going to have to give a heads up to the U.S. Attorney's office about this case. They don't know anything about it yet. They could be getting a call from her lawyer – or the doctors' lawyer."

"Sorry, but I have to go with the direction of our civil case counsel. There is some good news, though."

"What's that?"

"Satterlee told me that the project of cutting the Tech Tips edges off was Byrne's idea."

"Okay, I'll write that up. It could add to probable cause to search his house or any electronics we come up with. But Satterlee could have been covering her own involvement."

"True."

"Do you think she'll comply, or destroy the evidence?"

"I heard her give instructions to the receptionist – her name is Alice Wang, by the way – to bring all the documents in to her office. I also sat in the parking lot for a few minutes after I left and watched Byrne and Wagner get walked out to their cars by Satterlee. I think she kicked them out. She's probably preserving everything until she talks to the company lawyer. I told her that it would be obstruction of justice if she destroyed anything and that I had photos of it to prove they had it. I think she believed me, but it might not hurt to give her a call and tell her the same thing. I'm sure that if the lawyer hears that the FBI called and said not to destroy that stuff, he would advise her – and the doctors – not to."

"That's good. I will. And, Cliff, I'm going to interview Mel tomorrow."

"Bring smelling salts. You may have to revive him. Fortitude is not his forte. I don't know if he'll be at work or home. If he got kicked out, he'll probably be on leave tomorrow."

"I plan to stake out his house and catch him in the morning when he leaves. Or, whenever that is, if he doesn't go in to work."

"You don't have an appointment? He hasn't agreed to talk?"

"No, I want to do a cold call. I want to catch him leaving so I don't have to knock on the door and identify myself to his wife if she answers. He's probably in a bad place with her right now for being suspended. It might give me leverage if he doesn't want her to know he's under federal criminal investigation."

"Good idea."

"What are you doing tomorrow morning?"

Cliff smiled at this. He was hoping for this kind of cooperation, but didn't expect it. "Are you inviting me along?"

"No, of course not. I'll have another agent with me. The FBI is not working for or with a private company. We are simply investigating a possible federal crime. You do your investigation and we'll do ours." She said this as though reciting some formal doctrine. Then, changing to a lighter, almost playful, tone, "Of course, you're a free citizen. I can't prevent you from being across the street from his house at 7:00 AM sharp."

"Good to know. That's quite a coincidence. I was thinking of maybe getting up at 5:30 tomorrow morning so that I can drive out to the East Bay and take a stroll in his neighborhood tomorrow morning at exactly that time."

"Okay. I'll bring the smelling salts. You may want to bring snacks and something to pee in. We could be there a while."

"I was an agent for 25 years. I know the drill."

"I'm sure you do."

When the call ended Cliff looked up to realize the lawyers were filing out. The lecturer was handing out certificates of completion. He walked up, collected his, and initialed next to his signature on the roster to show he was there the entire time. In a colossal make-work exercise he was now officially educated in substance abuse such that he could practice law for another three years. If the bar ever decided to audit him, he had the magic paper to prove it.

He walked up to Vogel's office as he had been asked to do and briefed Vogel on the events of the previous day and the two calls this morning. Vogel was obviously pleased and actually clapped him on the shoulder.

As they were talking Sharon Perry called Vogel. He put it on speaker and told her Cliff was there, too. She explained that she had just gotten a call from the lawyer for the Fremont clinic, a partner at another big corporate law firm she knew well. He assured her that the radiology clinic would cooperate and would preserve the documents and the computer files. His position was that the doctors and Satterlee knew nothing about the project, that it was all Byrne's idea, and that he would be fired today. They weren't sure about Mel Wagner yet. He argued, however, that the material wasn't protected trade secrets and the clinic was within their legal rights to possess all of it. If Xlectrix agreed not to name the doctors, the clinic or Satterlee as defendants, they would give all the material back in exchange for a discounted rate on the annual service now that their lead engineer is not there. They also promised that if any other materials marked with Xlectrix's proprietary markings were discovered or came into their possession, they would be returned to Xlectrix, too.

Cliff laughed. "Ah, the old my-client-didn't-do-it-and-if-you-let-him-off-he'll-promise-never-to-do-it-again defense."

"Exactly!" Perry agreed.

"What about the receptionist, the one doing the actual cutting and scanning?" Vogel asked.

"He said they questioned her and she claimed it was Byrne who directed her to do it and when she complained to him about the markings saying it was proprietary he told her it was okay and that they had a license. He told her she'd be fired if she didn't do it."

"Did the lawyer say how they got the information? How they decrypted the Tech Tips?" Cliff asked.

"No. He said they don't know how it happened. The receptionist just gets a pile of printouts every day or two from Byrne and is supposed to clip the edges off, then when she gets a full stack, send that through a big scanner Byrne bought that has a sheet feed. The scanner has OCR software to convert the text to digital form."

"The lawyer said they aren't prepared to give back the documents or the computer files yet, but they will make copies of everything and provide that. He was obviously trying to use their possession of it as leverage to get that discount on service charges."

"Very ballsy," Vogel commented laconically. "Anything else, Sharon?"

"He was really worried about the criminal investigation. He hasn't heard anything from the FBI yet but he wanted to know if his clients were targets. I told him we wouldn't know, that he'd have to talk to the FBI or the U.S. Attorney's office."

"That's great, Sharon," Vogel continued. "We think he might have had a piece of our hardware called a dongle. Was there any mention of that?"

"No, nothing about a dongle."

"Okay, then. Thanks again."

They ended the call and Cliff left for his office. When he walked in, Maeva was on the phone, but she quickly said goodbye to whoever was on the other end.

"Who was that?" he asked innocently.

"Oh, no one."

"No one? As in a male no one?"

"Just some salesman. He was male, I suppose." She blushed and dropped eye contact.

"You suppose he was male. I see. Don't ever play poker." He retreated to his office.

After lunch he got another call from Sharon Perry. She had just gotten off the phone with the lawyer for the Fremont clinic.

"Cliff, listen to this. The computers in the engineering section were searched – there were three – and they found various Xlectrix files and various other files – from Xlectrix – 'Byrne wasn't supposed to have.' The lawyer wouldn't say what those were, but Byrne was fired for having those, not for the Xlectrix information, which they still maintain is rightfully in their possession. They also claim that he copied the Xlectrix materials without the company's knowledge or permission and that he therefore wasn't acting in the scope of his employment."

Cliff laughed. "Not in the scope of employment. Right. So he didn't do anything wrong, but whatever he did wasn't authorized so they aren't liable for his actions if it was wrong."

"That's their story and they're sticking to it."

"Let me guess. They're still asking for a discount on the service contract."

"Of course," Perry laughed.

"Did they find a dongle? Or the Tech Tips files or the IP list of the other Lilac owners."

"They said no to the dongle. They're still searching through the engineering section. What's this about a list of IP addresses?"

Cliff realized Sharon still didn't know about the overdose cases and he was not authorized to tell her. "It's a client list of sorts. It identifies who in the service region owns a Lilac 4. It could be of value to a competitor, either another manufacturer, or one of those third-party service people who try to underbid Xlectrix for the service contracts on the Lilacs. It was encrypted with the dongle, too." This was true as far as it went, but he said nothing about the real reason they wanted to know if that file was there.

"Well, the lawyer said he'd messenger over all the paper stuff they've copied so far by the end of the day. They have to bring in an IT specialist to copy the hard drives, CD's, and memory sticks, but they had the company computer guy print out a file directory from the three main computers so we should at least be able to see the names of those files today. When I get it, I'll call you. You can come over and see if it's there."

"Sounds good. So Byrne is officially fired, anyway. And they aren't defending him on the cross-complaint, either. He'll have to pay that boozer lawyer of his from his own pocket. That's one down. What about the others?"

"He didn't say, but I assume they're still employed or he would have told me."

"Okay. Thanks for letting me know. Give me a call when you have the material in hand."

"I will, but I don't know if I want you working on this case," she said with a tease in her voice.

"Why is that?" he replied warily.

"You're stealing all my billable hours. You got more information in one day than I would have gotten in weeks of discovery."

"A man's got to make a living," he replied, echoing her tone. "You know what they say, 'All's fair in love and war.'"

"And which is this?"

"Maybe you'll find out this afternoon."

"I'm looking forward to it."

The next hour was spent on reading through the mail, updating his legal education file with today's details, and, prompted by Sharon's remark, totaling his billing records for Xlectrix. This was shaping up to be his best quarter yet. He'd been working almost full-time on this case, and the client was a deep-pockets corporation. He'd already billed enough to earn the initial retainer and he expected billings to be even higher for the next few weeks.

The phone rang, and he let Maeva answer it. A moment later she stood in the doorway to his office. "It's Roger Vogel. There's been a shooting!"

He picked up the line. "Roger, what happened?"

"Someone took a shot at our building. It went through the window of the Software Design Manager, Byrne's old boss. The one who fired him."

"Was he hit?"

"No, the angle was too high. The shot went into the ceiling. No one was hurt. We think it was someone hidden in the shrubs across the street on the Hewlett-Packard property, but that's just a guess. The manager had just been standing near the window seconds before. It was a very close call. We called 911. They're en route."

"Do you want me there?"

"No, I don't think so. The police will do whatever they do. Crime scene processing, I suppose. You won't be able to do that independently I would guess."

"That's not my expertise anyway. I'm sure the police can handle it better than I could. How's the manager? Shaken up?"

"Very much so. Cliff, the main reason I'm calling is to warn you. If it's Byrne, and I think it is, you could be next."

"That's a possibility. Or Sharon Perry. I'll let her know. Thanks for the call."

Cliff looked up to see Maeva still standing in the doorway, concern distorting her features.

"What happened, Cliff?"

"Maeva, stay right here."

He rushed out into the hallway and downstairs to the building lobby. The building was too small to have a security guard or receptionist. At the entry, there was just a small lobby with a building directory, with stairs and an elevator to the left and a hallway with tenant offices to the right. He looked around for any sign of anything out of order, but saw nothing unusual. Standing to the side of the front door he peeked out into the parking lot. No one there.

He reflected that it was fortunate his office was on the second floor and had no exterior windows or doors. The only access was into the hallway next to the rest rooms, around the corner from Cross and Silver. The other end was the wall that had been put in to separate the two offices when the law firm had given him the library space. That also meant there was no emergency exit. If Byrne came for them, the only way out was through the office door into the hall, the same way he would have to come in.

After a few more minutes of looking, he ventured out into the parking lot. No one had passed him going in or out of the building during that time. He darted quickly left then right. Nothing happened. He felt foolish, and slowed to a normal walking pace. He circled the building trying to identify where a sniper might secret himself. He satisfied himself that there was no way for anyone to shoot into his office from the street, or even from a neighboring building. Someone could, however, shoot into Cross and Silver. If they could get onto the roof of the two-story building across the parking lot, they could even shoot at a downward angle. For now, though, there was no sign of danger. Byrne probably still thought Cliff was an employee of Xlectrix with an office there, based on the business card he had left, but he knew Byrne was sophisticated with computers. It wouldn't take him long to figure out where his real office was. Cliff had a website and a telephone directory listing.

He went back upstairs.

"Maeva, you're on vacation. Paid vacation."

"What? No, I'm not. I took my last day of leave for the Fourth of July when I visited my parents."

"I'm giving you a vacation right now. I want you out of here. Pack up your stuff and go."

"But if I use my leave now I won't have any more for Christmas. I only get…"

"Maeva, this is in addition to the three weeks I give you. I'm paying you to stay home – or go visit your parents again. For Christ's sake, just go."

"Cliff, you're scaring me. Is it safe to go out? This is about the shooting, isn't it?"

"I just checked; there's no one out there."

"Are you coming with me?"

"It's better if I don't. If the shooter is who I think it is, he's never seen the two of us together. He wouldn't know who you are. If I was with you, that might identify you as a target. Just take your car and go home. Don't come back until I tell you."

He grabbed her arm and led her to the front door. She had to break away to grab her purse and a sweater. They then both stepped into the hallway and she headed around the corner, looking back at Cliff over her shoulder as she turned. He gave her the thumbs up sign and she disappeared.

He went back to his desk. He had just cleared out all his email minutes ago and now there was another. It was a notification that he had received another email at the Xlectrix email address. He logged in there and found a single anonymous message with only a subject line and no body: "*You're next.*" He forwarded it to Vogel and Ellen.

He called the non-emergency number of the Los Altos police and said he wanted to report a death threat, adding that it was related to a matter being investigated by Detective Hanssen. Surprisingly, Hanssen came on the line almost immediately. Cliff started to tell him about the email, but Hanssen said to just wait there, he would be right over.

Since Cliff's office was in downtown Los Altos, a triangle four blocks or so on a side, and the police department was too, Hanssen was there in five minutes, a patrolman by his side.

"Where's your secretary?" Hanssen asked before anything else.

"I sent her home. I was afraid something like this might happen. I don't want her in the line of fire."

No sooner had he said that when his phone rang. He made his excuse on the grounds it might be important, and picked up the phone. It was Maeva telling him that she was now halfway home, waiting at a light, and wanted to let him know that she was safe. Cliff thanked her for calling, said that the detective was there, and that she shouldn't talk on her cell phone while driving. They hung up and he told Hanssen that was Maeva and she was okay.

He showed Hanssen the email, which he'd already printed out, including all the header information, and told him that he thought it was sent by Byrne, the same man whom he suspected of planting the isotope container in his car, as well as the likely suspect in the shooting over at Xlectrix. This time Hanssen took much more detailed information about Byrne, the Fremont radiology clinic, and the shooting at Xlectrix, which apparently was being handled by a different detective at that very moment, along with patrol officers.

Hanssen told him he thought it would be wise to stay away from the office for the near term, and maybe from his home which was also in Los Altos. He asked if Cliff's home address was listed. Cliff pointed out that it didn't matter since a simple check with any of dozens of Internet businesses could obtain his home address in a matter of seconds. Cliff gave him the address, which Hanssen recognized as a cul-de-sac. The detective told him that since it was on a cul-de-sac it would be much harder for a sniper to set up without someone noticing than in downtown with its relatively dense buildings and people moving around constantly. He told Cliff he would have patrol officers make a point to drive by the area frequently and be on the lookout for Byrne or anyone else who seemed suspicious.

After the police left, Cliff decided to take their advice and go home, but first he shot off another email to Ellen and Vogel saying he was going to stay away from the office for the rest of the day at least, but would be in touch from home. He left his home address and telephone with both. He closed down the office and walked out to the parking lot and drove home.

As soon as he got home, Ellen called him and asked if he was okay. He assured her he was.

"I'll make sure the whole squad knows about the threat, Cliff," she told him. "Don't be surprised if you see a bunch of agents doing drivebys. Nobody messes with the FBI family."

"Thanks, Ellen, it means a lot. It won't deter me from doing my job, though. Don't be surprised if you see an ex-agent out at Mel's house tomorrow."

"I expected no less. I'll take backup considering what happened today. Do you carry a weapon?"

"No. I don't have a carry permit. Maybe I could get one as a licensed private investigator, but I wasn't a particularly good shot when I was in the Bureau, and since my laser eye surgery I'm worse. I'd be more of a hazard than anything else."

"Remind me to stay away when they have ex-agents day out at the range," she laughed. "I shot a possible last year, by the way," she added after a beat. A possible is the FBI term for getting a perfect score on the handgun course.

"Why does that not surprise me?"

"Be careful, Cliff. See you tomorrow."

"See you tomorrow."

Chapter 32

The next morning Cliff was already on scene at Mel Wagner's house at 7:15 AM when he saw Ellen and Matt Nguyen pull up in front of Wagner's house. Cliff had parked three houses down, in front of a construction site where a home was being remodeled, and appeared unoccupied. He'd gotten up at 4:30 to make sure he'd have time to have his morning coffee and eliminate it before he got on site. He knew that public bathrooms were scarce in residential neighborhoods, and he wouldn't want to have to leave the scene for that purpose anyway. As it turned out, there was a Porta-Potty for the construction crew not ten feet away.

Ellen and Matt were soon joined by another car, which Cliff quickly recognized as FBI. That car drove up the street, made a U-turn, and pulled in behind Cliff. Cliff recognized the two agents in that car as squadmates from Palo Alto, no doubt the back up Ellen had mentioned. In the rear-view mirror he saw the driver grinning at him. The agent had obviously recognized him, too. They exchanged waves.

Fortunately, the wait was only a half hour before Mel Wagner emerged, his son in tow. Ellen judged the boy to be about nine. Ellen approached Mel as he walked down the front walk to the driveway, Matt standing next to the Bureau car at the curb, his right hand on his belt ready to draw if necessary.

"Colin, I just remembered I forgot something," Wagner, taking in the scene, said to his son in a calm voice. "Go back inside and find my blue pen. I think I left it on my desk."

The boy seemed puzzled, but did as he was told, disappearing onto the house. As soon as he was inside Wagner hissed, "Don't do this in front of my son... please."

"We're not here to arrest you," Ellen replied, displaying her credentials and badge. "I'm with the FBI. We just want to talk. I didn't want to do it in front of your wife. I wasn't sure she knew you'd been suspended so I thought I'd give you the option of doing it privately."

"This is hardly private. It's my front yard."

"Well, we could go inside then."

"No, don't. My wife doesn't know. I told her I'm on leave, that I had accumulated too many leave hours and was in a use it or lose it situation."

"Where are you going?"

"My son has judo class."

"I tell you what: we'll follow you to your son's dojo. After you drop him off we can talk there."

Wagner agreed and told them the name and location of the dojo. Ellen and Matt got back in their car as the boy returned with his father's pen. She radioed the plan to the other car. She watched as the agent behind Cliff got out and walked up to Cliff and said something to him through the window. Cliff nodded.

Wagner's car left, but Ellen held back in order not to bring unnecessary attention to the procession. When the car was a block away she pulled out, too, and then the three cars, Cliff's included, followed down the hill toward the school.

The martial arts school was in a suburban strip mall. After Wagner dropped off his son, he walked back to his car. Ellen and Matt were waiting there.

"Mr. Wagner," Ellen began, "We'd like to talk to you about the Xlectrix documents from your office. Why don't we sit in my car."

"Look," he replied, "I want to cooperate, but my boss said I can't talk to anyone. If I talk to you I could be fired. Please, just talk to the company lawyer."

"If your boss – or the lawyer – told you not to talk to the FBI, that's obstruction of justice," Matt warned.

"No, they didn't say it like that. They didn't say anything about the FBI. They just said not to talk about this until they'd talked to the lawyers." He had a hard time getting the words out, the dryness in his mouth evident.

"If you don't talk to us, you'll put yourself in the position of a prime suspect, you know that?" Ellen warned.

"I want a lawyer."

Matt and Ellen looked at each other.

"Do you have a lawyer?" Matt asked.

"My boss said…"

"Who?" Ellen interrupted. "Byrne?"

"No, Lynda. She said if I asked for a lawyer you'd have to stop questioning me."

"Is she a lawyer?" Ellen said scornfully.

"Actually, she is. At least she has a law degree. I don't think she ever practiced law."

"Well, she's got a few things wrong." Ellen knew the law. If Mel was in custody and they kept questioning him, anything he said would be excluded from evidence against him, but that wasn't quite the same thing. He wasn't in custody, and anything he said could still be used against someone else, like a co-conspirator, or as a lead. "What we're really interested in is Byrne, not you. You don't mind talking about him do you?"

"Am I under arrest?"

Ellen let out a big sigh before answering. "No."

"Then I want to go." He motioned toward his car door, which Ellen was blocking. Resignation on her face, she stepped aside. He walked up to his door and opened it a few inches, but she was still standing where he couldn't open it all the way.

"Mel, I'll let you go, but you have your lawyer contact us." She handed him her business card. "We think Byrne is the real culprit here but we're just as happy to prosecute two instead of one. Your lawyer will tell you the first one to cooperate is the one that gets the good deal. And remember this: your company's lawyer is not your lawyer. Neither is Satterlee. They'll tell you whatever's in the best interest of the clinic, not you. They'll hang you out to dry in a heartbeat. Get your own lawyer or come talk to us. Preferably both."

With that she stepped away and told Matt it was time to go. Mel got in his car quickly and backed out as the agents walked several aisles over in the crowded parking lot to their car. They all drove away.

Cliff watched the questioning from across the lot. He couldn't hear what was going on, but he could tell from the short duration and from Ellen's body language that she was not getting cooperation. He hoped someone would clue him in, but no one came over to talk to him. He knew Ellen would not want to create a record of providing information to the corporate victim's lawyer/investigator who was prepping for a civil case, so he was not surprised when she drove off without calling or texting him.

The agents all drove west toward Palo Alto. Wagner drove back uphill toward his home, to the east. Cliff followed him at a discreet distance in his rental car, a full-size Ford. When they got to a stretch of road over an arroyo, Cliff pulled right behind him, honked his horn, and flashed his lights. As he expected, Wagner thought it was the agents again, and pulled over to the curb. Although there was occasional passing traffic, they weren't right in front of any residences.

Wagner rolled down his window and waited. Cliff got out and almost sprinted to Wagner's door, reached in and pulled the door handle on the inside, thus preventing Wagner from locking the door and rolling up the window. Wagner was so surprised he didn't react in time to stop it.

"Hey, what are you doing?" he protested, then, recognizing Cliff, his eyes went wide and he cowered backward toward the passenger seat.

"Hello, Mel. I'm here to discuss a certain isotope pig that was planted in my car," Cliff announced in an ominous tone. He grinned down at Wagner as he reached in and unbuckled his seat belt. "Move over."

"You can't..."

"But I can." Cliff grabbed the front of Wagner's windbreaker and lifted him bodily from his seat and shoved him over to the passenger side like a rag doll. Then he sat in the driver's side and closed the door.

"I asked for a lawyer," Mel whined.

"That's nice. You're going to need one. So was that you who tried to give me cancer of the gonads or was it Byrne?"

"It wasn't me, I swear. He just asked me if that was your car and I told him it was. I didn't know he was going to do that. The container was empty, I swear. It was years old and the isotope had a very short half-life. There couldn't have been any radiation danger left. He just grabbed it off the shelf. I handle all the isotopes. We keep spare pigs around in case we need to divide up the sample."

"So I suppose you're going to tell me that whoever it was that took a shot at the Xlectrix building yesterday and whoever sent me the email saying I'm next, that wasn't you either." Cliff still held Mel's jacket with one hand.

"Jesus, I don't know anything about that. He's crazy. It wasn't me. It wasn't."

"Lucky for you I believe you, you little piece of garbage. The FBI is the least of your worries right now with their white collar case. A year in a federal resort at worst. If you helped him in any way with that shooting you're an accessory to attempted murder. That's ten years of hard time in San Quentin if you're lucky. Tell me what happened."

"Nothing. I don't know. I mean, after we were sent home I just went home. Brian didn't say anything to me or call me or anything. I have no idea what he did. He just left, like me. But he's a gun nut. He goes hunting for moose, bear, up in Canada somewhere and brags about his trophies. It must have been him. Are you going to hurt me?"

Cliff thought about that for a few seconds. "I am, but not in the way you mean." He let go of Wagner's jacket and reached into his own coat pocket. He pulled out a packet of photographs.

"Take a look at these." He spread out the photos on the console between the seats. The photos were from the compensation claims made by the overdose victims. There were autopsy photos of the two dead victims, several showing the deep burn marks from the X-ray beam, and several of the woman who lost her leg, one showing the amputated leg on the floor. Last was a picture of Ashley Bishop's leg, taken right after the first vein transplant, with the surgical scar prominently displayed.

Wagner got noticeably queasy after a quick glance and looked away. Cliff grabbed his hair and yanked his head back to the pictures. "Look, I said."

"What are these?" Wagner choked out.

"What if I told you these are the people Byrne's been killing and maiming with Crabbe's dongle?"

Wagner's jaw dropped and a look of total confusion enveloped his features as he made eye contact with Cliff again. He forced himself to look down again. Still, he said nothing.

"Do you know if he's been remotely accessing other clinics and causing overdoses with their Lilacs?" Cliff demanded.

Wagner's lower lip began to tremble. His nose started to run. "No. No... I ..." He wiped the slobber from his face with the sleeve of his windbreaker. "I didn't know. Oh God. Oh my God." He clasped his hands together, interlocking his fingers, bowed his head and started to pray.

Cliff concluded Mel was probably being truthful, although he wasn't one hundred percent convinced. He decided not to interrupt the prayer. If Wagner was religious, it would work in his favor.

When Wagner opened his eyes and looked up, Cliff resumed, "Tell me the whole story. How did he do this?"

Wagner looked up toward the sky, although the roof of the car was all he could see. "Dear God forgive me," he said out loud. He turned toward Cliff and in a calm voice, told him what he wanted to know in a long, rambling account.

He explained how Crabbe had come out for a service on the Lilac 3 and couldn't finish the repair. He needed a circuit board from back at the office. Since he was going to have to come back the next day, he asked if he could leave the laptop there in a safe place because he was going direct to some fancy dinner and didn't want to leave the laptop in his car. Mel told him yes and agreed to take the laptop back to the engineering section of the clinic. Mel watched him remove the dongle from the laptop bag and had asked him what it was. Crabbe told him it was a dongle and it encrypted all the sensitive stuff on the laptop. He didn't want Mel to take offense, but it was company rules that he could never leave the laptop and dongle together where anyone else could access it.

Mel took the laptop back to the clinic and when he walked in Byrne asked him what it was. He told him it was Crabbe's laptop and that he was coming back for it the next day. Byrne immediately said they should see what was on it. Mel knew this wasn't right and explained about the dongle, trying to convince Byrne that there wouldn't be anything useful on it. Byrne was Mel's direct supervisor, though, and paid no attention. He took the laptop and booted it up.

Byrne found that he could launch the normal applications, like Word or Excel. When he opened the Lilac 4 application, it opened, too. The interface was much like the Lilac 3 interface, and he quickly got bored with exploring that. There just wasn't much to see at first. Then when he read the Help file, he read about how the dongle needed to be plugged in when the program was launched in order to enable diagnostic mode. He also saw the Tech Tips file, but when he tried to open it, it just flickered and then shut down again. At that point, he decided to copy the whole hard drive.

Byrne was an expert with computers, Mel told him, better than the clinic's own IT guy. He had a spare hard drive on the shelf. He took that down, installed it on one of the computers in the Engineering section, and copied Crabbe's entire C drive to it, a complete image, then copied the Xlectrix directories to his own laptop.

When Crabbe returned the next morning, Byrne and Wagner were both at the hospital. They watched Crabbe put the dongle back in the laptop bag where it had been before. Byrne then distracted Crabbe with some questions about the L4 and how it compared with the L3 while Mel, acting under Byrne's orders, took the dongle from the bag. Wagner's lip started to quiver again at this point in the story. He swore he didn't want to do it and had protested strongly, but Byrne threatened to fire him if he didn't help. Byrne told him all they were going to do was learn how to service the L3 and L4 from the Tech Tips file, to save the clinic money. Mel surreptitiously handed the dongle off to Byrne, who raced back to the clinic and plugged the dongle into both computers, then relaunched all the Xlectrix applications. He then unplugged the dongle and checked the programs. He learned then that the programs continued to function normally. They didn't need the dongle to be plugged in after the program was opened. So he took the dongle back to the hospital where Crabbe was working on installing the circuit board.

This is where it got tense, Wagner explained. Crabbe finished up quicker than they anticipated. Byrne wasn't back yet when Crabbe was just getting ready to go. Mel called Byrne, who told him to stall Crabbe a few more minutes since he was already in the car and would be there very soon. Wagner then had Crabbe check out the printer that was attached to the L3. He made up some story about how it malfunctioned. Crabbe checked all the cable connections for a few minutes and printed something out but couldn't find anything wrong. Then Byrne showed up and secretly passed the dongle back to Mel as he questioned Crabbe again about the L4. Mel replaced the dongle while Crabbe was distracted. Crabbe never suspected a thing.

After Crabbe left, Byrne switched to the Tech Tips program. He tried to print out the information on the screen but there was no print menu. He tried to do a screen capture with the PrintScrn button, but it didn't work. He could minimize the Tech Tips window, but when he tried to paste the screen shot into the graphics program there was nothing there. So he maximized the Tech Tips window again, took out his cell phone camera, and starting shooting pictures of the screen – page after page of photos. When he realized how big the file was, he went out and bought a digital camera, OCR software and a sheet feeder for the copier/scanner. Byrne controlled the engineering budget.

He ordered Wagner to take photos of the Tech Tips screens whenever he wasn't busy with anything else. They divided up the chapters. Byrne would then print out the photos and give them to Alice, the receptionist. She was instructed to cut off the warnings on the edges that said property of Xlectrix, do not copy, and then scan them. The software would turn the image into text. Some of the pages didn't work very well, especially where there were formulas or Greek letters representing radiological symbols. Byrne had to review them and write in the corrected formula or symbol. It took a lot of time, and they were only about halfway through the file. Alice asked about whether it was okay to do this and Byrne told her they had a license to do it. She was totally clueless, Mel said, guilty only of stupidity, or at least naiveté.

Mel knew that Byrne had the L4 program running in diagnostic mode, but he never saw it used. They didn't have an L4, only an L3. Byrne told him he wanted to keep it running so that if they ever got an L4 he could do the diagnostics himself, saving the company money. He warned Mel not to turn off the computers or close the Xlectrix programs because they wouldn't work again without the dongle. For weeks the spare computer with the copied hard drive in it was kept running. The programs were never closed. Byrne would keep his company laptop plugged in during the day but at night he always made sure it was in sleep mode. Then one day they came into work to discover there had been a power failure overnight. The backup generator had kicked in, but not soon enough. The spare computer had shut down. Byrne rebooted, but he couldn't access the Tech Tips or other sensitive Xlectrix files because he didn't have the dongle. Fortunately, if that's the right word, the laptop was still in sleep mode and retained its state. After that, they only had the one computer, Byrne's company laptop, running the programs.

Mel stopped at this point in the narrative and reached into the console. Cliff was worried there might be a gun there, and grabbed Mel's hand as he reached in, but when he looked in there was no gun, so he let go. Mel pulled out a wad of tissue and blew his nose. Cliff took the opportunity to ask him about the remote access to the other clinic Lilacs.

Wagner denied knowing anything about that. He said he didn't even know that it was possible to remotely access a Lilac, much less one belonging to someone else. Byrne never let him read the Lilac 4 operation manual and Mel didn't have any interest in doing so. Mel's main responsibility was the isotope machines, not the Lilac, and they didn't have an L4. But he knew Byrne read it. He once overheard Brian talking on the phone about it, he said. It was obvious to Mel after hearing some of Byrne's end of the conversation that he was talking to a third-party service company, a group of ex-employees of Xlectrix who went out on their own and competed against Xlectrix for servicing the Lilacs. Byrne had obviously promised he could bring a printed copy of the complete L4 Tech Tips. From what he could gather, the job offer was contingent on him bringing that. After that he assumed that Byrne kept rushing him and Alice to finish the photographing and scanning so he could take the manual and jump ship. Byrne didn't want the Tech Tips to help the clinic, he wanted to go into competition with Xlectrix and get a higher-paying job.

Cliff asked him why Byrne might want to remotely access another clinics' system to overdose patients, Mel at first said he had no idea, but when Cliff asked him if Byrne had any financial incentive to increase business there in Fremont, Mel had an epiphany.

"Lynda and Dr. Gaur were seriously thinking of getting an L4," he said. "Brian told them he thought it was a bad idea, that it had a software flaw. He said he thought it would be unreliable and might even be recalled. He tried to convince them the L3 was good enough. That was his expertise, you know. He serviced L3's at Xlectrix."

"Go on."

"Well some of the doctors practiced at other locations sometimes, or went to conventions and talked to other radiologists, and they hadn't heard of any problems with the L4. They thought they'd be losing business because other doctors would refer patients to the clinics with the newest equipment. The hospital administrator was also giving them pressure to stay current with the technology. The L4 supposedly could be tuned more finely in dosage and aimed more exactly, so it was supposed to be safer for the patients, plus service costs were less, but Brian told them that he had heard different. He said if they waited another couple of months, he bet it would come out that the L4 had a safety flaw and patients would be flocking to clinics like ours with the L3's or other systems."

"Well, that doesn't seem like enough reason to go killing people. So what if he was wrong? He was salaried wasn't he? It's not like he was going to get fired if it didn't happen."

"Yeah he's salaried. But he hated the doctors. He hacked into the company payroll system and saw how much they make. Dr. Gaur makes over a million. The others all make at least eight hundred thousand. He didn't tell them he knew this, of course, but he told me and Alice. He was fuming that they only paid him seventy-five. So he made a deal. He said if patient traffic for the L3 didn't increase by at least ten percent over the next six months he'd take a twenty-five K cut for the year, but if it did, he'd get that much of a boost."

"You've got to be kidding. For an extra twenty-five grand he'd overdose patients? Even killing them?"

"I don't know. I never knew he was overdosing anyone. How is that even possible? And how would that increase traffic here?"

"Did you hear about the post in the cancer forum that said the Lilac 4 was overdosing patients and that it was unsafe? It implied that patients and doctors should avoid those treatment centers with L4's."

"Oh, my Lord, he was ranting about that a couple of weeks ago. He said the word was out and he'd soon be proved right. He was short on his bet, I know that. The patient load was up a little, but not the ten percent. It actually would have cost him fifty grand, too, not twenty-five. Remember, he would take a cut of twenty-five if we didn't hit the target."

"You're right," Cliff said, exhaling hard. "although I doubt the doctors would actually cut his salary since he could always leave if they did, but he may have thought they would take him up on the cut. How much longer did he have to get it up to the target?"

"I think another two months or so."

"Who else knew about the hacking into the payroll information?"

"Just Alice, I think. Brian told me not to tell anyone, and I didn't. But I heard him talking to her about it once or twice. They used to go out drinking sometimes after work. I think maybe he's poking her. She hates the doctors as much as he does. Satterlee makes over one-fifty. Alice hates her even more. Alice only makes forty-five. That's why she'd do anything to help Brian hit his ten percent target, and do his scanning, too. If they find out about that, him hacking the payroll records, they'll fire him."

This was the first time Cliff realized that Mel didn't know Byrne had been fired. He should have picked up on it when Mel said Byrne "is" salaried, not "was."

"He has been."

"Brian's been fired?" Wagner would have to have been a good actor to feign the surprise, Cliff decided.

"That's what I've been told. I think that's why the potshot was taken at the Xlectrix building, and he threatened me."

"So what happened to the patients?" Wagner asked, indicating the photos.

"I can't tell you everything we know. I can tell you what I suspect. I think Byrne remotely accessed the competing hospitals' and clinics' Lilacs during treatment, slaved the Lilacs to his laptop, then disabled the dose-per-pulse monitor and increased the current. I think he was trying to injure people and then spread the word that the L4's were dangerous so people would come to your clinic."

"And were patients hurt? Killed even?"

Cliff had skirted the edge of his attorney-client privilege already, probably crossed it in fact, but wouldn't go as far as this question required. "I can only let you draw your own conclusions," he finally said, tapping the photos, then picked them up and put them in his pocket.

"Jesus Christ," Wagner wailed, again clasping his hands in prayer and looking skyward. "Forgive me."

"Have you heard of the felony murder rule?" Cliff asked.

"Umm, I think so."

"The simplified version is this. If someone engages in a felony, like, say, trade secret theft, or conspiracy, and then he kills someone, even accidentally, he's guilty of murder."

"I never killed anyone, even accidentally. I'm no murderer." There was desperation in Mel's voice.

"Aren't you? There's more. The rule says that all the perpetrators, all the co-conspirators, are guilty of all the crimes committed by any of them. The getaway car driver is guilty of murder if the guy inside the bank accidentally kills someone during a robbery."

Wagner's eyes went glassy and he just sat there, defeated. "What should I do?" he finally asked.

"Get a lawyer, a good criminal lawyer. Go to the FBI now and make the best deal you can. You may have to do some time in prison, I don't know, but they don't have jurisdiction over murder, only the trade secret theft. They're going to find out everything sooner or later. Your best chance of making a good deal is in the next four to eight hours. And don't tell your wife or anyone besides your lawyer about the possibility of overdosed patients – and I'm not saying there were any."

"I swear I didn't know it was even possible to access someone else's system, much less cause intentional overdoses. I never thought I was hurting anyone. I just took a little computer widget from a bag and shot some photos."

"That may save your ass from prison, but you have a higher judgment to worry about." Cliff pointed a finger skyward.

After a long pause Wagner nodded and croaked, "I know."

Chapter 33

When Cliff returned home he was both elated and troubled. He had finally solved the mystery. Byrne had stolen the dongle and launched all the programs that used it. He'd remotely accessed the L4's of competing clinics and hospitals and caused overdoses in order to drive business to the Fremont radiology center. But what was he to do with this information?

He had to tell Vogel, but Vogel wouldn't want the information to be provided to the FBI or police. That would inevitably bring out the fact that patients had received overdoses and could make doctors and patients afraid to use any Xlectrix machine. They'd be viewed as vulnerable to hacking. The settlements in the overdose cases might even be challenged, with patients' lawyers claiming that the company knew there was a product defect and concealed that information. But this was murder. He would have been legally required to provide the information to authorities if he knew of a crime in progress, or one about to be committed, but he couldn't break attorney-client privilege just to report a past crime he learned about. Not without his client's permission, anyway.

First, he called Sharon Perry and told her that Mel Wagner had admitted stealing the dongle at Byrne's direction. She was ecstatic.

"Cliff, that's fantastic! That totally shoots down any defense Byrne might have that it wasn't a trade secret. That's asportation – when somebody physically steals something and carries it away. That looks like stealing to any judge or jury. We can prove the secret part of trade secret theft. The theft part, too."

"The clinic's on the hook, too," Cliff replied. "The theft was in the course of business."

"The clinic, too. Vogel probably still won't want to sue them, but now we've got leverage. I'll call their lawyer as soon as we hang up. Did you get this admission in writing?"

"No."

"Record it?"

"No. You can't do that in California without consent of both parties. I didn't think I could get it out of him if he knew it was being recorded." He didn't tell her that he didn't want a recording of his heavy-handed treatment of Mel, either.

"So it's just your word that he did this. How are we going to prove it if he recants?"

"He won't. I'm willing to bet he'll be spilling his guts to the FBI within twenty-four hours, trying to cut a deal. I told him to get a criminal lawyer and not let the company lawyer tell him what to do."

"That's great for the criminal case, but the FBI isn't going to give us any statements he makes."

"You can question Mel about it in the deposition. I served that subpoena. If he takes the Fifth, you've got my testimony as to what he said. If Mel's lawyer won't let him deny it under oath, which he won't with criminal charges possibly pending and the chance of perjury being added on, it's my uncontradicted testimony."

"That could work. It's enough to play the card with the clinic, too. They're going to have a hard time claiming this wasn't in the scope of employment with two employees involved."

"Three. Alice Wang wasn't involved in the theft of the dongle, but she knew the scanning she was doing was wrong."

"Right on!"

"One other thing."

"What?"

"That lawyer was probably telling the truth about why Byrne was fired. He hacked into the company personnel files and saw the salaries of the doctors. Eight hundred grand at the bottom end, over a million at the top. He told Mel and Alice. They were resentful at what they saw as the pittance they made."

"The doctors aren't going to want that made public. That'll also convince them Mel spilled the beans to us."

"I'll leave you to it, then. Hold their feet to the fire."

"I can hardly wait. Thanks again, Cliff. How about lunch again?"

"Not today. Too much going on."

"Okay. Talk to you soon."

"Later."

Cliff called Vogel next and left a message to call him when he couldn't get through. It was still only 10:30 but he'd gotten up so early he was hungry for lunch. He'd been up for six hours and only had toast and coffee for breakfast. He had put off lunch with Sharon not because he was too busy but because he was hungry and wanted to eat immediately. He knew she wouldn't be eating for another two hours or more. He also wasn't so sure he wanted to rush into anything with her. Lunch once a week was plenty of togetherness for now.

He fixed himself a sandwich and ate, then, with not much else to do, took a nap to make up for his lost sleep. He managed to get only forty minutes in before his phone rang. It was Vogel calling him back.

Cliff told him the whole story with Mel, except, of course, for the part about him picking Mel up bodily and shoving him into the other seat.

"You told him about the overdoses?" Vogel said with alarm. "If he tells the FBI that's going to come out in the criminal prosecution. If our clients hear that our systems can be compromised this way – were compromised this way – we're doomed. I never authorized that."

"I didn't tell him anyone was overdosed. I just told him I suspected that was what Byrne was intending to do, and I showed him the photos. I didn't confirm those were Lilac patients. He drew his own conclusions."

"Still, that could let the whole thing out. This could be disastrous."

"I think you're exaggerating. Now we know that it was an intentional act by a saboteur – just what you told me when you hired me. Not a design flaw." Cliff realized he had exceeded his authority showing Mel the photos, but it had done the trick. He got the confession. Now it was time to control the damage.

"It was a flaw to design it in a way that it could be compromised. At least that's what plaintiff's counsel would argue. We could still be liable in theory. But our settlement agreements are ironclad and there won't be new cases. Liability isn't the issue. I'm worried about future sales."

"Look, it was bound to come out sooner or later. These doctors all go to the same conferences and the rad techs move from town to town changing employers. Eventually it had to become known to the whole radiology community but you'll have months or years of safe operation to show it's no longer a problem. At least now you can point out how you fixed it. It was the act of a crazed thief, a brazen saboteur. You've got spin doctors for that."

"Do we know if he still has that laptop? Maybe he could still do it. Or destroy the evidence."

"You've reinstalled all the systems with the new dongle, so he couldn't hurt anyone even if he has it. Mel said it was just the one laptop. I watched Satterlee walk them out of the building. Neither had any laptop in their hands when they left. Didn't the clinic lawyer say they were turning over copies of all the files? Did you check to see what's there?"

"I don't know what's been turned over yet. We'll have to have our software people review it. From what you say, the files are going to be in there at least from the one desktop machine, so even if we get them, it doesn't mean the company has the laptop in hand."

"I'm more concerned about Byrne's rifle, especially since it's likely to be pointed my direction. Did you read the email I forwarded? Saying I'm next?"

"Yes. Jesus. I'm sorry."

"Did they find anything useful yesterday? The police, I mean."

"They traced the path of the bullet from the window up through the false ceiling into the ductwork of the HVAC. They'd have to disassemble our heating system to find the bullet, and we refused to let them. They told me they were pretty sure it was a high-powered hunting rifle based on how far it penetrated and the distance."

"Did you or anyone else get a threat like the one I got?"

"No. No one's reported it to me anyway. The police said we should consider getting increased security, maybe armed guards."

"You can talk to your security provider about that. They all have armed guards on call. A lot of off-duty cops or retired agents do that. But it gets expensive, and a stalker can just avoid them. You can't afford to have them everywhere indefinitely. If he wants to try again, he'll just wait until the coast is clear."

"How about you? What are you doing about security?"

"I'm staying away from the office, and Los Altos P.D. is doing increased patrols around my house. Some of the local FBI agents know about it, too, and may be coming by."

"Do you carry a gun?"

"No. Just a GPS unit."

"GPS?"

"That's a joke. Never mind." Cliff didn't feel like explaining geocaching to Vogel.

"So how long until the FBI arrests him?"

"Maybe a year. Maybe never."

"What?!! I hope that's a joke, too."

"Calm down. The FBI only has a case of trade secret theft started, not murder, and they only just got it. They'll have to investigate it, take it to the U.S. Attorney's office. Someone there will review it and maybe authorize prosecution, or maybe not. If they do, then they present it to a grand jury and get an indictment. Since Byrne is represented by counsel, they'll first issue a target letter and give him a chance to come in and testify to the grand jury if he wants, but that's highly unlikely he'd do that. Then they'll probably give him a chance to come in and self-surrender. There's usually no arrest. That's just the way it works. The prosecutors are more concerned with making nice with the defense attorneys than giving the agents stats."

"How about making nice with the victims' attorneys?"

"You're not a party in the criminal case. You have almost zero rights, at least until sentencing. You won't be standing up in front of the judge. The defense attorneys will be screaming about constitutional violations, ethical breaches, yada, yada. The AUSA's do what they have to do."

"So Byrne will be free to hunt us all down for the next year? We can't do anything?"

"You're the one who didn't want me to report the overdosing to the FBI. They still don't know about it. Once they know there were killings, things will change. Violent crimes are a whole other ball of wax."

"Murder is a local crime. Will they tell the police about the overdoses? Of course, we still think the deaths were a result of the cancer."

Cliff noticed how the cause of death conveniently changed according to Vogel's and the company's best interest. "I'm going to do my damnedest to pin the shooting on Byrne. The police can work on that for now. The FBI knows about the email, too. They'll take this seriously and light a fire under the AUSA."

"I still wish you hadn't shown Wagner the photos."

"You'd better change your security procedures so the overdoses can't happen again. You should probably disable the remote access feature."

"I don't know how technically hard that would be to implement, but I don't think I could get that pushed through. It saves us tens of millions annually. We've cut the average time spent by a service rep by fifty percent per service ticket. Half the calls we get now can be diagnosed remotely and the service rep can direct the rad tech or engineer at the client's location to make some small adjustment, or try this or that. Not only that, but now these centers don't have to wait hours or even days for a rep to get there, so their up time is much greater and service costs are lower. It's been a huge selling factor."

"Well at least make the programs password protected."

"That's what the dongle is for. It's got a digital password hardwired into it, something incredibly long and totally unguessable."

"You're missing the point. You need a belt and suspenders. When the dongle is stolen, it doesn't matter how strong the encryption is. I'm talking about a password typed in manually by the operator. Something that's not carried in the bag or on a disk or in a note. Something he can remember but not easily guessed, like a long phrase with digits in it, too. If Byrne had had to enter a password by hand in addition to the dongle, this would never have happened."

"I never thought of that. You may be right. I'll talk to my software people. It doesn't sound that hard to do. If the overdoses become public we can say we've already implemented that measure, so no one can do it, even with a stolen laptop and dongle."

"And maybe you can actually prevent anyone else from getting hurt or killed. Don't you think that's a bit more important?"

"Of course. Of course. That too."

"I have to ask you something else. Do you think Byrne knew he could be killing patients with what he was doing? What kind of training do the service reps get?"

"I don't know. They get trained in the hazards of nuclear medicine, of course. They're well aware that the Lilacs are dangerous, but I doubt they ever see them in clinical use much and may not realize how much more dangerous they are when unmoderated by the DPP. It might be like driving and drinking. You hear all the time it's deadly, but so many people do it all the time with no trouble they think the rhetoric is exaggerated or doesn't apply to them. He could have thought he was just going to administer a little burn, enough to get the patient to change to a different clinic."

"I hope you're right. He'd have to be a cold bastard if he knew he was killing people."

"Well, he obviously knows he's shooting at his old boss. We've relocated the manager temporarily. His family, too. But we can't afford that forever. You've got to get this resolved with Byrne sooner than a year."

"Wait a minute. *I've* got to get it resolved? Why me? I didn't turn him into a homicidal maniac. He was fired this last time for hacking into the company personnel records and sowing dissent among the clinic workers. That had nothing to do with me. And he was angry at Xlectrix and his boss long before I was on the scene."

"But you're the one who exposed it to the clinic brass and that's what got him fired. I expected you to investigate the cause of the overdoses, not put targets on our backs."

"Obviously the targets were on your backs before you hired me. Byrne was zapping your patient base with fatal doses of radiation trying to ruin your company. And I did what you hired me to do – find out the cause. Something none of your engineers or anyone else at your company was able to do, I might add."

"And I'm grateful for that. But he wasn't shooting at us until you went overboard."

"Went overboard! Jesus Christ! I solved the case. Now, he appears to be gunning for me, too. Are you going to relocate me?"

"You're not our employee. We hire people like you to protect us in situations like this, not the other way around."

"Thanks for nothing."

Vogel started to respond, but Cliff hung up on him mid-sentence.

He needed to blow off steam, he decided. He changed into his running clothes and headed out to the park, forgetting to look around for Byrne when he left his house.

He parked at the main lot at the same park where he had helped Ashley and Ellen with the geocache. He started running hard at first, expending the nervous energy he had built up. It felt good, but he soon got winded and slowed down.

Settling into a jog he approached the demonstration farm where goats and other animals are raised to show schoolchildren the agricultural heritage of the valley. Six miles later he was totally drained and thoroughly relaxed, bathed in endorphins to the point of nirvana. All the cares of the world had melted away.

He drove home, passing a police cruiser on his block, showered and changed clothes, and popped open a beer. He had just sat down in his recliner wanting to think about nothing at all when his doorbell rang. On instant alert, he moved from the family room to a bedroom from which he could see who was on his porch. It was Ellen Kennedy. She had rung the bell four times with no response, and was turning to leave, when Cliff rapped on the window and motioned for her to stay there. He went to the entry hall and opened the front door.

Ellen greeted him with a question. "Cliff, what the hell did you do?"

Puzzled, he hesitated before replying simply, "Come in." He stepped back.

Ellen stepped inside. Seeing his look, she continued, "Wagner's lawyer just called me. He wants to set up a meeting with me and the AUSA. He says Wagner's ready to cooperate fully and testify against Byrne."

"That's great, Ellen," he replied tentatively. He could tell there was another shoe to drop.

"That's the fastest I've ever solved a case. But what's this about killing people?" She gave him a stern look.

"Why? What did he tell you?"

"The question is, what aren't you telling me?"

"Ellen, come on, you know I'm bound by attorney-client privilege."

"Then let me make it easy for you. The lawyer said Byrne copied Crabbe's hard drive, then when he couldn't access the encrypted files, ordered Wagner to steal the dongle that decrypted it all. That's the part Mel knew about. Then, apparently, Byrne remotely accessed some Lilacs belonging to competing radiology clinics and caused them to overdose patients in order to drive business to the Fremont facility. The lawyer insists Mel knew nothing about this until yesterday when 'an investigator for Xlectrix' showed him some pictures of dead patients. That was you, I'm sure. Are you going to deny it?"

Cliff nodded throughout the recitation. "I can't confirm it, but I'm not denying it."

"And that's how Ashley got overdosed, isn't it?" She glowered at him.

He realized he was still standing in the entryway with a beer in his hand. "Come on, let's sit down. Would you like something to drink?"

"I didn't come here for a drink. I'm on duty." She followed him to the living room and accepted the invitation to sit down. "So are you going to tell me the whole story? If this is a murder case instead of a white collar crime the AUSA needs to know right away."

"You don't need me to confirm what Mel told you. Get Byrne's laptop and the documents from the clinic they took off of it. But I swear I didn't know Ashley or any other patient was being targeted. I had my suspicions, but it could have been a software glitch, a design problem, or something else. If I had known for sure Byrne, or anyone, was intentionally overdosing patients I would have taken action to stop it. I did try to stop it in fact, even without knowing the cause."

"Did some patients die from overdoses?"

"All I can say is probably, but that could be hard to prove beyond a reasonable doubt, which is what you'd need for a criminal case. Lilac patients have cancer; when they die soon after treatment, they usually die from cancer. If I were you, though, I'd leverage that in talking to Mel's lawyer. If they're worried about him going to prison or even get a death sentence for murder, the lawyer'd probably get him to agree to almost anything. No one's talked to Byrne yet since he got fired. He got fired for hacking into the payroll records, not for overdosing anyone. If anyone was overdosed – and I'm not saying anyone was – Byrne would assume no one else knows he did it. Have Mel wear a wire and meet with him to ask what he should do if anyone questions him."

"You told me you got a death threat email and there's that shot through the Xlectrix window. It now looks like Byrne is on a murderous revenge binge. I don't think I could put a civilian through that kind of risk."

"At least do consensual monitoring. Mel can call on the phone if that's what you're worried about."

"Thanks for telling me how to run my case. Would you like me to tell you how to run your business?"

He liked her independent spirit, even if her anger was directed at him. He would have reacted the same way in her position.

"Point taken. Sorry. But I'm the one with a death threat on my head. I have a right to want to get this over with, and quickly. Look, I can't tell you certain things, but I have a right to self-preservation. I can tell you this much. I have reason to believe Byrne has killed before and is fully capable of doing it again. I'm legitimately in fear for my life. More than I ever was when I was an FBI agent."

The scowl left Ellen's face at this. She knew that this was enough for her to get the Assistant U.S. Attorney to authorize search warrants and indictment on the trade secret theft. It might not be enough to arrest Byrne yet, but she could probably get the AUSA to cut Mel a deal if he knew that he'd get a murderer handed to him on a platter. Mel and his lawyer would first have to convince her and the AUSA that he really didn't know about the overdosing, of course. She had achieved her goal, for now at least, and, satisfied, finally smiled briefly at Cliff.

He noticed for the first time that she was letting her hair grow out. She no longer had that masculine look, but it wasn't just the hair. It took him a moment to place what it was. She'd had those Leonid Brezhnev eyebrows plucked! It gave her face a whole new look. Maybe Theresa inspired a bit of vanity in her.

"All right, I have to go," she said. "I'm sorry about the threat to your life. I know several of us from the R.A. have done some drive-by's here. I just hope you weren't too rough with Mel. If you forced a confession out of him and it gets attributed to us, we could lose all the evidence."

Cliff smiled back at her. "Let me know how it goes with Mel's interview. When is that going to be?"

"We've set it for tomorrow with the AUSA." After a beat she returned a wicked scowl. "I'll let you know, all right – like you've let me know how your investigation has gone."

He managed a wan smile. "Rules are rules."

"Exactly. Rules are rules." She stood up and left.

Chapter 34

After Ellen left, Cliff thought he'd had enough action for one day, but Sharon Perry called him at 5:30 and said there had been big developments in the civil case.

"I'm all ears," he told her.

"Look, I'm on my way out of the office. Can I stop by on my way home? I have some stuff to show you. If I stick around here, I'll get trapped in a management committee meeting."

"I guess that would be all right. Where do you live?"

"Does it matter?" she said coyly. "The question is where do you live?'

He gave her his address and she said she'd be there in a half hour. They hung up. Cliff was exhausted. The early morning expedition to the East Bay and the long run had taken its toll. The nap had helped, but forty minutes wasn't enough and the beer hadn't helped, either. Still, it sounded like the civil case could be winding up and he was anxious to hear what happened.

It took her forty-five minutes to go the fifteen miles from the Herrick offices to Cliff's house, Bay Area commute traffic being what it was. When she arrived Cliff opened the door without checking through the bedroom window as he had done with Ellen. He was just too tired to be paranoid, and, anyway, he was expecting her.

"Cliff," Sharon gushed, "we have some celebrating to do." She held up a bottle of champagne and stepped inside without waiting for the invitation. "Sorry I'm late. The police pulled me over just a few houses down the block. I guess they're taking this threat thing seriously."

Mixed feelings flowed through Cliff's system. It sounded like the civil suit was going to end well for his client, which was good news for him, but he just wasn't in the mood to sit and drink champagne with Sharon right now. Still, he didn't want to be rude and he definitely wanted to hear the developments.

"I'll get some glasses." He gestured to the living room for her to find a seat while he went to the kitchen. She sat on the sofa. He returned with two wine glasses. He didn't have champagne glasses. She handed him the bottle to open.

As he peeled off the foil he asked, "So is the civil suit settled?"

"No, I haven't heard from Byrne's lawyer, but I'm not worried about that right now. I have better news."

Cliff dislodged the cork and poured. He had no intention of finishing his glass. He didn't even like champagne, but he could sip at it as necessary to fake enthusiasm. "What?" was all he could think to say.

"The Fremont Radiology Group. Their lawyer called and said they want to settle any and all claims stemming from whatever Byrne may have done. They've dropped their demand for discounted services and offered to buy a Lilac 4 at full price – no haggling – and a five-year service contract. Of course they want a release from any claims. Roger is delighted. He has to clear it with the V.P. of sales and a couple of other people, but the deal should be wrapped up by tomorrow morning." She raised her glass.

Cliff clinked his with hers. "That's great. Is he returning all the original materials Byrne took – deleting all the files?"

"No, that's the funny thing. He's offered to delete all the files on Byrne's computers. Our people can watch and verify that the disk is reformatted and so on. But he doesn't want to give us a copy of what was on that. The initial materials he gave us had a copy of the desktop computer in the engineering section, but he hasn't turned over the clone of the laptop disk. He says it's just the same stuff as on the other computer."

Cliff realized immediately what this meant. Mel or his attorney must have told the clinic about Byrne's possible overdosing competitors' patients in order to increase business. They weren't about to admit that their employee did such a thing, or provide anyone with evidence of it. That would look like it was at the partners' direction and could lead to huge civil liability, not to mention criminal prosecution or yanking of their medical licenses. He'd be willing to bet they found evidence of that activity on the laptop. Still, Vogel hadn't authorized him to tell Sharon about the overdoses so he said nothing about it.

"Interesting. Maybe he's trying to conceal something there, something that makes them look liable. Maybe there's something that got stolen from another company."

"Come on, drink up. What's the matter, you don't like champagne?" Sharon held her near-empty glass up again. Cliff's sat untouched.

"It's just been one helluva day, Sharon. I'm sorry if I'm not very good company. I was up at 4:30 this morning so I could get on station at Mel's house this morning, then the whole business with Mel, then briefing you and Vogel, then I did a long run. On top of that I've been looking over my shoulder for an assassin all day. I'm just plain beat."

"Poor boy," she cooed. "It sounds like you could use some comforting."

She wasn't getting the hint. "Let's save the comforting for some other time when I can really enjoy it. How about if you put this champagne in the fridge for now and I'll take a rain check." He tried to convey a certain lustfulness in his voice, but wasn't sure he'd pulled it off.

"No problem, Cliff. I should have thought about the long day you put in before barging in here. That's terrific work you did today. I mean it. So much better than our usual investigator."

This piqued Cliff's interest. If he could secure the business of a big firm like Herrick, it would be a major boost to his income. "Who do you usually use?"

"Holden Boulter. He's ex-FBI, too."

"Boulter?! You've got to be kidding. He couldn't find porn on the Internet." Holden Boulter was a supervisor who had retired about five years before Cliff had. He was one of many who got promoted for no other reason than he drank with the front office brass. In addition to being lazy and never around, he'd been a terrible investigator and couldn't write a grammatical sentence to save his life. He'd been known around the office as Hobo, and it wasn't just a play on his name. Cliff had no idea how he'd gotten his P.I. license, much less gotten a major law firm as a client.

"My my. A little professional jealousy?" she teased.

"Hardly. How did you find him? He must be a drinking buddy with one of your partners."

"Golfing buddy, actually, if I remember right."

Ah, golf. They always say the real business gets done on the golf course. Boulter was a good golfer, Cliff remembered. Maybe he should take up golf, too, instead of geocaching. Naw. Geocaching was more fun.

"Anyway," Sharon continued, "I'll let you get some rest. I really am sorry for being too presumptuous." She rose to go.

"Not at all. Your timing just isn't the best." He walked her to the door. In the entryway he put his hands on her shoulders, intending to give her a warm hug, but she turned to face him, closed her eyes, and puckered her lips. He realized there was no polite way to avoid kissing her, so he bent his head and their lips met. She wrapped her arms around him and pulled him close.

"Are you sure you don't want that comforting?"

"Another day. Or night."

She smiled and let loose from the embrace. "Another night then. I'll save the champagne." She turned the doorknob and stepped out onto the porch. He stepped out with her, watched her walk down the walk to her car, and smiled weakly when she gave him a little wave as she pulled away from the curb.

Chapter 35

Cliff woke the next morning with a sense of accomplishment and satisfaction for solving the mystery, but it was tempered by the realization that the situation was far from resolved. Byrne, a killer, was still out there and even more enraged and desperate than before.

He got up and made his way to the kitchen where he fixed himself a small breakfast – half a bran muffin, juice, coffee and some strawberries. He was trying to be virtuous with his diet after the excesses of the past few days.

When he came out of the shower he found his answering machine was beeping. He was at first surprised anyone would call so early, but then he looked at his watch and realized it was after 9:00. He was normally in the office by this time, but he had slept late to make up for yesterday's early rise, and because he wasn't planning to go into the office. He dressed in jeans and a tee shirt and then went to the phone to play the message.

It was Ellen asking him to call right away. There was a distinct urgency in her voice. He dialed her number. She picked up immediately.

"Cliff, I have some bad news."

"Shoot."

"That's a bad choice of words. I got a call from the lawyer representing the Fremont radiology clinic. There was a break-in there last night. Byrne's laptop was taken from Satterlee's desk. There goes our search warrant justification, at least until we can find out where it is."

"That should increase your probable cause to search his house."

"Maybe, but do you really think he would steal it and keep it at home? We have PC to search his home anyway, but I don't really expect to find it there. It's probably at the bottom of the Bay or melted into slag by now."

"Okay, so you've got an evidentiary problem for the moment, but you still have Mel, and I'd be willing to bet whoever did the examination of Byrne's computer for the clinic knows what's on it. He or she can testify. Just find out who it was."

"That's the real reason I'm calling. I already know who it was. It was the regular IT guy for the clinic, someone named Garcia. But he can't testify."

"Why not?"

"He's dead. Shot through the head last night in his driveway. It was a rifle round. Whoever did it is quite the marksman. I think Byrne is out to eliminate the evidence against him. I'm calling to tell you that the death threat against you should be taken very seriously."

"I was taking it seriously."

"Well, take it more seriously. Are your curtains open?"

"Yes."

"Close them, and don't stand in front of the windows when you do. I recommend you don't go outside until we can get you an armed escort. Then you should find another place to stay. Does he know where you live?"

"I would assume so. He knows how to type my name into a search engine. My address would be one click and fifteen dollars away. I appreciate the warning, but I can't stay away from work and home indefinitely. Isn't this enough to get an arrest warrant for him?"

"For the trade secret theft, yes. For murder, probably not, at least not yet, which means even if we find him he won't stay behind bars for long. You'll still be at risk. Do you have another place to stay?"

"I don't have any relatives around here and he already knows where my office is, I assume. I stopped going there. I could find a motel somewhere. I can afford that for a while anyway."

"Do you or the lawyer have a copy of the hard drive from the laptop? Don't you do civil discovery?"

"Herrick, that's the law firm representing Xlectrix, got a big pile of discovery, including a ton of computer files. I don't know what's on them. I could go through them and see, but I think they only got the files from the desktop computer, not the laptop."

"Okay, that's something at least. Will they turn them over or are they going to claim attorney work product privilege?"

"If it means getting Byrne arrested for murder – and keeping him from hunting me down – they damn well better not refuse to turn them over."

"Can you work from there?"

"Probably. I'll contact Shar…, uh, the lawyer handling the case, to see if they'll let me set up there. I should probably stay away from Xlectrix, too, considering the shot that was taken there."

"Okay, good. I'll coordinate with Los Altos P.D. and Palo Alto P.D. so they can alert their patrol people to this latest development. Until we get Byrne locked up, you, the company people, and maybe the lawyer at Herrick could all be at risk."

"Okay. So is someone coming over here or what?"

"Yes, Matt's on his way right now with another agent. They'll make sure you get out of there safely."

"I really appreciate that. I'd better pack some stuff, then."

"Okay, I'll let you go. Stay safe."

"That's my plan."

After they hung up Cliff dug out a suitcase and packed it with a minimal supply of clothes, shaving kit and toiletries. His smart phone would suffice for a computer for now. He was still packing when the doorbell rang.

He went to the front door, stood to the side and asked who it was. Matt Nguyen yelled back that it was him. Cliff opened the door. In the cul-de-sac, idling at the curb were two Bureau cars. Dave Warner, the Arabic-speaking agent, was at the wheel of one. The other was obviously Matt's. Beyond them a Los Altos P.D. patrol car cruised the through street beyond.

They exchanged handshakes and the usual greetings. Cliff finished his packing and told Matt he would be backing his rental car out of the garage. Matt said they'd escort him out until he was away from the neighborhood and they were sure no one was following him. Then he'd be on his own.

Cliff made sure the house was locked up and emailed his neighbor asking her to pick up his mail for a few days. She'd accommodated him in that way several times in the past. Then he headed to the garage and backed out as planned.

When they got a mile or so from his house the patrol car peeled away into the left turn lane. Cliff waved his thanks at the officers who returned a thumbs up. Cliff drove to the rental car company, Matt and Warner still behind. There, he told them he was going to exchange his rental car for something else just in case Byrne had seen this one when he served the subpoenas. His own car was still in the upholstery shop. Matt told him he had to get back, and another round of thanks took place.

Cliff rented a big SUV with plenty of power. He wanted something more substantial and taller, with better visibility, now that he was a target. His insurance, which was paying for the first car while the vandalized Volvo was being repaired, wouldn't cover the more expensive vehicle entirely, but this was no time to stint. Vogel had said they wouldn't pay to relocate him, but this was damn well going on his next bill. They could argue about the money later.

He drove directly to the Herrick offices and was promptly ushered into Sharon's office. She was in court, but the two associates he'd met earlier came in to greet him and give him congratulations on solving the case. He explained that there was still a lot of work to do and he was there to review the discovery that had been turned over. Apparently they had already been doing that and they briefed him on what they'd found among the documents.

They told him they had found a gold mine of trade secret theft information: the Tech Tips and IP chart as expected, but also customer lists and the internal operations manual for the Lilac 4, all normally encrypted with the dongle and marked as "Xlectrix Company confidential, Do not copy." These were in paper form, but they were not a photocopy of the Xlectrix version. It was now obvious that these had been brought up on the screen, photographed, then the photos had been printed, the edges cut off where the Xlectrix warnings were, then scanned with optical character recognition software. Voila! Brand new documents containing the Xlectrix text had been created with a new format, and the evidence of Xlectrix ownership expunged. Byrne and his receptionist had been busy little beavers. They told him Sharon considered the counterclaim against Byrne a slam dunk.

Cliff asked them if they had examined the cloned hard drive of the desktop computer that Byrne used. He knew that had been turned over, although he would have preferred a clone of Byrne's laptop. They said they had not. He suggested that he do that while they work on the paper documents. One of them showed him the computer that now housed the cloned drive and set him up a workspace there.

He told them he'd be fine and to go on back to whatever it was they were supposed to be doing. They had said nothing about the shooting at Xlectrix, the death threat email Cliff had received, or the murder of the clinic IT guy Garcia. He assumed they hadn't heard about any of that and decided not to mention it now. It would only make them paranoid and he didn't think they were at any risk. Also, he didn't want them around while he examined the computer. They still didn't know about the overdoses, either, he assumed, and Vogel wanted that kept under wraps.

Once alone, he booted up the cloned computer and began to examine it. He didn't really care about the trade secrets. They already had more than enough evidence of that, and with the clinic making its settlement with Xlectrix, the suit against Byrne would never result in collectible damages. Byrne was broke – judgment-proof, in the legal jargon. Cliff mainly wanted some evidence that Byrne had used the computer to access the Lilacs at competitors' locations.

He wasn't a computer expert and wasn't sure exactly how that would be done. Maybe through an FTP client or, more likely, through the Lilac operations program itself. Since he didn't know how to use either, he decided instead to start with the browser. The Firefox icon was prominent on the desktop, so he double-clicked that. When it came up he clicked on the Most Visited button. At the top of the list was Byrne's Gmail Inbox. Then came Google, then Bing.

The fourth website was the one that caught Cliff's eye. He clicked on the link. It was a blog by a Canadian "pastor" about Positive Christianity, the religion Sharon had told him Byrne followed. Although it avoided overt hate language, it was remarkably foul stuff. The writer, who used the name Oberherr Franz, explained how positive Christianity was non-denominational, but enveloped the principles of all the Christian denominations, which, he explained further, were devoted to acting for the common good, as opposed to the evil "self-good" motives of the Jewish religion. He made clear that Christ was an Aryan, not a Jew, and lauded Adolf Hitler's many fine points. Cliff had never heard of this guy, but it was evident that he was an older male who was something of a leader in the movement, at least in North America

Much of the blog was not much different from that of any other blogger, recounting his day-to-day travels and problems. He railed against various stores when he felt he was treated badly by a clerk or cheated in some way, and railed even more at Canadian government agencies. Fascinated, Cliff read further. As he did so, he noted that two months earlier Franz mentioned that he had had to travel to California to get the medical treatment he needed since the Canadian system had put him on a wait list. He was staying with a "disciple" there. He regretted that he could not give a more specific location as "Jewish hate groups" would hunt him down and drive him from his doctors if they knew where he was. He bragged that he had fooled the incompetent American bureaucracy by driving across the border, ostensibly to shop for a day, but kept on driving until he got to California. Cliff reread the later posts. There was no mention of him returning to Canada. Could he still be in California? Could Byrne even be the "disciple?"

Some passages Cliff had read earlier rung a bell with him. He reread one blog entry, a quite recent one, about being assigned a doctor from an inferior non-Aryan race and complaining about the lack of Aryan doctors at the hospital. But, Franz explained, the doctor was from India, and despite their dark skin, since Indians are actually Caucasians, he deemed this acceptable. He mentioned how he had strolled the nearby campus and how the beautiful rolling hills reminded him of the Weinstrasse region of the Fuhrer's native Austria. Cliff looked up that region to get an idea of the geography.

When he had first read it, Cliff had assumed this hospital was somewhere in Canada, but now that he knew Franz was in California, it sounded like it could be Stanford. A hospital near a campus and rolling hills, with many non-Aryan doctors. Stanford Medical Center fit the bill, but probably several other places in California did, too. UCLA was certainly hilly enough, but was too urban and also too dry, being situated in the Westwood area of Los Angeles. USC had a medical school, but Cliff hadn't been there. He thought it, too, was too urban to meet the description. UC San Francisco had a major medical school with cutting edge research, but that was another one in an urban environment, not far from San Francisco Bay. Cliff thought a blogger would more likely comment on the ocean or bay scenery than rolling hills if that was his location. There were certainly many other hospitals near hills, and it was not clear that the campus was connected with the hospital other than being "nearby," but Cliff's gut instinct told him the dear Oberherr was getting treated at Stanford where many specialists practiced the newest forms of medicine.

How many "disciples" of a fringe cult leader from Canada could live within commuting distance of Stanford? Byrne's frequent use of this website certainly made him a prime candidate for that role. Cliff went from the blog to the website's main page. He found a Gallery section that showed photos. Many were of Nazi parades, Hitler saluting, a cross with a red and black swastika on it. There were even several of Oberherr Franz, but he was very young in the pictures. In one he had a Hitler mustache. In another he was working on a farm somewhere in Germany as part of an exchange program, if the caption was accurate. He was a scrawny youth with a pinched nose, tousled blond hair, high cheekbones, and piercing blue eyes. He would have been quite handsome had it not been for bad acne, but perhaps that had cleared up long ago. The man had to be at least in his sixties now based on the date of the photo.

Cliff tired of this, but figured he should find a way to get this information to the FBI. It was relevant to the original discrimination claim that cited religion as a grounds, giving him a possible revenge motive for the trade secret theft, and didn't give away anything about the radiation overdoses, so Cliff saw no reason why Vogel would object. Cliff moved on to examining the rest of the cloned drive, but nothing pointed to it having been used to access other Lilacs, at least nothing he could spot with his skill set. He knew it needed the FBI or a forensic evidence firm to do a thorough job. He would have to discuss that with Sharon and Vogel.

As if on cue, Sharon walked in, back from court. She smiled brightly on seeing him. She refrained from any display of affection since they were in a work area with glass walls, visible to the rest of the office. He explained that he had been examining the drive and further described what he had found. She was interested and agreed that the information on the Oberherr Franz site should be shared with the FBI, if Vogel was okay with that, but said it would hurt their case if they volunteered it. It might look like they were agents of the FBI, or using government influence.

"Now, if the FBI were to send us a letter asking us to turn it over and it said they'd have a grand jury subpoena issued if we refused, then I'd have no choice but to turn it over." She gave him an exaggerated sitcom wink as she said this.

"Fine," Cliff replied, not bothering to continue the charade. He looked around to see if anyone else was within earshot. "Did you hear about the killing?"

Sharon looked at him, perplexed. "What killing?"

"The IT guy over at the Fremont clinic. A guy named Garcia. He must have been the one who copied this hard drive. No doubt he examined what was on it, too, but I think whatever he saw on the laptop is what got him killed."

"You think Byrne killed him? For exposing the fact he had hacked into the doctors' pay information?"

Cliff realized he had made a tactical error. Sharon still didn't know about the radiation overdoses. It was the evidence of murder – the overdoses – that probably got him killed, but Sharon's suggestion made sense based on what she knew. He decided to play along. "Well, that's what got him fired. And there was that rifle shot at Byrne's old boss at Xlectrix. I got a threatening email, too. It's got to be Byrne, out for revenge."

"Omigod, omigod. This is for real. You think he could be coming for me?"

"It's possible, but I think he blames me, not you. He hasn't threatened you, has he?"

"No."

"Well, he's ultra-conservative. Maybe he doesn't believe in attacking a woman."

Sharon sat down heavily and the flush of fear colored her neck and cheeks. Beads of sweat appeared on her forehead. She said nothing for a minute.

"What are you going to do, Cliff?"

"For now I'm going to stay at a motel and stay away from my office and house. With this latest killing I have to believe the Bureau or the police will have enough to arrest Byrne. Until then, I thought I'd use this as my base of operations. Byrne might be looking for me at Xlectrix, so I don't want to go there."

"You want to work here?" The doubt in her voice fell heavily on Cliff's ears.

"Of course. You don't mind do you? You've got the space and the evidence I'm reviewing is here, too." He couldn't keep the anger from his voice as he saw her hesitation grow.

"Well… it's just that … I'd have to check with the partners. I'm not sure they'd agree if there's a gunman out after you. They have to worry about the personnel here." She made eye contact with him, barely, but was now blushing profusely.

"You're a partner, aren't you?"

"Yes, of course. And if it were up to me, you know I'd say fine, but I do have to check with them." For a trial lawyer she was surprisingly unconvincing.

"I can't do my job holed up in a motel." There was now an accusatory tinge in his voice.

"You were in the FBI. Aren't you used to this sort of thing? I mean, you carried a gun and locked up murderers and all. Can't you go after him or something?"

"I've never had anyone stalking me, an expert shot with a hunting rifle, no less. I've never been shot at and now I don't carry a gun or wear a protective vest. Look, that heroic bravado bullshit you see on TV is just that – total crap. Medals for heroism are usually given posthumously. No thank you. I'll let the FBI SWAT team handle that duty. They live for that kind of shit."

His voice level had risen to a point where others in the office were noticing. A largish male associate came over and gave Cliff a stern glance. "Are you okay, Sharon?" he asked.

"I'm fine. I'm fine. Leave us alone. We're just having a spirited discussion."

The man left but Cliff could see he was hanging out in the nearest hallway within easy shouting range.

"Cliff, I'm so sorry. This is not what I meant to happen. I think I can get it cleared, really, but for now, why don't you stay away from here. Just a couple of days until the weekly management meeting. I'll let you know then."

He stared down at her in disgust and shook his head. "Okay, if that's the way you want it. See you around." He turned on his heel and stormed out, without looking back to see if she made any further effort to remonstrate with him.

When he got out to the parking lot he was confused for a few moments. He couldn't find his rental car at first. Then he remembered he'd traded it in for the SUV. He drove to a nearby extended stay motel and checked in. This was going to get expensive fast and he had no idea whether Vogel would pay for his "travel." He was in a black mood as he unpacked what little he had.

He wanted to know what was going on with the FBI case. As he had told Sharon, he felt they should have enough to arrest Byrne now. He called Ellen, but only got her voice mail. Rather than leave a message, he hung up and called Matt. Matt picked up.

"Matt, I want to thank you again for this morning, for escorting me out."

"No problem."

"It meant a lot. Anyway, I need to talk to Ellen. Is she there?"

"Ellen's over at the U.S. Attorney's office getting a search warrant for Byrne's place."

"An arrest warrant, too, I hope?"

"I think she's pushing for it, but she wasn't hopeful about that. There's enough for the trade secret theft, she said, but they don't authorize arrest, as you know. This latest shooting... if she can convince the AUSA she has enough probable cause that it was Byrne, well, then she should be able to get a warrant for obstruction of justice at least, then maybe an arrest warrant. She said the problem was that Byrne never had any criminal record beyond some traffic tickets in Idaho. No violence. Motive, yes, but that's all."

"Look, I've got more information. Byrne has killed before."

"Seriously? You know this how?"

"Well, it was privileged information I couldn't give you before, but screw that. It's my own life on the line. He's a murderer, multiple murderer. I'll lay it all out, but Ellen needs to know before she leaves. She needs an arrest warrant for a murder case to keep Byrne locked up."

"You call her. There's no point in me relaying it." Nguyen gave him her cell phone number. "Hey, do you need a vest? I'm sure we can find a spare around here."

"I'm tempted to say yes, but if Byrne kills by a bullet in the head a vest isn't going to do much good. And you know how uncomfortable the heavy-duty ones are. What I could use, though, is some place to hang out and do my work. I got kicked out of Herrick, and Xlectrix and my house are both off limits for now, too. I need to see Ellen anyway."

"Just come on over here. I'll clear it with the supervisor. Like I said, you're still Bureau family. You should still consider that vest, too. You know head shots are rare because they're so difficult. We're taught to shoot center of mass for a reason."

"Much appreciated. I'll be over there in about a half hour."

"See you then."

He decided to stop by his house to get a few more things. Since he couldn't use the computers at Herrick, he needed his laptop. The FBI computers were for internal use only. They might let him hang out there at a desk, but not use their own intranet. He also figured he was going to be without any evidence to review for at least the next two days, but he was still going to need to stay current on his email, keep Maeva informed, and generally tend to business. He could do most of that from the hotel, but more importantly, he wanted to be at the FBI office because he knew he'd be able to overhear – or even be consulted with about – any developments in the case.

He called Ellen's cell. She answered with a curt "Yeah?"

"Ellen it's Cliff. I need to talk to you. Byrne's a murderer. You need to arrest him for that, not a white collar crime."

"I believe you but we don't have PC to tie him to the Garcia killing yet." Cliff could tell from the sound of her voice that she was in the car and using Bluetooth.

"Not him. Well, yeah, him, too. But he's killed before."

"He has no record."

"It's what I couldn't tell you before. Privileged information."

"Swell, now you tell me," she said caustically. "I'm almost back to Palo Alto. The AUSA would only authorize a search warrant, but he said if Byrne gave us any guff to arrest him for obstruction."

"'Guff?' Like shooting you through the head?"

"Yeah, that kind of guff. Look, I'm getting off the freeway. I can't talk right now. Can you come by the RA?"

"I'm already planning to. Matt said I could hang out there for now. I'll be over there as soon as I can."

"Okay, bye." She was off the line.

He drove back to the area near his house, but stayed two blocks away and cruised around, looking for any suspicious vehicle or person on the street. After his second pass around the area he saw a patrol car pull behind him, flashing its lights. He pulled over and the officers pulled up behind him, vehicle at an angle. Two officers got out, hands on guns, and approached his car, one on each side.

"Step out of the car empty-handed," the closest one ordered, thumping the left rear bumper.

He complied. "I'm Cliff Knowles, the reason you're patrolling here." He stood in the street, hands empty, fingers splayed so the officer could see them.

"Driver's License," the officer commanded, watching Cliff's hands, not his face.

Cliff gently reached his rear pocket and pulled out his wallet. He opened it, extracted the license and held it out to the officer. The officer examined it carefully while the other one kept his hand on his gun butt and never took his eyes off Cliff.

"Thank you Mr. Knowles," the first officer said with a hint of deference. "I'm sorry, but we were told you'd be driving a Volvo C70 or a rented Ford sedan."

"The Volvo's in the shop and I swapped the Ford for this GMC because I thought that Byrne might know what the Ford looked like."

"I'll update the other officers. Thanks for letting us know. We were told you had moved to another location. Why are you here now?"

"I need to go back to my house to get more stuff. I wanted to check out the area myself to make sure it was safe before going in."

"We'll escort you."

They drove around his block and into his cul-de-sac while he waited two blocks away. They came back and said things looked clear. They then led him back there and idled at the entrance to the cul-de-sac while he drove into his garage. He packed up some more clothes, including running clothes, the novel he was reading, his laptop, his GPS unit, his reading glasses and few of his favorite snacks for the motel fridge. It all went into a cardboard box and that was loaded into the SUV. The officers were still waiting when he came out. He drove away, waving at this pair as he had at the officers this morning. In twenty minutes he was at the door to the Palo Alto Resident Agency of the FBI. Ellen was already there.

"Cliff, how are you holding up?" she asked, genuine concern in her voice.

"So far so good. Except Xlectrix and Herrick have both made me *persona non grata.*"

"Well, you're *grata* here. But I have some bad news for you."

"What now?" he asked with an air of resignation.

"I got a call from Mel's lawyer. Mel's in the wind. It looks like Byrne scared him off. He must have heard about Garcia getting killed."

"Is he in hiding? Coming back?"

"The lawyer didn't know."

"So now the laptop is gone, the guy who examined it is dead, and Mel, your cooperating witness, has disappeared. I guess that puts me next on the hit list."

"Cliff, we've got a search warrant now for the Fremont clinic and Byrne's house. I'm sure we'll get what we need for the trade secret case, but what's this about him killing before? We need to know for our own safety – and yours. We don't have an arrest warrant yet, but we may be able to arrest him on the spot if he's there and we get the PC."

Cliff laid out the whole story for her from beginning to end. Matt Nguyen joined them in the middle. It took over a half hour. When it was over, Ellen and Matt exchanged looks that told Cliff they finally realized this was more serious than they had thought – a lot more serious.

"Why didn't you tell us this before?" Ellen asked.

"I couldn't. It was attorney-client privileged. And I didn't know the overdoses were intentional criminal acts until last week. By then the danger had passed since all the vulnerable Lilacs had been updated with reinstalled software. No one was at risk."

"So what's changed?" Matt asked.

"Now I'm at risk. The hell with Vogel. My life is on the line. The ethics rules allow breaking privilege where human life is at risk, anyway. I might lose a client, but I won't be disbarred."

"So that's why the laptop is so damaging," Ellen commented. "He's not worried about the evidence of trade secret theft. He was worried about whatever digital traces were there to show what he'd been doing logging onto the competitors' Lilacs."

"We still have no direct evidence that Byrne accessed those Lilacs," Nguyen replied. "Or even that the overdoses weren't just malfunctions of the machines or their software."

"Oh, come on," Cliff shot back. "You don't believe that. It had to be Byrne. He had the motive – fifty thou worth of motive, plus the revenge factor against Xlectrix. He commented to Mel about the post from ConcernedRelative, trying to spread the word about the Lilac 4."

"I agree, Cliff, but I'm just saying we don't have enough proof yet. We need to move fast and execute the search warrants before he has a chance to destroy any more evidence. There could be something in his house that ties him to those deaths – the overdoses or Garcia's murder."

"You could be walking into a death trap, Matt. He's a crack shot and proven his willingness to use violence."

"That brings up another problem," Ellen broke in. "We don't have a good photo of Byrne. He doesn't have a California driver's license. We need to be able to recognize him – for our own safety as Cliff said."

"You're kidding," Matt responded. "Is he still using one from Idaho?"

"Yes, but I can't get a photo from them on short notice the way I could from California DMV."

"I'll call over to Xlectrix," Cliff offered. "They probably have a photo, for their security badge system." He called even as he spoke. He got Vogel's secretary who put him on hold to find out whether they still had a photo. After a minute she came back to tell him that they had deleted his record from the security system after he got laid off. He relayed the information to Ellen and Matt.

"Cliff," Ellen said, "you can identify him. Can you come with us for the search warrant? You also know a lot more about this case than we do. You can help identify Xlectrix intellectual property."

"Sure, I can help. But I'm not armed and not an agent any longer."

"We'll secure the scene first, you know that. I'll go ask the Supe if we can get SWAT for this." Ellen went into the supervisor's office. It took her several minutes to explain the new developments. She emerged and said the supervisor called the ASAC, but it turned out the number one SWAT team was in Bakersfield in a SWAT competition.

"He said to take Dave Warner and anyone else we can round up. He agrees we need to move fast on this before Byrne can destroy any more evidence. Let's go do it."

"I'll call Gina," Matt said. "I know two of her guys are SWAT alternates. They work violent crime and have the MP5's and shotguns." He made the call to his wife in San Jose and she took only two minutes to tell him he could have Woody Braswell, the same agent who had helped Cliff at the bank robbery. She also said she had an extra protective vest for Cliff.

It took another forty minutes of working out the logistics and briefing the AUSA. The prosecutor said they didn't have enough to arrest Byrne for the killings, but he gave Ellen the authority to arrest him on sight for the trade secret theft. There was no warrant yet, but enough probable cause for the arrest to hold up. That would at least get him off the street long enough to find evidence of the violent crimes and get him held longer. In the meantime, he'd try to find a federal statute that covered murder by Internet.

They ended up with eight agents. Four were designated to search the Fremont clinic. The other four – Ellen, Matt, Warner, and Braswell would execute the search warrant at Byrne's residence. Warner and

Braswell were both ex-SWAT. Cliff was to go with the four to the residence and help them identify Xlectrix property or any evidence of the overdoses, and, of course, Byrne.

They headed out from Palo Alto in three cars. Cliff rode with Ellen and Warner rode with Matt. The third car contained two other squad members who were designated for the clinic search. It was always good to have at least one agent without a car in case you needed to put someone out on foot, and it was also helpful to have a passenger to work the radio and look things up on the briefing material, like license plate numbers, while driving. They stopped in San Jose and met up with the agents from Gina's squad. They got the protective vest for Cliff, which he donned immediately. All the agents had theirs on. Braswell told them he'd follow them in his car to Byrne's residence. The other San Jose agents joined the two headed for the clinic.

In the car Ellen kept the air conditioning cranked up to maximum. It was over 90 degrees and expected to get hotter during the day. Since Byrne lived in the south valley area it would be even hotter there. Wearing thick Kevlar vests in that climate was never comfortable.

"How's Ashley now?" Cliff asked her as they drove.

"She's almost back to normal. Her leg is still weak, but the doctors are very pleased. They expect a complete recovery."

"That's wonderful news. You know that if I…"

"Cliff, stop. Say no more. I realize now that you were doing your best to prevent what happened. And volunteering for the vascular transplant was above and beyond. I'm sorry for the way I treated you there for a while."

He said nothing for several minutes. Ellen got a radio call from the squad supervisor who said he had notified the Sheriff's office about the search. Some other radio traffic passed between the different cars. When there was a pause, he spoke up again.

"You're letting your hair grow out. It looks good."

"Thanks. Yeah, I donate my hair to Locks of Love. That's why it was so short when you met me. I'd donated two months or so before. It'll be months before I can donate again. They have minimum length requirements. I don't color it, either, for that reason."

"What's Locks of Love?"

"It's a charitable organization that makes wigs for cancer patients, the chemo patients who lose their hair."

Cliff realized he had misjudged Ellen, and in more than one way. She was obviously more giving, more caring, than he had given her credit for. Her tough exterior hid a selfless nature. Few women, young single women especially, would sacrifice something so critical to their appearance as their hair for the sake of some unknown strangers. From nun to FBI agent, and now to caring aunt, sister, and organ donor. This was a woman who put others above herself.

Chapter 36

The caravan wound its way up Dunne Avenue until they reached the junction with Finley Ridge Road. That took over twenty minutes from the freeway. Ellen sent Braswell in for a drive-by just to get the lay of the land. After a minute or two he radioed back that it was quiet, no exterior sign of any vehicles or people at Byrne's. There was a large garage, and a car could be inside. There was an SUV parked across the road on the shoulder, but it didn't match any cars registered to Byrne and he thought it was probably associated with one of the houses on the other side of the road.

They moved in. Since Ellen had Cliff in her car, she pulled over about fifty yards from Byrne's driveway and parked. She told Cliff to stay there with the car and out of sight until she came back for him. She got in Braswell's car and they all drove in and parked on Byrne's driveway.

Cliff watched from his vantage point. The house was on the uphill side of the road across what was a fairly substantial mountain. He could see the front of the structure, a 1920s-vintage wooden ranch house built by someone who would not qualify as a DIY instructor. The shakes on the roof were so warped it had to leak in the rain, which, fortunately, almost never occurred here. Up the hill two hundred yards or so from the house Cliff spotted two large hay bales positioned on top of a small rise. He recognized the papers fastened to them as targets – riflery targets. He couldn't see well enough from that distance, but he'd be willing to bet the bull's-eyes were obliterated.

As soon as the agents stepped out of the cars, the heat began to brutalize them. Matt Nguyen, sweat streaming from under his vest, moved around to the back of the house. The yard was clear. He stepped back to the side and signaled to Ellen that there was no sign of anyone in back. He moved to the corner so he could cover the back and left side. Braswell positioned himself back toward the road diagonally opposite Matt so he could cover the front and other side. He carried the Heckler & Koch MP5 at the ready position. Ellen and Warner approached the house. This was her case, so she was in charge. Warner held a shotgun. Ellen held her credential case in her left hand and pushed the doorbell with her right hand, which she then placed on the butt of her handgun.

They heard someone move inside. She moved to the side one step. Warner moved back further so he was out of sight of the living room window, but where he had a clear shot at the front door.

"Who's there?" a male voice called through the door.

"Open up, Byrne. It's the FBI. We have a search warrant."

"Brian isn't here," the voice replied.

"We're coming in to search one way or another. You have ten seconds to open up or we'll force the door."

They heard the rattle of a chain lock being slid, but they weren't sure whether it was sliding into the locked or unlocked position. Then the door cracked open about two inches. Ellen was gasping for breath from a combination of the heat and the tension. She saw one eye of the man as he peeked around the door right at her. She couldn't see his hands, which were still behind the door. She held up the credentials for the man to see.

Simultaneously, Warner ran low and fast from the other side and threw his weight into the door, knocking it open all the way. The man inside went sprawling, landing on his butt. His hands were empty.

Ellen rushed in, hand on gun, and quickly scanned the area. She could tell the man on the floor posed no danger, but she didn't know who else might be there. She moved through the living room to the kitchen, which had a door to the back yard. She opened that door and called to Matt that they were inside. He came to the door and stepped inside. Together they cleared the dining room and garage. No one was there.

Before venturing down the hall they stopped to question the man, whom Warner was now helping up. Matt kept his gun trained toward the hall while Ellen moved back to the front room of the house. The man told them there was no one else in the house. He identified himself as Frank Schultz, Byrne's roommate. Byrne was out and he didn't know when he would be back. Schultz had a wallet on him, which he offered to display. The Canadian driver's license confirmed his identity.

Ellen knew it was possible for Byrne to have false identity papers, but this man did not meet Byrne's description. Byrne was six three and in his forties. Schultz was five eight and much older. Byrne was bald; Schultz had plenty of gray hair.

Ellen explained to him that they had a search warrant for the entire house and that they would search his bedroom or other private area as part of that. He told her his was the one on the right. She asked him if he had any weapons or anything dangerous there and he said no. When she started questioning him further he said he didn't know anything about Byrne's activities and didn't want to talk to the FBI about him.

"Am I under arrest?" he asked.

"No. We're just here to search."

"Then I'd like to go. I'll come back later when you're done."

Although she was disappointed he wouldn't talk to her, it was preferable to have him out of the house during the search and she couldn't hold him anyway.

"All right, you can leave. How are you going to get out of here? It's a hundred degrees out there and too far to walk to anywhere except a neighbor's."

"That's okay. My car is parked across the street. I'll just drive into town."

Ellen would have liked to search his vehicle, but it wasn't named in the warrant nor was it on the premises, so they had no legal grounds. She was a bit uncomfortable with the fact they knew nothing about this roommate, but she'd done enough searches to know this wasn't so unusual. Cliff had told her Byrne had money troubles, so it wasn't particularly surprising he had taken in a roommate.

She called Matt over.

"Matt, why don't you take Mr. Schultz to his car and let Woody know we're inside and everything appears to be clear. Don't let this gentleman go until we tell you we've cleared the rest of the house, then you can send him on his way."

"Sure. Come on," he said to Schultz and took him by the arm and led him outside. "Do you have your car keys?"

The man nodded. Matt frisked him, then they walked out to where Braswell was standing. Matt told Braswell this was Byrne's roommate and he would be leaving when Ellen gave the all clear sign.

Braswell grunted an okay, sweat running off his brow in rivulets. He was clearly wilting under the heat. "I tell you what," Matt said. "I'll take the duty out here for now. The house has air conditioning. Why don't you go inside and cool off."

"Thanks, Matt. I owe you one."

Braswell headed into the house while Matt stood there with Schultz. After another two minutes Ellen yelled from the door that they had cleared the rest of the house and Schultz could go. Matt motioned to

Schultz with a jerk of his head to take off. Schultz walked across the road and got in the SUV.

Matt hadn't paid much attention to the vehicle before since he was focused on the house, but now something about it seemed familiar. It was the same make as Abboud's, but the color was slightly different; maybe it was a different year. It was a shiny black on top, but the lower section was lighter, because it was dusty and splattered with mud. It had a Canadian plate, but there was nothing suspicious about that since the man was Canadian. It could have been the one he'd chased at the bombing, but then he'd seen a lot of SUV's since then that could have been that one. He just hadn't seen that one well enough to make a positive ID on any of them. There was nothing to tie this one to that bombing either. This old, white Canadian was hardly Palestinian. He watched it drive off.

Inside Ellen and the others formed a search plan. Now that the house was clear they needed to focus on executing the search. Since the warrant included documents and electronic media, they could look anywhere without limitation, at least anywhere a post-it or SD card could conceivably fit. Warner stayed there while the others went back to their cars and got their search kits – the boxes, bags, evidence tags, gloves, and forms needed. The evidence clerks kept these kits ready for such occasions, so it had been quick work to grab a few on the way out the door.

Back at her car Ellen told Cliff he could come in now. His thanks were effusive, since he'd been sweltering in the car. She had considerately parked in the shade, but she'd taken her car keys with her so he had no air conditioning   He could see that she was perspiring heavily, too. Her bangs hung in wet ringlets around her forehead and her cheeks were flushed. Dark stains marred her shirt where it emerged from the vest. He thought she might take off her vest now that the house was clear and no one was home, as he would have done. But she kept it on, so he did too. She drove her car closer to the house and they went inside. Blessed relief!

Warner and Braswell, with their shoulder weapons, took turns guarding the front in case Byrne returned. Now that Schultz was gone, they assumed he would call Byrne and alert him to the search. She guessed he would avoid the area, but you never knew. Some subjects rushed back home to see what was going on. She instructed everyone to keep their vests on.

Cliff was ordered to stay just inside the front door and not touch anything. If they needed something identified, they would bring it to him. This would remove or at least reduce the chance that some defense attorney could contend he planted some evidence or took something that would cast blame on Xlectrix.

Braswell walked inside, trading places with Warner, cell phone to his ear. Cliff heard him say "no shit" a couple of times, then "he's right here." Since Braswell was looking straight at him when he said that, he got very curious.

"Cliff, you won't believe this," he said when he finished his call. "You know that bank robber you tackled?"

"The do-rag guy?"

"Yep. He was on parole when we caught him, so he got sent right back to San Quentin as a parole violator."

"That's good." Cliff waited for the other shoe to drop. This was not "no shit" news.

"Well, he's part of a gang. He and some of his crew got into it with a rival gang, some drug dealers from down south. They jumped one of them – that cop-killer Houck. Houck's in critical condition, not expected to survive."

"No kidding?! And they say our justice system doesn't work."

"God's honest truth. Didn't I hear that you testified against Houck?"

"I did, but it was just a routine pre-trial hearing. It didn't make any difference. He pled out to save himself from the gas chamber. The prosecutor said he'd probably have a higher chance of dying in prison if he didn't get the death penalty, since death row inmates are isolated from other inmates and never actually get executed. I guess she was right."

Braswell added, "And now the robber is up for both bank robbery and murder. His trial is scheduled for next month on the robbery. They'll re-indict to add the murder. That's three strikes – with violence. He'll be in the system for the rest of life."

A wistful smile crept up the corners of Cliff's mouth. "And to think some people don't believe in natural selection."

At that point Ellen called to Braswell, and he left.

Cliff pulled out his smart phone and logged onto a news site. Already there was a headline saying "Cop Killer Slain." It seemed Braswell's call was an hour behind times. Houck had died half an hour ago. Cliff noticed that his phone had already lost half its charge. He was far enough away from the cell towers on Highway 101 that the phone was using a lot of power to stay connected. He decided to turn it off to save the juice.

Ellen and Matt had been concentrating on searching Byrne's bedroom, where he also had a desktop computer. She was about to get Braswell started on the garage but a phone call had caused her to herd everyone back out to the front where Cliff was standing.

"That was the other search team. The clinic is cooperating fully, so there should be no trouble there, but I have some bad news. They did an inventory of their radiological isotopes and some are missing. So are some other medical supplies – scalpels, hypodermics, some powerful drugs. Byrne must have taken them when he broke in to steal the laptop."

"What does that mean?" Braswell asked. He had almost no background on the case.

"It means that there could be very dangerous radioactive materials on site here. The ones he took were the most dangerous – most radioactive – that they had. Everyone needs to be very careful. Cliff, do you know what we should look for? You had that container in your car."

"The one Byrne put in my car was like a little metal barrel. It's called a pig. I don't know whether that's what they all look like, though."

"Has anyone collected anything that looks even remotely like that?"

Everyone shook their heads no. The only things taken so far were address books, letters, and similar documentary items, all of which had been shown to Ellen for her to initial the evidence tag.

"Ellen," Matt said, "We have to suspend the search and get a hazmat team in here. If we open something up, or knock something over and it's radioactive, that could be a death sentence."

She hesitated for a few moments but the stern look Matt gave her convinced her quickly. "Matt's right. I'll let Dave know the score. We'll have to call for the county hazmat team. That could take an hour or more for them to get that truck up the mountain, assuming they're even available."

She went outside and told Warner the latest. When she returned she told everyone to gather in the living room and not touch anything. She pointed out they had to keep someone out front, since Byrne could come back at any time, but at least now all the agents could share the duty so no one had to roast for more than ten minutes at a time. The temperature was well over 100 degrees here.

She retreated to another room to make a call to her supervisor and ask him to get the hazmat team. Braswell went back to the front to watch for Byrne.

For the first time since they'd arrived, there was some down time, so the rest had a chance to compare notes.

"Cliff, did you know that Byrne had a roommate?" Matt asked.

"No. Is that who I saw leave in the SUV?"

"Yes. A Canadian guy named Schultz."

On the word "Canadian" Cliff's ears perked. He'd totally forgotten about Oberherr Franz in the excitement and hadn't noticed the Canadian license plate of the SUV when it passed him as it left the area.

"An older guy, first name Franz?"

"Frank, he said, but his license read Francis. That's the same as the German Franz, isn't it?"

"It's got to be Oberherr Franz. I forgot to tell you guys about him. He's a self-styled pastor, the spiritual head of Byrne's church."

"What church is that?"

"It's called Positive Christianity, or the religion is anyway. I don't think he had a specific church. It's supposed to be non-denominational. It's mainly just a quasi-religious rationalization of Nazism using biblical quotes and phony history. The main thrust of it is anti-Jewish. It was one of Byrnes's favorite websites. I read some of Oberherr Franz's blog. He said he was in California getting some medical treatment that wasn't available in Canada and was staying with a 'disciple'. That must be Byrne. From the sound of it, he was getting treated at Stanford."

At this, Matt jumped up and ran into Schultz's room. He had been out front when Ellen cleared that room, and he'd been searching Byrnes's room since he came back in. He hadn't looked in the other bedroom yet.

When he opened that bedroom door he saw nothing unusual at first. He began to open drawers. Ellen, now off the phone, came rushing in.

"What are you doing?!" she almost screamed. "You're the one who told me to stop searching."

"This is Schultz's room, not Byrne's. This guy could be the bomber. His car was identical to the one I chased." He continued to rifle through the contents of the chest of drawers.

"What are you talking about?"

Matt told her to go talk to Cliff about Schultz. She left. When he got to the bottom drawer, he no longer had any doubt. In it were two Palestinian flags with Made in China tags on them, appearing identical to the flag found at the Palo Alto bombing site. Right next to those were dozens of small containers of gunpowder and a packet of primers.

"Dammit!" he muttered under his breath as Ellen came back in. He pointed to the stash in the bottom drawer. "We let him go."

"Back off, Matt. You're too excited. This stuff explodes. This is all the more reason to bring the hazmat guys in."

"We have to put out a BOLO. He's not even to the bottom of the mountain yet. It's only been what – ten minutes? The deputies coming up this way could stop him."

"And do what? There's no warrant on him. He's just a suspect, Matt. Maybe he entered the country illegally, according to Cliff, but the locals aren't going to hold him for that. ICE won't hold a white Canadian for that. Not around here."

"They will if we tell them he's wanted for a fatal bombing, a hate crime. I'm going after him. He's the bomber, I know it."

He turned toward the bedroom door to leave, but Ellen put her hand on his arm. "Matt, think about it. You..."

But Matt shook off her hand and bolted for his car. Within twenty seconds he was racing down the street, lights and sirens full blast.

"You better go after him," Ellen called to Warner. "It looks like that guy Schultz could be the Palo Alto Jewish Center bomber. Matt's on a tear. He almost killed himself chasing him once. We can't let him make the arrest alone. Schultz could have a whole arsenal in his car. We never searched it."

"What about you guys? That leaves just one car."

"We'll be fine. We can't leave Cliff alone here and he can't come on an arrest, not for a bombing suspect. We'll stay and wait for the hazmat team. I'll call for more agents, too. The clinic team should be finishing up anyway. They told me the employees there had all the stuff in the warrant nicely organized for them. I'll have a team break off from there. Maybe if we're lucky they can intercept Schultz, or at least Matt, at the bottom of the mountain. If not, we can use the help finishing the search here. I'm going to call the ASAC myself. He'll send as many bodies as we need when he hears we've got the bomber identified. Now go."

Warner grabbed the shotgun and left. Within seconds they heard his car start up and spit gravel on the driveway as he rushed to catch up to Nguyen.

She pulled out her cell phone and started to call when she realized her battery was dead. They were just too far up the mountain. She should have thought of that earlier and turned it off. She walked into the kitchen where there was a wall phone. She called the Assistant Special Agent in Charge of the division and explained the situation. He told her to sit tight. He was sending everyone but the marines. In fact, he'd send a few of those, too, since many agents were ex-marines.

"Okay, help is on the way," she said to Cliff. "Let's go outside and I'll brief Woody. For chain of custody I can't leave you inside alone."

Cliff followed her out to the front driveway to talk to Braswell. No sooner had they gathered by the edge of the road when a rifle shot rang out.

Chapter 37

Braswell was knocked backward as the round penetrated his protective ballistic garment, then his shoulder, shattering his right clavicle, and passed out his back and came to rest inside the vest. Agents were warned that the Kevlar garments were good protection, but weren't really "bulletproof vests," at least not for high-velocity ammunition. Braswell had the unfortunate distinction of demonstrating this fact. He lay face up moaning, blood seeping from his wound, his right arm useless.

Braswell had been standing between Cliff and Ellen. Since he was holding the long-barreled weapon, he was the logical one to take out first. Instinctively, both Cliff and Ellen had dived and rolled from their positions, but in opposite directions. Cliff had launched himself into the shallow depression that ran along the side of the road, a rough gutter of sorts carved out by the running water when those rare rainstorms hit this mountainside. Ellen took two steps toward the house and dove behind a decorative boulder.

The second shot hit the pavement inches above Cliff's head. This was more than sufficient to remind him not to look up. He remained prostrate and immobile in the gutter. After this there were no shots or other sounds for half a minute that to Cliff felt more like a week.

Ellen couldn't tell where the shot came from, other than it was generally to the northwest, toward the intersection of this street with Dunne, the only exit from the area. She could see Braswell lying on the driveway, bleeding, but didn't dare expose herself to give him aid. She couldn't tell if he was alive or dead from where she crouched. From the blood she could tell he had been hit in the shoulder, and that alone probably would not be fatal, but he had fallen backward and hit his head on the pavement of the driveway as he went down.

She also didn't know where the second shot had hit. She had been behind the boulder and at least knew it hadn't hit in her immediate vicinity. She ventured a peek around the far end of the boulder. She saw nothing. She had been at firearms ranges enough to know from the sound the shot was from a rifle and not a handgun and wasn't very close, at least 200 yards away. That meant the shooter, Byrne or Schultz she assumed, hadn't just come upon the scene and spotted them, but had stopped well short of the house and set up an ambush.

A third shot kicked up dirt next to Cliff's position and this time she saw the impact. She decided to make her move while the shooter was looking the other direction. She sprinted for Braswell's position, scooped his MP5 from the ground, made a sharp left and ran back toward the front door of the house. Just before reaching the door, which she now cursed for being closed to keep in the cool air, another shot passed inches from her face, shattering the front window. She dove back the other direction and rolled, not letting go of the rifle.

Cliff, hearing the glass crack some distance away, took the opportunity to change his location. He jumped up and sprinted across the roadway. There was no house or yard there, just a barbed-wire fence, which he leapt clumsily, shredding his pants leg and tearing the flesh of his calf. There was some low brush for visual cover, and he could see some short ridges and shallow arroyos beyond that would provide better cover if he could get to them. He made it to the nearest bush, which hid most of his body from the shooter's direction.

His clothing was completely saturated with sweat, from both exertion and fear. He was pinned down by a marksman with a rifle in an unfamiliar area, unarmed. At least he had his phone. He pulled this out and turned it back on. Thank God he'd had the presence of mind to turn it off before the battery was drained. It came on and showed reception of one bar. He had a signal! He immediately dialed 911. It rang seven times before anyone picked up and then he was immediately put on hold.

An eon passed while the 911 operator dealt with preceding callers. He imagined them as lamebrains calling emergency services to get their cat out of a tree or to complain about the neighbor who threw his plastic trash into the garbage can instead of the recycling. Finally connected to a human, he managed only to give his location.

The next shot came before he could say more; it hit the gravel only six inches from his foot. He turned off the phone and scooted further behind the bush. The shot was clearly coming more from the northeast now. The shooter was circling around from west to east to get a better shot. The sniper had to be moving up the hill. Cliff's foot was the part sticking out the furthest and must have been visible. The shot had not ricocheted into his leg. It had either buried itself in the dirt or skipped over his leg, he didn't know which. The gravel that was kicked up, though, peppered his shin, shredding his khakis even more and producing stinging reminders that he was under fire.

Ellen, hearing the shot coming behind her now, felt relatively safe in moving since the house would block the shooter's view of her position. Still, she could not be sure, so she assumed a start position like an Olympic sprinter behind her boulder, then tore across the yard and around the north side of the house into the back yard. There was a shed of sorts, almost like a bus shelter, with a roof and three sides, filled with garden tools, paper targets, and hay bales. She positioned herself behind the hay bales, which she figured would provide the best protection. Then she peeked around the edge toward the direction of the last shot.

There was movement! High on the hillside a man was moving through the scrub oak that populated that side of the street. The downhill side, where Cliff was, featured only a few small bushes on the sere hillside, but up the hill, where the shooter was, the foliage was dense enough to provide some solid as well as visual cover. The trees were sparse, but they were trees with trunks, not bushes. Still, at least she knew where he was, and as he moved, he was coming further into her line of sight. She had been trained on the MP5 like every other agent, but she'd never had more than the minimum familiarity training – perhaps ten rounds once a year at a stationary paper target.

The MP5 was a top quality weapon, but it used 9 millimeter rounds, the same as her handgun. It was light, had little kick, and was remarkably easy to be accurate with up to 100 yards or so, which is why it was so popular with law enforcement agencies worldwide, but its range was nowhere near that of the hunting rifle that they opposed. She didn't know whether that was a .30-06 or a .308, or maybe something else, but it would have a much larger round, a longer barrel, and the advantage of the uphill position, allowing gravity to extend the range, rather than shorten it. In brief, it had more range and more killing power than her carbine. She had never tried to hit a distant target with the MP5, but she was quite sure she had little chance at the distance where she had seen the figure move, despite being an excellent shot with the handgun.

Then she spotted the man move again, and his silhouette appeared against the lighter soil behind him as he took a shooting position, rifle raised. She could tell he was aiming at Cliff across the street. She raised her MP5, sighted quickly, and cranked off a round toward the man. The shooter moved quickly in response, positioning himself so that a tree protected him from her direction. Ellen had no idea where her round had landed, but if she could keep the shooter distracted long enough for the cavalry to arrive, she might be able to save a life, either Cliff's or Braswell's, preferably both. Maybe even her own.

Chapter 38

Matt Nguyen caught sight of the SUV on East Dunne only three blocks before the entrance to U.S. 101. Matt had no doubt that if he did not make the stop, Schultz would be gone from California. However, this spot was right in front of an elementary school and the kids were being let out. He could not make the stop here.

He turned off his lights and siren, but moved up close behind the SUV, almost tailgating. When Schultz passed the school, he started to accelerate toward the freeway ramp, but Matt turned the siren back on and flashed his red light once. Schultz pulled over to the curb.

Matt unbuckled his seatbelt and pulled out his handgun, holding it in his right hand. With his left he reached across his body and flipped on the loudspeaker on the console, then lifted the microphone.

"FBI," he announced. "Get out of the car with your hands raised." He opened his own driver's door and stood next to the car. The echoing resonance of the amplifier made him sound more authoritative than he was. Still, Schultz did not get out.

Matt repeated the command. He saw the door open, but Schultz remained in the car. At that moment three Sheriff's vehicles came racing off the freeway toward them, on the opposite side of the street. Matt realized his Bureau car was unmarked and had no siren or lights going. He was afraid the deputies would race past, heading up the hill, and just mistake him and Schultz for a couple of motorists pulled over to the curb.

The first two vehicles, one of which was a hazmat team truck, did exactly that, leaving Matt behind; but the third car spotted Matt holding the gun and the mike and did a quick U-turn to come up behind him. Matt was wearing his FBI raid jacket, which identified him to the deputy without the need to show a badge. Schultz stayed in his car. As the deputy arrived, Matt announced again "FBI. Get out of the car with your hands raised." This was more for the benefit of the deputy than for Schultz, but it had the desired effect. Seeing the patrol car was enough to convince Schultz fleeing or resisting would not be possible. He got out of the SUV with his hands above his head.

Matt exited his car and approached Schultz. At the same time, the deputy who had pulled up behind, stepped out, hand on gun, and took a position at an angle so that Matt was not between him and Schultz. Matt handcuffed Schultz and began to frisk him. The old man did not resist or say anything. Matt found no weapon on his person, but he removed Schultz's cell phone.

The deputy approached. "You're Matt Nguyen." He said it as a fact, not as a question. "We received a dispatch call about you. Do you need assistance?"

"I might. I don't know yet. Don't leave." Matt then turned to Schultz and read him the Miranda warnings. When he was done, he asked if Schultz understood them. Schultz just nodded yes.

"Are you Oberherr Franz?"

"I write a religious blog using that name. I believe you have freedom of religion and the press in this country."

"Did you call Byrne to warn him about the search?"

Schultz took a moment to answer. Then he looked at his cell phone in Matt's hand and realized Matt could see the record of the last call easily enough. "Is it a crime in America to call a homeowner to let him know that police are executing a search warrant at his house?"

"I didn't say it was a crime. I asked if you called."

"I choose to invoke my right to remain silent, just as you told me," Schultz replied.

Matt tried several more questions, his accusatory tone increasing in intensity, but Schultz said nothing in response. Finally, in frustration, Matt informed him that he was being placed under arrest for illegal entry to the United States. He walked him back to the deputy and asked the deputy to maintain custody while he searched the SUV.

Dave Warner pulled up, tires screeching like a banshee as he almost overran the scene and had to brake hard. After a quick display of credentials to the deputy, Warner asked how he could help. Matt said he could help with the search of the vehicle.

They dug through the contents of the SUV and found nothing of evidentiary value. No explosives, no gas can, no Palestinian flags. Not even a suitcase or a toothbrush. Schultz had been surprised at the house with no chance to pack and was probably traveling with just the car, his wallet and passport, and the clothes on his back.

Matt consulted with Warner for a minute, then turned to the deputy. He told him to put Schultz in the patrol car and close the door so he couldn't overhear. The officer did so.

"Look, here's the story. This guy is a suspect in the Palo Alto bombing."

"The Jewish Center? I thought that was a terrorist thing – Palestinians or something."

"Right, that one. But he's some kind of neo-Nazi anti-Semite. We just found Palestinian flags in his room. I think he did the bombing and planted the flag to cast suspicion. I'm not sure we have enough to arrest him on that yet, but he's admitted to being this Franz guy, who bragged about entering the country illegally. We can start with that. I'm going to call the U.S. Attorney's office now to see if we can arrest on the terrorism charge. We need to complete the search of his room, but we're waiting for the hazmat team to clear it."

The deputy, tired of waiting, volunteered, "You'll be here all day if that's what you're waiting for. They take forever. I can transport him to main jail and he'll be held overnight on the immigration charge. You can get your authority worked out and either charge him with something else or pick him up in the morning. He'll go to federal court with the bus, and if you don't charge him with something else, he'll probably get kicked loose by the judge."

Matt and Warner exchanged looks and nodded. "Okay, thanks. That'll work. But make sure you don't release him before then. We have to get back up to the house to help complete the search."

BUSINESS REPLY MAIL
FIRST-CLASS MAIL   PERMIT NO. 865   NORTH HOLLYWOOD, CA

POSTAGE WILL BE PAID BY ADDRESSEE

PO BOX 17046
NORTH HOLLYWOOD CA 91615-9186

Chapter 39

Cliff now knew the shots were coming from the uphill direction, from the northwest. Hearing the exchange from the MP5 and the hunting rifle – the sounds of the two were distinctly different – he guessed the shooter was momentarily distracted – he made a break in the southeast direction, parallel with the street and going downhill.

He figured he had been saved largely because of the fact he was downhill. The hay bales with the targets on them at Byrne's home had been up the hill behind the house. Byrne was used to shooting that direction. The steep downhill changed his aiming point significantly and he hadn't yet adjusted for it. His best protection in this nearly open environment was thus distance, both horizontal and vertical. He wanted to put as much space and elevation between him and Byrne.

The sprint across the barren hillside was grueling. He realized that he was no longer sweating. He was too dehydrated. With temperatures in the triple digits and the humidity near zero, liquids disappeared from his body at near relativistic speed. He reached a barbed wire fence that marked a neighbor's yard and collapsed in a heap. All that was going through his mind was that he just had to lie down for a moment and catch his breath. He also knew he couldn't continue to wear the protective vest. It was causing heat exhaustion and really wasn't much protection against a rifle bullet anyway. He peeled it off and let it fall into the dust. The relief was immediate.

He could see a house on the other side of the fence about twenty yards. His best hope was to get help from the resident there. Maybe someone there would give him a ride out of the area. At least he could get out of sight, although he feared Byrne would have been able to see his direction of travel from his vantage point.

The front door of the house was on the street side, of course, which meant it faced uphill, and would be visible to the shooter. Cliff planted one hand on the fence post and tried to vault the fence. This attempt, too, was unsuccessful. His pants leg caught on the top barbed wire and he tumbled into the dirt on the far side. One of the fence barbs shredded the fabric along his calf and gouged another long scratch through his flesh. It was a superficial wound, but it produced quite a bit of blood. In addition, he sprained his left wrist when he landed. At least he heard no further shots. He no longer knew where the shooter was, or where Ellen was. He began to have hope that he had not been seen making his way here, but knew he couldn't continue to lie there in the dirt. He had no visible cover. He struggled to his feet and trotted – the fastest speed he could manage – toward the rear of the house, out of the sight of anyone uphill.

Then the most wonderful vision appeared to him. He wondered for a moment if he was hallucinating. There across the yard, or what he now realized was actually a corral, was a watering trough. Instead of diverting left toward the back door of the house he made a beeline straight ahead for the trough. It was full of water. Without a moment's hesitation he plunged his face in and drank deeply. Dirt, bugs, and horse slobber notwithstanding, it was ambrosia from the gods. Never had anything tasted so good – not even the wine Mark Bishop's father had imported.

He splashed his shirt and pants with the heavenly nectar; the evaporation provided immediate relief to his overheated body. He crumpled to his knees and gasped with gratitude. All he needed was another minute of this and he would be rejuvenated enough to think straight. He took another long drink and let out a loud, involuntary belch.

"Don't move."

The words came from behind him. Although he couldn't see the source, Cliff immediately recognized Byrne's deep bass voice. He could also tell that Byrne was close enough to put a bullet through his head at a whim, no problem. He froze.

"Now turn around."

Cliff did so. He saw Brian Byrne standing twenty yards away, panting heavily. His right hand held a hunting rifle pointed directly at Cliff. His left hand was fumbling with something in the pocket of his hunting vest. The pockets were bulging with shells, but Cliff could tell he wasn't trying to extract ammunition. He was digging deep for something else.

The water he'd drunk and soaked onto his clothing was having a distinct buoying effect on Cliff. He knew he could run at a sprint now and react faster than he might have minutes before, but Byrne was still too close – and too far away. This corral area was relatively level, open, and surrounded by barbed wire. Cliff would be gunned down before he could go more than ten yards. Byrne was obviously exhausted, not only panting heavily, but his face was flushed and his eyes glassy. Cliff saw an empty water bottle in a custom pocket on Byrne's hunting vest. No doubt he was dehydrated, too, but it looked like he'd had water and wouldn't be in overly bad shape. Cliff judged that if he could get to him, he would have an advantage over Byrne in a physical fight, but Byrne was too smart to get that close. He also kept his eyes on Cliff the whole time rather than look down to help him find whatever it was he was digging for in his pocket.

Then Byrne extracted from that pocket something ominous – a hypodermic needle, capped with a plastic cover. It was wrapped in some kind of foil-lined fabric, but the shape was still obvious. Byrne tucked the rifle under his right arm for a few seconds while he used his right hand to unwrap the foil and pull the cap off the needle, but never took his eyes from Cliff.

"You ruined my life," Byrne declared in a matter-of-fact tone, still panting.

"I'm just a process server," Cliff replied, "a small fry hired to drop off the papers. Your complaint is with Xlectrix or the clinic doctors who fired you."

"Bull shit. You're no process server. You're the hatchet man for Xlectrix. You left your card at the clinic. You're the guy they use to go out and destroy someone's life, and now you're going to have your life destroyed – unless you choose to end it right here by trying to run. Welcome to my world."

"Why did you kill those people with the overdoses? Was it really necessary just to get a raise at work?"

Byrne cocked an eyebrow at this remark and hesitated before replying. He looked genuinely puzzled. "Killed people? I never killed anyone. Not yet anyway. I'm hoping you give me a reason to change that."

"When you hacked into the other Lilacs and killed the power to the DPP, the overdoses killed two patients and caused another one to lose her leg."

"No way. You're lying. It would be all over the news if that happened. I calculated the doses. It should just have left a small burn – enough to make the patients afraid to go back there. I wanted to show the world that the design of the L4 is unsafe. If I could hack into it, anyone could. The whole remote access thing – that's like inviting disaster. I was doing the world a service."

"You're in denial. I'm telling you, two of the patients died. Another one had her leg amputated."

"It must have been cancer that killed them. I've always put patient safety first; I always made sure my machines were working perfectly, ... calibrated to exact specifications. That's why it was so unfair Xlectrix canned me. I was good at my job, the best they had. You're just playing mind games and it's not going to work. Come closer."

Cliff didn't move.

"I said come closer." Byrne raised the rifle to sight it directly at Cliff's chest.

Cliff started walking slowly toward Byrne.

"Stop there. Turn around."

Cliff stopped about ten yards from Byrne and turned his back to him.

"Now kneel down."

Cliff knelt.

Byrne shifted the rifle from his right hand to his left and took the hypodermic in his right. Cliff considered making his move. He could hear Byrne behind doing something that occupied his attention, but he couldn't see what. Byrne was obviously in a slightly awkward position, but the distance was just too great. Byrne's weapon was not a mere handgun. One shot would probably kill him.

Byrne advanced toward Cliff. Glancing down, he gently squeezed the plunger until a bead of liquid oozed from the tip of the needle.

"You want to talk about a radiation overdose? Cesium-137 brine. A little cocktail of my own invention. That's the real deal, not your bullshit. You shouldn't have searched my house. You were careless. You opened my experimental sample and accidentally stuck yourself. That was your mistake. You got a fatal dose."

Cliff still couldn't see what Byrne was doing behind him.

"I don't know what you're talking about. The FBI was doing the searching."

"I was shooting at burglars who were rifling my house. How was I to know it was the FBI with a search warrant? And I only fired warning shots. If I'd wanted to kill the agents back there I could have done it half a dozen times. With that pea shooter the G-girl's got, she was a sitting duck. She's still hiding in my hay shed, afraid to come out and play with the big boys."

"I never said anything about a search warrant. How'd you know about that? Oberherr Franz called you, didn't he? He told you the FBI was searching your house."

"Enough talk."

Byrne advanced toward him and tilted the hypo a few more degrees.

Chapter 40

After her shot Ellen had waited for several seconds. She was safe behind the hay bales, but was in a vulnerable position only partially covered, since her head and one shoulder were exposed as she leaned out to get a view. She had lost sight of the shooter as soon as he had ducked behind the tree. There was enough foliage up the hill that he could have moved left or right, ducking low, his outline blending into the shadows, so she had no confidence he was still in the same location.

Then another shot had rung out and she'd fallen to the ground. Sitting there stunned, it took her a moment to realize she had not been shot. Then what had knocked her over? She looked up and saw it. The hay bale on top of the stack she had been using as her shield was now overhanging the stack by about half its length. The stack was the third one from the shed wall. That meant the bullet had penetrated the shed wall, hit the top bale of the first stack, and either penetrated all the way to the third stack, or hit the first bale with such force that it had knocked the top bales of the next two stacks back a foot or two. It was the force of the bale hitting her shoulder that had knocked her over.

It occurred to her that the shooter could probably have put that round through her head while she was looking for his silhouette amongst the trees. She stayed sitting down for a good two minutes before shifting her position. She reached for her cell phone only to realize that the battery was still dead. She put it back in her pocket. Spotting a pile of paving stones stacked at the far side of the yard, she decided to move there and look for an escape route. She couldn't stay where she was forever.

She got into a crouch and sprinted for the pile, diving and rolling at the last few feet. There was no shot. She waited there for another minute and still heard nothing. She began to wonder what the shooter had done during the last several minutes. Was Cliff safe? What had he done? Her view toward the downhill side was now blocked by the house.

Because of the steep rise in the back yard her position crouching behind the paving stones put her head level above the sill height of the windows of the house. She could see into the back bedroom despite her crouch. Shifting her position a foot to one side she realized she could see through that window, through both bedroom doors, and through the window of the bedroom on the opposite side of the house.

This gave her an idea. She knew she couldn't go through the back door of the house without exposing herself to a shot in the back while opening that door, but the bedroom window area was mostly obscured by the paving stones and a tall bush near the edge of the back yard. Still, she knew it was shut tight to keep the air conditioning in and she wouldn't be able to open it from this side. At least, not the conventional way. She picked up one of the paving stones, a large brick essentially, and heaved it through the bedroom window.

There was no shot or other reaction from the shooter. She hurried to the window and, staying low, she reached her gun barrel over her head and ran it around the edge of the window frame to knock out the remaining glass shards, then dropped the gun softly on the carpet inside, just below the window. Then she backed up, took a running start, and leaped through the window, rolling onto the carpet inside the room. No shots. She picked up the MP5, dashed through the open bedroom door and slid left into the front bedroom, out of line of sight through the door. From there she could see Woody Braswell lying on the driveway. He was alive at least, she could see from his twitching movements. He still lay on his back, eyes closed; she thought she heard faint moans.

She moved to the kitchen and called 911, still staying away from the windows. She was lucky enough to get through to the operator within seconds. She quickly explained the situation and then said she was going to go provide medical aid to the wounded agent. The operator told her to take the phone with her, but she explained that it was hard wired and her cell phone had a dead battery. She left the phone off the hook, though, so that the operator could at least hear any shots, screams, or other sounds that might occur in the house. Then she grabbed some towels from the bathroom and cautiously opened the front door, standing to the side as she did so. Still no shots.

She ran to Braswell's side and knelt down next to him.

"Woody, can you hear me?"

His eyes fluttered open and focused on her face but he said nothing.

"You're awake. Good, that's good. You've been shot. The shooter is still out there. It's your shoulder. You're going to be okay, but you've lost some blood. It's still seeping. We need to get that stopped."

She unfolded one of the towels and lifted Braswell's wounded shoulder. He blanched to as white a shade as any dark-skinned black man could ever be. A gut-wrenching groan escaped his lips.

"Sorry," she said simply. "I've got the towel in place on the exit wound. Your weight should apply pressure to that side. Now I need to get some pressure on the entrance wound."

She unfastened the Velcro straps of Braswell's vest and eased it open. The protective vests had a clamshell design. It was essentially a front panel and a back panel connected at the top by a thin fabric piece containing a head hole. It slipped on over the head much like a smock or apron, and the front and back were then brought together at the sides with heavy-duty Velcro closures, protecting the sides with a double-thick layer of Kevlar.

Once the shoulder portion of the front panel was loosened she was able to inspect the entrance wound. For whatever reason, it was not bleeding badly, although there was some clotted blood around the wound. She positioned the second towel over this wound and then pulled the vest back over the towel. She tightened the Velcro closures, eliciting yet another moan from Braswell.

"Sorry again. That should do it. Don't try to get up. The vest should hold that towel in place. You need to lie still and keep your weight on the towel under your shoulder. That's where the bleeding was the worst, but I think it'll stop now. I've got to go help Cliff. The shooter's after him."

Without waiting for acknowledgment she dashed back to the house and through the front door, which this time she had left ajar. She went back to the telephone in the kitchen. The 911 operator was still on the line. She explained that Braswell was alive and conscious but badly wounded. She described his wounds and how she had placed the towels.

The operator told her that a SWAT team was on the way and reminded her that the county Hazmat team was already on its way up the mountain. The dispatcher had been able to reach that team and said they would be there with another unit in about ten minutes. One of the other deputies had radioed back that he was transporting a prisoner to the county jail and said Nguyen and Warner had headed back up the mountain to help finish the search.

Ellen told her that she was going back out to try to provide cover for the civilian witness who was assisting with the search. The operator told her to wait until backup arrived, but Ellen was no longer on the line by then. She didn't take orders from a county dispatcher, not when a life was at stake.

Chapter 41

Cliff didn't know whether Byrne really believed he could make that story stick about him accidentally getting exposed during a search. More importantly, he didn't know whether to try to fight, run, or let Byrne expose him to the radiation. He knew Byrne was behind him with what had to be an isotope, but could you really kill someone with that? Was Byrne holding it close to him now? Within inches of his skin? A chill ran up his spine at the thought.

A bullet would surely be lethal. Two of the four overdosed patients, including Ashley, had survived and were leading fairly normal lives. That was an X-ray beam, while this was a radioactive solution. Cliff knew nothing about how those compared but guessed radiation was less lethal than a bullet.

These thoughts flashed through Cliff's brain in a microsecond in only the vaguest of forms, but he had no time to come to a rational decision. He heard Byrne step up behind him. Instinctively, Cliff twisted his body to the left and swept his arm with a blinding speed in a broad arc behind him. As he struggled to his feet, he felt his hand make contact with the gun barrel as it fired, searing the skin on the back of his hand, but the shot went wide. The hypo landed on its side within six inches of Cliff's boot as Byrne dropped it to secure his gun with both hands. Cliff jumped right; simultaneously he heard a shot echo down the mountainside.

As he jumped, he saw Byrne drop his rifle and emit a grunt. Cliff was half deaf from the previous shot so near his ear but he realized the sound of the last shot was coming from a distance, not from Byrne's rifle. Someone had shot at Byrne. The rifle lay in the dirt with a big chunk of wood splintered out from the stock. The splinter, at least four inches long, was protruding from Byrne's forearm. The hypodermic was nowhere to be seen.

Ellen cursed inwardly when she saw the rifle splinter. She had been aiming at Byrne's center of mass. She had been trying to kill him and had hit the gun instead. But this was at least three times as far as she'd ever fired the MP5 and she felt lucky to have hit him at all.

Over the past few minutes there had been no more shots but Byrne had been moving southeast, following the tree line. She had moved up into the trees herself and followed what she thought was his probable course, the prey hunting the hunter.

After several minutes she had spotted movement down near the road, several hundred yards ahead. She ran toward the figures in the corral. When she saw Byrne approach Cliff with the hypo in his hand, she knew it had to be the isotope or something equally deadly. When Cliff made his move, she had taken her best shot.

She watched stunned as Cliff, now on his feet, lunged for Byrne. He was impressively fast. Float like a butterfly, sting like a bee; Cliff had a quickness she had not imagined. In a fraction of a second the two large men were falling in a heap to the ground, Cliff landing on top.

On hitting the ground, their momentum translated into a rolling motion, their combined mass moving toward the watering trough, first one on top, then the other, rolling toward the spot where Cliff had been standing, the spot where the needle had landed.

She wanted to shoot again, but she knew she couldn't while they were rolling around like that. She began to run toward them.

Cliff was surprised at Byrne's weight. He knew Byrne was taller and heavier – younger, too – but not in good shape. But he had underestimated Byrne's level of fitness. It was all he could do to keep Byrne from escaping his grasp. Cliff's sprained wrist and burn from the gun barrel made it excruciatingly painful to grip Byrne firmly with his left hand. Cliff had a vague sense of where they were. He knew they had rolled toward the isotope and that was not an area he wanted to be. He stuck out one leg to stop the roll.

Cliff had grabbed Byrne in a bear hug of sorts, encircling his right arm, pinning it against his side, but Byrne had managed to keep his left free. Byrne's right hand was pinned, and at the moment, not posing a danger. With his left, though, as soon as the rolling stopped Byrne began to pummel Cliff's head with surprisingly powerful blows. They were lying side by side, neither on top.

Byrne was too close to do serious damage from these punches but Cliff felt his right ear turning to cauliflower and blood beginning to seep from his eyebrow area. His wrestling experience and instincts kicked in. Without conscious thought, he pulled his arm from a grasping position around Byrne's torso and snatched Byrne's left wrist with his right hand. Byrne started to roll back the other way, pulling his now-free right hand out to club Cliff, but Cliff executed a near-perfect wrist-and-half-nelson by slipping around behind him and getting his left arm under Byrne's right and snaking the hand up behind his neck. Adrenaline dulled the pain in his wrist long enough for him to accomplish the feat.

Suddenly Byrne was almost helpless, but he used his considerable mass to thrash with a violence that nearly caused Cliff to lose his grip. Cliff used his leverage to turn Byrne over onto his back, slowly working the half-nelson into a reverse headlock. If this had been a high school match he would have tried to finish him with a cradle and pin, but Cliff could see that Byrne wasn't going to put up much of a fight from this point. Byrne's chest was heaving like the Pacific and his face was the color and texture of a ripe pomegranate. He still struggled, but more feebly now. Cliff just held him down, immobile.

"Freeze, Byrne," Ellen commanded as she arrived on the scene, looking almost as exhausted as Byrne. She, too, was flushed and sweating profusely. Her MP5 was in her left hand, depressed to the ground, her sidearm in her right hand, pointed directly at Byrne's forehead. Lifting his head, he stared straight up into the barrel.

Cliff released Byrne and stood up, taking the MP5 as Ellen held it out to him, keeping the pistol and her attention trained on Byrne.

"I thought you guys were burglars breaking into my house," Byrne declared, sounding almost sincere.

"Just hope that agent back there on the driveway survives. If he dies you're in for the death penalty. You may be anyway."

"No, no. I thought you were stealing my stuff, really. Of course I had to take out the guy with the rifle for my own self-protection. I shot him in the shoulder. I could have put that bullet through his skull if I'd wanted to kill him. I just wanted to disable him so I could approach safely. A big black dude like that with a gun – anyone would think he was a robber."

Cliff and Ellen exchanged glances, their distaste unhidden. The sound of a siren suddenly filled the air.

Chapter 42

The Hazmat truck rolled into the yard, sirens and lights going. Closely behind was the second unit, a patrol car. One officer, the passenger, had jumped out of the patrol car and run to assist Braswell back at Byrne's. In weak whispers Braswell told him he heard shots but didn't know what had happened and told the officer to go help Ellen and Cliff further down the road, but the officer told him the other deputies could do that. He checked Braswell's wounds as best he could and determined the bleeding had stopped. He stood next to Braswell to give him the shade of his body and waited.

Down the road at the neighbor's corral the Hazmat truck pulled into the driveway. Ellen signaled with one hand for them to come over. Byrne continued to lie on the ground, covered by both guns.

The deputies in the truck came over to Ellen. She explained that Byrne was under arrest for assault on a federal officer and may also be guilty of attempted murder. She pulled out her cuffs, wanting to make sure to get an FBI arrest. She didn't want the deputies to take him into local custody.

"Hold on," Cliff warned. "The isotope is somewhere in the dirt over there. Don't approach that area until the Hazmat team identifies where it is."

"Isotope? What's going on?" the older deputy asked.

"The subject worked at a radiology lab and stole some medical isotopes. He dropped the hypodermic there on the ground." He pointed in the direction of Byrne. "But I don't see it now."

"What kind of isotope? Did he say?"

"It was Cesium-137," Byrne answered. "It's very hazardous. I was using it for experiments. I'm a radiology expert. This guy – he's a flunky for my ex-employer who's suing me – took it from my room and when I confronted him to get it back he dropped it here. If you stick yourself, it's potentially fatal. Be careful."

The younger hazmat deputy, on hearing this, returned to the truck and began to don protective clothing. All eyes turned toward him.

Byrne stood up and moved backward slowly, but Ellen warned him with a gesture not to try to escape. He stopped. She noticed for the first time that the splinter of wood that had penetrated forearm was no longer there. It must have fallen free. Dangling from one buttock, however, was the missing hypodermic. In the excitement, apparently he had rolled over it and hadn't even felt it stab him. He seemed to be still unaware of it. She was unsure whether to say something, but decided to wait for the hazmat deputy to return suited up.

At that point Matt Nguyen rolled his car up to the scene, tires screeching. He had no idea why the Hazmat truck and Ellen were hundreds of yards from Byrne's house, but he had headed for the scene of the action.

Dave Warner stopped back at Byrne's house to help with Braswell. He, too, didn't understand what was going on. The deputy there explained to him that they had received a radio call of someone with a rifle attacking federal agents who were executing a search warrant. The deputy further explained that an ambulance was already en route. The FBI radio operator apparently had not been notified of these developments, since Warner had not heard anything about the rifle attack previously; he got on his radio and relayed Braswell's status with instructions to notify the Special Agent in Charge. When the operator asked him if the scene was secure he looked to the deputy, who shrugged.

Warner answered, "The house where the warrant was being served is secure, but there is some action about two hundred yards down the street. It appears to be under control, but I don't know yet what's going on there. The county Hazmat truck's there. We still have to wait for them to clear the scene. Radioactivity or something."

"10-4. There are five units en route to assist. Do you need more?"

"Negative. The Sheriff's department is sending more units, too, and an ambulance is on the way."

"10-4."

The Hazmat deputy in his full protective regalia looked like a cross between an astronaut and the Michelin tire man. Holding his Geiger counter out in front like a sword, he advanced toward the area Cliff was pointing out. The staticky clicking of the Geiger counter was already audible from ten yards away. Then as Byrne turned his back on him, the deputy saw it. The hypo was still dangling from Byrne's pants.

The deputy rushed up, grabbed it, and tossed it into a metal creel-like container by his side. He yelled, "I've got it!"

Everyone except Byrne jumped back, an instinctive reaction to possible danger. Byrne grabbed his buttock as he felt the needle being withdrawn. A haunting realization overtook his features.

"Check him," Cliff said, pointing to Byrne.

The deputy reached the Geiger counter toward Byrne, who stood stock still. The ominous clicking increased. The deputy began moving the detector around the top of Byrne's head and worked his way down the body. When he got to the area where the needle had entered the body the sound got louder. After a few seconds the deputy stood back.

"Throw me some handcuffs," he announced to the collected personnel in general.

"That's my subject," Ellen announced, "I'll cuff him now that we know it's safe." She pulled out her handcuffs.

"It's not safe. He's got the highest reading I've ever seen on a human body. It's right where his wound is. From the feel when I pulled it out, it hadn't penetrated very deeply; maybe it just nicked the skin. But if that got into his bloodstream, even medical personnel will have to use protective gear when they treat him."

Byrne's face contorted into an expression of rage at this news. He charged toward Cliff. "If I'm a dead man, I'm taking you with me," he snarled, but Cliff darted to one side, evading the clumsy attempt to grab him.

The Hazmat deputy tackled Byrne at the ankles from the rear and was able to bring him down, but then got up and stepped away. "Everybody else stay back," he huffed. "It's not safe to get in close contact with him. Seriously."

Byrne struggled to his feet again and for a moment did nothing. Then he realized his position of power – of a sort. The only officer who could get close enough to handcuff him was the deputy in the protective clothing, and that deputy was smaller than Byrne and encumbered by the heavy suit. By all accounts he was now untouchable. They wouldn't shoot an unarmed man, either, he felt sure.

Byrne suddenly made another run at Cliff, who once again dodged the charge, but Byrne kept turning and weaving to match Cliff's movements and continued the chase. The Hazmat deputy made another attempt to tackle Byrne, but he couldn't keep up with the two, outfitted as he was.

It looked to Ellen much like the cartoon she had watched on TV with Ashley only a few days ago, a hatchet-wielding farmer chasing a chicken to the tune of Turkey in the Straw. But here the hatchet was Byrne's own body and Cliff was the chicken. She had her weapon at the ready but she couldn't take a shot at Byrne – not because of any worry about him being unarmed – but because she'd be as likely to hit Cliff as Byrne, or even Matt standing on the far side of the duo.

Matt Nguyen, on the opposite side, had the same problem. He holstered his gun. Notwithstanding the warning from the Hazmat deputy, he charged Byrne from behind and was able to grab an arm momentarily, but Byrne outweighed Matt by almost 100 pounds and was able to throw him off with a twisting motion.

That distraction was just enough, though. As Byrne turned back toward Cliff his nose met Cliff's skull amid a sickening crunching sound. Cliff had launched himself back at his pursuer during the seconds Matt had him turned, and with a vicious head butt had made solid contact with the middle of Byrne's face. Byrne collapsed like a rag doll. Cliff could almost see the stars floating around Byrne's head.

The Hazmat deputy shouted, "Will somebody toss me some goddam cuffs…PLEASE."

Ellen didn't hesitate this time. Hers were the first of three sets that landed at the deputy's feet. He rolled Byrne over onto his stomach and cuffed him. Byrne was out cold.

The hazmat deputy returned to his truck and brought back a metal shield. He shoved it into Byrne's pants, over the needle wound. Finally, he ran Byrne's belt through the cuffs behind his back and rebuckled it in front. The arrangement should be enough to protect any personnel who had to come in contact with Byrne and prevent him from any further escape attempts.

The other two deputies moved in and retrieved their cuffs, then helped lift Byrne to his feet. His nose was a flattened mass of flesh and cartilage streaming blood from both nostrils. One of them retrieved gauze from a kit in the car and gave it to the hazmat deputy who shoved pieces hard into each nostril to stanch the flow. Then they gingerly hauled him to the patrol car and locked him in the rear seat as he groggily regained consciousness. Matt Nguyen dusted himself off and joined them, giving instructions about transport.

"Are you okay?" Ellen asked Cliff, who obviously wasn't. He was bending over holding the top of his head with both hands. She rushed to his side.

"Man, that smarts," he replied breathlessly.

"'Smarts' may not be the right word for it," Ellen quipped. "'Dumbs' is more accurate, but I have to admit, it did the trick."

"Thanks for the rescue." He was able to stand erect now, but still kept one hand pressing on his head. "That was some shooting, knocking the gun from his hand from 100 yards. Just like TV."

"I was aiming for his chest."

"Close enough for government work."

Ellen laughed. "Well, you look like you're going to survive. You'd better get checked out at the hospital, though. For a concussion, too, not just the radiation."

Almost on cue the wail of an ambulance siren could be heard in the distance.

"Make sure they take Woody first," Ellen barked at Matt as she saw the vehicle pull up in front of Byrne's house. "These two can wait." Matt headed back on foot to Byrne's.

The Hazmat deputy, his helmet now stripped off, came over to Cliff to recheck his condition with the Geiger counter and to warn him yet again to get checked out. Cliff thanked him for the help with Byrne.

"You need to wash off. Use this trough right now, avoiding the area near where the needle was, then go back to the house and wash more thoroughly with soap. The needle could have squirted some liquid into the air, a mist or droplets, or some droplets could have landed in the dust. If you breathed in any of that isotope, it could be lethal. External skin contact shouldn't be deadly, but you need to wash off to be safe. I still need to check the house. There could be more of that stuff. Here, wear this." He handed Cliff a face mask.

Ellen spoke up again. "He's right, Cliff. We have to stay and complete the search, but we'll have to wait for him to do his job first. This will take hours. Don't worry about staying around to help identify the documents. Clean up first like he says, then get to medical attention. When the other agents get here, I'll have them transport you. With what we have on Byrne now, attempted murder of an FBI agent at a minimum, the white collar stuff isn't even going to be very important."

"Yes, ma'am." Cliff had no desire to stick around. A nice cool hospital bed sounded just fine right now. He rinsed off with the trough water, then began walking back to Byrne's house.

Matt came running back. "They took Woody. They say he's in serious condition but think he'll make it. The bullet just missed his lung. The bleeding's stopped, thanks to you. That was the key thing."

"Working in a hospital for five years taught me something."

Within the next two minutes four more cars arrived, two with FBI agents, two with Sheriff's deputies. Ellen walked back to Byrne's house to await the results of the hazmat check.

Chapter 43

The next afternoon Cliff sat on the edge of his hospital bed tapping his foot impatiently. Matt was late. Cliff's clothes had been disposed of as hazardous waste even though they had not registered radioactivity. They said hospital rules required it. He was stuck until Matt brought him some of his clothes. In the meantime he had to endure once again the indignity of wearing nothing but a hospital gown. Matt finally appeared with a gym bag of clothes.

"Cliff, how are you feeling?"

"I'm fine. Or so they tell me. I didn't inhale any of it. That's supposed to be the worst. I had an open scratch on the other leg from the barbed wire, but there was no sign of radioactivity. How about Byrne?"

"I was talking with the guard. We've got agents on him twenty-four hours a day. The doctors won't tell us anything directly about his condition without a court order, but the agent up there says he's heard him vomiting all morning. And moaning."

"That doesn't sound good."

"Not for him, anyway."

"Cold, man. That's cold."

"There's a certain ironic symmetry. The hazmat guy said radiation sickness is a horrible way to die. Byrne was planning to stick you. That could have been you."

"What about Schultz? Is he being charged with the bombing?" Cliff pulled out some jeans, underwear and a T-shirt from the gym bag.

Matt's face fell and he squirmed uncomfortably in his seat for a few seconds. "No. Not yet."

Cliff could tell there was something more to the story. "Why, what's the problem?"

"It seems the jail let him go. They're under some court mandate to reduce crowding, and since the U.S. Attorney's Office has a policy of not prosecuting illegal entry cases unless there are felony charges pending, the jail lets them go after processing them. He wasn't even held overnight. We didn't find out until this morning when he didn't show up in court."

"Do you know where he is?"

"Back in Canada, we assume. He probably flew out first thing this morning. He still had his passport and wallet. We have his SUV so he didn't drive."

"Bummer."

"We've got agents sitting on the house, continuing the search. Once we leave the premises the warrant's no good any more. We should be able to get enough probable cause to charge him by the end of the day, but it may be hard getting him back from Canada."

"If you can prove he did it, you'll get him back."

"Maybe."

"And Braswell? How is he?"

"He lost a lot of blood, but he'll be okay. He got lucky. The bullet didn't penetrate his lung."

Cliff finished dressing. "There's a blessing. Let's get out of here."

When Cliff got home he called Maeva and told her the danger was past. He asked her to go back to the office and get things back to normal as soon as she could.

Then he called Vogel.

"Cliff, how are you? I heard you had quite an adventure."

"I'll be fine. What's the status there?"

"Our manager is back, safe and sound. Things are back to normal. I just got off the phone with Sharon. She's been talking to the Assistant U.S. Attorney. It looks like Byrne is going to be charged with shooting the FBI agent."

"What about the trade secret theft? They've got him cold on that. And killing the cancer patients with the overdoses?"

"We're hoping they don't pursue that now. It could bring some unwanted publicity to the problems we had. It won't affect his sentence anyway, they tell me. The shooting of the agent should be a life sentence."

"I doubt he'll ever see the inside of a courtroom."

"What do you mean?"

"Some of the cesium got into his bloodstream. It looks like he's got radiation poisoning. He's barfing his guts out now."

Long pause. "That's terrible of course. But if he passes away before charges are made public, it would make things a lot easier for us.

This is turning out very well. The Fremont clinic bought a Lilac 4 and a long-term service contract. That's over three million, and of course we're not suing them for the trade secret theft. Here we started with a lawsuit against us and we end up with a multi-million dollar sale. Sharon really did a terrific job for us."

Cliff couldn't believe what he'd heard. "Sharon? You think Sharon did this?"

"And you, too, of course. She couldn't have done it without your help. But, Cliff, I have to say I was not happy about your unilateral decision to tell the FBI about the overdoses and the dongle problem. That could have ruined the company. It still could if it comes out. You violated attorney-client privilege. I'm not going to complain to the bar, since it looks like no harm will come of it, but I have to wonder about your moral compass."

"*My* moral compass? *You* have the gall to question *my* moral compass? You were willing to hide the fact of your faulty Lilac system while patients were still at risk, letting Ashley Bishop almost lose her leg. The other patients might have lived, too, if you had come clean earlier. I find the problem so you can fix it. Who knows how many others would have died if I hadn't? And then when I'm being hunted by a crazed killer, you leave me hanging in the wind, totally on my own, and you think I'm the one without a moral compass? I tell you what. Please complain to the state bar. Try to get me disbarred. The Code of Ethics allows breaking attorney-client privilege if a life is at risk. Let's tell the world the whole story and let them decide."

"Now, Cliff, you're not talking rationally. You're still excited from the recent events. You misunderstood me. I'm just glad you're okay. I have no intention of causing you any trouble with the bar. You earned your fee on this, no question – and a handsome fee it is, I must say. Just send me your bill and your final report. The investigation stage is over. Sharon and the AUSA can handle it for now. And of course everything you've learned about the Lilacs and the overdoses is still privileged and confidential."

Cliff slammed down the phone.

He made himself a sandwich and opened a beer. Looking out the kitchen window he saw a Los Altos Police Department cruiser drive into his cul-de-sac and make a slow turn. The officer was looking at his house. He remembered the extra patrols and hurried out his front door, beer still in hand. The officer driving the cruiser spotted him just as he was completing his turn, and stopped. Cliff walked over to him and thanked him for keeping such a good watch out, then told him the shooter had been arrested and was in custody. They could discontinue the watch on his house and street. The officer said he was just doing his job and thanked him for letting them know.

Cliff went back inside and finished his beer. Then he called Ellen. When she didn't answer he left a message. An hour later she returned the call.

"Cliff, I'm sorry I couldn't answer before. It's an absolute madhouse here. How are you doing? Matt said you were looking good."

"Did he? He's not my type."

"Always the joker, aren't you. If you have your sense of humor back I guess that means you're okay."

"I am, thanks to you. I wanted to call to thank you again. I'd be the one dying of radiation poisoning if not for you."

"A lucky shot. I'm the one who owes you the thanks. Look, I really have to go. I'm doing the criminal complaint now. We don't have time for an indictment. The grand jury doesn't meet until next week. We at least want to get him charged before he croaks. The AUSA is all over me to finish writing this up. But I'm really glad you're okay."

"Congratulations on the case. Take care."

"You take care."

Chapter 44

Cliff spent the rest of the week writing up his final report for
Vogel. He spared no detail. He was getting paid by the hour and made
sure to take as long as his conscience would allow. He'd have written
Moby Dick if he could have.

He didn't hear from Sharon Perry for the entire week. When he'd
finished his report, he printed it out – Vogel still didn't want anything
about the Lilac investigation in electronic form. Then he made an edited
version for Perry that didn't mention the Lilacs. She still didn't know
about the overdoses. He called her up and said he had the report to
deliver. Her assistant said she could see him at 2:00. She didn't take the
call herself, and apparently lunches were no longer on the agenda.

He appeared at the Herrick offices right on time and walked right
past the receptionist to Sharon's office. She was on the phone, but waved
him in with a big smile. He walked to her desk and stood. She ended the
call, stood, and walked around the desk to stand close to him.

"Here," he said, before she could say anything, and handed her
the report.

Nonplussed, she replied "Cliff, how are you? I heard you were
attacked and had to go to the hospital. I'm sorry I couldn't get over there.
You have no idea what it's been like around here."

"I'm fine. Vogel fired me, so I'm just delivering my final
report."

"Cliff, you did absolutely terrific work. You turned this case
from a money loser to a money maker. We all know that. You make it
sound like he's mad at you. Did something happen?"

"I doubt he'll be hiring me again, but that's fine with me. Look,
I'm not going to be able to go with you to Santa Barbara."

Sharon flushed and stepped back. "Cliff, what's the matter?
You're not still mad about that problem about you working from here are
you? I mean there was a gunman after you."

"I'm not mad. I just don't think it would be a good idea. The
relationship, I mean."

"That's only two weeks away. What am I supposed to do now?
Cliff, you have it all wrong. I just needed to clear it with my partners

before I authorized that. And I would have gotten the okay, but everything happened the next day and it became moot."

"Moot it is. Have a good life, Sharon." He turned and walked out.

Chapter 45

The Santa Barbara weekend came and went with no further word from Sharon. Cliff was back to doing special appearances. His bills to both the Herrick firm and Xlectrix were paid within a week of being delivered. That was lightspeed by normal standards. It usually took sixty days. Xlectrix even added a twenty-five grand bonus. He realized they wanted to keep him happy – or quiet, at least.

Two weeks earlier the newspaper said that "Brian Byrne, the suspect in the shooting of an FBI agent, died in the hospital of wounds sustained in the gun battle." No mention was made of the radiation poisoning. Cliff was sitting at the same booth at The Jury Room where he had first met Ellen. Today, though, it was just the three of them – Cliff, Gina, and Matt. This had been Cliff's first chance to talk to them since that article had come out.

"Yep, he died within a week," Matt said, matter-of-factly. "It wasn't pretty. If I described it to you, you wouldn't be able to eat your lunch."

"You obviously don't know me as well as you think you do." He took a big bite of his club sandwich as if to emphasize the point. "But that's okay, I don't need the grisly details," he managed to mumble through the mouthful. "How's Woody?"

"Back on duty, although strictly at his desk. No field action," Gina replied. "The shoulder should heal normally."

"That's wonderful news. It's a shame he had to be the one to take the bullet. This wasn't even his case. Speaking of which, is Ellen getting any credit for breaking the Lilac overdosing? I know they can't charge a dead man, but did the investigation show he remotely logged on and caused those overdoses?"

"He gave a complete confession before he died," Matt answered. "He says he didn't know it would kill anybody. He was just trying to cause some nasty burns and scare those patients over to his clinic. He was an engineer, not a radiologist. He just didn't realize what that beam could do to a live patient at the doses he was administering. Once he figured out how to use the dongle and log on, he was able to buffer the real operators' keyboard commands and replace them with his own. That's what caused the 'hitch' they talked about. Mel and the others at the clinic knew nothing about the remote logons, so there's no one to charge. Mel's plea deal held up on the trade secret theft, so he won't even be charged on that."

"So Ellen gets no credit? She solved a serial murder case. That doesn't seem right."

"Ellen's report went all the way to the Director. Remember, he's a close friend of the Bishop family. I found out he's actually Ashley's godfather. He knows that Ellen is the one who caught the guy who almost killed his goddaughter. Even though there are no headlines for her on this one, her star is shining brightly. She's been told she can have her OP and go back to Utah if she wants, but she said she's going to stay out here – for family reasons."

"You should call her," Gina said with an uncharacteristic gentleness.

Cliff shrugged. "Gina, you don't have a future as a matchmaker. I'm a hopeless case. You've tried to hook us up before, but Ellen told me in no uncertain terms that I'm not her type."

Gina and Matt exchanged looks then both looked down at their plates, eating. "Gina's right. You really should call her, Cliff," Matt echoed.

Cliff grunted an acknowledgment, but had no intention of following through. "So what's the story on Schultz?"

Matt shook his head with disgust. "He's in Canada like we thought. The AUSA says we don't have enough to charge him. We can't link him or his car to the bomb at the Jewish center. Byrne drove that car sometimes. His prints are on the steering wheel. The Palestinian flags and reloading gear in the house were in Schultz's room, but there's no way of knowing whether they were there before he came to stay with Byrne, so even if we could link the car or those materials to the bombing, which we can't, the defense could argue that Byrne used Schultz's car and did it. It's circumstantial at best and with Byrne's access, proving beyond a reasonable doubt is impossible."

"Did Byrne admit to any part in it? You said he confessed."

"No, he confessed only to the Lilac sabotage. He denied any knowledge of the bombing. But that's not proof Schultz did it."

"It gets worse," Gina interrupted. "Matt, tell him about the insurance."

"Yeah. It seems Byrne's employer provided a $250,000 life insurance policy for senior personnel. As a department head, Byrne qualified."

"But they fired him," Cliff objected. "Wouldn't the policy terminate immediately?"

"Well, yes and no. They fired him, but legally they had to give him two weeks notice, which they did. He was told not to come back, but officially he was on the books as an employee for two weeks, and he died before the two weeks ran out. The insurance company had to pay."

"So who got the money? His estate? If so, Xlectrix or the clinic could sue him and get that."

"No, his church. He named his church as the beneficiary. The good pastor in Canada gets it. It's already been paid."

"Nooo." Cliff put his palms to his temples. Some things in life just weren't fair.

They finished their lunches and exchanged hugs and handshakes.

Chapter 46

Two weeks later Cliff returned to his office from a weightlifting workout at the gym to find Maeva on the phone. It didn't take a trained detective to discern that the call wasn't business related. She was blushing even before he stepped through the door, and only got redder when she saw him, if that was possible. Quickly she told the person on the other end her boss just walked in and she had to go.

Cliff mumbled that it was okay, she could finish her call, but she had already hung up.

"You had a call from some weird guy who said he wanted to talk to you about a due diligence investigation. But I don't know if he was serious."

"Who was it?" Cliff asked.

"That's what was weird. He wouldn't give a name. He just said he was the ruler of the Queen's Navy and you'd know who he was. He left a phone number." She handed him a note.

Cliff broke out in a broad smile. It had to be the Herrick partner who had thrown him the Pinafore line. He didn't remember the man's name, but he knew he could look it up. The firm's website had pictures of all the partners. Due diligence investigations were the goal of every private investigator in the valley. Corporations considering mergers, acquisitions, or takeovers spent big bucks investigating the other company, its officers, key employees, and investors. If he did a good job for a major valley player like Herrick, the work would be steady and lucrative. Safe, too.

He sat down at his desk and thought for a moment. Life had its trying times, but in the end, he reflected, life was good. And it wasn't to be wasted. He picked up the phone and called Ellen. She picked up on the third ring.

"Hi, it's Cliff."

"Cliff. Well… hello."

"I've been wanting to make a geocaching run over to Half Moon Bay. Saturday morning looks like perfect weather. Would you like to join me?"

There was a long silence on the other end.

"Pick me up at 9:00."

Author's Note

My years on the FBI's High-Tech Squad in San Jose were the most rewarding of my career. I had the good fortune to be the case agent on the first prosecution in California under the federal Economic Espionage Act of 1996, one of several cases that served as inspiration for this story. That act defines two crimes: Economic Espionage, where the theft of economic secrets (not classified information in the hands of the government) is directed by a foreign government; and Trade Secret Theft, the home-grown variety. The defendant in that case received a four-year sentence for trade secret theft.

This story is wholly fictional. The events described here did not happen. The characters are not based on real people and any resemblance to real persons is wholly coincidental.

I want to thank all those who helped me to write this story. It would not be possible to list all the FBI agents, supervisors, and support personnel who were critical to the successful investigations and prosecutions that inspired this story. Special thanks should go to the lawyers, both prosecutors and the civil attorneys working for the victims, who pursued the cases through the courts.

I owe a huge debt to David Knapp, probably the smartest person I've ever known, for all his technical assistance. Any mistakes in the story are entirely mine; if you choose to be charitable, you may attribute them to my desire to put narrative over accuracy at times. Chris Lawson, another beta reader, also improved the story greatly with his many excellent suggestions. Lastly, David Clark provided invaluable service as my copy editor.

Made in the USA
San Bernardino, CA
26 December 2016